# THE SHOE QUEEN

Anna Davis

**BLACK SWAN**

TRANSWORLD PUBLISHERS
61–63 Uxbridge Road, London W5 5SA
A Random House Group Company
www.rbooks.co.uk

**THE SHOE QUEEN**
**A BLACK SWAN BOOK: 9780552773348**

First published in Great Britain
in 2007 by Doubleday
a division of Transworld Publishers
Black Swan edition published 2007

Addresses for Random House Group Ltd companies outside the UK
can be found at: www.randomhouse.co.uk
The Random House Group Ltd Reg. No. 954009

The Random House Group Limited makes every effort to ensure that the
papers used in our books are made from trees that have been legally
sourced from well-managed and credibly certified forests. Our paper
procurement policy can be found on www.randomhouse.co.uk

Typeset in Goudy by
Falcon Oast Graphic Art Ltd.

Printed in the UK by CPI Cox & Wyman, Reading, RG1 8EX.

2 4 6 8 10 9 7 5 3 1

Anna Davis lives in London with her husband and two children. She is a former *Guardian* columnist and works part-time for a leading literary agency.

*Also by Anna Davis*

THE DINNER
MELTING
CHEET

For the two Shoe Queens in my life:

Carole
whose collection rivals even Genevieve's

&

Natalie
whose first word was 'shoes'

# I

# Quarters

# 1

THE FANCY-DRESS THEME WAS REFUSE AND WASTE PAPER.
Genevieve Shelby King's kingfisher-blue dress was all
patched over with pages from old literary journals. Her blue
silk dancing slippers were embroidered with fragments of
poems and tipped with bows made from sonnets. She was
one big mass of poetry.

Handing her fur to the man by the door, Genevieve
entered the marble-floored hall on the arm of her best
friend, Lulu. Count Etienne de Frémont's grand house was
all dressed up like his guests. High above their heads,
suspended on invisible wires from the ceiling hung a
selection of bicycle wheels, empty bottles and ancient
boots.

'It's very Dada,' said Lulu.

'Dada was over years ago,' said Genevieve. 'Why didn't
someone tell Violet de Frémont?' And they swept through
to the party, leaving Genevieve's husband Robert back in
the hallway, fumbling for change to tip the coat man and
muttering under his breath. It was often this way – the girls

whispering and giggling together, scheming and sharing secrets, while Robert followed behind.

In the ballroom, they hovered by an enormous collage of old theatre programmes, sipping champagne and getting their measure of the room. The chandeliers had been removed for the evening and replaced by crazy garbage copies of themselves made from a million glittering fragments of coloured glass. Genevieve's gaze moved swiftly over the room to spot her many rivals – the daughters, wives, lovers and darlings of Parisian culture, American shipping, Italian motor-car manufacture and English blue-blood. The refuse theme, as it turned out, was an interesting leveller. The Princesse Martignac was hung with an assortment of buttons in place of the family diamonds, and looked less than happy about it. The famously exquisite Harriet Dupont looked – well – bottle-shaped in her shiny-green-bottle dress.

Genevieve, while not entirely satisfied that her costume was more glamorous than anyone else's, nevertheless perceived that sheer, bold confidence might give her the chance to out-dazzle the pack. They're feeling small, she thought. Take away the finery and they're nothing.

'Everybody's here,' said Lulu, nodding in the direction of Ernest Hemingway, who was dressed entirely in brown paper. Tristan Tzara and Francis Picabia were used métro tickets; Paul Poiret was a bizarre multi-coloured tangle of fabric – was he a piece of carpet fluff? A fur-ball? 'Of course, nobody can afford *not* to be, or Violet will stop the money for their next little exhibition or journal or show.'

Genevieve frowned. 'Where *is* Violet? I can't see her.'

The band was striking up a Charleston and couples

moved out across the sprung dance-floor, bird-stepping and flapping their arms.

'Come on, Vivi, let's find some pretty boys to dance with.' Lulu's dress was covered in shiny sweet papers. Her earrings and necklace were strung sweets, which sparkled in the glow of the garbage chandeliers as she headed off into the crowd without looking back. Perhaps there was one woman in this room capable of competing with Genevieve . . .

'Ah, there you are.' Robert was dressed in a silver suit that was supposed to look like a trashcan. He'd refused to wear his 'lid', thereby rendering the costume unidentifiable. 'Great party, isn't it? Say, isn't that Harry Mortimer over there? In the newspaper suit? Looks kind of like a fish supper.'

But Genevieve wasn't looking at the man in the newspaper suit. She was watching Lulu dancing with two men at once. The short one was the painter Joseph Lazarus, a long-term admirer of Lulu's. The other, taller man, wearing a cream suit, was someone she hadn't seen before. She would certainly have remembered him. He had a broad, handsome face, somewhat in the classical Greek style.

'*Is* it Harry, do you think?' Robert was still peering off into the far corner.

Genevieve seized his arm. 'Come on. Let's dance.'

'Oh, honey. You know I don't like to.' Gently, he removed her hand. 'Listen, I'm going to say hello to Harry. Why don't you go on and dance with your friends? I'll be just over there.'

'If that's what you want.' Genevieve pursed her lips in irritation. 'There are men who'd kill to dance with me, you know.'

*

'Chérie!' Lulu was shimmying wildly with the tall man in the cream suit.

Genevieve allowed Joseph Lazarus to take her hands and draw her close. Even as she began kick-stepping with Lazarus, her gaze was fixed on Lulu and the tall man.

'Isn't she a marvel?' Lazarus was dressed like a waiter, and Genevieve wasn't entirely sure whether this was a costume or merely his terrible fashion sense. 'Look at the way she moves. She's an empress. She should be in that fresco.' He pointed at the ceiling overhead. Genevieve glanced up at jackal-headed men among pyramids and palm fronds. Men with enormous eyes standing sideways on. Lulu's eyes were enormous too, and surrounded by a layer of thick black kohl that was certainly reminiscent of Ancient Egypt.

'Ladies and gentlemen.' The band-leader lowered his trumpet. 'As I'm sure you've noticed, we have in our midst that spectacular cabaret star, the most painted and photographed woman in the whole of Paris – Lulu of Montparnasse! Hey, Lulu, let's have you up here. Come on, girl, give us a song.'

And before he'd even finished speaking, Lulu was up there on the stage, saying something to the pianist, who nodded. Turning to face the room, she announced:

'This is a song about Paris. It's a special time, my friends, in this most amazing of cities. And 1925 will be the most amazing year of them all. The song is called, "C'est Nous Qui Avons de la Chance". In English, that's "We Are the Lucky Ones".'

Her voice, when she began to sing, was fine silk thrown over broken glass – covering but not truly concealing it.

The words blurred together; you couldn't make them out, but it was the voice that counted. Its pain, in spite of the cheery song title. It was the heartache in the big eyes that counted – belying the smile on the red lips, the frivolity of the painted-on beauty spot.

Genevieve was holding out her glass for a champagne refill and looking around for Robert when a deep, American voice just by her ear said:

'What's that supposed to be, do you think? An egg or a head?'

It was the man in the cream suit. He pointed at the Brancusi bronze atop its plinth.

'It's an egg that looks like a head that looks like an egg that looks like a head,' said Genevieve. He really was very handsome, this man. Broad shoulders, the nicest kind.

'You say that with such authority. Perhaps it's the English accent.'

'I have it from Violet. But that's just my précis. Her version took a good twenty minutes.' She showed her surprise at the lack of recognition on his face. 'Violet? The Countess de Frémont?' And then, when he continued blank, 'Our divine hostess. Were you actually invited to this party, Mr . . .'

'Monteray. Guy Monteray. And no, I wasn't. Not directly. I'm the guest of a guest.'

'I see.' She wanted to ask him who he was here with, but drew back. Tried once more to spot Robert.

'This is my first time in Paris,' said the man. 'I'm fresh off the boat. Practically a virgin.'

She sipped her wine and looked at him sidelong. 'I'm Genevieve Shelby King.' She tried his name on her tongue. It had a familiar sound to it. 'Are you a poet?'

The whitest of smiles. 'Would you like to dance, Miss Shelby King?'

'*Mrs.*'

'Oh.' The smile flickered for a moment. 'I do apologize. Where's your husband? Is he here?'

She gestured vaguely. 'He'll be over there somewhere. He doesn't dance.'

'Pity.'

'Yes,' said Genevieve. 'Yes, it is.'

Robert puffed on a cigar, sipped his bourbon and watched his wife dancing with an incredibly tall, broad-shouldered man in a cream suit. 'Fellow's like a skyscraper.'

'What a sharp observation.' The speaker was so insubstantial that Robert hadn't even noticed him. 'Mind if I borrow it?'

Robert's head was a little swimmy with the bourbon. He hadn't realized he'd spoken aloud. 'Borrow it?' He frowned, puzzled. 'They're only words. Don't belong to me any more than they do to you.'

'A dangerous point of view, that one.' A soft voice. A narrow face with glittering eyes and a high colour in the cheeks. 'If there were many people who spoke that way, well, what would become of *us*?'

'Us?' Robert watched the skyscraper man lift his wife clean off the floor before setting her down again and spinning her about. He made it look so effortless.

'Us low-down scribbling types who make commodities of

words. Not to mention literature. You don't remember me, do you, Robert?'

The fug in his head was thickening. 'You're a friend of my wife's, aren't you?' It was a safe bet. Everyone was a friend of Genevieve's. That was how it had been ever since they'd settled in Paris two years ago – ever since she'd taken up with that Lulu creature. He did his best to accept the situation. If you marry a woman as beautiful, clever, out-going and thoroughly modern-thinking as Genevieve, you can't expect to hide her away at home. You might as well ask a bird not to fly. But sometimes, just sometimes, he wished he could.

'Norman Betterson. A friend of Genevieve's and a recipient of your great generosity, sir.' His smile was almost manic. 'The magazine?' he added, by way of explanation.

Magazine . . . Robert groped about in his memory.

'The work's starting to dribble in now. I already have stories from Hemingway and Scott. And poetry from Gertrude Stein. I expect to have enough material to go to press in another month or two.' The fellow broke off at this point and erupted into a coughing fit which made him bend double.

'Are you OK?' asked Robert.

'Oh, don't worry about me.' He dabbed at his mouth with a large white handkerchief. 'I have five years to live. Plenty of time for you to make good on your investment.'

'Right. Of course.' Dry-mouthed, Robert smacked his empty glass down on a little table. He would have to speak to Genevieve. She was susceptible to men like this – men with fancy ideas and poetic aspirations in need of a few quick dollars. He hoped to God that it was only a

15

*few* dollars . . . Wasn't her fault – not exactly. Trouble was, she had dreams of her own. Dreams of becoming a poet. Her literary ambitions made her easy to exploit. And increasingly her vulnerability was rendering him vulnerable too. What would his daddy have to say about this if he was still alive?

He tried for another glimpse of her on the dance-floor, but couldn't see her.

'Your wife –' the eyes were glittering fiercely – 'is the most beautiful woman in Paris. She's got that aristocratic British thing, hasn't she? Like a racehorse. A real thoroughbred. You're a lucky man. Oh, don't look like that, Robert! I'm not saying she *looks* like a horse. Far from it. I—'

She had vanished. And so had the skyscraper man.

'Excuse me.' Robert straightened his jacket and cleared his throat. 'I must go and find—'

The man – Betterson, or whatever his name was – was already wandering away.

Robert wished nobody but himself could see Genevieve's beauty – its full, powerful dazzle. He liked to think that he was the only man who really knew her. He was ninety per cent sure he did. Or maybe ninety-five. There was just the tiniest bit of doubt in him, and he couldn't work out what it was all about.

At the moment when Robert set down his glass and began to search for Genevieve, she was standing with Lulu over by the Brancusi sculpture. A waiter on stilts came teetering by with a tray of canapés, all of them coloured green, and the girls raised their eyebrows in bemusement. Even if they'd wanted a snack, they'd never have been able to reach the tray.

'Well, that's about the stupidest thing I've ever seen,' said Genevieve. 'Must have been Violet's idea.'

'She's a singularly stupid woman,' said Lulu.

'But not so stupid that she can't throw the best party of the year. How could I possibly compete with this?'

Lulu flapped a dismissive hand. 'Oh, chérie. Don't even bother *thinking* about Violet de Frémont. She's nothing. Violet's trying to buy her way in but she can't get at the *real* Paris.'

'So what about me? Am I a part of the real Paris?'

'Ah, chérie. Stick with your friend Lulu and you won't go wrong. Live your life at night-time in the 6th, where Violet de Frémont is nothing but a tourist. The rich are mere consumers here. The real Paris is about the art that's in your heart and your mind.' She winked. 'Anyway, tell me about Guy Monteray.'

'You seem to know more about him than I do.'

'Come on, Vivi. You know what I'm talking about.'

'Do I?'

'I saw the way you were looking at each other.'

'Window-shopping, that's all.'

'If you say so.' But her face still wore that expression – suggestive, mischievous.

'Stop it!'

'Stop what?' But now the mischief was evolving into something approaching sympathy. 'Oh Vivi, this insistence on the sanctity of your marriage – it's sweet but ultimately . . .'

'Ultimately what?'

'Unrealistic.' The smallest sigh.

Genevieve pursed her lips and scanned the room again.

'So where's Camby tonight?' Lulu was in love with the renowned photographer Frederick Camby. Had been for years.

'How should I know? The man's a fool.' No discernible emotion from behind the make-up mask.

'There's Norman Betterson.' Genevieve touched Lulu's arm. 'I need a word with him. I gave him some of my poems to read a while ago, and . . .' But the sentence was left unfinished. She'd caught sight of something unmissable. A pair of shoes . . .

At the Shelby Kings' apartment on the Rue de Lota in the fashionable 16th Arrondissement, a whole room was devoted to Genevieve's shoes. Floor-to-ceiling shelves and each shelf crammed with wooden boxes. Boxes that were cushioned on the inside with velvet and silk. Inside each box, a pair of shoes. The boxes multiplied, week on week, month on month. Hundreds of boxes. Shoes made especially for Genevieve by the world's most exclusive designers. Shoes with glass heels. Shoes studded with gems. Shoes so perfect that Genevieve could hardly believe they really existed, so that she'd have to keep taking them out of the box and touching them and then putting them away again – afraid of soiling them, ruining them.

Shoes that, for the most part, had never been worn.

The shoes were somewhere between ivory and silver, and appeared to be made entirely of lace. Lace layered upon lace, spidery and fine. A slipper shape and a Louis heel – not too thick, not too high, not too low. Delicate toes. There was something about these shoes . . . Beautiful but subtle. Quietly calling all attention to themselves without the need to scream out. Genevieve's heart ached for them. She wished so much that she was wearing them in place of her own purpose-built poetic pumps. She'd been proud of them at the start of the evening but now they seemed, frankly, childish. They were no more than fancy-dress accessories, and this was wrong. Shoes should always be more than accessories.

She absolutely longed for those lace slippers to be on her feet, and instead . . .

Instead they were adorning the feet of her hostess, Violet de Frémont.

The countess was wearing a black dress overlaid with paper doilies, and had a doily hat perched on the back of her head. She was a good-looking woman but with features a touch too soft to be conventionally beautiful. That nose was almost piggy. She had something, though. She'd been painted and sculpted by everyone, and not just because of her money. And her ankles were perfect, her feet tiny. The shoes were divine on her.

'Genevieve, I'm so glad you could come.' Violet, clutching a glass of champagne, was making her way over. 'Oh, and Lulu, darling, the singing was wonderful. I wish I had a voice like yours.'

'Sensational party,' said Genevieve. 'And may I say, those shoes are *adorable*.'

Violet almost purred with pleasure. 'Aren't they?' All three of them looked down as she turned her feet this way and that to be further admired. 'You know, last night I had to get out of bed at some ungodly hour just so that I could take them out and put them on and look at them in the moonlight. Etienne woke up and found me dancing around in my négligé with the curtains open, gazing at my own feet. Can you imagine? He thought I'd gone stark staring mad!'

'I hadn't realized you were such a shoe connoisseur, Violet,' said Genevieve.

'Really? You must come round to see my collection some day. Oh – oh!' And now she seized Genevieve's arm. 'But look, here comes their creator! Genevieve, Lulu, this is Paolo Zachari.'

A velvety-looking man stood before them. Thirty-five or so. Soft black eyes. Black, tufty hair that was slightly too long – you wanted to stroke it, smooth it. His unusual suit was very dark – almost black but with a luminous glow that just hinted at blue. No refuse-costume for him. His face was serious but with something subtle happening at the mouth, something that was not quite a smile. His face was somehow familiar.

When he bent to kiss Genevieve's hand, she almost felt the tip of his tongue against her knuckles. Almost.

'Have we met before?' she asked, as he straightened.

'We have indeed.'

She frowned. He was raising Lulu's hand to his mouth. Complimenting her singing. He was too thin to be conventionally handsome, but was attractive all the same. One of those men who make themselves more attractive by dressing cleverly and by flirting. Yes, very flirtatious. Even as he was talking to Lulu, Genevieve saw his gaze flick across to her. He gave another of those almost-smiles and looked her up and down. Blatant. Impudent.

'It's strange,' she said, after a moment. 'I know we've met but I can't recall the exact occasion.'

'Can't you?' He turned to Violet and whispered something in her ear. Something that made her laugh out loud.

Genevieve felt herself blush. But why should she be embarrassed?

Now he bent to whisper to her, his mouth close. 'Am I so forgettable?' And his lips actually brushed against her ear.

'Of course not!' The words came out too loud, but the countess seemed not to have heard. She was deep in conversation with Lulu. And as Genevieve lowered her voice, words started coming out of her mouth. Words that she hadn't meant to say. 'I've heard all about you,' came the words.

'What have you heard?'

'That you choose your clients like you'd select a piece of fruit, just because you like the look of their feet. That you only make shoes for twenty women. That once a woman has worn a pair of Zachari's shoes, nobody else's will do.'

'Is that so?' He raised an eyebrow.

'You're a very talked-about man, Mr Zachari. Some people say you're from Italy. From Calabria. Or maybe Naples. Other people say you're from the East Indies. Or else that you're an East Indian from Calabria. Or a Neapolitan from the East Indies. I've heard so many stories about you.'

'My, my. All those rumours.' Zachari shook his head sadly. 'I know a little about you too, Mrs Shelby King.'

'What do you know?'

Again he bent to whisper in her ear, and she felt his breath hot against her neck.

*

21

'That man, Zachari.' Genevieve leaned against a marble pillar while the room began gently to turn.

Lulu shoved a canapé into her mouth. 'What about him?'

'What do you think of him?'

'Dark horse. Perhaps a little too deliberately so. He likes to hand-pick his clients, I gather. Obviously enjoys the exclusivity. I'm suspicious of his criteria.'

'I can't *believe* he makes shoes for Violet de Frémont,' said Genevieve. 'And not for me.'

Zachari and the Countess de Frémont were dancing together. He held her close, his hands planted firmly on her back.

'I've heard he's sleeping with her,' said Lulu.

Genevieve groaned. 'How could the man who made those delectable shoes have such appalling taste in women?'

'Jealous, chérie?'

'I must have a pair. I simply *must*.'

Lulu shrugged. 'Well, go right over and tell him. Sometimes a girl has to swallow her pride and speak out. Tiresome though that may be.'

But Genevieve was shaking her head. 'He hasn't chosen me. And now he never will. On our way in here tonight I mistook him for the footman. I shoved my fur at him, Lulu, and asked Robert to give him a tip.'

22

## 2

'YOU HAVE TO TAKE ME AWAY FROM HERE.' THAT WAS WHAT
Genevieve said when Robert got down on one knee in the
drawing room of her family home in Suffolk. Her breath
quickened, her chest began to heave and her eyes were a
deep wild blue. 'You have to take me away from here and
never bring me back.'

He was gratified by her enthusiasm. Her passion, one
might say. But the level of desperation was unsettling, and
inexplicable. What could be so awful about life in an
English stately home? Sure, it was a little damp and
draughty, but grand too. Her father, the Viscount Ticksted,
was something of an old buffer, but amiable with it. He'd
been tickled pink by the engagement, cracking open the
single malt and slapping Robert on the back, calling him
'my boy' and grinning so much that Robert could almost
see the blood vessels popping under his skin, while Lady
Ticksted had wept in a sunshine-and-rain sort of way and
kissed him on the cheek with thin, trembling lips. What
could be so awful about these people? They'd been a

positive boon so far as he was concerned. If only Daddy could have lived long enough to see this Boston boy marrying English nobility.

But there was Genevieve, seizing his hands with a strength that was, frankly, astonishing. 'I'll die if I have to stay here one more month, Robert. I want to live in Paris and write poetry and be among writers and artists and designers. We can be Bohemians together.'

Robert had no particular objection to a spell in Paris. It was cheap, for one thing. Post-war, the franc was practically worthless against the dollar and consequently the city was full of Americans. Home from home. And then, he had a fondness for Old Europe. He'd come to the continent in 1918, when he drove ambulances at the Italian front during the Austrian offensive at Piave, and fell in love, for the first time, with an English nurse called Agnes, who had a face like an angel and an air of gentle, exquisite sadness. The sadness concerned a fiancé who'd gone missing in action. Robert made it his personal mission to cheer the girl up and show her that there could be life beyond Edward. Gradually the colour returned to Agnes' cheeks and her laughter came much more freely. He intended, when the war was over, to ask her to marry him. But just before he was able to pop the question, she received a momentous letter. Edward was alive. He'd spent most of the year in a German prison camp, and was now a free man again. He declared himself 'not quite the ticket' but eager to 'pick up where we left off, dearest'.

Agnes could hardly get the words out. When Robert asked her what she planned to do, she simply hung her head and allowed her tears to roll down her nose. It was only later, too late, that Robert wondered if she had in fact been waiting for him to say something – do something. Declare his love once and for all and reassure her that yes, there still *was* a life beyond Edward. He didn't, of course. His sense of honour and duty forbade it. And that was the last time he ever saw her.

Really the most sensible thing he could have done was go straight home to Boston. But something made him stay on in Europe, travelling about, seeing the sights, wandering from country to country with an air of melancholy brooding. Some instinct made him believe that if he was ever to find that kind of love again, it would be here, amid the wreckage of war, in one of these strange old countries. Gradually, as he travelled and read and thought, the idea began to torment him that he'd inadvertently been entirely *dis*honourable in his dealings with Agnes – that it was the girl to whom he had a responsibility, not the unknown Edward. That he had abandoned her in the most dishonourable manner just when she needed him most. He would never make a mistake like that again, that was for sure. The next time he fell in love there would be no procrastination, no delay. He would seize his moment and secure his happiness. Newly resolved and in better spirits, he sailed to England, where he was introduced to the Viscount Ticksted, and invited to come for dinner one night at his house on the flat grey marshlands of Suffolk.

And there she was.

Looking back, Robert fancied that even on that very first night, watching the twenty-year-old girl smiling pleasantly and eating her roast pheasant with quiet precision, he could discern the real Genevieve beneath the demure exterior.

When he visited again and again in what became a three-month courtship, his own feelings developed rapidly. What a contrast to the vulnerable, watery Agnes this girl was. This beautiful girl, with all her fire and passion – the Honourable Genevieve Samuel, as she was then – well, this was the girl for him. For keeps. He'd give her whatever she wanted if only she'd agree to be his.

'I have to be free,' she said, on that momentous day in the drawing room, and she gripped his hands so hard he thought she would break them. 'I can never be free here.' And then she told him a story. An anxious, incoherent story about a horse she had as a child. 'I'd ride for miles and miles and hours and hours,' she said. 'I've never felt so free in my life.' One day, she said, there was a gunshot. A poacher, perhaps. The horse, frightened, threw Genevieve. She wasn't badly hurt but she never saw the horse again.

'You have to take me away from here.' (He was wondering, now, if she had a fever.) 'How quickly do you think it can be arranged?' Finally she released his hands, and her eyes looked liquid and dreamy. 'When we get married, I'll wear my cream silk shoes with the rhinestones by Alfred Victoria Argence. Paris isn't just a city, Robert. You'll see.'

Robert was watching Genevieve out of the corner of his eye, as they were driven home from the party in the Bentley. There was a restlessness about her tonight. She kept running her right hand through her glossy, bobbed hair. When he first knew her, in Suffolk, her hair was long and luxuriant, but perhaps little-girlish. Now it was cut short and chic, fashionably waved at the salon of Lina Cavalieri on the Rue de La Paix. It showed off her long neck.

Her left hand was held to that long neck – to the throat, where it agitated her necklace (large glass beads wrapped in snippets from poetry journals). It was something her mother did too – this unconscious clutching at the throat. Genevieve wouldn't be pleased if he were to point this out to her.

'Did you see Violet de Frémont's shoes?' she said suddenly, without turning to look at him. They were driving past the Hôtel de Ville and up the Rue de Rivoli, and it was raining. The streetlights blurred and seemed to dance.

'Can't say I did.'

She made a noise that was somewhere between a tut and a sigh, and straight away he felt he'd let her down. He'd never noticed shoes until he met Genevieve. Dresses, yes. Jewellery, yes. A neat figure and a pretty face – yes, of course. He was a man, after all. The mid-1920s had seen hemlines rising up towards the knee, drawing the gaze to the ankles, their narrowness, their fine bones. But Genevieve had taught him to look, too, at the shoes themselves. Beautifully designed, flamboyant shoes, made from expensive, richly coloured materials, promised a sensuality in the wearer. High heels were so provocative – the way they emphasized the arch of the foot, the fulsome curve of the calf. Genevieve prided herself on being one of the first women to really understand that shoes could be the focal point of an outfit. She was way ahead of the pack.

'Were they special in some way?' he asked, eventually.

'They were special in *every* way.' She pulled so hard on her necklace that the string snapped and the beads scattered. 'Don't!' she said, as he bent to gather them. But he did it anyway.

'Robert – what's more important, do you think: to be beautiful or to be talented?'

'Well . . .' He slipped some beads into his coat pocket and bent to retrieve more.

'Beauty's enough to make a man want to marry you, but it doesn't win respect, does it? It doesn't make people take you seriously. Not the people who really count.'

'Which people?' There was a bead stuck down the side of the seat. He was almost getting his fingers stuck, too, as he tried to fish it out.

'Oh, for heaven's sake leave it!'

'Got it.' The bead lay in the palm of his hand. It was wrapped in paper, like the others.

'If you're talented but ugly, you can be who you want to be. You can live like a man if that's what you want. Take Gertrude Stein, for example.'

'Must I?' He hadn't the first clue what she was talking about. Perhaps she'd had too much champagne. 'She's that poet who looks like a bulldog, right?'

Now she giggled and reached over to kiss him lightly on the lips. 'Quite so, darling. You're so sensible. My rock-solid husband.' She snuggled in close to him, laying her head on his shoulder. 'What would I do without you?'

'Well, you'd need to find someone to keep you in shoes, that's for sure.'

'Lulu has it all,' she murmured into his shoulder. 'Beauty, talent, fame, experience . . . She's not much older than me but I feel like a child in comparison to her. There's so much she *knows*.'

The bead in his hand had the one word, 'tenderness', written on it.

The apartment in the Rue de Lota had been redesigned by Eileen Gray. Genevieve's idea, though Lulu had more than a hand in it. The renovations took over a year – a year of living at the Ritz at great expense – and went way over budget. The result was a symphony in lacquer. The salon's shining black walls with silvered geometrical landscape, the study with parchment-covered ceiling and handsome bookcase, the famous canoe-shaped 'Pirogue' sofa in tortoiseshell. The equally famous, artfully curved 'Bibendum' leather seats, the ostrich-egg lampshades ... The apartment was photographed for many a style magazine and society page, with the happy couple posing arm in arm in the foreground.

Privately, Robert thought he'd preferred it before. It just wasn't very homely now. They'd stay a good long time, though, to justify all the money and time that had been lavished on it. In the mean time he had to run his sewing-machine manufacturing business from the wrong side of the Atlantic, relying more than he wanted to on Bram Fairley and certain other key employees, and on creaky communications systems. The telephones had a tendency to go dead in the middle of an important call and the electricity seemed to fling itself through the wiring in fits and starts so that you were nervous to so much as touch anything. All far from ideal, but it was what he wanted because it was what *she* wanted. Nothing made him more fulfilled than to see his wife happy.

'Are you happy, honey?' They were standing just inside

the front door, kissing. His arms were tight around her and his hands cupped the back of her head, holding it like it was a precious, fragile egg. His pockets were full of paper-wrapped glass beads.

'I'll be happy when I get a pair of Paolo Zachari's shoes.' She pulled away from him as she spoke, and headed for her room. 'That sow Violet de Frémont has him at her beck and call, apparently.'

'Ah. Shoes again.' They were both reflected, dimly, in the tiny golden tiles that covered the walls. Two vague shapes, some distance apart from each other. He watched his reflection moving towards hers.

'It's late.' She had her hand on the doorknob now. 'Time for bed.'

He felt sad and heavy. Even his reflection looked sad. He thought about his wife giggling with her appalling friend earlier that evening. He remembered the contempt he'd seen in Lulu's black-ringed eyes, the sneer at the corners of those red lips. Lulu was his enemy. He knew it now, with great clarity. And she was ever-present, or so it seemed. He could almost see her reflection in the golden wall-tiles, along with his own and Genevieve's.

'But you can join me,' she said. 'If you want to, that is.'

# 3

ON THE AFTERNOON FOLLOWING THE COUNTESS DE Frémont's party, Genevieve made her way to Rumpelmayer's, an Austrian *salon de thé* on the Rue de Rivoli, where she and Lulu met regularly – often when Lulu had just ended a love affair, and wished to celebrate or console herself with a dessert.

She took a seat at her favourite corner table, beneath an arch, with a prime view of the comings and goings of the room, and was already halfway through a *chocolat l'Africain* (Paris's best hot chocolate in a cup, prepared to a secret recipe) and a praline cake filled with almond meringue when Lulu arrived, still wearing her dress from the previous night. Some of the sweet papers had gone, leaving only dangling threads. Her make-up looked thick and crumbly and her curls were flattened.

'I'll have a chocolate mousse,' Lulu called to the waitress. 'And a *café noisette*.' And then more quietly, to Genevieve, 'Am I being followed?'

Genevieve peered without seeming to peer. 'Who should

I be looking for? A gendarme? A fanatic? A wronged wife?'

Lulu shrugged. 'Any of those, I suppose. But particularly Joe Lazarus.'

'Oh dear. Has something happened?'

'He just won't take no for an answer.' Lulu took off her wrap and sat down. 'He's following me about as if he's my shadow. I should never have slept with him, Vivi. I don't know what I was *thinking* of. He has such short legs. And his feet turn out. Walks like a penguin. I didn't really notice until I saw him without his trousers, but once you've seen it you can't ignore it. And he does this thing. He—' But a waitress came over with cutlery and napkins to set her place and she let the sentence go.

'So the mousse is for poor old Lazarus.'

Lulu flapped a hand. 'He's a very unfortunate individual, let's leave it at that. New subject, please.'

'Last night?'

Another flap of the hand. 'Oh, you know. The usual.'

'Tell me everything. I want to know what I missed.'

'No.' A sulky pout. 'You should have been there with me. It's not enough to listen to stories. You have to be a part of them.'

The waitress brought the coffee and mousse.

'Don't be like that, Lulu.'

'Like what? You keep telling me your husband is enough for you. If that's true, then you won't need my stories to keep you happy.' She stabbed at her dessert with a spoon.

Genevieve sighed. 'Why do the two things have to be linked? Am I not allowed to be interested in your night?'

'Come on, Vivi. You know you didn't want to go home at the end of the party. Admit it.'

Genevieve drained her hot chocolate. 'I was quite ready for bed.' There was a stiffness in her neck that made her want to shrug her shoulders and roll her head around. She could still feel Robert's hands, holding the back of her head when they kissed in the hallway. Why did he have to do that? It was like being trapped in some kind of brace.

'And it was very exciting in that marital bed, eh?'

Robert had 'before' rituals. The special knock on her door – one light knock, one heavy, like a heartbeat. Always the same. Then, as though there was a further need to identify himself, he'd call, 'Only me,' before coming in. He'd get into the bed on the left side, always the left, and he'd warm his cold feet against hers.

There were 'during' rituals too. First the whiskery kisses that made her want to gasp for air, then the interminable fumbling below the sheets. She'd tried to speak to him gently, in the hope of improving the experience for both of them, but such discussion was unacceptable to him. This came as an unpleasant surprise after her early impressions of him as someone you could talk to about anything. Eventually he'd just hitch up that nightshirt of his, climb on top and do the business. Heavy, red-faced, mechanical. And the knocking would start. Exactly which *component* of the bed made that strange noise? She'd tried to figure it out during the day, peering at the legs, the mattress . . . Knockety-knock, faster and faster. It was like making love with an overwound clockwork toy.

Afterwards, he would trace circles on her bare shoulder and try to talk to her, just when she didn't feel like talking. Small circles. Large circles. Always circles. He hummed too. The humming would almost be a recognizable tune, but not quite.

'You seem . . .' he began, last night, as he traced those damn circles.

'What?'

'Distant.' Tonight's humming was very nearly a Charleston. One of the dance tunes from the party.

'I'm just thinking about the evening. Mulling things over.'

'What things?' The circle-tracing continued.

'Nothing much.'

'But I like to know what you're thinking,' he said. 'I want to be as close to you as one person can be to another.'

'We're close enough, aren't we? Do I have to tell you every single thing that pops into my head? Can't I keep just a *few* things to myself?'

'But, honey.' He was still humming. Perhaps he didn't know he was doing it. 'You're my wife.'

I'm trying to be, she thought. I'm really trying.

When Robert had finally – *finally* – left her room, Genevieve lay on her side with her eyes closed, thinking about what Lulu and the others might be doing. They were heading off to the Select as she waved goodbye and got into the Bentley with Robert. Lulu's long-term lover, Camby, would be there and she was clearly desperate to see him, though she'd never have admitted it. First there'd be a couple of drinks, and then a whole lot more. There'd be some dancing, and maybe a fight. And suddenly it would be morning, and they'd all go off to Les Halles for onion soup at one of the market cafés or buy a picnic breakfast and take taxis out to the Bois. Eventually they'd return to the Boulevard du Montparnasse for coffee at the Dôme or La Rotonde. The Quarter would be back in full swing and all of Paris would be rushing by, and they'd just sit back with the papers and watch and nurse their aching heads, till one by one they peeled off to bed, leaving only Lulu, still partying, still wanting more.

'I bet he's a red-hot lover, eh, Vivi? Your Robert?'

'Your make-up's crumbling into your coffee,' said Genevieve. 'Look at all those little flakes floating about.'

'A truly feeble attempt at changing the subject.' But Lulu was staring into her coffee, and then squinting myopically at her reflection in the gilt-framed mirror that hung just behind their table.

'Lulu, I think you might need spectacles.'

'Shut up.' With a growl, Lulu bent and peered under the table.

'What now?'

'I'm having a look at today's shoes.'

Relieved, Genevieve turned her feet this way and that. High-fronted court shoes, covered in pearls, stones and gold decoration, with outlandish corkscrew heels.

'Now those really are amazing.'

'They're by Salvatore Ferragamo. I had them specially imported from California. He designed them for Gloria Swanson and she doesn't know he made a second pair for me.'

'I've never seen anything like them.'

'Ferragamo's a genius. He's discovered that the weight of a woman's body isn't carried on the ball and heel of the foot alone, but on the entire arch. He puts a thin strip of steel into the soles of his shoes to support the foot. If the sole is stronger there's not so much pressure on the heel so you can play with the shape – make the heel thinner, make it into a corkscrew, whatever.'

'You could almost be talking about buildings, chérie. Strengthening the foundations so you can build higher. Your Ferragamo is like an architectural engineer.'

'But so much more sexy. All the Hollywood stars want his shoes.'

'Well,' said Lulu, 'who needs Zachari when you've got Gloria Swanson's corkscrew heels?'

At the mention of that name, Genevieve's smile went slightly askew.

'What is it now?' asked Lulu.

'Well,' said Genevieve, 'my first thought, when I woke up this morning, was about those shoes of Violet's. I have to have a pair of Zacharis, Lulu. And I was feeling defiant. I decided to go over to his shop and talk him round.'

\*

# Paolo Zachari
## *World's Most Expensive Shoes*

The sign took up half the shopfront. Genevieve peered in at the window. It was dark and cloaked in deep purple velvet on the inside. There was no display of any kind. And no clear indication of whether the shop was open or closed. It seemed very quiet though. Nothing to do but try the door.

Nervous, and irritated with herself for this nervousness, she reached for the round brass handle.

The door opened smoothly and she stepped into a square room hung all over with the same purple velvet that shrouded the inside of the window. No natural light was allowed in, and the room flickered in the glow of various candelabra positioned on ebony side tables among copies of *Vogue*. Genevieve wrinkled her nose at the hot, sweet odour of melting wax. Further light came from a cluster of five or six twisted candles in an ornate silver cage, suspended on a chain from the ceiling. How quaint, like stepping back into the last century.

White wax dripped, slow and globular, pooling on the ebony tables and dark wood floor – oak perhaps – which was uneven and highly polished. The zebra-skin rug in the centre of the room made a better impression. Much more modern. There were a couple of Napoleon III couches upholstered in the purple velvet, and Genevieve wondered if she should sit down on one of them and wait for someone to come. But did anyone know she was here? The door had made no sound. There was no bell to ring for attention.

And there were no shoes. Not one.

'Hello?' Her voice was over-loud in the stillness. '*Bonjour?*' She caught her reflection in the long silver mirror at the far end of the room. She was visibly tentative, damn it, and she didn't want to be. She looked very good, though. Beneath the long cuir de laine coat with collar and cuffs in squirrel fur was a dress of Canton crêpe in Copenhagen blue, the Jenny collar in fine cream lace and tucked georgette softening the daring V-neck, the low waistline encircled with a band of shirring. The outfit was topped off with a cloche hat in crêpe de Chine, slightly rolled, and on her feet were Gloria Swanson's shoes with those revolutionary corkscrew heels. Surely even an élitist like Zachari would be impressed.

'Yes?'

Genevieve wheeled around, mortified at having been caught admiring herself, one hand moving defensively to her throat, to find herself facing a thin, elegant woman of forty or so, with clear blue eyes and long hair swept back in a chignon. The hair was remarkable for its strangely in-determinate colour – neither blond nor silver nor brown nor grey but somehow all of these one by one, changing from moment to moment. Spun gold in the flickering light of the candle flames, and then cold, shining steel as she stepped back into the shadows.

'Yes?' the woman repeated – adding, with a slow, sarcastic insolence, 'Madame?'

'I'm here to see Monsieur Zachari.'

The woman blinked and slowly looked her up and down. As she shifted from one foot to the other, the light changed again and for a second her hair was almost the same iridescent blue as her eyes. She said nothing.

'I would like to see Monsieur Zachari, please.'

The gaze was disconcerting. She seemed to look right through and beyond Genevieve.

'Is there a problem?' Genevieve was snappish now. 'Am I not making myself clear?'

'Quite clear. But you don't have an appointment.' A heavy accent. Russian? Polish?

'I most certainly do.' She felt foolish the moment the words came out, but she couldn't stop herself in time. There was something about this woman that made her want to argue, even if she had no grounds for doing so.

'No. You don't.' There was a smile on the pale face, but the eyes were crystal cold.

Genevieve, struggling to conquer her embarrassment at her own foolishness, attempted a polite smile. 'Could you tell me, please, whether Monsieur Zachari is here?'

'It makes no difference whether he's here or not. You don't have an appointment.'

'How do you know that I don't have an appointment? You haven't made the slightest attempt to check in a book or speak to Mr Zachari. You haven't even asked me my name.'

'I know about the appointments. I know that you don't have one.' A sharpness in the woman's expression. Something jagged. With her colourless hair, her pale eyes, her coldness, she put Genevieve in mind of shards of glass.

Genevieve opened her calfskin clutch-bag and delved about for a card, holding it out stiffly.

'Please take this to Monsieur Zachari. Tell him that I am a friend and client of Coco Chanel and Paul Poiret. Tell him . . .' (and this stuck in her throat), 'tell him that I'm a close friend of the Countess de Frémont, and that I would be most obliged if he would give me a few minutes of his time. I would like to order a pair of shoes.'

The assistant made no move to take the card and Genevieve thrust it further – holding it almost under her nose.

'Will you please take my card to Monsieur Zachari?'

The woman raised her hand, and it seemed as though she might be about to take the card, but instead she touched at her hair, tidying invisible stray strands. 'He's not here.'

Genevieve's hand dropped. 'Well, when *will* he be here? Can I make an appointment?'

A sound from somewhere in the building. Hard to say whether it came from above or below or just behind the shop room. A cough.

Genevieve frowned. 'Are you *sure* he's not here?'

'There is no one here.'

And another cough. There was no mistaking it. A man's cough.

Genevieve took a step sideways and tried to peer down the narrow staircase at the back of the room, as though if she tried hard enough she might be able to see through the closed door at the bottom. The woman also moved, blocking Genevieve's view. She looked suddenly weary.

'This is ridiculous. I don't know why you're lying to me, but let me tell you that you're not doing Monsieur Zachari any favours. I will not forget this discourtesy.' She slapped her card down on the tallest of the little tables. 'Please show this to Monsieur Zachari and ask him if he would be so good as to telephone me. I intend to order a pair of shoes from him. That is my intention.' A quick glance at the mirror showed that she was white in the face. The woman also looked into the mirror. They stood for a moment, both gazing at Genevieve's reflection. She was smaller than the woman, and for perhaps the first time in her life she felt truly diminutive.

She made for the door.

'If you or Monsieur Zachari cared to make an enquiry or two, you would discover that I am not a woman to be trifled with. Not a bit of it.'

And she blundered out, tripping on the edge of the step.

'Oh dear.' Lulu set down her coffee cup. 'Not so good. But perhaps he'll telephone.'

'No,' said Genevieve. 'I doubt that awful woman will even give him my card.'

'You think she's that arrogant? Failing to pass messages to her boss – she could find herself out of a job.'

'I don't know if it's arrogance, but there's something about her. She took an instant dislike to me.' Genevieve helped herself to another spoonful of Lulu's mousse. 'And I to her. No, she won't give him my card, I'm certain of it. I shall have to find a way to bypass her.'

Lulu raised her cup in salute. 'I'll come with you, chérie. Tomorrow. This woman is no match for the two of us. Let's have a drink. Fighting talk gives me a thirst.'

'Isn't it a bit early for alcohol? Even for you?'

'You forget, I haven't been to bed yet. It's still yesterday as far as I'm concerned. If anything, it's very late.'

Genevieve frowned. There was just a touch too much bravado in her friend's voice. 'Is something wrong?'

Lulu made a face. 'Oh, you know. The usual.'

'Camby? What's he done now?'

But she just shook her head as though it was far too complicated for Genevieve to understand. 'I wish I didn't care about that man. Typical, isn't it? Practically all the men in Paris are in love with me and I want the one man who isn't!'

'He's in love with you all right.' Genevieve reached over and squeezed her hand. 'Frankly, you're as bad as each other. Neither of you can stand being taken for granted. You enjoy being mysterious and unpredictable. And you hurt each other because you'd rather feel pain than feel nothing.'

'Maybe you're right, chérie.' Lulu smiled. 'How do you know me so well?'

'I just do,' said Genevieve. 'And you know me too – better than anyone.'

Lulu eyed her. 'If we weren't such good friends, we would have to be enemies.' And then she was back to talking about Camby again, and what a bastard he was. 'I'm so angry with him, Vivi. I don't know what to do about it. What would you do?'

Genevieve shrugged. 'I don't know. Write a poem, probably.'

'I can't write poems. Something happens – I get all the words back to front. The letters go twisting away from me.'

'Sing about it, then. Put the emotions into your art. That's what Camby does, after all.'

'Yes. The swine.'

Genevieve gave her hand another squeeze. 'Buck up, darling. I've decided to throw a party. A grand costume party, like Violet's but bigger and better. The theme will be Cubism.' She'd only actually had the idea this very second but she was already warming to it. 'What do you think?'

Lulu clapped her hands in delight. 'What fun!'

'I'll have to settle on a suitable venue, of course.'

'Of course.' She looked quite restored now. 'You could commission some special works. Something by Braque or Derain. Oh, and Sonia Delaunay. Have you seen her latest fashion designs? Very Cubist. She's going to be the star of the Exposition, you know.'

'Excellent. Would you help me, Lulu? You know all the artists, after all.'

But Lulu was distracted again. Her gaze darted about before she seized Genevieve's arm and whispered in her ear.

'Don't look now, chérie, but that damn penguin just walked in.'

# 4

ROBERT CAME UP WITH THE IDEA AT THE END OF ONE OF HIS poker nights. These were regular monthly jaunts with Harry Mortimer and his pals at a tiny club in Montmartre. They ate supper and had a few drinks and played a little poker. Robert wasn't a cards man: he'd never played until he came to Paris and met Harry. The evenings at the club – all that drinking, the great haze of smoke, the chips pushed back and forth over the green baize, and a certain kind of talk … these things were a form of holiday decadence, so far as he was concerned. Permissible during the extended sojourn in Paris, but due to end for ever with the inevitable (though not scheduled, as yet) return home to his family and the factory and his Boston way of life.

Harry was at least ten years older than Robert – a stout, balding newspaper-man with quick wits, a quicker temper and sufficient experience held under that straining belt to justify his strong opinions. He was a dissolute version of Robert's own father, and this made him attractive company.

The poker was a challenge. Robert played too cautiously, and knew it. Sometimes, when he'd folded again and yet again, he'd catch Harry raising an eyebrow just ever so slightly, egging him on. *Go on*, Robert. Get in the game. Be a devil. But he didn't seem to have it in him – that devilish streak. That was real money on the table. If his two cards weren't obviously good, he just wouldn't play. Sometimes the flop would be laid out and he'd see he could have had a straight, after all, and taken the hand. But other times his cards turned out to be worth diddly-squat and he'd sip his drink with quiet satisfaction that he was right to stay the hell out.

Genevieve knew about the poker, but she didn't know what else Harry and the guys got up to at the club in Montmartre. To start off with, the girls would bring the drinks up to the cards room, light the cigars and replace the ashtrays, smiling sweetly all the while. But later on, when the smoke was thicker, Harry's voice was louder and the chips were shuttling back and forth in bigger and bigger stacks, they'd linger on, waiting for their cue to sit down on an ample lap, drape an arm around a thick neck and start whispering and giggling – before leading the boys one by one up the little staircase at the back of the club to the rooms above.

And here came Robert's favourite moment. The moment when he got up from the card table and stepped out into the cool, dark, smoke-free night air or the lovely new lilac of approaching dawn. He'd wander down the hill to look for a cab home, all alone in this great city but for the occasional passing motor car or chirping bird. His money would be safe in his pocket (for he always knew when to cash in his chips) and his virtue still intact (the girls quickly learned they were wasting their time dallying on this boy's lap or whispering in his ear). Sometimes he'd walk the whole way home, whistling.

'How's that gorgeous filly of yours?' Harry had asked tonight as he shuffled the cards. 'Got her tightly reined in, I hope?' He was drunk already, and leering, but it was just his manner, his way of being friendly.

'You can't rein in a girl like Genevieve,' said Robert. 'That's the last thing to do with her.'

Harry shrugged, and dealt to the five players. 'Well, my advice to you, my boy, is to keep a close eye on your lady. Those artistic types she pals around with ... Well, I certainly wouldn't trust a man who wears a beret or a cape.' As he said this, he looked up and winked at a pretty redhead who was lingering in the doorway.

'I don't need to trust them,' said Robert. 'I trust *her*.'

'Very admirable, I'm sure. Say, why don't you bring her round to my place some time, eh? We could have a little dinner, and the girls could gossip about babies or flower-arranging or whatever it is they like to talk about.'

'Sure. That'd be nice.' Robert could imagine only too well what Genevieve would think of the idea of spending an evening with Maud Mortimer. Maud, with her charity committees and her tapestry-work. They just weren't Genevieve's kind of people, the Mortimers. None of his friends were. That was immediately obvious when he first introduced her around, soon after they arrived in Paris. And after all, what did he expect from marrying someone of her quality? Why, he'd never have fallen in love with the sort of girl who'd be bosom chums with Maud

46

Mortimer, or possibly even with any of the girls back home.

'Firm handling, Robert.' Harry picked up his two cards. 'That's what they need, these women.' Again he winked at the redhead. 'And, hey, I'm going to call you tomorrow, with the number of a friend of mine.'

'What sort of friend?' Robert heard the wariness in his voice.

Harry tapped the side of his nose and leaned closer so the others around the table wouldn't hear what they were saying. 'I'll explain when I call you.'

Robert picked up his cards, frowning.

'Let's talk tomorrow.' Harry glanced down at his. 'You in?'

'Nope. I'm folding.'

Out in the street just before 4 a.m., under a night sky covered in dense cloud so that it looked like a heavy velvet cloth thrown over the rooftops, chimneys and towers, Robert wandered through the sleazy, brothel-lined streets of Pigalle, more or less in the direction of home, thinking about the way Harry had kept on about Genevieve.

Harry just doesn't understand, he decided. It's not his fault – not exactly. It's the way he is.

He stuck out his arm to hail a taxi, and allowed himself a smile. She's lucky to have chosen a man like me.

The taxi pulled up – one of the old horse-drawn kind that you barely saw any more.

Does she know just how lucky she is? he thought, as he opened the door.

And then he had his idea.

*

It was on the day after the Countess de Frémont's party that Robert's idea came to fruition.

Genevieve returned home in the late afternoon, after listening to Lulu trying out some new numbers with her pianist at the Coyote on the Rue Delambre. She was stepping out of the lift when she saw her own front door opening just a crack. A small face – surely that of Céline, the maid – peered out, and then the door was slammed shut again so quickly that Genevieve was uncertain as to whether it had really happened.

'Céline?' Genevieve rapped smartly on the door. 'Céline!'

But it was Robert who opened the door and stepped outside, pulling it to behind him. He had an odd look about him.

'Are you ill or something?'

'Close your eyes,' said Robert, grabbing her by the hand. 'I have a surprise for you.'

'What sort of surprise?'

'Just close your eyes.'

She heard the creak of the door being opened again, and his muffled footsteps on the hall carpet. He was breathing through his mouth – the way he often did when he was nervous. There were other times, too, when he breathed that way . . . She saw him in her mind, close up, his face right above hers, his weight pinning her down. The moustache smelling of cigars and bourbon and his dinner. That breathing . . .

'Come on, Robert.'

Why was her heart thudding like this?

48

There was a rustling sound from inside the apartment. A papery sound.

'Can I open my eyes now?'

Standing there, with her eyes still shut, she felt her surroundings fading away. The floor beneath her feet seemed less solid than it had a moment ago. She could almost be drifting off, up to the ceiling – perhaps down the lift shaft. She wanted to reach out, put her palms against the silk-papered walls, grab hold of something so she could be sure of where she was.

'All right.' He was close by again. His hands landed, heavy, on her shoulders and he gave her a little shove forward over the threshold. 'Open your eyes.'

The surprise was towering over her so that she thought, for an instant, it would crash down on top of her. She let out a little squeal and tried to step backwards, but the heavy hands pressed her to the spot, and Robert's body was like a wall behind her.

'I've never forgotten that story you told me,' he said, in a whisper. 'About your horse. It touched me in some way I can't explain. I've imagined you as a little girl, riding out across the land, free as a bird. I've thought about it a lot.'

It was really there, in the middle of the hall, rearing up in front of her on its marble pedestal. It had to be eight feet tall. Bronze.

'You see?' And he nuzzled the back of her neck. 'You have a husband who understands you absolutely. Did you know that?'

Fixedly crazed eyes, enormous teeth, hideous flared nostrils. How could he *possibly* think . . . ?

49

On the night when Genevieve first met Robert, as her father's dinner guest, she smiled at him across the table and knew straight away that he had come to rescue her.

She was sorely in need of a rescuer. Even before her troubled summer she had begun to long for escape. She'd been getting through the interminable days by reading, dreaming about the life she could one day have, and scribbling her fantasies in her notebook in the form of poems. And then Robert arrived, with his easy laughter and his gallantry and his kind smile. How relaxed he seemed beside her pinch-faced, neurotic mother. How straightforward beside her double-dealing father. She'd grown up in a house full of secrets where nobody ever spoke their mind. And here at last was a man she could really talk to.

During their three-month courtship, she'd sat back from their conversations, trying to assess him seriously and not allow her judgement to be coloured by her eagerness to get away from her parents. She wasn't in love with him – not in an explosive, earth-shattering way, at any rate. But she felt a tremendous fondness for him, and she sincerely believed she could make this evolve into the Real Thing. At the time he proposed, she thought she was halfway there.

The horse was life-size but with nothing of life about it.

'I guess I don't know much about art,' Robert was saying, 'but I took some advice, and I can tell you this is a sound investment. More so than those literary magazines you have me funding.'

One afternoon, late on in their courtship, Robert and Genevieve were walking together in Lady Ticksted's rose garden. The sky had been getting progressively darker, and then thunder rolled overhead.

Genevieve turned her face up to the sky. The storm would be magnificent. 'Do you know how hungry I am?' she whispered. 'For life, I mean. For the world.'

'We'd better get back,' said Robert. 'It's going to rain.'

'Then let's get wet.' She had a tight hold of his arm.

'Your mother won't be pleased with me. What if you got a chill?'

'Oh, Robert. Don't be boring.'

The rain came suddenly.

'Quick,' he said. 'We'll be drenched.'

'I don't care.' And then she put a hand against his cheek. 'I'm suffocating in that house. My life is moving further and further away from me.'

He frowned, and gave her the look. The lost-dog look. It said, 'What are you talking about?' It said, 'Poor me.' It was the first time she'd seen it.

She stopped in her tracks. One word sounded in her head. The word was NO, loud and clear.

'Genevieve?'

Within seconds, she'd rallied. Swallowed heavily. Sent the word away. Made herself forget it.

He was the man who would take her out of this place for ever and show her the world.

He squeezed her hand.

And she let him lead her back into the house.

*

'Genevieve? Aren't you going to say something?'

She couldn't go on pretending to herself.

He didn't know her. He would never know her.

## 5

GENEVIEVE WAS TO MEET LULU MID-MORNING FOR THE assault on Zachári's shop, but in the event she was already there, alone, before even the weak March sun was properly up. She'd had a poor night's sleep. Every time she closed her eyes she saw those hooves rearing up above her. Her head was full of whinnying and snorting. It was as though that monstrosity in the hall was laughing at her. Unable to bear the thought of more hours lying awake, followed by breakfast with Robert (what would she say to him over the breakfast table? What would she *do*?), she'd bathed, dressed and left the apartment.

A lamp glowed from a basement window below the shop. His workroom? He must be there on his own. She contemplated ringing the bell, but was discouraged by the 'closed' sign. She didn't want to aggravate him more than she had already. After circling the tiny courtyard a couple of times, she walked back out of the passageway.

The Rue de la Paix was quieter than she'd ever known it. The shutters of the great fashion houses were all closed, the air still. She stood for a moment, gazing out across the Place Vendôme. The famous column looked somehow pudgy this morning. Soft. Like a bolt of cloth standing upright at the centre of the eight-sided piazza. Must be a trick of the light.

As she stood there in dreamy contemplation, a long black Lea Francis car passed by, too close to the kerb, and splashed dirty puddle water all up her legs. Her unique court shoes by André Perugia, *the* Paris shoe designer – impossibly high Spanish heels and pointy toes; the softest leather overlaid with a mass of brilliantly coloured and intricately worked triangles in silk, suede and brocade, inspired, so Perugia said, by Matisse's painting, and worn especially to impress Paolo Zachari – were drenched and mud-spattered. Outraged, she stepped forward, opening her mouth to shout something, but the car was already disappearing down a side-street. There was a woman sitting in the back. She wasn't clearly visible but Genevieve thought she knew who it was, all the same.

After two fortifying coffees and a *croissant beurre* consumed at one of the window tables of a nearby café with a lurid green interior, Genevieve made herself bend down to peer at her sodden shoes. It was as she'd thought. They were ruined. She'd wet her hankie in a glass of water to dab at them, but what was the point?

'You'd better look on the bright side.' A male voice, nearby. 'They weren't so lovely, were they? A little clownish. Harlequin shoes, one might say. Not a great loss.'

'Not a great loss! Do you have any idea how much

these . . .' And, straightening, Genevieve found she was talking to Paolo Zachari.

'They're André Perugia's, aren't they?' he said, looking amused. 'So you've certainly overpaid.' And then he removed his overcoat and sat down at her table without even asking permission to join her.

At first she couldn't speak. His arrogance had swept all her words away and left her gaping at him. He was wearing what she supposed must be his work clothes – some tweedy brown trousers, good-quality but faded and baggy, and a loose-fitting cotton shirt, open at the neck. But with all that swagger, you'd have thought he'd never lower himself to any actual work. His black eyes gave away nothing of his thoughts, his true intentions.

A pigeon-chested waiter with melancholy moustaches brought over an almond croissant and a *café espresse* and set them down in front of him. Zachari's regular daily breakfast, it seemed – the order so unchanging that it no longer had to be spoken.

'Did you win yesterday, Anton?' Zachari asked.

The waiter shook his head. 'It's a sad business, Monsieur Zachari. Fabienne's going to kill me when she finds out how much I lost. I was so certain, you know? I really thought I knew what I was doing.'

Zachari gripped the waiter's sloping shoulder. 'Nothing is ever certain, my friend.' And as he spoke, he was looking over at Genevieve again, narrowing his eyes.

This was the moment when Genevieve spotted the freckle at Zachari's throat, just above the shirt collar, nestled into that little hollow where the skin is at its softest. Somehow that small freckle changed everything. It was friendly. It hinted at another side to the man – a vulnerability. Genevieve, fixing her gaze on it, began to relax.

'I'm throwing a costume party,' she told Zachari. 'The theme will be Cubism. It will be a party to dwarf even Violet de Frémont's. A *legend* of a party. Everyone will be there, and everyone will be looking at me.' She took a breath. 'And I will be wearing a pair of your shoes, Mr Zachari. What do you think?'

Zachari's mouth stretched into a smile. He took a cigarette from a packet in his jacket pocket and tapped it on the box. 'Do you mind if I smoke?'

Emboldened, Genevieve reached for his box and took a cigarette for herself too.

'So shoes are important to you, then, Mrs Shelby King?' He held a lighter to her cigarette, and then to his own.

'Absolutely.'

He leaned back in his chair and raked a hand through his tufty black hair.

'Why?' He blew out smoke and quietly scrutinized her.

'*Why?*' she repeated. The cigarette was stronger than she'd expected. It made her feel slightly nauseous. She took another drag, none the less. 'Does there need to be a reason? Shoes can be beautiful. We both know this. They can be works of art.'

'But so can dresses, can't they? So can necklaces and rings and perfumes. Why the particular interest in shoes?'

'I'm a collector,' said Genevieve, slightly put out now. 'I have a room full of shoes. Over five hundred pairs. Shoes are my passion.'

'Yes, yes. But you're still not telling me *why*.'

The cigarette was making her head spin. 'Perfume means nothing to me. I wear it, of course, but that's as far as it goes. Dresses, jewellery – well, they're important, but they're so *obvious*. Truly beautiful shoes are so much more fascinating. Why, a few years ago you could have worn hobnail boots or clogs under your dress and nobody would have been any the wiser. But now ... Now an outfit is nothing without the right shoes.'

The smile stretched a little wider. 'Go on?'

She realized she was being tested. Her answer had better be the right one. 'And then, good shoes aren't merely beautiful. The fit must be perfect or the most fabulous party can be utter torture. Shoes connect us to the world, you know, in the most direct physical sense.' She liked this last pronouncement. It had a profound quality to it. Her head was swimming all the more, though. She stubbed out the cigarette.

'That's all very interesting and pretty.' Zachari put out his own cigarette. 'But it's not the real reason, is it?'

Genevieve was becoming exasperated. 'Look, I just like them. All right? What more do you expect me to say?'

'Nothing.' He drained his coffee cup. 'Nothing at all.'

The silence between them was abruptly broken by a loud tapping on the window. Genevieve, startled, twisted round to see Zachari's glassy assistant standing in the street outside. Her hair was silvery in the cold sunlight. Her face was sharper, somehow, than Genevieve remembered it. Ignoring Genevieve and focusing solely on Zachari, she gave a little jerk of the head and pointed meaningfully at her wristwatch. Then she turned and walked away.

'I must go.' He reached for his overcoat.

'Because that woman says so?'

'Because I have an appointment with a customer.'

Genevieve searched for the freckle but it was obscured, now, by his shirt collar.

'And what about me?'

'You?'

'The shoes for my party?'

Zachari frowned. 'I haven't promised to make you any shoes, Mrs Shelby King.'

'But you will – won't you?' She smiled in as coquettish a manner as she could.

Zachari put his head to one side and appeared to be considering the issue.

'Please?' Genevieve hated the smallness of that word.

Zachari put his head to the other side.

'Look, I know I offended you at Violet de Frémont's party. If there was any way on earth that I could go back to that moment and unmake that mistake, then I would. It was just a mistake, Monsieur Zachari. A plain, simple mistake for which I am most terribly sorry.'

'And what makes you think I care about that, madame?'

Genevieve's smile had taken on a beseeching quality. My goodness, she realized. I'm practically begging! And the realization brought her to her senses. He was just a shoe-maker, after all. He might be immune to her charms, her apologies, her willingness to humble herself, but she still had one thing that he couldn't possibly be immune to. The dollar. King of all currencies.

She reached for her bag and brought forth the wad. Letting the money talk for her.

But now he got to his feet and turned to leave. It was

as though he hadn't even seen the cash in her hand.

'Good-day to you, madame. It's been an unusual breakfast. Entertaining, but ultimately a little disappointing. For both of us, I suspect.'

The girls ate lunch at the Dôme, seated at the table that the management kept permanently reserved for Lulu. Today she was wearing a silly black hat decorated with peacock feathers. Her eye make-up was more Egyptian and elaborate than ever.

'I've found out some more stories about Zachari,' she said, pushing her plate away.

'What kind of stories?'

'That he came to Paris because he was running from the Mafia. That his life was forfeit as part of a blood feud between his family and another, and he got on the boat with another boy's blood still smeared across his face. That his mother sent him over here in a basket when he was only a baby because she was mad and couldn't take care of him. That he was brought up by Calabrian wolves.'

'So what's the truth?'

Lulu shrugged. 'How should I know? He must enjoy the rumours, otherwise there wouldn't be so many of them. I think you will have to be the one to find out, chérie.'

'I can't bear him,' said Genevieve. 'He's the rudest, most arrogant . . .'

Lulu leaned back and smiled. 'Admit it, Vivi. You find him irresistible.'

'I do not.'

'Of course you do. All that mystery, those eyes . . . And

he's refused you. An unavailable man is all the more attractive for it.'

'It's his shoes I want, not him. I *must* have the shoes. And once I've got them, I'm going to tell that swaggering little cobbler exactly what I think of him!'

But Lulu wouldn't let it go. 'Now I come to think of it, unavailability must be the most attractive thing of all for someone like you. Someone who only toys with the idea of having an affair rather than really doing it. All that hopeless longing and sighing. All that fantasy. Why, Zachari is just perfect for you.'

'For the last time, Lulu . . .' But Genevieve's voice lacked conviction, and she knew it. She looked down at her fingernails, newly manicured at Lina Cavalieri's salon just before lunch. She made her hands into fists.

'Vivi? What is it?'

'If only Robert hadn't bought me that horse. I can't bear it. You should see it. You should see its eyes. Whenever I look at the ghastly thing—'

'Come on.' Lulu gestured for the bill. 'You'd better show me.'

'It's changed everything,' said Genevieve. 'I can't ignore it. I don't know what I'm going to do.'

# 6

THE NEXT MORNING GENEVIEVE SKIPPED BREAKFAST AND went straight to the study in her dressing gown. Sitting at her desk (amboyna with dark *acajou* and slim *sabot*-footed legs) she started writing a poem about a girl who didn't know her own name. The words came rapidly. By the time she paused to read over it, she already had over twenty lines and was practically breathless with the intensity of it all. How wonderful it was to be able to find such a release for her most troubling emotions. A release which, as a kind of bonus, was also an act of creation. This was the best thing she'd ever written, it had to be. This was the poem that would establish her as a real figure on the Anglo-American writing scene here – not just a would-be or a hanger-on.

She'd been striving for acceptance by Paris's artistic élite ever since she and Robert first arrived. In those early days, while still registering the full extent of her disappointment with Robert's drab circle of mediocre acquaintances, she'd walk for miles along the Seine, over to the Left Bank and past the Métro Vavin into the 6th Arrondissement. She'd peer through the windows of the Café Select, the Rotonde, the Dôme, and scan the pavement tables for the more famous writers and artists who passed their days there, scribbling and sketching in their notepads. She'd take her poetry notebook into whichever café she'd chosen, order a *café au lait* and settle back to write and to eavesdrop. She was here, in the city of her dreams, but only as a spectator.

It was four months – four months which were fun and frustrating in equal measure – before Genevieve met Lulu of Montparnasse in the bar of the Ritz. Lulu took an instant liking to her, and began straight away to introduce Genevieve around and bring Paris alive for her. Now Genevieve knew everybody and went everywhere, thanks not to Robert, her bright white hope of a husband, but to Lulu. There was nowhere else she wanted to be; no city in the world that was the equal of this one. And yet she was still, to an extent, pressing her face up to the glass. She was not *one of them*.

In order to gain acceptance from the writers she admired so much – in order to be allowed into their discussions, their talk of meaningful things, clever things, beautiful things – in order to be really listened to by Betterson, Pound, Ford and the rest – she must write a poem that was truly brilliant. A poem that would show them she was not just another rich woman with ridiculous aspirations, to be humoured and flattered for her patronage – not just Lulu's pretty, English sidekick – but a real poet in her own right.

Today's poem would be the one. The written evidence of her talent, her genius.

Wouldn't it?

As Genevieve read through her masterpiece, the

excitement in her eyes began to dull. The poem was losing its form before it had even found it. By the sixth line, it was more a series of rambling, disjointed thoughts than a poem. By the tenth line it had become a whine. At the thirteenth line she gave up reading altogether, struck a line through it and started doodling in the margin. She drew a comical little sketch of Joseph Lazarus, Lulu's admirer. Lazarus the penguin, holding a fish in his long beak, with a confused expression, as though he couldn't work out what it was doing there.

'When did you say the horse is coming back?' Robert had appeared in the doorway.

'I'm not exactly sure.'

'They must have given you some idea, Vivi.' He was straightening his tie with the use of the hall mirror. She knew this without looking up: it was what he always did on his way out to work.

'I think the man said three weeks. Or was it four?'

'Four weeks! Four whole weeks just to clean a statue?'

'Three, more likely.' She drew Lazarus's wings and dipped her pen in the ink again, her head bowed a little so that Robert couldn't see her face.

'That really is an awfully long time.' He was brushing crumbs off his sleeves. 'I fail to see why the thing needed cleaning in the first place. Looked just fine to me.'

'Oh, it was very smeary.'

'So what was wrong with getting Céline to give it a wipe?'

'Darling!' Genevieve widened her eyes to show how shocked she was. 'I couldn't let an amateur loose on a piece

63

of fine art like that horse! Why, I'd never forgive myself if some sort of harm came to it. A delicate job like that requires skill, care, expertise.'

'Well, I suppose you know best.'

Soon he'd be out the front door with his hat and his briefcase, and she could let the breath go.

'So what are you thinking of doing today?' he asked.

'I need to finalize the party venue. The invitations will have to go out soon. And then this afternoon I'm going along to Natalie Barney's salon. Paul Valéry's giving a reading. And Norman Betterson will be there.'

'Ah, yes. That magazine fellow.' He'd come right into the room now. He bent to kiss the top of her head.

'He's not just "that magazine fellow", Robert. He's a poetic genius.'

'Of course he is, honey. Whatever you say.'

American arts patron Natalie Barney regularly hosted poetry readings at her three-hundred-year-old mansion on the Rue Jacob, but this was the first time Genevieve was to attend. Eager to make the right impression, she spent a long time over her outfit, eventually choosing a two-piece grey Chanel suit in imported tweed with a mannish notched collar which made her feel intellectual, and a pair of court shoes in snakeskin by an English shoemaker, Sebastian York. Their shape was conventional but the choice of materials lent them a certain pizzazz. They had a naughtiness that she enjoyed. She liked to think of the snakes slithering over her feet.

The audience at Miss Barney's salon was almost entirely female. And Genevieve was about the only non-Sapphic woman present, so far as she could judge. This made her uncomfortable, perhaps because she had no sway with them. She was a nobody, only there at all through Norman Betterson's recommendation. Yet she knew that this was one of the places that she, as a poet, should make her own. If only Lulu was here to get her a few introductions. Lulu knew everybody. But then again, Lulu was full of devilry just when you needed her to be serious. She'd probably go waltzing off with one of those women in monocle and cravat, just for the novelty.

The reading was late to start. Women dressed as men drifted among the dated, turn-of-the-century furnishings, or lounged against Turkish cushions on the couches. Genevieve, ignored, took a seat and gazed up at the domed, stained-glass ceiling. There was an ancient mythological feel to this place, she reflected. Though tiny, fierce Natalie was no Greek goddess. If only Norman Betterson would turn up.

Tea was served from a silver urn, but Genevieve remained glued to her seat. All around her, poetic lesbians nibbled on harlequin-coloured cakes and limp cucumber sandwiches, lamented the demise of the *Transatlantic Review*, welcomed the arrival of *This Quarter* and gossiped about other events at the respective salons of the Princesse de Polignac and Gertrude Stein. Genevieve stared glumly down at her own hands folded in her lap, wishing her host would serve up something more potent – a little Dutch courage.

At length, Valéry emerged from a back room, looking pale and shaky, as though his collar was too tight, and clutching a sheaf of papers. The audience began to take seats, perching with their teacups on chairs arranged in neat rows, or lolling on those couches.

And now – hurrah! – a small oriental man bearing a magnum of champagne entered at the rear of the room, followed by a maid with a tray of glasses. Then came Ezra Pound, wearing a ridiculous beret and greeting Genevieve, along with practically everyone else in the room, with one all-encompassing, 360-degree wave. And finally Norman Betterson, in cape and bow-tie, emerged from behind Pound, accompanied by the handsome Guy Monteray in his cream suit. Things were definitely looking up.

Genevieve couldn't follow the reading, try though she might. She wasn't sure whether the problem lay with her failure to grasp the complexities of the French language or with her inability to properly grasp poetic expression itself. Eventually she brought her notebook and pen out of her bag, thinking it might help to try to jot down a few of the more memorable phrases. But this proved too tricky, and so she gave up altogether and began sketching a little line-drawing of Ezra Pound, showing him simply as a huge beret with some unruly hair, a pointy beard and a pair of feet protruding from beneath – a sort of animated wig – while Valéry's poetry drifted and scattered over her like so much blown blossom. She only realized he'd finished when everyone began clapping.

'Why, hello, Mrs Shelby King. Did you know that I was watching you throughout that interminable reading? You're about the only thing worth watching here, after all.'

'Thank you, Mr Monteray.'

The audience were all moving about again and Genevieve had extended her glass for a top-up just as the champagne bottle ran dry. When the man in the cream suit came over and tapped her on the shoulder, she'd been contemplating the disappointing prospect of the tea urn. Now she smiled uncertainly up at him, not entirely sure how much of a compliment this actually was, in present company.

'You looked . . .' He lowered his voice, making the space between them seem smaller, more intimate. 'You looked as though something profound was happening to you, right there inside your head, while the poetry rushed on past you like a train, like life itself. As though you'd hit on something important.'

'Well . . .' Genevieve wondered whether to confess that she'd simply been doodling.

'You looked as though you were considering what would be the best way to die.'

'I beg your pardon?'

'Genevieve, my dear.' It was Betterson, smiling out of one side of his mouth so that he looked lopsided. The bow-tie too was crooked. 'I see you've met Guy. He's one of our best poets, you know.'

'Yes, we've met. Norman, I was wondering . . .'

'About the magazine? Let's have a talk about it later, shall we? After this shindig? A few of us are going over to the Select, if you'd like to join us.'

'Actually, it wasn't about the magazine. Not really.'

'I was thinking we might feature some of Guy's poems in the first issue.'

'That's nice.' Genevieve sucked in a breath and watched

Monteray head across the room to join Pound. 'It was about my poems, Norman.'

'Ah, yes.' Betterson patted her on the arm and winked as you might wink at a child. 'Later? The Select?'

A gong sounded loudly. A woman dressed like an English butler declared, 'Ladies and gentlemen, this afternoon's pageant is shortly to commence. As we've been favoured with beautiful spring sunshine, we will move out to the *temple à l'amitié*, so may I ask you to process to the garden, taking your teacups with you? Those of you vulnerable to the cold might like to collect your coats and wraps as we go. We have some rugs that you could put over your legs, but I do assure you that it's wonderfully warm outside.'

'Fantastic,' said Betterson. 'I do love it when Natalie puts on a show.'

Genevieve looked around for Guy Monteray, but he seemed to have slipped away.

The *temple à l'amitié* was a mock-Greek temple, complete with pillars and statues, the front steps decked out as a stage. The audience sat, protected from the breeze by the tall, ivy-covered walls of the neighbouring houses in the Rue Visconti and Rue de Seine, on folding chairs arranged in concentric semi-circles. Genevieve sat by Norman Betterson, who was allowing his leg to press against hers, just a little.

A man in a dinner jacket, whom she recognized as the composer and musician Virgil Thomson, sat down at the grand piano positioned beside the temple, and struck up something modern and experimental-sounding.

When Genevieve attempted to shift in her seat to avoid

the physical contact with Betterson, his leg inched across still further to rest against hers once again.

With a flourish and a tweak of the hat, Natalie Barney emerged from behind a curtain, dressed as a shepherd, complete with crook, and leading a shepherdess, her stick-thin lover Renée Vivien, in bonnet and numerous petticoats, by the hand. As the piano music softened, the shepherd knelt on the floor, declaiming loudly in French something-or-other that might have started out as a Greek classic, and reached out to touch the shepherdess's pretty ankle.

After an end-of-afternoon Chambéry and cassis at Café Prés aux Clercs, and with a glass of crisp Sancerre cold in her hand at the Select, Genevieve was feeling restored. Robert was out for dinner tonight and wouldn't be home until late, so she could sit back and enjoy herself. Guy Monteray had just materialized again and was in conversation with a couple of men she didn't know.

'What do you think of Monteray?' Betterson was following her gaze from behind a cloud of cigarette smoke, his knee finding hers under the table once again so that she had to draw right back.

'He's interesting.'

'I think he rather likes you,' said Betterson, and broke into a round of coughing.

'Goodness, are you all right? Can I get you some water?'

Betterson held up a hand and mopped his mouth with a handkerchief. 'I'm fine. Would you like to go to bed with me, Genevieve?'

'Oh, Norman . . .' Was he drunk? To be talking like that

even though his wife was just across the room, sitting up at the zinc bar with his secretary?

He saw where she was looking. 'You needn't mind Augusta. She'd be fine about it. She can be ... quite welcoming, actually.'

Genevieve had heard things. About the wife and the secretary.

'I want to talk to you about my love poems,' she said firmly.

He widened his glittering blue eyes. 'I'm very good, you know. Don't let the illness put you off. It's not catching.'

'Have you had a chance to read them yet?'

'I only have five years to live, sweetheart. When it comes to beautiful women, I like to seize every opportunity.' And again he was coughing violently.

Genevieve waited for him to finish, letting the coughing itself serve as a conversational full-stop. Ernest Hemingway had once referred to Betterson as 'the man marked for death'. The tag was so apt that it was becoming more famous than Betterson himself. His 'markings' could hardly be clearer.

'Norman, you're the only person who's ever seen my poems. Well, except for Robert, but he doesn't know anything about poetry. I need to know ... I need to know if you think I'm any good.'

'Oh, I'm sure you're *splendid*.' But he was just being smutty again.

She closed her eyes for a moment. When she opened them, his expression had changed.

'You're a sweet, sweet thing, Genevieve.' He shook his head and smiled sadly. 'Trouble is, you've never been in love, have you? And it shows, honey. It shows.'

'I see.' She thought about Robert proposing to her – the way she'd weighed up her decision, tried to convince herself that he was more than just a means of escape.

'Now I've upset you. That was the last thing I wanted to do.'

She shook her head. 'I'm not upset. I needed to know.' There was too much laughter in the bar, and too much smoke.

'Look, Genevieve.'

'I'd like to go home now, Norman.'

'Sweetie.' He put his hand on hers. 'Why don't you try writing about something else? Something closer to your own experience?'

Genevieve pulled her hand away. 'Stop patronizing me.'

He reached for his drink. 'All right, then. I'll be straight with you. The poems are no good. They're like some tired old meal that's been dished up again and again. What else do you have?'

'Well.' Hesitantly, Genevieve brought out the notebook and started flicking through. 'I really thought the love poems were my best, but . . . I suppose I could copy out some of the others, and . . .'

'Are they all in there?' asked Betterson.

'Yes.'

'Then let me take the book. If there's anything good in there, I'll find it.'

'Oh, but there's a lot of very rough material too. I'm a bit embarrassed to—'

'Come on, don't be coy.' He reached out his open hand.

71

Blushing, she pushed the book across the table to him. 'Do take care of it, won't you? It's . . . personal.'

'Of course.' And he gave another lopsided smile. 'Now, let's talk about the magazine, shall we?'


'Mind if I share?'

Genevieve, still a little rattled from her conversation with Betterson, was getting into a taxi on the Boulevard du Montparnasse, outside the Select. Turning, she saw Guy Monteray standing there.

'Where are you going?' she asked.

'Shakespeare and Company.'

Sylvia Beach's bookshop and lending library on the Rue de l'Odéon was so much more than a mere shop, forming the hub of the Left Bank Anglo-American literary scene. Genevieve's interest was pricked as to what business the man in the cream suit could have there after hours. In spite of the fact that Shakespeare and Company was not remotely on her route home, she nodded to him to get into the taxi.

'I can't believe it's taken me so many years to come to Paris,' he said, extending his arm along the seat behind her. 'I've been here just a few days and I've never been more at home in my life.'

'I feel the same,' she said.

'Things are so much more intense here.' His mouth was close to her face. 'Life happens fast and furious. Don't you think?'

And then she knew that he was about to kiss her, and that she wasn't going to stop him, in spite of her marriage, in spite of the fact that they were out in public. And God, it felt good – his mouth. His heat. He reached to touch her breast, and again she let him. She let him put his hand inside her coat, inside the tweed two-piece suit, until he found flesh. She wanted the abandon of this. She wanted him to touch her and kiss her here, in the taxi, moving through the city. And while they were moving through the traffic, giddy with alcohol, she could allow herself to just let it all happen. Because in any case, it was hardly real. It was barely more than a blur.

The taxi drew up outside Shakespeare and Company. They got out and Monteray paid.

'Sylvia said I could stay a night or two in the apartment above the shop,' he explained. 'Until I get myself properly set up, you understand.'

Out on the pavement in the chill evening air, she felt less sure of herself. She put a hand to her mouth, wiping away the smeared lipstick, while he searched for his keys.

'I know I've got them here somewhere . . .'

This seemed to go on for ever. She shivered.

He turned and shrugged. 'Seem to have mislaid them.'

'Perhaps we should go and knock at the apartment across the road. Sylvia's bound to be there.'

'Nope. She and Adrienne were going out. Only one thing for it – I'll have to climb up.'

'You can't be serious.'

He put his hands on his hips and gazed up at the first-floor window. 'It shouldn't be so difficult. I'll swing up by the sign.'

The taxi was already gone. The alcohol was wearing off. He spat on his hands and found a grip on the shop's windowframe, getting a firm footing on the ledge.

'Hope you're watching,' he called out. 'This is my best angle.' From there he lunged for the sign that was swinging from an iron hook just at the top of the door, the shop's name on one face of it, a portrait of the bard himself on the other. As Monteray trusted his weight to it, the hook bent alarmingly and creaked, and Genevieve gasped and covered her eyes.

'Keep watching,' came his voice again, as though he had eyes in the back of his head and was monitoring her every response.

She peeped through her fingers and saw that he was clambering up above the sign, using the shop's closed-up awning for purchase, and reaching for the balcony of the first-floor window. She allowed herself to breathe. Seconds later he was safe and fumbling with the window catch.

'Hang on there and I'll come down and let you in.'

Things got better once they were inside. Genevieve hadn't been in the apartment before, though she'd visited the shop downstairs hundreds of times. It was cosy – a single bed in the corner, an armchair, a table and two wooden dining chairs, and then a little kitchenette. There were two doors off the kitchen area.

'Perfect for me,' said Monteray. 'Everything a man could need, and enough books downstairs to last me a lifetime.' He produced a little flask from his jacket pocket and then started searching about in cupboards for a couple of glasses.

'Here you go.' He poured. She sipped, enjoying the burning in her throat, welcoming the return of the giddiness. She was staring at the single bed when he came up behind her and started kissing her neck. She allowed him to run his hands down her body, her legs. As he brought his hands up under her dress, she gasped.

What was she *doing*?

'You like that, don't you,' he whispered. 'You're going to like this even more.'

She could hear Lulu's teasing voice: *It was very exciting in that marital bed, eh?*

Even as she considered leaving, she was already bending forward for him, holding on to the edge of the table to keep her balance.

She thought about Robert's habitual knock on her bedroom door. The rituals – before, during and after.

She was pushing herself against him. Letting it happen.

*Trouble is, you've never been in love, have you? And it shows, honey.*

She was practically in a frenzy for it to happen. And so, it seemed, was he. He was inside her before she even got a proper look at him. She had to brace herself against the table, which inched forward, grinding over the wooden floorboards. In fact it was the table, rather than Genevieve, that groaned as they did it. Not that she wasn't excited. She relished the illicit nature of what they were doing. Her wickedness. And the more it hurt, the more she liked it.

When it was over, he started pulling at her clothes, fumbling with buttons.

'Haven't you got this the wrong way round?' she said. 'Isn't it more usual to undress *first*?'

'You think we're done?' he said.

This time it was their two naked bodies entwined in the bed. Fingers running over skin. Eyes locked on eyes. Tongues finding secret places. A long, slow, sensual kind of sex.

Afterwards, as they sat crammed together in the tiny bed, she started to shiver uncontrollably.

'You're something else, you know that?' He had a dazed, dizzy look in his eyes.

'Am I?' That second time had got to her. The first time – well, that was just lust. But that 'love-making-without-the-love'. What was *that*?

'Hey. You're cold.' He splashed some whisky in her glass. 'This'll warm you up.'

'I'm not cold.' But she put the glass to her lips anyway. 'I'm afraid.'

'Afraid of what?'

'Of what I've done. Of what it means.'

'It can mean whatever you want it to mean.' He kissed her shoulder. 'My sweet girl.'

*You're a sweet, sweet thing . . .*

'I'm talking about my marriage.'

He took a swig straight out of the flask and she noticed a tattoo on the inside of his arm.

'Let me see that.'

It was a skull. A black skull.

'I had it done in North Africa. It's part of a pact I have with someone.'

'What kind of a pact?'

'A death pact.'

Part of her wanted to ask more, but the rest of her didn't want to know. It was too spooky. He offered her the flask again but she shook her head. The whisky was too much now. The smell of it on his breath, on her own body where he'd kissed and licked her. Saying she needed some water, she wriggled over him and got out of the bed, hating the fact that he was watching her while she struggled into her crêpe-de-Chine lace-edged chemise, clambered into her absurdly formal, crumpled suit.

The tap squeaked in the kitchen and the water looked a little rusty, but she drank it down all the same.

'Bathroom?' She had her hand on the knob of one of the doors.

'That's right,' he said lazily. But it was a broom cupboard. She tried the other door, increasingly uneasy.

From the bathroom, where she peed, washed her face and hastily reapplied her make-up, she heard him talking:

'Have you read any of my poetry? It's kind of metaphysical but it's not quite there yet. I can't seem to reach the right state in which to truly touch the thing that needs to be touched. Opium is useful but it's not enough. Have you tried opium?'

'No,' she called out. Her face, in the mirror, looked foolish. She thought wistfully of Robert. He might already be back from his evening out. He could be sitting with the papers – the *New York Times*, the *Boston Chronicle* and *Le Monde*, with a cigar in his mouth, slippers on his feet and a cup of coffee or a bourbon at his side. She wanted to be home with him now, curled up with a book in the Pirogue couch. She wanted everything to be as it was before.

Most likely, he wasn't home yet. If she went straight back, she could draw a bath and wash it all away – the smoke, the whisky, the sweat.

'You stupid girl,' she whispered to her bedraggled reflection.

'I can't wait to meet Sylvia,' came Monteray's voice.

77

She frowned. 'But . . .' But this was Sylvia's apartment. Over Sylvia's shop. He had surely met her already. He *must* have.

She saw him again on the pavement, keyless, climbing up to the window.

He hadn't known where the bathroom was.

'Oh my God.'

Emerging from the bathroom, a false smile on her face, she found he was no longer in the room.

'Guy?' Where could he have gone?

Something – instinct – made her pick up his cream suit jacket from where it lay on the floor. Something – instinct – made her reach inside it, feeling her way into the inside pocket, finding . . . a heavy metal object, as familiar as an intimate friend although she'd never touched a thing of this shape before.

Heart thudding hard, she almost dropped the gun, but managed to get a hold of herself just in time, replacing it and laying the jacket down silently. Searching across the floor for the remainder of her things.

She had to get out of here. But he must surely be downstairs in the shop, browsing naked among the books. How could she get past him?

'Guy?' She tried to make her voice sound bright. 'Where are you?'

'I'm in here.' He didn't sound like he was downstairs.

'What are you doing, Guy?'

'I'm thinking. There's a poem in my head and I'm trying to make it come out. It's good to think in small dark places.'

He was in the broom cupboard.

Quick as a flash, she was out of the apartment and running down the stairs.

'Genevieve?' came his voice, distantly, as she ran through the empty shop and fumbled with the catch on the front door. 'Don't you want to hear my poem? It's awfully good.'

## 7

ROBERT WAS MORE THAN A LITTLE SURPRISED, ON ARRIVING home just before eleven, from an awful evening at the snootiest kind of restaurant (the waiter really could have dropped him a hint that steak Tartare comes raw. Not just rare. Actually *raw*) with the worst kind of British industrialists (a toad-faced, swaggering, Yorkshire textile manufacturer and his smarmy, snaggle-toothed assistant, neither of whom appeared to possess even the slightest degree of human warmth. My, but those Dark Satanic Mills loomed with startling clarity in his mind's eye) to discover that his wife was not in.

The sound of distant humming as he passed through the hall (so empty and cavernous now, with the horse away at the cleaner's) turned out to be Céline. The footfalls from the salon must have been from the floor above. Could the sigh that seemed to emit from the shoe room possibly have been one of Genevieve's *shoes*? Perhaps he himself had sighed without realizing it.

Reflecting gloomily that this place was unbearably lonely

without her in it, he fixed himself a bourbon. Where *was* she? She'd told him she was going to a poetry event of some kind in the afternoon, but had said nothing about the evening. Lulu was behind this, he'd bet on it.

He was considering whether or not to ask Céline to light a fire when the telephone rang. He hoped it would be Genevieve, apologizing for her lateness and saying she'd be home directly, but no such luck.

'I'm thinking of changing the layout of my rose garden,' said Lady Ticksted, after a stiff exchange of greetings.

'And you want to speak to Genevieve about it?'

'Why on earth would I want to do that?'

He scratched his head. 'You mean, you want to speak to *me* about it?'

'To *you?*'

This was going nowhere. She was most likely drunk as a skunk, though he couldn't hear the booze in her voice. 'Genevieve's not here at the moment, Lady Ticksted. And it is rather late. Shall I get her to call you?'

'Well, where is she?'

'I'm not exactly sure.'

He heard her catch her breath. 'Don't you think you should keep her on a rather shorter leash?'

Even knowing them as he did, he was shocked. 'She's not a dog.'

'It was a figure of speech.'

'I'm aware of that.' He found he was grinding his teeth.

'Robert – my husband and I entrusted you with the safety and well-being of our daughter. And you know that Genevieve is *fragile*. You're not going to let us down, are you?'

'Lady Ticksted.' He was thundering now. Really thundering. 'With all due respect, Genevieve is a fully grown woman.'

'Yes, but—'

'And she's *my wife*.'

Another sucking-in of the breath. And then, 'Bess has had her babies. Four of them.'

Talking to this damn woman was like some cryptic puzzle. Chinese boxes or something. 'Bess?'

'Our darling little dog. We shall keep two, I think. I wonder if you'd like to have one?'

'I don't think so.'

'They're quite small dogs, you know. Beagles. Do you have them in America? Perhaps you call them something else.'

'I'm sorry, we can't take one.'

'You will tell Genevieve, won't you? I'd like her to phone me some time.'

'About the puppies?'

'About her father. He's not well.'

At the end of the call he went straight back to the bourbon bottle, none the wiser as to what was the matter with the viscount, and indeed still uncertain whether the real reason for the phone call was his mystery illness or the puppies or something else that she didn't mention. He often had the sense, when he spoke to Lady Ticksted, that she talked in code. These smoke signals about the rose garden and Bess's pups might convey an altogether different message to Genevieve.

If only they were plain, simple people who talked plain,

simple English, then his life would be a whole lot easier. Instead, Pop was the stiff-upper-lipped aristocrat and Mom was quite, quite mad and a little too fond of the juice. And somewhere beneath all the evasion and the madness and the veiled comments was something Unmentionable. Something that had to do with his Genevieve – about the need for her to be looked after.

He'd known almost from the start that there was something the family was hiding. Even during the courtship Lady Ticksted made occasional references to Genevieve's 'delicate health' and alluded to an 'ongoing condition'. When the viscount gave his blessing to the engagement, he had laid great emphasis on the need for Robert to 'take care of' his daughter. Not such an unreasonable request, perhaps, but he did keep on. It was as though he saw Genevieve as a little girl or an invalid, more in need of a nursemaid than a husband.

Robert did his best to probe further, but no elucidation was forthcoming, and he didn't wish to seem disrespectful or overly suspicious. Ultimately he put the whole thing down to a sort of nameless, damp Englishness. Certainly there was no evidence of illness in Genevieve. Quite the contrary. And once he'd got his bride away from Viscount Ticksted's house in the flat, grey marshes, she positively thrived.

It was a long time since he'd given much thought to the 'Unmentionable' in Genevieve's past. But tonight, alone in the apartment, it was back in his mind again, and he found he couldn't stop himself from thinking about it. He could ask Genevieve directly, of course, but he'd tried that before and it hadn't got him anywhere. She was as difficult to pin down as her parents, and had lately begun to form a whole set of her own new Unmentionables . . .

Whenever he tried to bring up the issue of their settling in Boston, she'd immediately change the subject. She'd do this so fluently and effectively that he wouldn't realize until later that it had happened. Another Unmentionable was to do with Lulu – he wanted to know where exactly they went on their evenings out, who they talked to, what they talked about. He wanted to understand why his wife had established such a close friendship with someone she had so little in common with. Couldn't she see that if she volunteered a little information, then there might be no need for him to ask all these questions?

And then there was the incident a few weeks ago.

It had begun with one of those phone calls from her mother, rather like tonight's, which prompted her to announce, 'Mummy's so manipulative. She doesn't even realize she's doing it half the time.' And then she seemed to sink into herself for a moment and said, 'I'm not like her, am I?'

He shook his head, no.

'I know I behave badly. Sometimes. Often.' She reached out and stroked his cheek. 'I'm so frightened of turning into her.'

'Don't be silly. You're nothing like her.'

'She's *in* me. It can't be helped. No matter what I do. No matter how much I struggle against it. In fact, the more I try to be different from her, the more I turn out the same.'

He didn't understand what she was talking about. But he liked the way she softened as she spoke. The air itself seemed to relax and purr, and they talked quietly for a long time, as they seldom did.

She hardly ever came to his bedroom, but that night she did. What a treat it was to have her lying in his arms in his bed. And there came a perfect moment. Her head on his chest. Her gentle breathing as she slid towards sleep. He felt he knew the precise second when she began to drift off. He wanted to keep her safe and warm, his Genevieve. For ever. He wanted . . .

'Honey?' he whispered. 'Are you still awake?'

'Mm?'

He stroked her soft hair, playing with a few strands, putting them behind her ear. 'I was thinking . . .'

'Uh.'

'Let's have a baby.'

And that was it. Moment over. She went stiff in his arms, like a dead person. Then she was pulling away from him, muttering something about having to go to the bathroom. And he was left alone in the bed, gazing forlornly at the light shining through his half-open door, listening to the muffled thuds of her feet as she moved determinedly away – not to the bathroom as she'd said, but to her own bedroom at the end of the corridor.

Robert was on to his third bourbon now and was winding himself up into a fury. He badly wanted a son. And she'd practically forbidden him to talk about it! How *dare* she make an unmentionable of this most natural of desires?

He got up and started pacing the room, giving vent to two opposing impulses.

When your goddamn wife *finally* deigns to come home – said a voice in his head that sounded for all the world like Harry Mortimer – just drag her straight to bed and show her who's boss! Before you know it, she'll be pregnant and happy. There'll be no more gallivanting about town. No more secrets with Lulu. She might think she doesn't want a baby, but she's a *woman*, after all.

The other impulse was more moderate – more his own. Calm down, it said. What good will it do anyone if you start behaving like a brute? The way to win your wife over to your point of view is to find out what's troubling her. Then you can give her the reassurance she needs and be a good, strong husband to her. It doesn't make any kind of sense that a woman like her wouldn't want a baby. There has to be more to this than meets the eye. If she won't tell you directly, there are other ways to discover the truth. Subtler ways. For now, just calm down and sit down and make a plan.

'Céline?' Robert opened the salon door and peered out into the empty hallway. 'Would you come and light a fire before you turn in, please?'

Then he returned to the bourbon bottle, and poured himself another finger.

## 8

THE TAXI WAS ALMOST AT THE RUE DE LOTA, BUT GENEVIEVE needed a few minutes to steady herself before she could face Robert. The taxi was one of the new kind, fully motorized but styled like the old horse-drawn variety, with the passenger completely encased and protected from the elements at the back while the driver was stuck out front in the cold. Genevieve had to bang repeatedly on the little screen to attract his attention.

They pulled up under the spreading branches of a plane tree, alongside a street carousel. Genevieve watched a pair of sweethearts laughing and reaching out to each other as their horses went up and down. A group of giggling girls were using the ride as an excuse to reveal an expanse of leg which would be concealed by their dresses when they dismounted, while a bunch of young lads standing near by looked suitably appreciative.

What damage had been done, really, by the events of the evening? The only people who knew about what had happened were herself and Guy Monteray. And he was clearly as nutty as a fruitcake. This was unsettling, of course, but she felt increasingly certain, now that she was safely out of that apartment, that he would have little interest in making trouble for her. He was surely far too wrapped up in his own insane world to bother much about hers.

She would tell no one that she'd cheated on Robert. Not even Lulu. *Especially* not Lulu. That way, the matter could end right here. She'd made a mistake but she would not make the same mistake again. She'd put her marriage to rights. It simply *had* to work, or what would become of her? And Robert, poor Robert – well, none of this was his fault. Why should he have to suffer unduly? It would be much better for him if he never found out.

Perhaps, after all, it was a good thing that this had happened now. She'd 'got it out of her system', whatever 'it' was, and had emerged unscathed.

She was about to ask the driver to move on when a tall, slender woman came walking down the street, holding the hand of a girl of perhaps nine or ten years of age. The woman wore a long woollen coat with a high collar trimmed with opossum fur, and a matching cloche hat. There was something regal in her bearing. The little girl, in a coat that was almost a miniature version of the woman's, was all but skipping just to keep up with her long stride. As Genevieve watched through the taxi window, the child looked up at her mother with an expression of utter adoration, and the mother smiled back down at her. The little girl had endearing knee-socks, and on her feet were a pair of black patent-leather Mary Janes.

Something stirred in Genevieve. A very particular sadness. A long-nursed memory.

'Driver?' Genevieve rapped on the screen. 'Turn around please.'

'You don't want to go to Rue de Lota?' came the gruff voice from out front.

'No. Not yet.'

She got out at Place Vendôme, and paid the driver. Through the eight-sided piazza she walked, gazing up at the infamous column. It had started out as a statue to the Sun King, Louis XIV, before being torn down and replaced with a column made from 1,250 Russian and Austrian cannons celebrating the exploits of Napoleon. It was then pulled down again and, later, rebuilt yet again as a replica of its last incarnation. She'd had a good view of the column from her suite at the Ritz, just across the way, beside the Ministry of Justice. Those were fun times at the Ritz. She'd had her first encounter with Lulu there, late one night in the bar. Lulu was barefoot, followed by a black panther on a leash. She carried a bowl and was calling to the waiter for some water for her '*chat noir*'. When the waiter became nervous, Genevieve stepped forward and filled the bowl from her champagne bottle, to the apparent approval of the '*chat noir*', which lapped it up instantly so that she felt obliged to provide a top-up, muttering, 'Your panther has expensive tastes.'

'Absolutely,' said Lulu. 'That's why we get on so well. We could be sisters, she and I. We have the same blackest black hair, as you can see, the same angry eyes, and the same way of dealing with difficult men.'

The next time Lulu appeared in the Ritz bar, a few nights later, she came straight over to Genevieve's table and greeted her warmly by name as though they were already old friends. She had no memory of the panther.

'I must have borrowed it from someone,' she said vaguely.

Genevieve delighted in Lulu's spontaneity and frivolity. You never knew what she'd say or do next, particularly when she was drunk. And yet the friendship gained substance too. Lulu had plenty of friends but most of them were as unreliable as the weather. She had real need of someone steadfast and trustworthy. Someone she could confide in. Someone who didn't want to paint her or exploit her or sleep with her or betray her or even just laugh at her. And Genevieve needed someone to take her out and about in Bohemian Paris. Someone to show her the world.

Past grand houses with smart façades, multi-coloured histories and innumerable ghosts, walked Genevieve. Most were now swanky costumiers, perfumers and jewellers, and those few which were still private residences had become the homes of dubious money-grabbing surgeons, renowned astrologers, and strange old dames left over from another era with only their cats and their memories for company.

On went Genevieve, and out on to the Rue de la Paix, where she entered a discreet passageway, unnoticed for the most part by the tourists and daytime shoppers who flocked to the great fashion houses of the street. A passageway leading to a small courtyard whose tall walls were covered with ivy and other creepers which rustled and whispered in the night breeze. A courtyard unknown to Genevieve until just a few days before.

Standing before Zachari's shop, she stared up at that overblown, taunting sign of his, and then looked in at the window, trying to see through the little chinks in the purple velvet curtains. All was dark inside, which was perhaps unsurprising, as it was almost ten o'clock.

Bending, she peered down at the tiny basement window, and dimly made out that a light was still on inside. She couldn't see much – the high backs of chairs, the edge of a workbench, the shapes of tools. Listening carefully, she could just about hear the sound of soft violin music played on a gramophone. A figure was moving about the room, settling by the bench.

Genevieve knew she had lovely legs: shapely calves and slender ankles with the finest and most delicate of bones. Her feet were small, her arches superb (she'd been told many times that she should have been a dancer with arches like that), and her toes pretty and correctly sized, running in a gentle slope from largest to smallest. Her stockings were all of the finest silk, and today's were no exception – the seams ran absolutely straight up the backs of her legs. She was still wearing the Sebastian York snakeskin shoes, and she could almost hear those snakes hissing in delight at her cleverness as she stepped closer to the iron grille covering that tiny basement window. Zachari chose his clients like you might choose a piece of fruit, that was what she'd heard. Because he liked the look of their feet. Well, any true connoisseur would be incapable of ignoring a pair of feet like these . . .

For a time, she simply stood there, with her shoes and ankles in full view of the window. Then she paced a little, back and forth. The evening was growing colder, and she drew her fox-fur stole closer around her neck, feeling self-conscious and praying to herself that nobody was watching her from any concealed window high up in one of the neighbouring buildings. She walked some more, wondering how long it would take for Zachari to glance up.

She paced and paced, counting quietly to herself, allowing her heels to knock against the grille, making a clanging sound that he might be able to hear from inside. Anything to get him to look.

She thought about Robert arriving home from his evening out, and wondering where she was, perhaps giving up on her and going to bed. Then her thoughts moved to her father. He wasn't well, so Mummy said in her latest letter. His bronchitis had been bad and he'd been almost three weeks in bed. Her mother was patently hoping she would come and visit, but the very thought of that silent house and its miserable inhabitants made her shudder. Chances were the whole thing was a ruse to try to trick her into coming home. It was typical of her mother. If Daddy was seriously ill, someone would telephone. The ever-reliable Dr Peters, perhaps. Lady Ticksted was odd about illness in general, and had spent a good page of the letter fretting pointlessly about Genevieve's own health. The fretting made her furious – she could hear that whining voice, see the hands twisting around each other. *There is nothing wrong with me*, she wrote in her reply. *There was never anything wrong with me.* And then, *Give my love to Daddy. I'm sure he'll be on his feet again soon.*

A poke at her back. Someone's hot breath, very close by. She jumped, thinking for one ridiculous moment that it was Guy Monteray pointing his gun at her, but when she whipped around she discovered that of course it was Paolo Zachari, standing with his arms folded and an amused expression on his face.

92

'Have you taken to street-walking?'

'I came here to talk to you, Mr Zachari.'

'The shop is closed, madame.'

'But you came outside all the same.'

'I was trying to work,' he said. 'But there was a terrible clattering noise at the window and a pair of hideous reptiles kept going back and forth outside. Spoils the concentration, you understand.'

She nodded sympathetically. 'Would that café with the green walls still be open? I'd like to have a drink with you.'

He gave a half-smile and she thought she could just about glimpse the freckle at the base of his neck, even through the darkness. 'Are you trying to seduce me, Mrs Shelby King?'

She made a face. 'I've been thinking about our last conversation. I want to tell you the real reason why shoes are important to me.'

## 9

IT WAS THE SPRING OF 1913. THE HONOURABLE GENEVIEVE Samuel, aged nine, was spending the day in London with her mother. They were currently in Harrods, where Mummy was having the final fitting of an outfit for her forthcoming birthday party.

'What do you think, darling?' Lady Ticksted emerged from behind the curtain and stood before the mirror in a hooped dress of aquamarine and gold chiffon with iridescent sequins.

'It's beautiful.'

'And what about these?' She lifted the dress to reveal delicate satin dancing slippers in the same aquamarine.

'Gorgeous!'

'Walk around for me,' said the stern-faced assistant. But Genevieve's mother went one better, and began to dance a waltz around the changing room, bobbing and twirling, the sequinned chiffon twinkling and shimmering so that Genevieve thought of water in motion. Every so often she glimpsed the divine satin slippers, but mostly they were hidden by the dress.

'It's a shame Daddy's such a dreadful dancer,' said Genevieve later, as they wandered through the children's department.

'Genevieve!'

'Sorry. I just—'

But Lady Ticksted had already moved on. 'Now, darling,' she said. 'You've been so patient this morning that I think you deserve a little something for yourself. How about these?'

She had picked up a pair of Mary Jane shoes from a nearby display table. They were black patent leather and as shiny as mirrors.

'I love them!'

There was something very special about getting your feet measured – having an adult bend down and actually *kneel* before you. The slide rule was cold against Genevieve's foot so that she wanted to wriggle her toes. But it was a nice kind of cold. The lady with the grey hair told her that her feet had grown a whole size. Not just half a size – a *whole* size.

'Walk around for me.' The assistant sat back on her heels. 'See how they feel.'

The shoes had that perfect new stiffness. They pinched a little but it was a good sort of pinch. Genevieve examined her feet, turning them this way and that. They looked almost like proper grown-up feet. She glanced at herself in the mirror and thought she was very nearly a proper grown-up. One day she would be just like her mother, waltzing around in a floaty chiffon dress. She would be beautiful like her mother, but happier.

'What do you think, Mummy?' And she twirled around fast to see what Lady Ticksted's face was doing. But her mother wasn't looking at her. She was talking to a man.

'Mummy?' she called again, more loudly.

'Oh, they're very nice, dear,' said Lady Ticksted, looking flustered.

'Pretty as a picture,' said the man, in a voice that had an odd twang to it. 'Say, how would you two ladies like to join me for tea at Fortnum's?'

Mr Slattery – for that was the man's name – was a 'gentleman from New York'. The fact of his being from New York rendered him very glamorous. Genevieve had never met anyone from America before. She was particularly impressed by the description he gave of his boat journey across the Atlantic Ocean, by the strangeness of his accent, and by the size of his shoulders when he removed the big overcoat. Also, he ordered a huge plate of cakes, and she was able to eat three before her mother noticed the way she was cramming them in and warned her to slow down.

'Which is better – New York or London?' asked Genevieve.

'Well, that's a very difficult one to answer.' Mr Slattery stroked his big chin. 'They're both fine cities. London has all those centuries of history but New York – well, nowhere buzzes like New York.'

'What a silly question.' Lady Ticksted kept touching her hair. Her movements had a shy girlishness to them that Genevieve had never noticed before. And although she kept her gaze mostly on the bunch of flowers on the table, she was casting Mr Slattery odd sidelong looks. 'New York is Mr Slattery's home, after all.'

'Oh, I'm not sure that it is, these days.' His cheeks turned pink. 'Not any more.'

'Do you have a wife, Mr Slattery?' asked Genevieve.

'Genevieve!'

But he seemed unperturbed. 'No, I don't, honey. But I hope I will, some day. A wife and a daughter and a son and a pretty house to live in. Isn't that what everyone wants?'

'And will you all live in America?'

'Perhaps.'

'I should like to live in America,' said Genevieve. 'I'd live in one of those covered wagons like in the films and my husband would be the sheriff. Are you a sheriff, Mr Slattery?'

On her way to the lavatory, Genevieve took a sneaky peep over her shoulder at her mother and the man. They were laughing together like old friends. Lady Ticksted seemed so young and carefree. And as for Mr Slattery – he could easily be a sheriff. Or a film star. She'd never seen a man so handsome before. And neither, she supposed, had her mother.

'You'll think me terribly ignorant.' Her mother's voice had risen in volume. 'I can't think when I last read a book. Magazines, yes, but books . . .'

Genevieve was the kind of child who makes wishes, just in case. She made them when she blew out the candles on her birthdays, when she threw coins into fountains and wells, when she lost a tooth, and at moments when she felt especially happy.

'Well, you should read this one,' said Mr Slattery. 'Even if you never read another.'

Now, wearing her perfect new shoes and watching her mother giggling with a handsome American stranger, Genevieve decided there had never been such a glorious day as this. She closed her eyes, wriggled her toes inside the new Mary Janes, and wished.

They were the last remaining customers at the café with the green walls. Anton, the waiter with the pigeon chest and the melancholy moustaches, was stacking chairs and sweeping the floor. Now and then he looked at the clock above the bar and sighed. His sighs were loud, but the couple at the table in the window either didn't hear or didn't care.

'So this Mr Slattery . . . He was your mother's lover?' asked Zachari.

'I don't know.' Genevieve trailed a finger through some spilt sugar. 'They might have just been friends. Perhaps she met him for the first time that day. They were attracted to each other, I'm sure of that. But as to the rest . . . I was only nine years old.'

'Do you suppose a beautiful woman like your mother could really have been "just friends" with a man like that?'

'Well, when you put it that way . . .' She was keeping her gaze on the freckle. She couldn't look him in the eye. 'I hope they were lovers. I'd like to think she was happy with someone, however briefly. My mother was – *is* – a very unhappy woman. My father's a terrible philanderer, you see. And a bully.

'There was an argument when we got home from London

that evening. I was supposed to be in bed but I heard them and I crept out on to the landing and leaned over the banisters to try to listen. It was very bad. I couldn't hear what it was about, but he was shouting and she was crying and shrieking. And then she went quiet and it was just him shouting.' Her fingernails scratched, now, at the tabletop. 'She didn't come down to breakfast the next morning. She stayed up in her room for the whole day. The birthday party was cancelled. She never wore the dress or the satin slippers.'

'Do you suppose your father had discovered something?'

'Possibly. She was already changing, on our way home from London. Changing back to her usual self. We sat in the back of the Daimler together, and I watched her face closing down. It was like watching someone die.' She sipped her cognac. 'Back then, there was always a lot of space and silence around my mother. A remoteness. She hardly ever played with me or talked to me. I'd play the clown, misbehave – anything – just to make her *see* me. There were moments when she'd really come alive. Just a scattering of moments through my whole childhood, that's all. And that one day in London.'

She raised the glass to her lips again but it was empty. 'She's different now. She used to hide herself in the space and silence but now she's afraid of it. She fills it with ceaseless, pointless wittering. She's a bag of nerves and she tries to calm the nerves with drink.' Suddenly she frowned and looked up at him. 'But I'm getting away from the point of this. It was about the shoes. The reason shoes are important to me.'

'Your perfect Mary Janes bought on the one perfect day when your mother was happy.'

She was staring into his eyes now. His unfathomable eyes.

'Your wish didn't come true, did it?' he said. 'Your mother carried on being unhappy and the man never came back.'

*Shoes lined with silken flower petals. Shoes made out of dreams. Shoes that burst like soap bubbles when you reach out to touch them.*

His hand covered hers. She flinched at his touch and pulled away, her head suddenly awash with all that 'love-making-without-the-love'. She should have gone straight home.

'I'm sorry,' he said. 'I wasn't—'

'It's quite all right.' Her hands were in her lap now, rubbing at each other.

Zachari motioned to the waiter. 'It's late. We should go.'

*Go where?* she thought. *Home?* But what she said was, 'What about my shoes, Mr Zachari?'

'Come to the shop in the morning,' he said. 'At eleven.'

When at last Genevieve arrived home, the apartment was dark and quiet. But in the salon grate, the embers still glowed red hot.

# 10

HER OUTFIT WAS CAREFULLY CALCULATED. SHE HAD excelled herself. The Paul Poiret dress was of chiffon and the scarf was lynx. Her shoes – Oxford ties in Sauterne kid with a swirling appliqué pattern in tan calf and spike heels – were beautifully designed and custom-made, but subtle. The designer, one Wilfred Hargreaves of London, was a quiet man, uninterested in fashion fame, and would not pose a sufficient threat to Zachari's ego to make him bridle. As if to compensate for the subtlety of the shoes, Genevieve was dripping in diamonds – from her fingers, ears, wrists and neck.

When Robert looked up from his morning paper to see her standing in the hallway adjusting the scarf, he seemed, for a moment, to forget himself, and let out a loud whistle.

She glanced over, startled. He was blushing. So was she. And then they both giggled.

'Down, boy!' she said.

'You look fabulous,' he said. 'Where are you going?'

And then she was chattering about the shoe-fitting and

with every word that she uttered, her confidence grew a little more and she knew that it would be all right between them. He would never guess what she'd done. She would never feel compelled to tell him. His whistle had saved her.

'Back again, madame?' The assistant, when she opened the door, was as steely as ever. She began to close the door on Genevieve, her face showing a quiet pleasure in being able to do so.

But now there was a sound from inside. Zachari's voice calling, 'Olga?' And the woman paused with the door still half open and turned her head to await instruction.

'I think you'll find,' said Genevieve, 'that I have an appointment.'

'Good-morning, madame.' Zachari extended an arm to show her into the purple interior of the shop. There was a formality about him today. A brusque quality. It was as though those hours last night in the green café had never happened. Well, thought Genevieve, that suits me just fine.

Olga was still lingering by the reception desk, and Genevieve felt her every movement being scrutinized by those cold eyes. But then, to her delight, Zachari told his assistant to go and wait downstairs until after the fitting.

'Well, Mr Zachari. As I told you before, I'm throwing a Cubist costume party. It's taking place in six weeks' time and what I'd like—'

'Take your shoes and stockings off, please, Mrs Shelby King.' Zachari took her by the arm as he spoke, and directed her firmly to one of the purple couches.

She kept her eyes on her feet while removing her shoes,

dimly aware that he was moving about the room, bolting the front door. An odd flutter of nerves went through her when it came to removing her stockings. She wouldn't have thought they would need to come off for his purposes – and if they really had to be removed, shouldn't she be shown to a changing room? She was damned if she was going to be coy about this, though. And presumably Violet de Frémont had been given the same treatment. What was good enough for the countess . . .

Not knowing whether or not Zachari was watching her, having to trust solely in his professionalism, Genevieve lifted her skirt and unbuttoned the suspenders on her right thigh. Slowly, she rolled the stocking down and slipped it off, then started on the left. The wood floor was cold under her feet. She felt shy, as though more than just the legs, under the Paul Poiret dress, were naked. Unconsciously she curled her toes.

'Are you cold?' came Zachari's voice. She detected a faint smoky odour, and saw, when she looked up, that he was sitting just across the room in a Napoleon III chair, smoking a cigarette. He'd cast the formality aside now, like an old coat, and had become casual almost to the point of insolence. He had – would you credit it? – his right leg slung over the arm of the chair and was lolling back, his head to one side.

'Not at all.' And indeed the room was, if anything, rather warm. 'I'm ready to be measured.'

'I'd like you to walk for me.' Zachari gestured with his right hand, still holding the cigarette, indicating that she should go up to the mirror at the far end of the room and back. 'And stop clenching your toes.'

Genevieve looked down at her toes, and worked hard at relaxing them. Standing up, she realized she was afraid of disappointing him. Starting her walk to the mirror, she felt she was on a tightrope. Shoulders back, head straight, remembering those deportment lessons, the feel of the book on her head, the need to keep perfect balance. Arriving at the mirror, she glimpsed her flushed face, her whiter-than-white legs, her expression of vague discomfort. Then she turned and walked back.

Zachari smiled lazily. 'Now do it again, but naturally. You look like you've got a rod stuck up your back.'

Anger flashed and she had to work hard to suppress it and keep her concentration on her walking.

'And again,' he said when she got back to him. 'In fact just keep on walking up and down the room until I tell you to stop.'

Back and forth she went, time and again, wondering dimly if this was a deliberate move of his – a little light humiliation to keep her in her place. He was so changeable, this Zachari. She had no idea what he really thought of her and she wished she didn't care. But as she continued walking, the self-consciousness, the irritation, the embarrassment began to slip away, until she was no longer aware of anything very much. Only the smooth, cool boards, the rough softness of the zebra-skin rug, the slipping and sliding of her dress against her bare legs. The presence of Zachari, silently watching her, his gaze fixed on her feet.

'Good.' His voice was harsh. 'Now sit down again.'

She sat on the couch, and he came and crouched by her, putting a long velvet-covered footstool in front of her, indicating that she should place one foot there while he himself perched on the back of it. He produced a little slide rule, such as other shoemakers used. She placed her foot against it and he slid the marker down to the top of her toes. Then he used a tape to measure the width of her foot in three places. After the strangeness of the walking up and down, this was rather pedestrian and commonplace. She was disappointed.

'I can judge the measurements by eye but it's best to double-check.' It was as if he'd heard her thoughts.

'Did you judge right in my case?'

But he just smiled.

She began to move her foot down from the stool but he put out a hand to stop her. The hand touched her foot, and then slid to hold her ankle. She thought about that hand touching hers last night. The fingers were strong, presumably from all the work.

Lifting her foot and holding it gently, he slipped one hand under the arch and one under the toes. She imagined his hands shaping leather, knocking in nails. The broad palms. The arms, under his shirt, would be finely muscled. She allowed her foot to relax, to go limp.

And then she felt the most exquisite sensation, as though heat were passing from his hands into her foot, making it tingle, the tingling passing up through her leg. Slowly he moved his hands around her foot, pressing here and there with his thumbs, feeling for the shapes of her bones, separating her toes and exerting a light pressure between them. He stroked, he pressed, he felt his way around her foot until she sighed audibly with pleasure. She allowed him to run his hand up the back of her calf, feeling the shape of the muscle.

When he placed her foot back on the stool, she instantly missed his touch, but of course there was still the other foot . . .

'Don't stop,' she said, without thinking, when he had finished.

He laughed. 'I'm not a masseur, Mrs Shelby King.' And he was up and wandering away across the room, carrying the footstool with him. 'You can put on your stockings and shoes now.'

As she glanced up, she caught sight of Olga. She'd come halfway up the stairs, and was watching. Rapidly, she turned her back. How long had the woman been there? She hated the idea that Olga may have watched while Zachari was holding and caressing her feet. Yes, caressing. No lover had ever touched her feet that way.

When she'd finished fastening her stockings, she saw that Olga had come right into the room, and was standing with Zachari at the reception desk, checking through a diary and talking to him in a low murmur. Looking up at Genevieve, Olga cleared her throat and jabbed at Zachari with her elbow. Finally he too looked up.

'Thank you, madame. We're all finished. So nice to see you again.'

Genevieve's business head was on now. 'But we haven't discussed anything.'

He raised his eyebrows. 'What is there to discuss?'

'Well, the kind of shoes I'd like, of course. And the price. And you're to tell me when they'll be ready.'

'We will telephone you when the shoes are ready,' said Olga.

Genevieve continued ignoring her. 'We haven't settled any of the details, Mr Zachari.'

Zachari frowned. 'I don't work that way. I'd have expected you to know that, since you profess to have such a liking for my shoes.'

'But I need the shoes to work with a Cubist theme, and the colours—'

He held up both hands, signalling for her to stop. 'You must leave all this to me. My design will be perfect for the shape of your foot. That is all I can say for the moment. And I do not make any guarantees as to when the shoes will be ready. I must obtain the right materials, the right fabrics. This can take some time.'

'What *is* this? I'm commissioning a pair of shoes for my party.'

'Nobody dictates to Paolo.'

Zachari put a hand on Olga's arm to silence her. 'I'll make you a pair of shoes. I think you'll like them.'

'And the money?'

'Five hundred dollars now, and the rest when the shoes are ready.'

'How much will "the rest" be?'

He shrugged and spread his hands wide. 'I don't know yet. I might be working with plain leather. I might order in silks from overseas or buy lace and brocade from one of the flea markets.'

'Flea markets!'

'The money's not a problem, is it?'

'That's hardly the point.'

'*Madame*,' said Zachari, 'my shoes are magic shoes. They'll make you happy. You want to be happy, don't you?'

# II

# Vamp

# 11

EARLY MAY. PARIS IS WARMING UP, READYING HERSELF FOR summer's giddy party. The trees out on the boulevards and down by the Seine are decked out in their prettiest pink and white. The café terraces are crammed with people from dawn to dusk, and beyond (all through the night in Montparnasse). The people at the tables are laughing louder than they did last month or the month before. The sun shoots dazzling shafts between buildings, across rooftops, around street corners.

The windows are wide open at the Shelby Kings' apartment on this sunny May evening. The nets hanging inside are floating on the breeze and billowing into the rooms. To anyone passing along the Rue de Lota it would be obvious that this is a place where foreigners live. A Parisian would never tolerate the *courant d'air* – those unhealthy draughts and the possibility of getting a chill. But the movement of Parisian air, with its heady cocktail of flowers, traffic fumes, baking, cigarette smoke, coffee, eau-de-cologne and the river, is something both Robert and Genevieve enjoy.

The rooms themselves are quiet. Genevieve has gone out and taken the car. Céline, the maid, is visiting her mother. Only Robert is at home. He's in Genevieve's shoe room, taking down boxes at random and peeping in. He gets a thrill out of this – a sexy little tingle. It's not the shoes themselves which excite him. It's not even the thought of his wife wearing the shoes or taking them off. It's the thrill you get from trespassing, from reading someone's diary. He would never dream of coming in here when she's at home. She makes it abundantly clear that this room is her private domain. And she doesn't let him touch the shoes. It's as if he's some boy with dirty hands who can't be trusted. But he comes in here a lot, when he's alone.

Now, where to begin? Third shelf up, second box from the left: a pair of green satin party shoes, the front panel inlaid with strange Egyptian motifs. No mark at all on the soles – she's never worn them. Most likely, she never will.

Two shelves further up the wall and five boxes to the right, here are a pair of buckled evening pumps in blue brocade. At least he thinks they're pumps. He doesn't quite understand the difference between a pump and a court shoe, though Genevieve has explained. Both kinds of shoe are enclosed and hold to the foot without a fastening of any sort. See, the ornate buckle on this pair is purely decorative and serves no practical purpose. His friend Harry would make a quip if he was here: That's how women are – pretty but useless. Not that he agrees with Harry. Harry is Harry, that's all.

One shelf down and one box back: grey silk – court shoes, possibly – decorated with a diamond pattern in black and crystal bugle beads around a rhinestone flower. He

112

remembers these shoes. She was wearing them on the day he proposed to her. He noticed them as he knelt – you couldn't help but notice shoes like that, the way they glittered. Very dressy for what should have been an ordinary Sunday. Now he knows her so much better, he wonders if her choice was a calculated one. She'd seemed so amazed when he popped his big question – the heaving chest, the wild eyes. But perhaps she sensed, somehow, that he was going to propose that day . . .

Three up and four to the right: a pair of sugar-pink dancing slippers with bow trim. The label says HELLSTERN & SONS. Demure. Virginal. She might have worn them to a school prom. Did they have proms at those fancy English schools? He couldn't see it somehow – Genevieve dancing with some pimply boy. It wasn't her style. And she wasn't the kind of girl who shone at school dances, in spite of her looks. They'd have been terrified of her. She'd have been stuck at the side, poor thing, while the plain girls waltzed around the floor. And later, she was left stranded at home while her old schoolfriends married those boys. But what did they know, eh? Their loss was certainly his gain. Not that he was the dancing type himself.

Next door to the dancing slippers is a pair of black suede shoes with a curved heel decorated with tiny sequins clustered together like flowers. For some reason he lifts one of these shoes to his face, breathes in the scent of the leather inner. He doesn't know when she wore them but he can see them on her feet. She is sitting with one leg crossed over the other, swinging her foot. She is laughing.

She's never worn the boots one shelf below but he remembers how much he paid for them. Made of maroon

113

satin with floral embroidery and ribbons for laces, they date from the late 1800s. She tried to present them to him as a hot investment, and the notion tickled him, he had to admit it. Until he saw the price tag.

Robert puts the boots away, and pauses for a moment to think. There's more to this than the pleasure of sneaking about and nosing into Genevieve's private world. Each of these boxes holds a secret. If he wants to truly understand his wife, he has to learn how to interpret what he finds. He knows precisely which pair he wants to look at next.

Here on the bottom shelf, right in the corner, here is his favourite pair of Genevieve's shoes. He gets them out every time he comes in here. Flat, black patent leather, with an ankle strap and a cute little button. The toes are scuffed and the soles worn. He can just imagine her in them – running about, hopping, jumping a rope. She must have been eight or nine years old when she wore these shoes. The thought of her as a little girl, wide-eyed, makes him melt.

She would have put on her mother's shoes, the child-Genevieve. Clopping about and pretending to be a grand lady. Admiring herself in the mirror. He remembers his sister doing this, back when they were kids. He supposes it's a game all little girls play. But Genevieve has carried on playing it.

Robert stands looking at the Mary Janes for some time. Relishing the intimacy of the moment. He smiles to himself, and acknowledges the smile.

## 12

MARCEL HAD SPINDLY YELLOW FINGERS, LONG ENOUGH TO spider up and down the piano keys while his wrists hardly moved. His shoulders were hunched up from the many thousands of hours he'd spent playing. His back was permanently bent over and his legs stiff. For years he'd sat on a stool that was too high and by the time he'd been told as much it was too late to change his habits. And he had a way of peering at people like they were notes on a stave and he was trying to decipher them through myopic eyes. In truth, the piano-playing was slowly destroying him. But it was his whole life.

People found Marcel creepy but Lulu liked him. His conversation wasn't up to much, but then it wasn't companionship she was after. He always turned up on time and didn't try to sleep with her. And he could play. Sometimes, leaning against the piano and reaching for the high notes, she'd glance down at his arachnoid fingers capering back and forth and the sight of them would give her the cold shudders, putting her in mind of those nights when she'd earn a few francs by showing her breasts to old men behind the Gare Montparnasse – maybe letting them have a little feel. Shadowy nights that were long ago in a not-so-long-ago way. She gave up the old men when she discovered the artists. They didn't have much money but if you posed nude for them they'd buy the drinks and something to eat and give you a bed for the night. And then she met Camby and he sat her down in front of a mirror and set to work on her with black kohl and white powder and red lipstick, giving her the amazing cat-like eyes and beauty spot that were her trademarks, and introducing her to everyone as 'Lulu of Montparnasse, the face of NOW'.

Lulu sang several nights a week at the Coyote, an old and rather cramped bar in the Rue Delambre, just along from the Métro Vavin, and tucked away from sight of the tourists who now packed out the Quarter each night, flocking along the main streets, the Boulevard du Montparnasse and the Boulevard Raspail, herding into the larger terraced cafés and the new American bars. The Coyote had always been the domain of those in the know – the artists and writers. Though increasingly there were also a lot of rich hangers-on, predominantly from the US and England. Many came to get a look at the better-known artists who were Coyote regulars, but most of them came to see her sing. She was famous – the Queen of the Quarter. The Coyote pretty much owed its new popularity to her. The Dôme kept a table permanently reserved for her. Monsieur Select would smile when she walked into his joint, and cook her up a Welsh rarebit free of charge and without being asked on his little stove behind the bar. She was the most sought-after artist's model in Paris. And Camby needed to be reminded of that.

There he was, sitting up at the bar with Kisling, drinking Rémy Martin. Laurent, the one-eyed barman with the Croix de Guerre (two palms), poured shot after shot into tiny thimble-shaped glasses for the two artists, keeping the bottle out on the bar for easy access. Camby had given her a cheeky pinch on the bottom when he walked in, but was now deep in conversation with Kisling and paying her no attention.

Lulu sucked in her lower lip and tapped her foot impatiently on the floor. How can that bastard just sit there with his back to me all this time? Who does he think I am? Some little nobody to be picked up and dropped whenever the mood suits him? Well, not this girl. Not Lulu!

'"Lost Love"?' Marcel glanced at the set list she'd scrawled down for him.

'You're damn right,' muttered Lulu. And then, loudly, to the packed room: 'Here's a song for all of you who have loved someone who doesn't deserve to be loved. Some lousy, low-down swine . . .'

Readying herself to sing, she switched her gaze to the other side of the room – to her best friend, Genevieve, radiant as always in an emerald-green dress. She couldn't see the shoes from here but they'd match the outfit exactly. Genevieve would dress beautifully even for an afternoon alone at home. Lulu, whose personal style was vivid but haphazard, was strongly drawn to her friend's aesthetic. But sometimes she wished she could catch Genevieve looking sloppy. Just once. Genevieve was a girl whose world needed to be shaken. Shaken enough so that people would glimpse the cracks.

*

'A truly fascinating female, that one,' said Betterson. 'Just look at those eyes of hers . . . It's like she's seen everything there is to see in this world and felt everything there is to feel. And it's all there – there in those heart-breaker eyes.'

Genevieve twisted round to look at Lulu, up at the piano. You could barely see her eyes through all that black Egyptian make-up and the thick cloud of smoke in the air. But Betterson was right. There was a *quality* about her. Something quite extraordinary. It was this quality that made men want to paint her and sculpt her and write about her. Everyone was rapt when Lulu sang 'Lost Love'. Even Janine, the hard-as-nails barmaid with the scar and the broken nose. Laurent's little poodle, down there on the floor, had stopped licking at a puddle of spilt drink in order to watch. Genevieve felt a pang of jealousy.

'Don't you think it's amazing how she takes her pain and turns it into something exquisite?' said Betterson. 'That's what writers are supposed to do, but so many of them just sit back on the sidelines of life, coolly observing. Novelists especially. It shows in the writing, you know.'

'Indeed.' Genevieve was struggling to suppress the jealousy, to squash it out of existence.

'There are books so cold, they're like butterfly collections,' said Betterson. 'A lot of dead, pretty, lifeless things stuck on pins. Maybe that's why I'm a poet rather than a novelist. I'm a hot-blooded creature.'

'On the subject of writing,' said Genevieve, her voice falsely bright, 'I've been thinking about a title for the magazine. What do you think of *The Gallery*?'

'Which gallery?' Betterson was still scrutinizing Lulu.

'Someone really ought to put her in a book. She deserves her immortality even if it's one of those cold butterfly books.'

'She's hardly hiding her light under a bushel. She's Lulu of Montparnasse! She'll live for ever.'

'Nobody lives for ever, honey,' said Betterson. 'Least of all me.'

Genevieve tried not to be annoyed. 'Yes, yes. Five years to live – we all know about that. I'm attempting to suggest a title for our joint venture. *The Gallery* has a dignified feel, don't you think? And it tells you just what the magazine will be.'

A surge of applause. Lulu had finished her song. The applause stretched on and Betterson let out a wolf-whistle. From the back of the room, someone threw a single rose. Lulu stooped to pick it up, plucked off one of its petals and ate it. The petals were the same red as her lips.

'And another thing, Norman . . . Have you had a chance to look at my poetry notebook?'

Betterson twisted around in his seat, perhaps to see who had thrown the rose. 'Hey, look who's here! Come join us, you old dog.'

Genevieve wasn't sufficiently interested to turn around. Instead she looked over at the bar, where Camby was demonstrating something to Kisling with the use of a fork and a wine cork.

Up by the piano, Lulu ate a second petal. 'Bring me a drink, won't you, Laurent? My friend at the bar will pay. The fellow who's brandishing cutlery and taking himself too seriously.'

The war hero winked his remaining eye in assent.

' "Girl from Clermont"?' asked Marcel.

'No. I'm so bored of that one. I never want to sing it again.'

A glass was passed across from the bar, hand to hand until it reached Lulu. She held it up to the light, examining the round brown fruit rolling around in the amber liquid.

'Did I ask for a cherry?' she called out to Laurent.

'That's what the gentleman ordered for you,' said the barman.

'Camby's no gentleman.'

'No, not him. The gentleman over there.' Laurent pointed across the room.

Norman Betterson was raising his glass. '*Vive la France et les pommes de terre frites!*'

Lulu plucked the cherry from her glass, sucked it till her mouth was all burning brandy sweetness and then spat the stone across the room in Betterson's direction. '*Vive l'Amérique et le chauffage central!*'

'What am I playing?' asked Marcel.

Lulu sipped her brandy. 'Let me think a minute.' Absently, she ate another petal from the rose and glanced again at Betterson, a man she'd rarely given a thought to. Then, inadvertently, she caught Genevieve's eye. Something rather like panic had come over Genevieve. Her hand had flown to her throat, her movements were edgy and nervous, and all in all she looked as though she wanted to escape. But the room was crowded – there was barely standing room, let alone a clear passage to the door.

'Very mysterious,' said Lulu.

'What? Do I know that one?' Marcel was rustling through his music sheets.

A tall man in a cream suit had appeared at Genevieve's table. He was talking to Betterson, and Betterson was laughing at some remark he'd made – trying to include Genevieve in the joke. Genevieve was ashen-faced.

'Well, well,' muttered Lulu. 'Genevieve and Guy Monteray . . . What's all *this*?'

'Lulu?'

'All right, Marcel. I'm going to try something new. Forget the set list. Play that slow old Lyonnaise number you like so much, and keep playing it until I'm done.'

Marcel nodded and his fingers touched down on the piano keys, rippling back and forth. The melody was melancholy and complex. Instead of singing, Lulu started to speak across the music in a dry, rasping voice that made the bar fall instantly quiet.

'On the Rue de la Huchette stands a hotel called Sadness,' she began. 'The rooms are small and dark and the people stay inside them all day to hide from the sun. The owner beats his wife every night and then goes to the next room to make love to a girl who likes men and money and cherries, but can't hold on to anything in her life. While the owner makes love to her, the girl can hear his wife crying through the wall. She moans louder to block out the sound. The wife hears the girl's moans of pleasure and this makes her cry all the more. It's very loud at night in the hotel called Sadness.'

'Why did you run away?' Monteray whispered into Genevieve's ear. Genevieve darted a look across the table at Betterson, hoping he would rescue her. But he was watching Lulu.

'Women don't usually run out on me quite so literally. I had rather thought you were enjoying yourself. I know *I* was . . .'

'There's someone in the bathtub at the Hotel called Sadness,' spoke Lulu. 'She's been lying there a long time. First there was a lot of steam, and some of it was her breath. But now the steam has gone and the water is cold . . .'

Genevieve tried not to let herself think about that gun. Perhaps it wasn't real, she told herself. Just a stupid prank.

'Do you know what I want?' Monteray's hand closed over hers. His hand was hot and heavy. She wanted to flinch away but the hand stopped her.

'It was all a mistake,' said Genevieve. 'I was drunk. I'm married.'

'Let me tell you what I want, Mrs Shelby King.'

'She's been lying there all night.' Lulu stepped forward and stretched out her arms to two burly men sitting smoking at a table in front of her, gesturing for them to lift her up on to the marble-topped, Dubonnet-stained bar. 'The bath is full but the tap is drip-dripping. And now it is morning and there's water on the floor, seeping down through the boards. Down through the ceiling of the reception hall below . . . seeping and creeping and dripping . . . on to the bald head of the owner as he writes out the bills for the guests who are leaving. And he looks up at the ceiling, at the wet patch that's growing, and he thinks, Where is my wife? How can she allow this to happen? This anarchic leaking? This bathroom unruliness in my respectable hotel?'

'What I want,' said Monteray, 'is to get inside of you again. Inside where it's hot and tight. You understand?'

'Let go of my hand,' said Genevieve through gritted teeth.

Lulu was up on the bar now – reclining full-length while the hard-as-nails barmaid tutted and put her hands on her hips. Laurent smiled and shook his head and stroked his moustache.

'He's banging on the door of the bathroom. He's demanding they open up, whoever they are. But that's what she's done, you see. She's opened up her wrists and let it all flow out with the water. The drips downstairs are landing rusty-red on the hotel diary.'

'I have to get home, Norman.' Genevieve yanked her hand free. But Betterson was too busy watching Lulu to acknowledge her.

'Sweetheart!' Monteray's face was all concern. 'Have I upset you? It was meant as a compliment, I assure you. A discreet exchange between two people who've *known* each other.'

'Please, Guy. I don't want to talk about what we did.'

'Oh. Pity.' He shrugged. 'Women like you don't grow on trees, and that's a compliment too. But *c'est la vie*. Tell me we're still friends, Genevieve.'

'Of course we are.' But her tone said the opposite.

'Well, that's something. I'll see you at your party next week. It *is* next week, isn't it? I've got that right?'

'There's nobody to help the owner as he tries the handle of the bathroom. The hotel is silent and still. He realizes he has not seen his wife this morning. *He has not seen his wife this morning.*'

Lulu was lying flat on the cold bar, heedless of the puddles of drink, the mess of cigarette ash. As she continued her story, she stared up into the eyes of her lover, Frederick Camby.

'The door finally comes open. Bang!' Lulu sat bolt upright, her eyes huge. 'She is there. Lying in the bath.'

She surveyed her audience through long lashes. Across the room Betterson and Monteray were both still at their table, but Genevieve's seat was empty.

'Later that day, the owner's wife cleans up the mess with a mop and bucket. Now she will have to find another girl to live in that room.' She lowered her head. The bar was completely silent. Even Camby and Kisling were paying attention. 'You can stop playing now, Marcel.'

At home, in her bedroom, Genevieve allowed herself to be comforted by the sound of Robert's gentle snores from the other side of the cornflower-blue silk-covered wall.

It's all right, she told herself. It doesn't matter if he comes to the party. He understands that it's over between us.

Putting one foot up on the low table in patinated bronze, she gave her full attention to a nasty stain on her green suede Jules Fernand T-strap shoe. Someone amongst that solid wall of people at the Coyote had spilt a drink on her foot as she blundered to the door.

It's all right, she decided. It'll come clean. Best to try a soft cloth or a little wire brush in the morning.

Setting the shoes down, she began peeling off petal-like layers of silk, draping them over the oriental screen, dropping them on the African rug. When she was down to her slip, a small, balled-up piece of paper fell out on to the floor.

Carefully she unravelled it, and smoothed it out on the bedside table.

It was a sketch. Just a small one, in pencil. A death's-head.

# 13

VIOLET DE FRÉMONT'S SHOES. GOSSAMER-LIGHT. THEY might have been spun by a spider rather than a mere man. They were magical. Unobtainable.

With only five days to go until the party, there had still been no word from Zachari. Once Robert had left for work, Genevieve went to the telephone and asked to be connected to the shop. Again.

'Good-morning. This is—'

'Good-morning, Mrs Shelby King. And the answer is no.'

'Olga . . . May I call you Olga?'

'He's not here.'

'Of course not. He never is, is he? It must be very difficult for you, having to fob people off all the time. He shouldn't treat you that way.'

'We will call you when your shoes are ready.'

'Olga, when one is to host an important event, one needs to look one's best. Don't you agree? What one needs are Zachari's shoes. Brand-new, delicate as a flower, glamorous beyond all imagining but fitting like the softest glove.'

'Certainly.'

'I expect he listens to you, doesn't he? I should think if you were to explain to him just how much I need these shoes, he'd get on with it. Wouldn't he? I expect you'd benefit from an extra dollar or two, eh?'

'Madame . . .'

'How about five? Ten?'

'Keep your dollars, Mrs Shelby King. You may need them later.'

'Did you know that new shoes bring good luck, Olga? In England during the last century, people used to give each other miniature wooden or china shoes as lucky charms. Tiny shoe-shaped snuffboxes. Have you heard the stories about girls putting a clover leaf in their shoe when they wanted to meet a man? Children putting their shoes on the windowsill at Christmas hoping they'll be filled with presents in the morning? It's all true, Olga. I've read the books. I know about these things. And then there's the fairy tales – Cinderella's glass slippers, *Puss in Boots*, *The Elves and the Shoemaker*. Why do you think we're so obsessed with shoes, Olga, if not because they're *genuinely magical*?'

'Goodbye, madame.'

'Would you at least *ask* him for me? If I only knew for *certain* . . .'

'Perhaps you should buy yourself one of those lucky charms, madame. Shaped like a shoe.'

The big day arrived. Genevieve had summoned Lulu to come and help with the final preparations.

Lulu protested. 'I'll be no use to you, chérie. I'm no

society woman. What do I know about organizing parties? I *am* the party.'

'I need your moral support, Lulu. I need you to turn up in the morning and sweet-talk the artists and hold my hand through the day.'

'*Morning*? You need me in the *morning*? Oh no, chérie. Not this girl.'

But Genevieve was not to be refused. She collected Lulu in the Bentley at 8.30 a.m. (only four hours after Lulu had got to bed) to go over to Count Maurice Duvel's mansion on the Rue Cambon, where the party was to take place. Fernand Léger was already there when they arrived, looking in his flat cap and baggy trousers like any old removal man as he helped to unload his specially commissioned creations – monumental three-dimensional versions of his own paintings made from perforated metal plates, girders and grids. Sonia Delaunay was there too, hanging her gaudy fabric collages from the high balconies in Duvel's ballroom. The colours were so bright for Lulu's early-morning eyes that she felt compelled to slip the maid a few centimes to add a shot of vodka to her coffee.

Genevieve would not stop fretting. 'I should have thrown this party months ago, before the Exposition opened.'

They'd attended the opening of the Exposition Internationale des Arts Décoratifs et Industriels at the Grand Palais last month (along with anyone who was Anyone), while Genevieve's party was still an idea in bud. In the Pavillon de l'Elégance, created by Armand Rateau, Lulu dimly remembered trying to dance an inebriated Charleston with one of Jeanne Paquin's dressed mannequins. They'd caroused for many hours on one of Paul Poiret's three exhibition barges on the Seine, decorated by Dufy and the Atelier Martine. And Genevieve had begun worrying about whether anything would ever seem truly impressive again.

'Chérie, you are throwing a party,' Lulu said now, 'not an international *exposition*!'

Genevieve spoke slowly, as to a small child. 'Who is going to care about my little party when everyone went to *the* party? I'll be lucky if anyone even bothers to turn up.'

'Vivi.' Lulu put a hand on her shoulder. 'It's going to be fantastic.' And she drained the last grainy dregs of that potent coffee.

Lulu had her second vodka-laced coffee when Robert dropped by unexpectedly and got into an argument with the caterers over the vast quantity of caviar that had been ordered. He thought there must be some mistake and said so. Lulu, who had been present when Genevieve finalized the order, knew better. Robert took some placating, but Genevieve was a past master at handling him, and soon he was dispatched to the office and the caterers expertly soothed.

The third vodka-coffee came after a phone call concerning the enormous abstract ice sculpture Genevieve had ordered. The call came from the sculptor's mother.

'I felt it my duty to warn you, madame.'

'Warn me of what?' asked Genevieve.

'I was alarmed at the shape of your sculpture when I saw it there in the cooler.'

'The shape?'

'I shall ask my son to make some alterations before the evening.'

'Madame, what is wrong with the shape?'

'Well, it resembles a . . . a certain part of the male anatomy.'

By noon, when they arrived at the Atelier Martine for Genevieve's dress fitting, Lulu was carrying a small bottle of vodka under her coat. After the fitting, they were due to return to Count Duvel's place to watch the dress rehearsal of the specially choreographed Cubist dance piece. Then it was Richard Hudnot's perfume shop on the Rue de la Paix; and finally, if Lulu could still see straight, both girls were having their hair, nails and make-up done at Lina Cavalieri's Salon de Coiffure, Lulu's to be paid for by Genevieve as a thank-you.

At the Atelier Martine, Lulu reclined on a *chaise longue* while Genevieve was helped into her new dress.

'So, what do you think?' She emerged from behind the Chinese screen in a stunning flapper dress in flame-coloured velvet, ostensibly a rich orange, but gold wherever the light fell on it.

Paul Poiret wandered over to take a look, cocked his head and sucked on his fat little finger. 'If we just—' he beckoned to the pin-laden girl to adjust the sash.

'I'm not sure.' Genevieve peered into the long, gilt-edged mirror.

Below the waist, the dress was a mass of jagged downward-pointing velvet flames, edged in gold beading. Or perhaps they were more like icicles in their shape and effect – but hot flaming icicles, rattling and rippling as she moved, allowing daring views of her legs, right up to the thigh.

'Chérie.' Lulu tipped vodka into her glass of champagne, under cover of the latest issue of *La Vie Parisienne*. 'What is the matter with you? Are your eyes defective? The dress is sensational. *You* are sensational.'

'Do you think so?' Genevieve's face was sulky.

Lulu's lip tightened. Spoilt little rich girl. I knew I didn't want to come here today. She thought about her own party dress on its hanger back at her tiny apartment. A shimmering silver sheath from a flea market, on which she'd daubed her best approximation of an early Picasso painting. It had cost next to nothing, but who cared about that? She'd look a million dollars because she was Lulu of Montparnasse.

'It's not the dress I'm worried about,' said Genevieve. 'It's the shoes.'

'Genevieve, darling.' Paul Poiret bit his lower lip. 'They don't come better than Perugia.'

'Yes,' said Genevieve, 'they do.'

They were gold kid dancing pumps. Louis heels and a stitched-on flame motif in orange velvet. Not so long ago Genevieve would have been delighted to go to her party wearing Perugias. But that was before she saw Violet de Frémont's pair of Zacharis.

When the fitting was over and the exasperated Poiret had waddled away, Lulu dismissed the girl with her pins and went behind the screen herself to help Genevieve out of the dress.

'He's ruined everything,' moaned Genevieve as Lulu struggled with her fastenings. 'How can I be happy tonight without my Zacharis? I wish I'd never set eyes on that damn shoemaker!'

'Here.' Lulu produced the bottle of vodka and shoved it at her. 'It's medicinal.'

'Lulu!'

'You'll never get through the day without it. And neither will I. Go on, have a drink and stop worrying. Everything will be fine.'

With a sigh, Genevieve reached for the bottle. 'Oh, Lulu. You don't know the half of it.'

'Half of what?' Lulu frowned.

Genevieve seemed about to confide something, but then appeared to change her mind. 'Nothing. I'm sure you're right. It'll all be fine.'

The clock in the hallway chimed eight. Robert was out in the Bentley with Pierre, waiting. They already had the engine running – Genevieve could hear it purring away down in the street. Sitting at her dressing table, she patted at her newly waved hair, adjusted her sash, tried to enjoy the gold kid pumps.

The countess's shoes – those layers of spidery, silvery lace, their delicacy . . . They might break if you so much as touched them, they might vanish like a broken spell . . .

A horn sounded outside.

And then there was that other worry. Guy Monteray and the skull. She'd been feeling nervy this past week, since their encounter at the Coyote. Often in the street she'd hear footsteps close behind and think she was being followed. She'd tried to send her worries away, reminding herself that Monteray was a poet and a playboy. He liked games and she'd allowed herself to be drawn in. That's all it was – a game. In time, it would fade away.

But still she'd resolved to instruct the doormen at Count Duvel's mansion not to let him in.

The horn came again.

'All right,' she muttered. 'I'm coming.' Gathering up her wrap, she headed out into the hallway, only to draw up short at the half-open door to the shoe room.

A girl was standing there, gazing into the long mirror. So tiny that she might have been an elf. Bathed in the weak evening light, she stared at her feet in the mirror, turning them this way, that way . . .

Genevieve caught her breath. And it was then that Céline, the maid, looked up.

Céline was wearing Genevieve's Joseph Box court shoes. Shocking pink with dusky green piping, a Louis heel and a ribbon tie. Genevieve had been wearing them earlier and had left them lying on the floor before the mirror. Céline had been hitching her skirt up to admire her gently curving calves and delicate ankles. Her hair, normally worn in a tight little bun at the back of her head, hung in soft curls around her face. Her cheeks were red, even before she looked up and exclaimed. Genevieve couldn't quite see her eyes before she started and span around, but she could guess how they would have looked – how much Céline would have been revelling in this secret moment.

She'd never taken much notice of the maid. Why should she? She was a twitchy little thing of fifteen or sixteen, with mousy hair and a scuttling way about her. Genevieve had grown up in a house full of servants and was only truly aware of them when they made mistakes. This, of course, was Céline's biggest.

'Madame! I'm so sorry.'

'Do they fit?' whispered Genevieve.

'Please, madame.' The shoes were already off and Céline was replacing them in their open box. 'They're so beautiful. I couldn't help it, madame. I—'

'They do, don't they?' said Genevieve. 'They fit you perfectly.'

'You won't sack me, will you?' She was sliding her feet back into her own shoes – flat brown lace-ups with a square toe. 'I've never done this before. I won't do it again.'

Out in the street, the horn sounded again.

'I find that difficult to believe.'

'I thought you'd gone down to the car with Mr Shelby King. I never imagined ... My mother is ill, madame. I don't know what we'll do if I lose my job.'

The horn sounded yet again.

'*Please*, madame.'

Genevieve felt strangely moved by the scene. It was partly the way the shoes looked on the girl, but it was more than that. She had stumbled inadvertently on someone else's secret life – become suddenly aware of another person's most potent and covetous desires and fears at a moment when she'd been subsumed by her own. Céline had woken her out of herself in a way that was surprising and strangely delicious.

'Genevieve!' came Robert's voice from below.

'It's all right,' she said, softly, to the girl. 'You can keep your job. And the shoes. Not a word to Mr Shelby King. It'll be our secret.'

Somewhere in the background the telephone was ringing.

# 14

RAIN FELL ON THE GOLDEN VELVET WRAP WITH THE sumptuous Australian opossum edgings, on the André Perugia gold kid shoes. Rain fell on the heavily jewelled satin headband and the Lina Cavalieri coiffure. Rain fell on Genevieve as she knocked on the door of Paolo Zachari's shop and waited, sodden, nervy, excited – perhaps ever so slightly unhinged.

At last, a fussing with bolts on the other side.

'Mrs Shelby King.'

'Mr Zachari.'

'You're very dressed up for a visit to the humble shoe-maker, if you don't mind my saying so.'

'Let me in. I've had enough of your games.'

'And I of yours. May I take your wrap?'

She shoved it at him – remembering with embarrassment the last time she had done this – and pushed past.

Inside, the shop was completely dark. Not a chink of light showed through the curtained, shuttered windows.

And when Zachari closed the front door, the darkness was complete.

His voice, close by. 'Take your shoes and stockings off, please.'

'I can't see a thing. Could you open the curtains or turn a light on?'

'Take your shoes and stockings off.'

Robert would be arriving at the Rue Cambon by now, without her. The dancers would be setting up.

'Put a light on, Mr Zachari.'

'Take your shoes and stockings off. Surely you can manage something so simple.'

She sighed – 'All right' – and bent to remove the damp Perugia pumps. 'May I sit down?'

'Of course.'

But she couldn't see her way to a couch and he made no move to help her. Stiffly she began to unfasten her suspenders. She could hear his breathing now. He had moved further away from her.

She peeled off one stocking, then the other – this time almost losing her balance. 'You'd better have some shoes here for me, Zachari.'

A chuckle. And he took her arm and guided her across the room.

'Take a seat.'

She placed a hand on the couch to check it was there, and sat carefully. She heard his footsteps walking away from her across the wood floor, caught the tiniest glimpse of his moving figure, and then ... he was going down the stairs.

'Hey! You're not going to leave me up here on my own!'

136

'Scared of the dark?' A door squeaked at the foot of the staircase.

Genevieve was acutely aware of the ticking of a clock, the murmur of traffic and a church bell striking the hour. Nine o'clock! The first guests might be arriving at her party.

A groan of floorboards. He was coming back up the stairs. And then he was down on the floor at her feet. She could just about make out his kneeling shape.

'Give me your left foot.'

His hand. The strength in his fingers. And now ... a sensation of ... It was as though he had taken her whole foot into his mouth.

'And your right foot, please.'

She thought of the silky skin of babies. She thought of downy feathers, softest fur. She thought of clouds.

'Please put a light on, Mr Zachari. I'd like to see if these shoes of yours look as good as they feel.'

'Well, now we have a problem.'

'What problem? Open the curtains. I must see my new shoes.'

A sigh. 'The problem, Mrs Shelby King, is your dress.'

'What about my dress?'

'From what I could see, it clashes badly with my shoes. I think you'd better take it off.'

She laughed. She had to.

'I am quite serious, madame.'

'Do you want to see me in my slip? Is that it?'

A silence. Genevieve felt her heart begin to thud.

'I want to see you in my shoes.'

'Well you'd better give me back my wrap then. I'll have to put *something* on.'

137

'Your wrap and your dress are that same lurid orange, are they not?'

She wished she could see his face.

'I want to see you in my shoes,' he said. 'And you want me to see you in your slip. In fact, you want me to see you without your slip.'

'Oh, you think so?'

'Yes. I think so.'

'Well, I'm not that sort of woman, Mr Zachari. Now put a light on, please.'

Silence. The *zeeshhh* of cars on the wet roads. The tapping of rain against the windows. The creak of floorboards as Zachari wandered around the room. Two people breathing.

Genevieve removed the jewelled headband from her hair and laid it down on the couch. Her hands were shaking as she reached up to the back of her neck and began unclasping the hooks on her dress. The man is an artist, she told herself. It's just the same as posing for a painter. I've done this before. Lulu does it every day.

I have nothing to be ashamed of. She unclipped the hooks of her corset.

A scraping sound, and across the room a match flared. She saw his face by its light – the thin wide lips, not quite smiling. The soft eyes, not looking at her. He lit a taper and blew out the match. He reached up and – one by one – lit the six candles twisted around each other in the silver cage, suspended from the ceiling by a chain. He span the cage gently with his left hand, sending light and shadows dancing crazily across the walls. Then he turned and moved a little to the left, revealing the long silver mirror at the end of the room.

138

She took a step forward and then another, seeing herself: her skin honeyed in the candle-light, her eyes black and smudged, the curves of her body – her breasts, her hips – gentle, almost blurred.

She looked down at her feet. Deep red shoes like tongues, like blood, with the fierce sparkle of huge jewelled buckles. Spike heels.

'The shoes are made from Genoese velvet.' He was standing behind her, placing his hands on her bare shoulders. 'The heels are glass.' He pressed his lips to her neck. 'But the buckles are set with diamonds.'

Now his hands were on her waist, pushing her gently towards one of the purple couches. She tried to look into his eyes as she sat down and reclined, extending her legs and flinging her arms behind her head – but she couldn't make out their expression. He took hold of her left foot under the arch, raising her leg so they could both admire the shoe, and then bent to kiss the toe, the buckle, the heel, her ankle bone, the inside of her knee . . . She was naked but for the shoes. Their vivid red against her white feet made her feel *more* than naked.

She looked at his hand, holding her foot. The party didn't matter any more. None of it mattered. Not Robert and certainly not Guy Monteray. Only Zachari's hand holding her foot. Only his touch. His mouth. She'd been born for this moment. For him.

## 15

IT WAS ALMOST ELEVEN WHEN GENEVIEVE'S TAXI DREW UP outside Count Duvel's house in the Rue Cambon. The rain was sheeting.

She took a mirror from her tasselled bag and checked her face. The newly applied make-up was pristine, as was the hastily restyled hair. But still there was something disordered about her appearance.

I'll tell Robert I've been robbed . . . I was coming out of Zachari's shop with my new shoes and a man came at me in the dark street and demanded I hand over my purse. Yes, that's it. No – no, he'll want to get the police involved. Can't have that.

Two doormen descended the steps, their feet squelching on the drenched blue carpet. One of them carried a cushioned dining chair.

The driver opened her door and held up an umbrella while the doormen set down the chair.

'If Madame would like to sit, we will assist her to the house without damage to those beautiful red shoes.'

'Thank you. Don't mind if I do.'

Lifting the hem of the crimson silk Natalia Goncharova dress with daringly low cowl neck, and gathered slightly at the left hip beneath a pearl decoration (she'd had it made for the opening of the Exposition but in the end had worn Chanel), and taking very special care of the Zachari shoes, Genevieve slid out on to the dining chair and was lifted up, one man to each side of her.

I'll say I fainted at Zachari's and had to go home for a lie-down. I threw up. I was all over the place – it took all my strength and determination to get here at all, I'm still so very wan . . .

They set her down in the hallway, and she handed her cloak to an attendant. She could hear music and voices.

The doors to the ballroom were opened for her entrance.

The band was playing something frenzied and experimental while dancers, dressed in dizzy stripes, mad zigzags, disc-shaped and conical hats, capered about the dance-floor. Nouveaux-riches flirted with Old Money beneath the towering Léger metal sculptures. Beauty conversed with Bohemia against a backdrop of Delaunay fabric collages in green, red, blue and shimmering yellow. The serving staff wove back and forth, bearing their trays aloft. Norman Betterson stroked his chin. Violet de Frémont, in a pair of perfect hot-pink pumps that could only have been made by Paolo Zachari, clawed at the arm of Count Etienne, her portly husband. Guy Monteray, in a far corner, raised one hand to his forehead in a strange salute. The ice phallus dripped.

Robert had broken away from Count Duvel and was striding across the room.

Genevieve panicked. 'I . . . I was sick on a man in a dark alley.'

Lulu rushed forward. 'Vivi . . .'

'I had to go home and change. I . . .'

'My darling.' Robert put a hand on her arm. 'I think you'd better come with me.'

'What the—'

'You should do as he says, chérie.' Lulu had the other arm.

The band struck up a jazz number with an infectious, toe-tapping beat, and the dance-floor instantly filled with people. Genevieve glimpsed their swirling dresses and laughing faces as she was led from the room.

# III

## Sole

# 16

ROBERT TOOK HOLD OF GENEVIEVE'S HAND ON THE WAY BACK. They were the last to leave the family mausoleum and everybody else had already got into their vehicles or wandered away on foot to the house. She hadn't wanted to travel in the Daimler with the rest of the family, and he could understand that. He was touched, really, that she wanted to be with him and him alone.

Her hand was tiny and cold; the eyes looked empty. He wanted to gather her to his chest, squeeze her hard. But he sensed that she wouldn't want him to and he respected that. There are times when a person needs room to breathe, to remember, to grieve. If only he could find the right words to comfort her.

'My darling,' he tried, as they passed along the gravel path between insignificant gravestones, ornate marble crucifixes, statues of angels; walking under the shade of silver birches and horse-chestnut trees, and on towards a huge oak. 'I remember, when Daddy died, getting this feeling like someone snatched the ground from under my feet. I couldn't see how any of us would survive without him. He was so *big* in every way. His intellect, his character. He had such stature. But we carried on, Genevieve. I don't suppose I will ever fill his shoes, but I did the best I could. We all did – Mama and my sister and—'

But Genevieve pulled her hand away and went darting across to the oak tree. He watched, confused, as she searched over the trunk for something, and then, seemingly having found whatever it was, stood quietly, running her fingers over the bark.

'What is it, honey?'

She made no reply. Just kept on looking at the tree trunk. Stroking it.

At length he cleared his throat. 'Hadn't we better be getting along to the house? They'll be wondering where we are.'

'Let them wonder.'

The sunlight was darting in fierce shafts between the branches, through the leaves. Robert, hot in his heavy black suit, loosened his collar. 'It doesn't seem right that it should be such a beautiful day, does it? The sky should be weeping right along with us. Of course, it was a real scorcher on the day we buried my daddy. Well, it—'

'Would you just shut up for *one minute*? Would you?' A sound came up from her throat, like an engine that wouldn't start. And he knew, as she turned and ran away down the path towards their car, that she was crying. At last. She had not cried when they told her the news. She had not cried during the service or at the graveside. And she *should* cry. It was only natural. It would do her good.

He took a moment to examine the oak tree before

146

following. There was something scratched into the bark –
one word – a name: JOSEPHINE. That was all.

When he arrived at the car, she was powdering her face
with the aid of a vanity mirror.

'We have to get back,' she said. 'They'll be waiting for me.'

For the remainder of the afternoon, he watched her carefully. Saw her making conversation with aunts and uncles,
only some of whom he remembered meeting at their
wedding. Saw her exchanging pleasantries with the vicar,
bending down to kiss the cheeks of tiny cousins, shaking
the hands of well-wishers from the village. Nodding
politely, smiling bravely. Going through the motions.

At some point he became tired of struggling to make
small-talk, and took himself off for a walk outside. In the
rose garden he sat down on a bench for a smoke, and was
surprised to be joined by a thin man whom he recognized as
Dr Peters, the family physician, and who was lighting a
cigar of his own.

'Sad business.' Dr Peters had a pronounced lisp and spat
slightly as he spoke.

'Isn't it. You must know the family pretty well.'

'Oh yes.' Peters nodded emphatically. 'I brought young
Genevieve into the world, you know. A difficult birth.'

Robert puffed on his cigar. 'I didn't know that.'

'Well. She's not the type to slip out easily, is she? Not our
Genevieve.' The doctor seemed to realize, as soon as he'd
spoken, that he'd presumed too much with that pally tone.
His smile was twitchy.

'I suppose not.' Robert gave him a sidelong look. He
didn't like the 'our'.

147

Dr Peters cleared his throat. 'Genevieve is a lucky girl.'

They were quiet for a moment. Robert looked across the sea of roses in varying shades of pink, red, yellow and cream.

'How so?' he said.

'Pardon?' It was one of those occasions when a person says 'pardon', not because he hasn't heard the remark, but because he isn't sure of how to respond. It was something Robert had encountered a lot in his business life. It enabled the speaker to play for time, and it usually meant he was not being entirely straightforward.

'I said how so?'

'Well . . .' Another clearing of the throat. 'You're obviously a devoted husband, sir. Genevieve is lucky to have found a man who cares for her so completely and unconditionally.'

'*Unconditionally?* What the deuce are you getting at, doctor?'

'Oh dear me. Nothing at all, sir. I'm sorry to have . . . It was, as I say, a very difficult birth. For a while it looked unlikely that either Genevieve or her mother would pull through.' He knocked the burning end off his cigar, wrapped the remainder carefully in a handkerchief and placed it in his breast pocket.

Robert, sensing that the doctor was about to beat a retreat, and seeing an opportunity opening up, put a hand on his arm. 'No, *I'm* sorry, doctor. You delivered Genevieve into the world. You've known her all her life. It's natural that you should speak about her in a friendly and familiar tone.' And then, 'She looks up to you, you know. Holds you in the highest possible esteem.'

'Does she?'

'Oh yes. I should have thought that would be obvious. After all, you've stood by this family through thick and thin, haven't you?'

'Well, I suppose, I . . .'

'There was that other *difficult* time, wasn't there? A few years ago, when Genevieve was still a girl?'

Dr Peters was looking uncomfortable. 'I should go back inside.'

But Robert wasn't ready to let it go. 'Were you called to attend her much during that time?'

'I'm not sure I understand what you're referring to.' He wasn't looking Robert in the eye. And Robert knew what it meant when a man couldn't look you in the eye.

'Yes, you do.'

'Well.' The doctor loosened his tie a little. 'Then you'll appreciate that I can't discuss the matter. No offence intended.' He was up on his feet now, and starting to walk away, but Robert quickly stubbed out his own cigar and fell into step alongside him.

'So.' He struggled for a change of subject that would keep Dr Peters talking. 'A sudden death, was it? Bolt out of the blue?'

'Absolutely. A terrible shock to all of us. Her health was pretty good right up until the end. Headaches, trouble with sleeping – all the sort of things one might expect from a woman of her age with a nervous disposition. But nothing serious. Her heart – well, there was never any hint of a problem.'

'I gather she was found out here.' Robert gestured at the roses. An almost obscene proliferation of life and colour.

149

'That's right. It seems she was cutting a few blooms for the house. She was very fond of her rose garden. It would have been quick. No pain.'

'Be sure and tell that to my Genevieve, doctor. She was close to her mother, as you know. And she's a high-strung girl.'

Almost imperceptibly, the doctor quickened his pace.

'There are things I need to know about. So I can be a good husband to her.'

'Goodness, look at the time! You'll have to excuse me—' These last words were uttered as the doctor suddenly broke away.

'Dr Peters!'

He was scampering off with an odd bow-legged gait – first of all towards the house, but then, with a crazy zigzagging change of direction, to the main gate.

The dinner table was too long for three people. If it was down to Robert he'd have had the servants lay a small table in the living room and kept things informal and low-key. But here they were, in the dining room, eating off the best silver, surrounded by the family portraits which had so impressed him at one time but which on reacquaintance were gloomy and forbidding.

'How's business, Robert?' Lord Ticksted was poking at his food and eating nothing.

'Oh, you know. Fine.'

'Robert is doing *incredibly* well,' said Genevieve. 'He's quadrupled the size of the company since he inherited it. Isn't that right, darling?'

'I don't like to brag.'

'Well, I shall brag for you. He's quite a genius, Daddy.'

Robert felt himself blush. Genevieve had a high colour in her cheeks tonight, and he wondered how much wine she'd had. Lord Ticksted, on the other hand, was grey and wan. He looked as though his mind and his heart were far away. And so thin . . . His skin hung in loose pockets around his chin and neck. They were eating dinner with a ghost.

'How do you find Paris?' Lord Ticksted addressed himself solely to Robert.

'Well . . . It's not really *home*, but—'

'We love it.' There was a note of defiance in Genevieve's voice. 'One can live vividly there. We're surrounded by worldly people. Writers and artists. People who have something *real* to say for themselves.'

'Not that there aren't some very interesting people here too.' Robert was thoroughly embarrassed.

'There's a different code of ethics there,' Genevieve continued. 'Not like this small-minded backwater.'

'Genevieve!' Robert could hardly believe his ears. 'Sir . . .'

But the old man appeared unaffected by the outburst, and was quietly sipping his wine. 'I'm glad to know that Genevieve is in such good hands, Robert. Her mother – God rest her soul – never ceased worrying about the girl. Not until her dying day. But I can see that she is well looked after.'

Genevieve stood up too quickly, knocking her wine over. 'Nobody *looks after* me. I do not need to be *looked after*. Robert lets me live my life the way I want to. You, on the other hand – well, you know very well what you did to me.

You and Mummy. I can never forgive you – neither of you! God, this whole place is rotten to the core.'

'I'm sorry, sir,' said Robert, after the door had slammed behind her. 'I guess she's upset about her mother. She's not at all herself.'

'Quite so, dear boy.' Lord Ticksted pushed his plate away. 'Quite so. And she's always had a delicate disposition, little Genevieve. She was dreadfully ill as a girl, you know. We had to take her out of school in the end, and have her educated at home.'

'Yes . . .' He clenched his toes inside his shoes. 'What actually was wrong with her?'

'Oh, well, it was very complicated. All sorts of complications.' And then the tears were running down the old man's face. 'I'm so sorry.' He drew his hand across his eyes. 'My wife . . . I don't know what I shall do without her, Robert. You will stay a few weeks, won't you? You and Genevieve? I'm so alone here.'

## 17

Dear Lulu,

I've been here for just over a month now. Why haven't you written? It's occurred to me that there might be a problem with your post, so I'm sending this letter care of the Coyote. Please try to reply, dearest, even if it's just a postcard. I'm dying to know what's been happening while I've been here. I shall want to know <u>everything</u>. I'm afraid I don't think I'll be back until late July, so I'm going to miss Bastille Day. I feel as though I'm just a shadow, hiding away here. The real me is still in Paris with you. My life is going on elsewhere while I sit here.

I've been sorting out Mummy's things. It has to be done, after all. Putting together little parcels of trinkets and keepsakes for friends and relations. The vicar couldn't believe his luck when he came to collect, yesterday morning. The poor and needy of Ticksted and surrounds will be very well dressed for a while, that's for certain! I shall keep some things for myself, of course. Jewellery mostly. She had some lovely shoes but her feet were quite a bit bigger than mine. It's sad, dusty work, this clearing out. It makes one think, what *is* there to a life? What do we leave behind? Not much, in Mummy's case. Some clothes and jewels and a great many bottles hidden at the backs of cupboards and wardrobes (it seems the drinking was even worse than I'd suspected). You will leave a really fine legacy, Lulu. All those paintings and sculptures and photographs. Not to mention your brilliant songs. You'll never be forgotten. As for me – well, who knows? I'd like to think I'm a poet, but this seems far from certain. If you see Norman Betterson, would you remind him that he still has my poetry notebook? I'm waiting for his verdict. I don't seem to be able to write any more poems without it.

It's very quiet here. Just me and Daddy and the servants. Daddy seems genuinely desolate. It's as though someone has cut off one of his arms. He's become terribly thin. Often, he cries. It appears he *did* love her, after all, though I doubt she knew it. How strange people are.

I didn't love my mother. How could I, after what happened? Sometimes I think I hated her. I am sad for her, though. She was young and beautiful once but it was all wasted. She must have yearned for something more than she had.

I'm yearning too. For something beyond this place – beyond the constraints of my married life, even. I feel so lonely. Robert went back last week. He was very sweet, I have to say. And yet I was lonely even when he was here.

And I am grieving – yes I *am*. Though not for Mummy. *You* know why I'm grieving. You're the only person I've confided in. The only person I can really trust. I miss you so much, Lulu.

Write soon.

Much love,

Genevieve

## 18

THE MODELS STALKING AROUND THE HEAVILY MIRRORED first floor of Madame Hélène's Salon de Couture were in swimwear. Stripy costumes, made of the jersey fabric popularized by Coco Chanel and showcased in *Le Train Bleu*. Everyone would be dressed this way on the Riviera. Down the carpet they strolled, rounding the intricate glass fountain at the far end of the room, and back.

Genevieve had returned only two days before. This was her first outing with Lulu, and it should have been the perfect antidote to Ticksted: an afternoon of high fashion, offering the opportunity to show off something special from her extensive wardrobe. The dress, by Madeleine Vionnet, was a cascade of delicate chiffon petals. On her feet she wore a pair of spectacularly high heels by Ferragamo in precisely the same elusive hue (hovering indeterminately between cream and pink). But Lulu thought Genevieve looked pale in the dress today, and somehow uncertain. She might have been longing to be back in Paris, but her eyes had a remoteness about them.

It was a hot July day and the room was stuffy. Lulu was making good use of the gaudy Chinese fan that she'd brought along, fanning both herself and Genevieve.

'What you need,' she whispered to Genevieve, 'is a holiday. Why don't you buy yourself one of these costumes? We could go down to the coast for a few weeks. Swim in the sea, laze about on the beach.'

'But I've only just got back,' said Genevieve. 'This is where I want to be.'

'Is it?' Lulu looked at her sidelong.

'Of course. I still can't believe I missed Bastille Day.'

Lulu smiled at the memory. 'Ah, chérie, it was fantastic. The parties went on for three days. I hardly stopped singing. The Coyote, the Jockey Club, the Dingo, Bricktop's . . . Made a packet but then spent it all. So many Americans, though!' Her volume had risen. People sitting near by were turning around and staring their disapproval. 'Paris isn't what it was. There are too many guidebooks, giving out the names of all the best places. The Quarter's overrun with despicable tourists. If it carries on like this, we'll have to find somewhere else.'

Genevieve looked stricken. 'You wouldn't leave, would you?'

'Of course not, chérie. Not really. What's the matter? Something's wrong.'

A woman with jowls and scaly skin turned around and shushed them.

Lulu pulled a face at her.

'Did you get the letters I sent you?' Genevieve asked in a whisper.

'Yes, yes.'

'Then why didn't you write back?'

'Oh, I don't pay much attention to the post.' Lulu flapped a dismissive hand. 'It's never good news if it comes in an envelope.'

'Lulu! Did you even read them?'

'Ah, chérie.' A shrug. 'I'm not much of a one for words.'

Genevieve seemed angry now. 'Well, if you had, you'd have known how desperate I was to get back. You'd have known how hideous it was being stuck there in that house full of bad memories, trying to say the right things to a barrage of visitors who kept telling me what a wonderful lady my mother was. Actually, she wasn't.'

'Vivi.' Lulu put a hand on her arm. 'I'm sorry. Our lives are so different. Family . . . duty . . . I've never known these things. It's hard for me to understand how it is for you. I will try though, I promise. Shall we get out of here and go somewhere we can talk?'

'I can't get rid of the memories!' Genevieve was twisting her hands around each other, knotting her fingers. 'Being there again – it brought it all back so vividly. And there's something else.'

'What? What is it, Vivi?'

'Kindly save your conversation until later.' It was the jowly woman again. 'There's a show in progress here, or perhaps you hadn't noticed.'

'Show?' Lulu raised her sculpted eyebrows and leaned forward. 'Do you want to see a show, you old lizard? Do you want to see a *show*?'

The woman's ugly face twisted into a scowl, and she turned away.

Genevieve laughed. It seemed to have lifted again, what-ever it was that was troubling her.

'Now,' said Lulu. 'What were we saying before we were so rudely interrupted?'

After the show, wine and refreshments were served on the floor below. Clients milled about, browsing the dressed mannequins, attended by their individual *vendeuses* who advised on the suitability of the outfits and took orders. While Lulu seemed determined to drink as much wine and eat as many canapés as possible, Genevieve tried to rise to the occasion. She soon had her *vendeuse* – a tiny woman with thin hair and a pink, sore-looking scalp – running back and forth to get the answers to a number of detailed questions about the garments. No, she couldn't have a tennis dress in crêpe de Chine. And no, they didn't do the strappy sandals in silver. But was she interested in the swimwear? How about the beach wraps? . . .

'Genevieve, darling.' The Countess de Frémont, in un-becoming lilac, followed closely by a *vendeuse* bearing a pile of newly bought clothes so huge she could hardly carry them. 'What a pleasure it is to see you.'

'Violet. How delightful.' Genevieve darted 'Help me' looks at Lulu, but her friend was fading slowly away from them. Lulu was a past mistress of the 'gradual fade'.

'I'm so sorry about your mother. It must have been dread-ful for you.' There was an unbearable, exaggerated sympathy in the countess's voice.

'Thank you.' Desperate to change the subject, Genevieve looked down at the countess's feet. Four-inch spike heels and a mesh of thin black shiny straps criss-crossing back and forth across her feet, like a beautiful, intricate cage.

'My new Zacharis. What do you think?'

Genevieve flinched as though a bright light had been shone into her eyes. She hadn't heard that name spoken aloud since leaving his shop with her red velvet shoes and her secret almost two months ago. In England, she had done her utmost to banish all thoughts of Zachari from her head, telling herself it had been another mistake – the second of this kind. As with the first transgression, she had kept it to herself. As with the first, she had told herself it should not happen again. It *must not* happen again.

But Zachari was not Monteray. This was different. Time and again, she dreamed of his mouth pressed to the small of her back. Time and again, she ran her hands over his chest, tasted his skin, sighed against his neck. These were the most vivid, sensuous dreams she'd ever had. And over and over again she found herself waking from them alone – or worse, lying next to Robert – bereft. Guilty.

'Do you think it's true that Zachari's making special booties for Josephine Baker's pet leopard?' came Violet's brash voice.

'How should I know?' Genevieve put a hand to her head. 'I've been away. Anyway, I barely know the man.'

'Of course, my dear.' Violet was peering over Genevieve's shoulder now. 'Well, look who it is! I might just go over and ask him.'

'He's here?'

But Violet was already off, pushing her way through groups of people, followed by her *vendeuse*.

He had his back to her but it was an unmistakable back.

He was standing in the doorway, talking to Madame Hélène. He was wearing light grey trousers and a shirt of the cleanest white, ever so slightly translucent, which emphasized the long back, the broad shoulders. He was demonstrating something with his hands.

Genevieve raised her wineglass to her lips to try to hide the tremor in her face.

'That's Paolo Zachari over there.' Genevieve's *vendeuse*, clawing at her arm.

'Yes. What's he doing here?'

'I think he has some business with Madame Hélène,' said the *vendeuse*. 'He wasn't at the show.' And, with a touch of envy in her voice, 'Do you know him?'

'A little. He made me a pair of shoes.' As Genevieve spoke the words, Zachari turned around and looked right at her. Those dark, unknowable eyes . . . Her breath caught in her throat and she quickly looked away.

'I'd give anything for a pair of his shoes. Let me get you another, madame.' The *vendeuse* snatched Genevieve's empty wineglass and disappeared before she could say anything else.

I mustn't look again, she told herself. We have to leave. But where's Lulu? And before she could stop herself, she did look at him again. Damn it, Violet was there now. She was touching him on the arm as she spoke to him and he was looking down at her. Genevieve could hear her over-intimate tone of voice, her terrible, frivolous laughter, even from here.

'Did you know your friend Zachari is making shoes for the Marchesa Casati's boa constrictor?' It was Lulu, back at her side, flushed with all the wine.

'He's no friend of mine.'

'Oh, really?' All her expressions and movements were overdone. 'I think you're a little bit . . . sweet on him.'

'Do you?' Genevieve feigned uninterest. 'Anyway, snakes don't have feet.'

'Maybe they dream of having feet,' said Lulu. 'Maybe it's their secret fantasy.'

'Snakes don't have dreams or fantasies.'

'No, but women do.' Lulu stroked her chin, thoughtfully. 'Zachari's business – maybe his whole life – is built on women's dreams and fantasies. You know that, don't you, chérie?'

Genevieve glanced up at the doorway again. Violet de Frémont was still there, talking with Madame Hélène. Zachari had gone.

By mid-evening Lulu had staggered off in the company of a dark stranger with nice eyes and thick arms, and Genevieve headed home. She arrived to find Robert lying on the Pirogue couch, reading and smoking a cigar. She'd been snippy with him in the couple of days since she'd been back, and he'd become hangdog in response. She didn't know why she'd kept on at him. He was kindness itself. And tonight was no exception: as she walked through the door, he gave her his warmest smile.

'Are your feet sore, honey?'

The Ferragamo shoes had indeed been rubbing at her heels and she was hobbling a little.

'Come over here.'

She lay back in the couch with him and closed her eyes while he worked on her feet, inexpertly but lovingly.

162

Massaging her insteps, manipulating the joints of her toes. She tried not to let herself think about those other hands on her feet, that other touch . . . 'Feet are amazingly complex things,' said Genevieve, quietly. 'There are more bones in the feet than in any other part of the body.'

'Is that true?'

'Maybe.' She longed for Zachari's touch. *Longed* for it. How was she to get rid of this longing? She needed something to happen to reawaken her interest in Robert – something that would really focus her attention on him.

'I'm glad you're not an artist,' she said.

He stopped his massaging. 'Are you?'

Those doleful eyes of his, bagging slightly, the moustache that she'd never liked and which he'd stubbornly held on to. The large earlobes. She was fond of him, she always had been. But there had to be more to a marriage than that.

'You've got your feet on the ground,' she said. 'That's a good thing.'

He patted her foot. 'I'm glad you see it that way. I'm not sure you always do.'

'I know. But that's all going to change now.'

'It is?'

She took a deep breath. 'I've been thinking. I know how important family is to you . . .'

He sat up straight, snapped to attention. 'Yes?'

'Well, it's difficult for me. But still . . .'

'Genevieve, are you saying—'

'Get me a drink, will you?'

'Of course.'

She could see how excited he was, and how he was

struggling to contain it. He didn't want to frighten her with his eagerness, bless him. But it frightened her all the same.

He went to the ivory-veneered drinks cabinet. 'What'll you have?'

'I don't know.' She blinked away a tear. 'I don't know.'

# 19

THE MORNING BROUGHT WITH IT A SENSE OF REGRET AND dread. She'd felt so sure, last night, that she was doing the right thing – that a baby would be the answer. But she'd fallen asleep to dream, yet again, of Zachari, of his eyes – the way he looked at her across the room at Madame Hélène's. Between the two of them, in the dream, was a mass of women, frenziedly grabbing at dresses and shoes. Fighting over them, ripping them, flailing at each other with nails and fists and teeth. There was no way to get through to him.

And then she stopped dreaming about Zachari and instead dreamed of herself carving the name 'Josephine' into the bark of the great oak tree – the knife slipping and cutting her hand. Pulling out her handkerchief to dab at the blood, and then glancing back up at the tree to discover that the name had vanished.

Over breakfast Genevieve hid herself in the latest issue of *La Vie Parisienne* and gave one-word answers to each of Robert's cheery questions and remarks. After a while he gave up and sat peering at her in silence. This was what she'd wanted – his silence – but it didn't make her feel any better. He was so confused and despondent. Who could blame him?

Getting up to leave for the office, he hesitated at the door.

'What is it, Robert?'

'Well, that's rather what I should like to ask you.' He raked his hand nervously through his hair. 'You're so changeable, Genevieve. Last night you were . . . But now this morning . . .'

'Is that surprising? I've only recently lost my mother.'

'Yes, of course. Of course.' He was peering at her again. 'Only . . .'

'What?'

'If there was anything else – anything I ought to know, I mean. Well, you would tell me, wouldn't you, darling?'

'I don't know what you're talking about.' She turned her gaze down to the magazine, flicked irritably at a page. 'Are you dining out with Harry tonight?'

'Yes. I suppose I might be late. You'd better not wait up.'

'Fine. I've arranged to go out with Lulu in any case.'

'Good,' he said – though it didn't sound as if he meant it. 'By the way, Genevieve, I'd appreciate it if you'd look out the number of that bronze-cleaner. He's had the horse far too long and I should like to call him.'

As soon as the front door closed, Genevieve went to the little telephone table in the hall and shakily asked the operator to put her through to Paolo Zachari's shop. At length, there was a click at the end of the line and the familiar, vaguely insolent greeting from Olga.

Slamming the receiver down, Genevieve stood chewing

166

on a nail and staring distractedly into the salon, where Céline was dusting the ornaments on the mantel.

What am I *doing*?

Lulu was in the mood for devilry that evening. She wanted to go 'somewhere fancy' and to dress the part too. Arriving early at the Rue de Lota, she went riffling through Genevieve's wardrobes, settling on an Atelier Martine sheath dress in black lace that had never been worn.

It was Genevieve's idea to go to the bar at the Ritz. She'd told Lulu she felt nostalgic for the night they first met, but the real reason was its nearness to Paolo Zachari's shop. Maybe, just maybe . . .

She couldn't help gazing about her as they got out of the cab, but there was no sign of Zachari. Would he be in his workshop this evening? Or upstairs above the shop in what she now knew to be his apartment? Perhaps, later on, she'd look for an opportunity to slip away – just to take a look and see if his lights were on, if any sounds were being made within . . . No. No, she mustn't do that. She had to stay away from him.

But then she noticed something which completely took her mind off Zachari for the time being. Something which had not escaped the notice of the hotel doormen, the cab driver and several passing officials from the Ministry of Justice.

Lulu was not wearing any underwear beneath the lace dress.

'What does a grapefruit look like?' asked Lulu, as the girls sipped their Chambéry and *fraises*. 'What colour is it?'

'Yellow,' said Genevieve. 'Big and round and yellow. The taste is very sharp. Sour, really. Why do you want to know?'

'Sour.' Lulu closed her eyes and seemed to be trying to imagine the taste. 'Yes, that makes sense. They're Camby's favourite fruit. So he says. I'd like to try to get some for him.'

'In Paris? I doubt you'll find any.'

'That's a shame.' Lulu frowned. 'He's not been at all himself lately. I don't know what the matter is but there's something, that's for sure. I wanted to get him a present to cheer him up. And I remembered him talking about these grape fruits, whatever they are.'

Genevieve smiled. 'I suppose we could try the Necessary Luxuries Company. If anyone has grapefruit, they will.'

'Excellent, chérie.' Lulu downed her drink. 'I knew I could rely on you.'

'Come on,' said Genevieve. 'Let's have another. I want to get tight.'

Two drinks later, they were both becoming shrill. Genevieve knew that most of the men in the bar were watching them. Peeping from behind newspapers, openly gazing, or looking sidelong as if considering the merchandise. Young English aristocrats, just out of Eton. Americans 'doing the Tour', sharp French boys on the make. Their elegantly coiffed, heavily jewelled lady-friends looked on edgily.

Lulu was talking about Camby again. 'It's strange. I can't trust him as far as I can throw him but he is the whole world to me. You know that? I don't know what I'd do without him.'

'Sometimes I envy you.' Genevieve fixed her gaze on the bar – on a young barman with slicked-back hair shaking cocktails and pouring out pink liquid into a row of glasses. 'Your feelings for him run so deep. I've never felt that way about a man. At least . . .'

The barman dropped cherries into all of the glasses but one. He placed them on a round tray for the waitress and then pushed the remaining glass across the bar to a woman perched up on a high stool with her back to the girls. The woman had fair hair. She was wearing a simple blue dress, unadorned.

'Well . . . Not until now, that is.'

'Now? *Chérie?*' Lulu clapped her hands in excitement. 'I knew it! Who is it? Guy Monteray? I knew you slept with him!'

'Lulu, shush!' Genevieve glanced about. 'I did *not* sleep with Monteray. I have no interest in that dreadful man.'

'Then who?' Lulu looked a touch put out. 'Oh, *I* know who it is.'

The woman on the stool was talking to the barman. He was listening to her but was trying to look as though he wasn't.

'It's that Zachari, isn't it?' said Lulu.

Genevieve swallowed. 'It started out as an itch. I scratched it to make it go away. But the more I scratched, the itchier it became. Now I want to rip my skin to shreds and I know it'll only make it worse.'

'So you've slept with him, then?'

'Just once. The night of my party. The night I heard about my mother. It was amazing. And now I don't know what to do.'

A triumphant smile. 'Well, isn't it obvious? You must sleep with him again. Just as soon as it can be arranged.'

'No, Lulu. I absolutely must *not*. I can't let it go any further. It's practically turned me into a wreck as it is. And what about Robert? What about my marriage?'

'Zachari has touched you.' She put a hand on Genevieve's. 'He's touched you in a way that Robert never has – and never will.'

'That's just what I'm afraid of.'

The woman with the fair hair reached into her handbag – presumably for some money to pay her bill. But the barman, after checking to see if anyone was watching, indicated with a curt shake of the head that she should put her money away. The woman made to touch his shoulder but he pretended not to notice. Busied himself with polishing a glass.

'Do you love him?' Lulu's face was unusually serious.

'I don't know . . . Maybe.' Genevieve had one eye on the fair-haired woman, who was getting down from her stool.

'Perhaps you'd better sleep with him again just to be sure.'

'Oh, Lulu!'

'Chérie, you can't walk away from something so good. It's just not natural.'

'But I *have* to.'

Lulu rolled her eyes.

'This is precisely why I didn't tell you. And now I've told you, you have to help me.'

'Help you do what?'

The woman was heading out of the bar.

'Help me forget about him. It's not so easy when I dream about him practically every night. And then I ran into him at that fashion show and I couldn't even bring myself to speak to him. I can't shop on the Rue de la Paix without having to walk right past his door. I can't come here for a drink without that *woman* turning up.'

'What woman?'

'Her.' Genevieve pointed at the fair-haired woman, who was almost at the door now. 'That's Olga, his assistant.'

'*That* woman?'

'The barman was giving her free drinks. I wonder what she's up to.'

'Let's find out.' Lulu seized Genevieve's hand. 'Come on, chérie!'

Olga walked fast across the Place Vendôme, past the column (which, this evening, put Genevieve in mind of pictures she'd seen of totem poles) and out of the south side on to the Rue Castiglione. The sun had just set. The sky was an odd, heavy mauve and the great piazza was shrouded in shadows.

'Hurry.' Lulu hitched up her dress and half walked, half ran after Olga. 'We're losing her.'

'Lulu!' Genevieve could barely manage to walk from car to bar in these heels. And yet here she was, wobbling along behind Lulu in her royal-blue D'Orsays. She'd be lucky if she didn't twist both her ankles.

'Quick!' shouted Lulu.

'Lulu, stop!'

She did stop, but only for a moment. 'Don't you want to know where she's going?'

'Well—'

'Vivi, I'm doing this with or without you.' And she was off again.

The rain came suddenly, a great swirling torrent, as they headed down the Rue de Rivoli. Waiters ushered grumbling customers in from the terraces. Squeals multiplied and echoed from every direction. The street flashed and flickered with lightning, and thunder rolled overhead. Dogs howled and yapped. People scurried, covering their heads with their newspapers, their bags, their hands. Diving into doorways and under awnings.

'Where did she go?' In a matter of seconds, Genevieve was soaked to the skin.

Lulu was turning this way and that, the dress clinging to her body. 'She's vanished. We've lost her.'

Robert was dining with Harry Mortimer at Michaud's, on the corner of the Rue Jacob and the Rue des Saints-Pères.

To begin with, he thought the heaviness was inside his head. The restaurant seemed loud: the clattering of the kitchen, the shrill laughter of the girl on the next table, the scraping of metal on china. He and Harry had been having a pleasant meal, but now everything was subtly oppressive. A waiter rushed past their table, leaving a tangible sweatiness in his wake. It was enough to put you off your *tournedos*. Robert wondered if Harry had noticed. No, Harry had other things on his mind.

'It's due in January. Maud's busy organizing the nursery. Worrying about French doctors. Searching for an English nanny.'

'That's nice,' said Robert. 'Real nice.'

'Is that all you have to say?'

Then the rain came. It thrummed against the roof and the windows, so loud that it was as if someone was drumming on the inside of Robert's skull. Hysterical squeals carried in from the street.

'What's up?' Harry's voice was reassuringly solid. 'Something's going on with you. What is it?'

Robert fretted that one of those squeals might be Genevieve – that Lulu was dragging her through the streets. Lightning flashed and the thunder rumbled in his ribcage.

'Robert, old pal?'

Here was the problem. Even if she wasn't out in the storm, she was always *out there* to an extent. Because of the things he didn't know about her. 'You once talked to me about a friend of yours,' he said. 'A friend I could call on if there was ever something I was . . . unsure of.'

'His name's Felperstone,' said Harry. 'He's English, like your wife. He's expensive, but he's good.'

'Good at *what*, exactly?'


Two old men on stools twisted around to stare at the girls as they entered the little bar. Three laughing whores in the far corner fell quiet, nudging each other. A bald barman breathed on a glass and rubbed it with a grubby cloth. All had a dusty look about them, as though they'd been stuck here, unmoving, for many years.

'This place stinks of wet dog,' said Lulu. Sure enough, lying on the straw-covered floor was a matted-looking hound, scratching.

'I'll have an Armagnac,' said Genevieve. 'To warm up.'

'That's two,' said Lulu to the barman, and led the way to the only empty table.

'Where are we?' Genevieve looked around her. The dog yawned and closed its eyes. 'What is this place?'

'Somewhere dry,' said Lulu, and sneezed. 'But wet in one crucial respect.'

The barman brought their drinks over. Water dripped through the ceiling and plopped into an enamel bowl on the floor.

'It's your fault we got soaked,' said Genevieve. 'I'd never have followed her if it wasn't for you.'

'Well, I'd never have followed her if you hadn't slept with that shoemaker,' snapped Lulu.

'And now we've lost her anyway.' Genevieve eased off the D'Orsays and set them down on a stool beside her. They were several shades darker than earlier, and splattered with mud. Another pair ruined for ever ... She looked under the table at her feet, which were stained an odd blue – and then back up at ...

Olga!

She was coming out of what must be the WC, closing the door behind her. Being wet through made her look darker – the hair, the eyes – though still with that translucent quality. Oil in water.

'Well, well!' Genevieve did her best at wide-eyed surprise. 'Fancy running into you.'

'Yes. How strange,' said Olga.

Genevieve moved her D'Orsays down to the floor. 'Olga, meet Lulu of Montparnasse.'

'I know who she is. Doesn't everyone?'

'Come and join us.' Lulu gestured to the empty stool. 'Vivi will buy you a drink. Won't you, chérie?'

*

One hour and several drinks later, nobody had entered or left the steamy bar. Lulu was chain-smoking, lighting each

174

new cigarette from the end of the last. She was trying to soften Olga up, but Zachari's assistant remained stiff and guarded. As did Genevieve.

'I like you, Olga,' Lulu was saying now. 'We're two of a kind. Two women who've known hard times. You can't appreciate how good life is until you've seen the darker side. Don't you think?'

'I suppose so. Yes.' Olga looked edgily at Genevieve.

'Why don't you get us another drink?' said Lulu, adding, 'Lady Ticksted?'

'I'm not—' But Genevieve stopped herself from going any further. Took a breath. After waving at the barman two or three times and failing to get his attention, she went up to the bar and ordered three more Armagnacs. By the time she returned with the drinks Lulu was really hitting her stride.

'As for my mother – well, she couldn't wait to get rid of me. And I couldn't wait to get away from her, from the very moment I was born. I pushed my way out of that woman's body so fast that she didn't even have time to get home to bed. I landed in the street!'

Olga drained her brandy in one gulp. Her face was flushed and hot-looking.

'She sent me off to be a maid when I was very young,' Lulu continued. 'What was the point of me if I didn't bring in some money? I went to work for the local priest, cleaning his filthy house, cooking his filthy meals. He was a total bastard. I got away as soon as I could, of course. At sixteen, I was binding copies of the *Kama Sutra* for a living. I knew about all the sexual positions you can imagine, and more, but I was still a virgin. Ironic, eh? Just goes to show that appearances can be deceptive. So, what about you, Olga? What's your story?' She pushed her drink across the table to Olga, and gave Genevieve a little wink.

Olga gulped at Lulu's Armagnac, seemingly without realizing it wasn't hers. When she placed the empty glass down, her eyes had an odd sparkle. 'I came here from Russia. Some years before the Revolution. Before the war.'

Lulu nodded. 'I thought as much.'

'My husband, Viktor – he had some troubles. I don't want to tell you about them. He was worried he would have to go to prison. But he was more worried about what would happen to me and the children if they took him away.'

She broke off to cough – a nasty, hacking, persistent cough. Genevieve exchanged a glance with Lulu and pushed her own glass across the table.

'We fled here, to Paris. We used all the money we had just to get here. It was a long and difficult journey.'

'That must have been—' Genevieve began. But Olga didn't wait for her to finish.

'Viktor fell ill. He died shortly after we arrived.'

'How tragic,' said Genevieve.

A snort. 'He was a bastard pig! I was left alone to look after the children, with no home, in a foreign country where I barely even spoke the language!'

Genevieve chose her next words carefully. 'That's such an awful story. I can't imagine what it must have been like for you.'

And now the oil seemed to clear from those eyes. 'I couldn't have done it without Paolo. He's been like family to me.'

She was interrupted by another coughing fit, and Lulu gestured to Genevieve to return to the bar and buy yet more drinks. When she got back, the conversation had moved on. Olga was asking Lulu about the artists who'd painted and photographed her, and Lulu was off on one of her many stories – clearly enjoying the attention too much to stay focused on their objective of digging for information.

'. . . Yes, he wanted to sleep with me – of course he did – but you have to understand that sleeping with artists is different from sleeping with other men. They're looking for inspiration – the muse, you know. Sometimes they find it in bed with a woman. It's . . . better, somehow. It's art.'

Olga huffed. 'Artists are just the same as all the others. When you've lived as long as I have, you'll know what I mean.'

'Perhaps you're right.' Lulu looked remote suddenly.

How old *is* she? Genevieve wondered. Forty-three? Forty-five? Hard to say. Good bones and a good figure. Intelligent-looking too. But faded – worn out by experience.

'People don't think of shoemakers as artists,' said Genevieve. 'But they are. Paolo Zachari is. You must know him better than most people, Olga. You must have been working for him for a long time now.'

'The rain has stopped,' said Olga, without looking at Genevieve. 'I have to be going.'

'But it's still early.' Lulu gave Genevieve a swift kick under the table. 'Come with us to Bricktop's. Maybe I'll get up and sing.'

'I need to go home.' She started coughing again, and this time swallowing her drink didn't seem to help. She was still coughing when she stood up.

177

'Are you all right?' Genevieve asked.

Olga banged her glass down on the table and made to walk to the door. But the walk was more of a lurch. Her feet were clumsy, as though they'd been borrowed from someone else and didn't fit her properly. As the girls watched, her legs appeared to crumple beneath her, she lost her balance, and in trying to correct herself stumbled over a stool leg and went flying.

The whores were laughing, whether at Olga or at some joke of their own it was impossible to tell. The barman shook his head and tutted. The old men didn't so much as bat an eyelid. Olga lay absolutely still where she'd fallen.

She was slumped between them in the taxi. She was no longer unconscious, but she wasn't exactly conscious either. Her eyes were shut. Occasionally she murmured a few words in Russian.

'What makes you so sure Zachari will even be there?' said Lulu.

'I'm not. But what else can we do? It's our fault she's in this state. And I'd sooner take her to Zachari than back to the Rue de Lota. But maybe you'd like to take her to your apartment?'

'You must be joking!' Lulu squeaked. 'She's your problem, not mine. This has nothing to do with me.'

The taxi took a corner too sharply and Olga's head flopped forward. Gently, Genevieve eased her upright and used her handkerchief to wipe away a trail of spit. 'This isn't just the drink,' she said. 'Feel how hot she is.'

Lulu felt the forehead. 'Let's hope your cobbler is still at his cobbling.'

They turned into the Rue de la Paix, and Olga's face was illuminated by the bright streetlights. She looked ethereal, almost ghostly. And yet there was a softness about her that Genevieve hadn't seen before.

'She must have been a real beauty once.' Genevieve absently smoothed a few loose strands of Olga's hair behind her ear.

'Genevieve.' Zachari stood in the shop doorway. He was dressed in his work clothes and his sleeves were rolled up to the elbow. His smile, on seeing her, was almost more than she could bear.

'It's not what you think.' She was trying not to look at his eyes, scared that her own would reveal too much.

'Come inside.' He put out a hand to touch her arm, but she took a couple of steps back, shrinking away from him.

'I can't.' It was too awful – what she and Lulu had done to Olga. It was shameful. And for what? If Zachari knew . . .

He shook his head. 'I don't understand.'

Truly this was the most exquisite torture.

'I heard about your mother,' he said. 'I knew you must have gone back to England. I thought maybe you wouldn't come back. And then yesterday, at the fashion show –'

'I'm not here for you, Paolo.'

'– There you were! You looked . . . I wondered if you'd come here. I realize I've been waiting for you.'

Genevieve thought about Lulu. She'd be drumming her fingers impatiently on the upholstery and swearing to herself, Olga's head heavy on her shoulder.

'I *can't* be here for you, Paolo. It can't happen again.' Her voice, when she spoke again, was cold. As cold as she could make it. 'Your assistant's been taken ill. We've brought her back here in a cab. It's out on the Rue de la Paix.'

The driver refused to help extract Olga from the taxi. Lulu too was next to useless, announcing that she needed to smoke a cigarette before she could do anything further. Zachari and Genevieve worked together to drag her out.

'We'll help you get her inside,' said Genevieve. She retrieved Olga's bag while Zachari semi-propped her up against the cab.

'It's all right. I can manage.' And now Zachari scooped Olga up in his arms, like a doll. As if she weighed nothing at all. Her head flopped against his chest.

'Thank you,' he said. 'Thank you for bringing her here.'

'We didn't have much choice.'

'Yes, you did. There's always a choice.' His face was more open at this moment than Genevieve had ever seen it. 'I'm very grateful.'

'What about her bag?' Genevieve asked. But he was able to take that too, looped over one arm.

'Aren't you even going to offer us a drink?' called Lulu.

'Good-night.' Zachari started walking down the passageway, back to the shop.

Lulu exhaled a plume of smoke. 'Well, there's gratitude!'

Genevieve felt something tighten in her chest. 'Finish your cigarette and get in the taxi. I have to go home to my husband.'

180

# IV

# Collar

## 20

MRS GALLER WAS A STEAM-SHIP OF A WOMAN WITH A BIG white face, a plain brown hat and an enormous bosom, over which her blouse strained so that one caught glimpses of strong utilitarian underwear between buttons.

Before getting up from his chair, Robert turned the photograph of Genevieve in her wedding dress face down so he didn't have to look her in the eye. Then he came out from behind his desk, proffering a hand. 'How do you do, ma'am. I'm very grateful to you for making the long journey.' And he *was* grateful, though he couldn't help but blanch a little at the sum she'd demanded for her expenses. He still didn't quite understand why they couldn't simply have had this conversation on the telephone.

'She thinks it's a new-fangled, untrustworthy machine,' Mr Felperstone had explained. 'She's worried the operator may listen in. She wanted to speak to you in person. Wouldn't tell me a single thing ahead of meeting you.'

She had a vice-like handshake. 'Not at all, sir. Pleased to meet you, I'm sure.'

He called out to Marie-Claire, his secretary, for coffee for the two of them. And one for Mr Felperstone, who was waiting in an empty office down the corridor. Then he raised his eyebrows expectantly. 'Right then.'

The woman sat po-faced, her brown hat on her knees, silent.

Robert cleared his throat. 'Perhaps you could tell me what you remember about my wife?'

'Well, sir. I'm the matron at the school, you see. I'm responsible for the girls outside of lessons. Their health, welfare, laundry and suchlike.'

'Yes, yes.' Robert knew this much already. 'But what specific recollections do you have?'

Mrs Galler looked put out to have been interrupted. She fiddled restlessly with her hat. 'Miss Samuel was a pretty girl, very good with her lessons, but rather flighty, sir, if you'll pardon me for saying so. And she did have her airs and graces. I mean, I know her father was nobility and everything, but she wasn't the only Honourable in the school at that time.'

Robert wondered if she had an axe to grind. 'Let's leave the character assessment, shall we? Did she have many close friends?'

'Well, there was that little whatshername.'

She laid her hat on his desk. There was something nasty about that hat. It refused to make any concession to fashion or attractiveness. It was an obstinate, embittered hat, and it reminded him of his own schooldays – of women like her, women with bad tempers and rough hands and a military manner. Women without a single ounce of love in them. Who could blame his Genevieve for displaying certain airs and graces around Mrs Galler? For thinking herself better than the matron?

There was a knock on the door and Marie-Claire brought in the coffee, serving it out with much rattling of cups before retreating again. By which time Mrs Galler seemed to have lost her thread.

Robert decided to try another line of questioning. 'It's my understanding that Genevieve didn't finish her schooling – that her father took her away from the school for some reason to do with her health.'

'That's right.' The woman nodded. 'Though I'm not sure "took her away" is entirely accurate.'

'Are you saying Genevieve was expelled?'

'Well, I don't exactly know. It was all handled very discreetly, you see. Her father didn't come up to the school himself – he sent the family doctor instead.'

'Him again,' Robert muttered.

'They were in with the headmistress for a long time – Miss Samuel, her friend little whatshername, and the doctor. Then they called me in and asked me to help her pack her things. She left that day with the doctor, and we never saw her again. The friend – she was very upset.'

'But what actually *happened*? What was wrong with my wife?'

Mrs Galler looked down at the floor. 'There was an incident in the bath.'

'In the *bath*?'

'One of the girls said that the friend – whatshername – had walked in on Miss Samuel in the bath, and saw something that upset her. It wasn't long after that that Miss Samuel left.'

'Do you have any idea what the girl saw?'

Mrs Galler leaned forward conspiratorially. 'Well, sir. The other girls – they said there was blood in the bath. One or two of them thought that Miss Samuel may have been . . .' and she lowered her voice as though someone might be outside the door listening, 'that she may have been cutting herself.'

Robert's fists tightened. It had to have been something like this, didn't it – to warrant all that secrecy, all that cloak-and-dagger behaviour. And yet . . .

He got to his feet. 'Thank you, Mrs Galler. I'm grateful to you for making the journey.'

She looked perplexed. 'Is that it? I'm to go now?'

'Apparently.' Robert took up the dreaded brown hat and handed it to her. Then he went to the door and held it open. 'Do enjoy the rest of your stay in Paris.'

After she'd gone, he had Marie-Claire fetch Felperstone.


When Robert had repeated the gist of Mrs Galler's half-story, Mr Felperstone smiled a yellow-toothed smile. Robert was revolted by the long, yellow teeth. He was revolted too by the thought of the scrawny hands, the mean little eyes searching through his wife's life like a down-and-out going through a trashcan. He was revolted by himself for hiring the wretch in the first place. And yet . . .

'It's a start, sir.'

'Is it?'

Felperstone took his snuffbox from his jacket pocket and snorted a hefty helping before sneezing into a grubby pocket handkerchief. Robert, needless to say, was revolted by this filthy English habit.

'Remember that old saying, sir? Where there's smoke . . .' There was anxiety in the yellow smile. And well might the detective be anxious. The more Robert thought about it, the more the story did not sit well with him. The notion of his wife – his Genevieve – hurting herself deliberately. This couldn't be right.

'The story was paper-thin,' he pronounced. 'The woman knew nothing.'

'Nobody likes to hear such things about their nearest and dearest, sir.'

'I expect it's her first time abroad,' said Robert. 'How convenient for her that this should have come up mid-August. The school would have broken up for the summer. A pleasant little holiday, wouldn't you agree? All expenses paid. Very nice.'

'That's as may be, sir, but I don't think we should dismiss this out of hand. People who fabricate stories usually offer a more complete version of events. Sometimes *too* complete. Whereas Mrs Galler's story – well, it's an odd little fragment and I'd say it has a ring of truth about it.'

'*Ring of truth?* I didn't pay all that money for mere gossip. She offered no means of corroboration – not even the name of the friend, "little whatshername".'

'Names can be discovered, sir.' And he sneezed a second time into the dirty handkerchief.

'So you think it's worth pursuing this.' It was a statement rather than a question.

'Don't you worry, sir. The headmistress has passed away, unfortunately. But we shall uncover "little whatshername", wherever she's hiding. We'll find out the whole story, sir. We're close – I can smell it.'

Those yellow teeth again. And another big pinch of snuff.

He covered his face with his hands, hoping that he could remain that way until Felperstone had gone. But the detective lingered on.

'I was wondering, sir . . .'

'Your fee?' He peeped through his fingers as he asked the question.

'Not to put too fine a point on it, sir. With your permission, I shall involve a colleague of mine in England – very reliable he is, and he'll be wanting . . .'

But Robert had stopped listening. He was lost in the horror of it all. Those evil images.

A nasty, rusting old bath smeared with Genevieve's blood.

## 21

GENEVIEVE HAD HARDLY SEEN LULU FOR WEEKS – JUST THE
occasional chat over desserts at Rumpelmayer's. She'd been
keeping to the apartment in the evenings, only going out
for a dinner or trip to the theatre with Robert. Nights
out with Lulu had become dangerous – they led to places
she couldn't allow herself to go. Robert was delighted that
his wife was staying at home more and spending less time
with her flighty friend. But Lulu was far from happy about
it.

'There's a party tonight,' she told Genevieve, at their
usual table in Rumpelmayer's. 'It's on a barge owned by a
crazy Dutch couple. It's going to be fantastic and we have
to be there!'

'I can't.'

'Why not? You've already told me that Robert is going
out for the evening. He wouldn't mind, surely? It's due to
start at seven – you can leave when you want to but you
*must* come. It's been *for ever*, chérie.'

'It's not that.'

'Then what is it? You can't mope around after your shoe-maker for ever. Oh yes, I'm well aware of what's behind this, Vivi. You don't fool me.'

Genevieve stared into her *noisette*, saying nothing.

'He's just a man, chérie. He's not important. I, on the other hand, am your best friend.'

The barge was moored near the Pont Neuf, at one of Genevieve's favourite spots. Often she would take a walk to the Ile St-Louis to wander its narrow streets and gaze at its tall, elegant houses. She'd cross over to the Ile de la Cité, passing the gloomy giant, Notre Dame, and over to the Quai St-Michel to walk along the river, browse among the book stalls and go down the steps to the little park by the Pont Neuf, where she'd watch the long cane poles of the fishermen and bask in the leaf-dappled mid-afternoon sunshine.

She descended those steps now, hitching up her Chanel evening dress – Etruscan red silk patterned all over with intricate embroidery and crystal bugle beads – revealing her delicate Rambaldi satin shoes with Louis heel and hand-painted bird motif. But her excitement faded somewhat at the sight of the rustbucket barge.

'Is this *it*?' After the way Lulu had been raving on, she'd expected something highly glamorous – along the lines of the three barges Paul Poiret had kitted out for the Exposition.

Lulu, resplendent in a jewelled turban and shocking pink dress with plunging neckline (she even had a beauty spot painted on her cleavage tonight), affected not to have heard. 'Come on, Vivi. Let's go aboard.'

There was barely room to swing a cat on the poky barge. But as they climbed aboard, a man in an artist's smock was doing just that – swinging a cat by its hind legs while it yowled and squealed.

'Don't worry about her,' he called. 'She loves it.' He set the cat down on a canvas that lay on the deck and let her stagger dizzily about, leaving little red pawprints wherever she trod.

The boat was crammed with people and there were many more on the shore. They paddled at the river edge and stood about on the shingle, drinking white wine out of glasses, teacups and in one case a bucket.

'Now for the blue.' The man scooped up a nearby kitten and held her over a paint pot so that her paws were coated all over.

'You see?' Lulu nudged Genevieve. 'What did I tell you? *Crazy* people. This is going to be quite a night.'

After an hour or so of dancing tight up against people like so many dancing sardines while a couple of old men played the accordion; drinking champagne from a case brought on by some people from the Moulin Rouge; and eating cherries and scraps of Brie which were being passed around from hand to hand on ugly chipped blue dinner plates, Genevieve couldn't tell if it was the boat that was rocking, or herself. Squeezing her way out of the crush and back down on to the shore for some air, she found Norman Betterson and Robert McAlmon sitting together on a bit of old wall, smoking and sharing a bottle of wine.

'Come sit with us.' Betterson patted the space beside him on the wall and she was only too glad to acquiesce. 'Here.

You can take the minutes.' He shoved a pencil and a small notebook at her.

'Minutes? Are you having some sort of meeting?'

'So anyway,' said McAlmon, 'Scott was so tight he fell off his stool – right on to the dog. Tiny little thing it was. Size of a rat. And sure enough, the titch is dead. Stone dead.'

'What did Scott do?' asked Betterson.

'What *could* he do? Said he was sorry and offered to buy her another one. And you know Scott – gets the money out then and there. She wasn't impressed. And then Charlie starts talking about *cooking* the damn thing. Can you believe it?'

McAlmon passed the wine bottle over to Betterson, who took a swig and passed it back again without offering it to Genevieve.

There was something unpleasant about McAlmon. Tall, dark and lean, he ought to be handsome but wasn't. It was to do with the mouth, she decided. Thin lips with a slight downturn at the corners, and with an odd bulbous quality about the flesh. He looked permanently as though he'd shoved a small, live creature into his mouth – a mouse or a chick – and was waiting for the creature to stop struggling before swallowing it whole. Meanwhile the eyes had a guilty innocence to them – as if they were trying to deny what the mouth was up to. Genevieve opened the notebook and began a sketch of him.

'Have you ever tasted dog?' asked Betterson.

'No,' said McAlmon. 'But I know a man who has.'

'Ah yes – if you can believe that story.'

'Who's tasted dog?' Genevieve didn't look up from her caricature as she asked the question.

'Guy Monteray,' said McAlmon. 'Or so he says.'

'I should have guessed.'

'I'm surprised he's not here tonight,' said Betterson. 'Aren't you, Bob?'

'He's not been about much lately. Not since his woman came in on the boat.' McAlmon swigged at the wine. 'What's her name again?'

'Whisper,' said Betterson. 'At least, that's how she was introduced to me. Pretty girl. Filthy rich, too.'

'Not for long,' McAlmon said. 'I hear the husband's stopped her money and ordered her to come home.'

'Poor Guy.'

Genevieve gave a snort of derision. But actually she was pleased to hear that Monteray was busy with another woman. The death's-head still hovered at the back of her mind.

Mosquitoes darted about at the water's edge, their number swelling as the light slowly faded. Genevieve felt them nibbling at her calves and ankles as she put the finishing touches to her caricature. 'How's the magazine coming along?'

'Well,' said Betterson, 'the line-up's almost complete. There are Guy's poems – but then you know about those already. I have Gertrude Stein's latest – really superb stuff. There's a new story from Ernest Hemingway; the merest snippet of a thing from Fitzgerald – not a proper story but nice. You'll see what I mean when you read it. There are a few poems by yours truly, and Bob here gave me his story yesterday.' He peered over at the notebook. 'Say, that's really funny! Take a look, Bob.'

McAlmon peered across. 'You're a cruel woman, Genevieve. Is that a *claw* sticking out of my mouth?'

193

'She has you nailed.' With that, Betterson burst out coughing and had to get his hanky out.

More and more people were packing on to the boat and milling around on the shore. Some men dressed as sailors were dancing on the shingle with three girls in tennis dresses. A further few were in swimwear – they might have been dancers from the cast of *Le Train Bleu*, still in costume.

'So, it's almost ready,' Genevieve said. 'Our first issue.'

'Yup. Just about. And Bob came up with the best title. Tell her, Bob.'

'*Fiesta*,' said McAlmon with a flourish. 'What do you think?'

'Well, I was rather keen on *The Gallery*.'

'*The Gallery*.' McAlmon seemed to be testing the words out. 'Don't you think *Fiesta* has just that little bit more drama? Think about it, Genevieve. *Fiesta*.'

'Is this really any of your concern, Bob?' Genevieve closed the notebook and handed it back to Betterson. 'It seems to me this is for Norman and me to decide.'

'Ah.' Betterson patted her hand. 'There's been a development. I'm very pleased to say that McAlmon is joining me as co-editor. And he's putting a little of his own money into the pot too.'

His own money indeed! Robert McAlmon's money came in the form of regular payments from his wife or ex-wife or whatever she was. Everybody knew it.

'It rather sounds,' said Genevieve, 'as though you don't need me any more.'

But Betterson was quick to jump in with 'Vivi, you've no cause for getting all twitchy. Of course we need you.'

'We value your contribution greatly,' echoed McAlmon.

194

Genevieve looked only at Betterson. 'You told me I was to be more than just The Money. But you're keeping me well away from the creative side of things.'

'Nonsense, honey,' said Betterson. 'We love it when you create. Don't we, Bob?'

'Absolutely.' McAlmon smiled, and the creature in his mouth almost broke free.

Darkness crept over the party, broken only by an occasional flash from the photographer. The trees in the little park were strung with coloured lights which swayed in the breeze. People thronged on and off the rustbucket barge with their drinks and cigarettes, their cherries and pieces of Brie, arms slung around each other's necks and waists, lip touching lip, thigh rubbing up against thigh. Suits and summer dresses, rags, riches . . . They were such a disparate crowd – how was it they all seemed to know each other so well? Genevieve, wandering along by the water, took one of her jade earrings off and absently tossed it into the air. She watched it make a high arc and drop down into the river.

'Hey, Genevieve.' Betterson had followed her down the shore.

'What?' She didn't look at him. Didn't feel like talking to him.

'We got a bit carried away, Bob and me. You see, we go way back. He's good for the magazine, trust me on that. And he writes like a dream.'

'Unlike me.' Genevieve kept her gaze on the water, not wanting to look Betterson in the eye. 'My poems are no good. We both know it.'

He took a moment before speaking – trying, no doubt, to

think of a way to be tactful. 'No, my darling. And I'm afraid there's nothing you can do about it. This game isn't about how nice you are or how deserving or even how hard you work – though God knows you *do* have to work. None of it's any use if you don't have the gift in the first place.'

Genevieve felt heavy. Her mouth felt too heavy to smile. Even her individual fingers and toes felt heavy. Betterson moved closer to her. She sensed he wanted to comfort her with some simple physical gesture – to put an arm around her or take hold of her hand. But he held back.

'Why should you care if you can't write good poetry? You're a beautiful girl. What's more, you've got character. And money too.'

'You don't understand.'

'Don't I? It seems to me that you're labouring under a common illusion. Writing doesn't make us happy. Usually it makes us miserable. We do it because we *have* to.'

'Norman, when I sit down to talk to you and Bob McAlmon, I want to have something to *say*. Something valuable. I want to be a part of something important – a magazine, a book, a dialogue, *something*. To contribute ideas, not just money. And to know that my ideas are good. I thought if I came here, to Paris – this quarter – that it could happen for me. I want my life to *mean* something.'

A jazz trio in bow-ties and tuxes had rolled in from nowhere – guitar, double bass and trumpet, *tootle tootle*. And now a lone voice joined the music – soaring up above the party, strong and clear. Unmistakable.

Lulu reclined along the crumbling wall where Betterson and McAlmon had sat. Slowly she extended one provocatively bare leg into the air and pointed her toe. Her song, about two stray cats roaming the streets of Paris, was frisky, impish. She flung an arm behind her head as she sang. Now she was up on all fours on the wall, arching her back just like the cats she was singing about.

'Look, honey.' Betterson's face was in shadow, and Genevieve couldn't quite discern his expression. 'You wrote a few poems that are no good. Come on, that's not the end of the world. You can't tell me it's a dream you've had your whole life. Try something else. What about your drawings? There were some great caricatures in your notebook. And that sketch of Bob – it was right on the button. Maybe we could put a few in the magazine.'

'Oh, please,' said Genevieve. 'Spare me your pity.'

But Betterson's attention was on Lulu now. She was standing on the wall, pouting and high-kicking as she sang of how, at dead of night, the cats became kings of the city. A swarm of people were capering around on the shore, trying to dance on the shingle. They looked like so many crabs darting about.

Betterson mumbled something and headed off to get closer.

Genevieve turned to walk back along the water's edge. But as she neared the crowds, she spotted a familiar figure descending the steps by the Pont Neuf, dark head bowed, one hand holding a cigarette, shirt loose and unbuttoned at the neck.

Something inside her leaped up and fell again.

Zachari stood alone, watching Lulu's act. His cigarette end glowed yellow in the dark. Several weeks had passed since the night she and Lulu had got Olga drunk and then brought her back to his shop. She had successfully avoided him throughout that time, but she'd known she couldn't avoid him for ever. He was standing with a couple of the women in swimwear now, drinking from a bottle of champagne.

I could just leave, she thought. But something stopped her from moving. It was impossible to walk away from this party now she knew he was here. She took off her remaining earring and hurled it hard, as far as she could, out into the river.

'What are you doing, crazy girl?'

The voice was close by. She turned around to see Guy Monteray standing just behind her, hands thrust deep in the pockets of his cream suit trousers. Handsome face smiling and amused.

'Oh. It's you.'

'Could you possibly sound *less* pleased to see me?'

Suddenly there was a scrabbling and a yowling. People nearby were trying to get out of the path of two mad cats – one launching itself at the other, all teeth and paint-covered paws.

'I thought we agreed to be friends, Genevieve.'

Standing here by the river, looking up at Monteray's tanned face, his sparkly, humorous eyes, it was difficult to think her way back into the apartment over Shakespeare and Company, difficult to really recall her fear on finding that gun in his jacket. He looked so sane, so thoroughly *normal*. Betterson and McAlmon thought well of him. And he had a woman now – one who had left her husband and fortune and crossed the Atlantic just to be with him.

'What did you think you were doing, putting that stupid death's-head drawing down my dress?'

'Oh God!' He put a hand up to his face. 'I'm so sorry, Genevieve. I was drunk. I guess I thought it was funny, which shows how drunk I must have been!'

He looked genuinely embarrassed. She allowed herself to feel relief – decided to put the skull firmly from her mind. Zachari was still talking with those women. They were laughing together.

'Where's your new lady-friend tonight?' She heard the child-like note in her voice. 'She's got a funny name, hasn't she – Slippy or Tickle or something?'

'Whisper,' he said. 'She's not here. She and I have . . . an arrangement.'

'I see.' She didn't, of course, but did it matter?

Another frenzied squeal – a flash of claws and yellow eyes and the cats came pelting straight at them. Genevieve, alarmed, tried to take a step back and almost toppled. They flew by so close, she felt fur brush against her legs.

'Hey. Easy.' Monteray grabbed her arm to steady her. And as she righted herself – his hand still on her arm – her eyes met Zachari's.

Quickly she looked away, down at her feet. There was a bright blue paint smear on the toe of her Rambaldi satin shoe. Damn it!

Lulu gestured to the band and they swung into a new number – one with an irresistible, catchy rhythm that drove the dancers wild. She leaped off the wall and flung herself into their midst.

Taking a deep breath, and not allowing herself to look at Zachari again, Genevieve smiled at the easygoing Guy Monteray.

'Dance with me,' she said, and led him by the hand away from the water.

At some drink-sodden, danced-out stage of the night – maybe 2 a.m., maybe 3 – the barge began to let in water. Its owner, the man in the artist's smock who'd swung the cat, started panicking and shouting to everyone to go home, while his wife, a sloe-eyed woman with frizzy hair, bailed bucket after bucket of water out of the boat.

Up on the Quai de Conti, an inebriated Lulu was running around telling as many people as she could get hold of, including passers-by who had nothing to do with the barge party, that they should come along to a place on the nearby Rue de Lille for a late-night 'gathering'.

'I'd better get home,' said Genevieve. 'Robert will have got back hours ago.'

'Oh, don't be boring, chérie! Anyway, he'll have gone to bed, won't he? So what does it matter if you stay out another few hours?'

'I suppose you're right.' She should go home all the same, she knew it. But she was giddy with drink. It was easier to let herself be swept along by Lulu than to make the decision to go home. She didn't want to have to think about Robert.

'It's a great place,' said Lulu, excitedly. 'Wild! You'll see.'

'Whose house is it?' asked Genevieve. They were arriving, at the head of a motley and raucous procession, at a white-fronted mansion that was loud with jazz, the front door wide open.

'I don't remember,' said Lulu.

'So how do you know it's so great?'

'I don't remember that either. Anyway, who cares, chérie? It's party time!' And in she ran.

'Genevieve.' A hand on her arm. Zachari. 'I've wanted to speak to you for hours. But you were always with that man. The American in the cream suit. Who is he?'

'Jealous, are we?' She heard the petulance in her voice. She'd wanted him to be jealous, of course she had. But she hadn't meant to say that.

He withdrew his hand. 'Be careful, Genevieve. Of that man.'

Again the death's-head sketch was behind her eyes. 'Why? What do you know about him?'

A shrug. 'Nothing. Call it instinct.'

Genevieve moved away from the doorway and the stream of partygoers, and leaned against the trunk of a plane tree. 'I wish you'd just leave me alone.'

'You don't mean that.'

'I *have* to mean it.'

He took a step closer. 'I know you're frightened, Genevieve. Of me, and of yourself.'

'That's rubbish.'

'You're frightened of your passion. Of what it could do to you and your marriage. If you set it loose again.'

She let herself look at his neck. There was the freckle. If she kept her gaze on the freckle, it would be all right. She could stay in control.

'I was fine before,' she said. '*Fine.*'

The party grew louder. People were shouting and whooping inside. Sounds of glass shattering.

'But you want to let it loose again.' He moved still closer.

She tried to take a step away but her back was pressed against the tree. 'We both know how it was between us.'

'I can't. I . . .'

His breath was in her face. He was so close, she could bend her head and kiss that freckle. Or she could kiss his mouth.

'Hey, Genevieve!' Monteray's voice, from the house. He was leaning out of a ground-floor window.

Zachari put a hand on her shoulder. 'Him again. I want to speak to you alone, Genevieve.'

'You coming in?' called Monteray.

'Yes, I'll be right there.'

Zachari frowned. 'Be careful of him. Meet me tomorrow afternoon. The Jardins du Luxembourg.'

'Is that man bothering you, Genevieve?' shouted Monteray.

'Two o'clock,' said Zachari. 'I'll be by the Cyclops at the Fontaine de Médicis.'

'I don't think so.' Genevieve wriggled her shoulder free of his hand.

'Do you want me to come out and hit him?' Monteray again.

'No. I'm coming.'

'Good. See you tomorrow.' And Zachari was walking away, quickly.

'I wasn't talking to you. You know that!'

'I'll be waiting for you.' He tossed the words back over his shoulder.

Inside the mansion, a jazz ensemble – now joined by the musicians who'd been down by the barge – was letting rip in the grand salon. The room was hung all over with African and Egyptian artefacts. Palm trees grew in china pots. Creepers twined around gaudy marble pillars. Wall murals showed Egyptian gods, and a golden statue of a pharaoh might easily have been imported straight from Tutankhamun's tomb. The crowd, mostly wearing masks, were dancing a Charleston.

'You want to dance?' asked Monteray.

'Not just now.' Genevieve was still shaky. 'Have you seen Lulu?'

'Nope. How about we have a nose around this joint?'

'I don't know. I might go home.'

'Ah, come on.' He bent to whisper in her ear. 'Aren't you even *slightly* curious about this place?'

'Well . . .'

He put one hand on the small of her back and propelled her out of the doorway and into the hall. 'You know what I always say? "The only way to get rid of a temptation is to yield to it."'

'Wasn't it Oscar Wilde who said that?'

'Clever girl,' said Monteray. 'Come on. Perhaps we'll find Lulu.'

As Genevieve led the way up the sweeping oak staircase she realized again just how drunk she was. There seemed to be more and more stairs every time she looked up. An impossible number of them. It was like climbing a mountain.

'Oscar Wilde is something of a hero of mine,' Monteray was saying. 'He's better than anyone, dead or alive, at blending the sharpest wit with the most tender sentiment.

And somehow he's never cloying. *The Portrait of Dorian Gray* is just fabulous. I'm a little like him, wouldn't you say?'

'Like Wilde?'

'Like Dorian Gray.'

Genevieve, at the top of the staircase, turned to look at him. 'What *do* you mean?' But then she had to catch her breath.

'What's wrong?' Monteray asked.

'Look!'

A skeleton was strung from the ceiling. A skeleton dressed in a yellow raincoat with a contraceptive dangling from its mouth.

Monteray chuckled. 'Oh, that. Don't you think it's funny?'

'It's horrible.' She made to run back down the stairs but he was blocking her way.

'He died in Paris. Wilde, I mean. At the Hôtel d'Alsace on the Rue des Beaux-Arts. You know what his last words were? "My wallpaper and I are fighting a duel to the death. One or the other of us has got to go." Apparently the wallpaper won.'

'I'm going.' Genevieve tried to push past him but still he blocked her.

'Did you like my little death's-head sketch?' He was speaking in a whisper now. 'Did you keep it? I do hope so.'

'You said it was a joke!'

'It was a gift, sweetheart. Especially for you.'

'What are you *talking* about?'

'You know.'

With an effort, Genevieve shoved him aside. But as she reached the foot of the stairs, Lulu came catapulting out of another room on the ground floor and seized her by the hands. She'd lost her turban and her feet were bare.

'Chérie, you have to see this!'

'Lulu, where have you *been*? We have to go.'

But Lulu was dragging her through the double doors.

At the centre of the turquoise tiled floor was a vast sunken tub with four naked people in it – two women and two men. One of those men was Norman Betterson. A further naked couple were sitting at the edge, dangling their feet and drinking cocktails, and yet another nude pair were in a fierce clinch over in a corner, partially concealed behind the fronds of a tropical plant.

'Come on, Vivi!' Lulu was pulling down the straps of her dress.

'Whose house is this?' Genevieve was trying not to look into the room.

'What?' Lulu struggled with a fastening.

'I said, whose house is this?'

'An American woman with a funny name,' said Lulu. 'Who cares, anyway?'

'Don't be scared of the skeleton.' Guy's voice from the stairs. 'She's just a little girl. I got her from a medical supply house.'

'Come on!' laughed Lulu. 'What are you waiting for?'

## 22

THE APARTMENT WAS DARK AND SILENT. GENEVIEVE CLOSED the front door as quietly as she could, slipped off her shoes and tiptoed to her room. Still half dressed, she sat on her bed, staring into space. She was home, safe and sound, so why didn't she feel safe? Why couldn't she just laugh off the evening, feel relieved that Robert was fast asleep, and then go to sleep herself?

Two knocks at the door. 'Genevieve?' A fumbling of the doorknob. 'It's locked! What do you think you're at, locking the door against me?'

'Darling, it's nothing personal. I always lock my door at night. It's just a habit.'

'A *habit*? Open it at once.'

She made a yawning sound. 'Oh, Robert, can't it wait till morning, whatever it is? I was sound asleep until a moment ago.'

'That's rot. It's not fifteen minutes since you came through that front door. I heard you.'

'I'm so tired, I just flopped on the bed and went straight off to sleep.'

A creak of a floorboard. Was he returning to his room?

'It's after four, Genevieve!'

'Goodness, is it? No wonder I'm so tired.' She pulled off her slip and reached for her nightdress. 'Do go back to bed, there's a dear. I'm frightfully exhausted.'

'Genevieve!' He was shouting now. 'I order you to open this door. Immediately.'

And now a thud, as though he'd hit it with his two fists. Or his head.

'All right, I'm coming. Just calm down.' She tried to keep her voice even – tried to stop her hands from shaking as she turned the key in the lock.

His face was pale. His fists clenched and unclenched. And yet there was something lost about him. He was unable to sustain his fury now that the door was open and they were facing each other. 'Where have you been?'

'I was at a party with Lulu. You know that.'

'For all this time?'

'Then we went to another party. I wanted to come home, but I was worried about her. She gets herself into such scrapes. She'd had rather too much to drink, you see.'

He sighed. Raked his hand through his hair.

'Do you want to come in?' She did her best to soften her tone but it wasn't easy.

'Thank you. Yes.' He was shuffling about the room now, his hands thrust deep in his dressing-gown pockets. 'Frankly, Genevieve, I'm getting mighty sick of your independent ways.'

'It shan't happen again. I promise.' She stared down at her hands and lectured herself. Go to him. Put your arms around him. Soothe his anger away. But still she sat there, picking at her nails.

'I don't want you gadding about town with Lulu. Not any more.'

'No. Of course.' There's only one way this can end. Go to him. Get it over with.

'I mean, what kind of woman goes out without her husband until four in the morning?'

'I'm truly sorry, Robert.'

And now it was Robert who came to her. Pushing her gently back on the bed and clambering up to straddle her. His mouth on her neck – the bristling moustache. His sighs in her ears. A fumbling with the dressing gown and his hand coming up under her nightie, between her legs. She started to cry, silently – not wanting him to know she was crying – as he pressed down on her.

Let it happen, she told herself. Just let it happen. Soon it'll be over, and he'll go away again, and you can sleep.

His weight seemed to press all the breath out of her body. And then he was inside her so that she couldn't hide from him. His mouth was all over her face. The bed began its knocking. Knockety-knock. It was always this way with Robert. And yet tonight it was different too. More mechanical, perhaps. Less tender. Worse. But maybe it was her that was different.

'Frightened,' Genevieve whispered to herself, when Robert had finally gone back to his room. 'Really frightened.' She lay curled on her side, gripping the sheets, unable to fall asleep.

## 23

ON THE DAY OF THE SCHOOL PHOTOGRAPHS, THE Honourable Genevieve Samuel woke up to find she had a spot on her chin.

'What does it matter?' Irene Nicholas was sitting on the next bed. 'It's just a stupid photograph.'

'That's not the point.' Genevieve dabbed cologne on the spot and winced. 'Oh, look, I've made it worse now.'

'What *is* the point?' But then Irene gave a knowing smile. 'Ah, I see. It's about that boy, isn't it?'

'What boy?'

'You know what boy. The photographer's son. Alexander, isn't it? Honestly, Jenny, he's so common.'

Genevieve set her hand mirror down and gave up on the spot. 'He has the most beautiful brown eyes.'

'So do puppies,' said Irene. 'And cows.'

The stage was set up in the same way as the previous year. A high-backed wooden chair was positioned in front of a black velvet curtain. Mr Giles was fiddling with the camera on its tripod, while his seventeen-year-old son adjusted the heavy lights which starkly lit the chair.

'Miss . . . Samuel? The *Honourable* Miss Genevieve Samuel?' Mr Giles read the name from his list without looking at her.

'Yes, that's me.'

Alexander was looking at her, though. Alexander with the beautiful eyes.

'Sit down on the chair, please,' said Mr Giles.

Genevieve climbed up on to the stage and sat, aware as she did so of the spot throbbing. Perhaps if she tilted her head just a little – like this – perhaps Alexander wouldn't be able to see it.

There seemed to be a technical problem with the camera which delayed the taking of the photograph, and the solving of which required Mr Giles's total concentration. His son, meanwhile, wandered closer.

'I remember you from last year,' he said quietly. 'You're very photogenic.'

'Thank you.'

'I'd like to take your photograph. I'm usually at the shop on Sunday afternoons doing my developing. Alone. You should come by.'

Mr Giles straightened up. 'Right then. Let's get on with it.' Mr Giles had white skin and a prominent widow's peak which made him look like Count Dracula. 'Miss Samuel, I'd like you to sit at slightly more of an angle – very good – and fold your hands in your lap. Yes, fine. Turn your face a little towards me.'

Alexander, who also had a widow's peak, though less pronounced, gave Genevieve a sly, secret wink.

Mr Giles tutted. 'Alexander, do stop fraternizing and get over here, there's a good boy.'

It seemed all the girls in the dormitory had new and exciting romantic possibilities. Millicent Hornby (at seventeen, one year older than Genevieve) had just received a letter from her young man, Edward – formerly a childhood friend – and insisted on reading it aloud to the rest of the dormitory and talking about him incessantly. Sophia Harker (one year *younger* than Genevieve) would not stop bragging about her blossoming friendship with one Julian Chesterton from the boys' school in the next village, with whom she was due to have a secret rendezvous at the weekend.

Irene Nicholas was talking about Alexander Giles. She claimed he'd been trying to pass her a note at the photography session.

'Are you sure?' said Genevieve.

'Of course I'm sure.' Irene was lying on her bed with *Jane Eyre*. She didn't even bother looking up from the page as she spoke. 'He couldn't take his eyes off me.'

'But you didn't actually get the note, did you? I mean, it could have been a shopping list for all you know.'

'Genevieve.' She laid the book down. 'Don't be jealous. He's just not worth it.'

'Jealous? Me?' She tried to laugh but it didn't come out right.

Sunday afternoon found Genevieve catching a bus to town, flouting the rule about not leaving school without permission. She didn't really intend to go to see Alexander

– just to get away from those girls and their incessant boy-talk for a few hours. But when she got off the bus, her feet carried her straight to the tatty little photography shop. She chose not to see the CLOSED sign, and tried the handle.

The door opened on to a reception room with an unmanned desk, on which sat a telephone, an appointments diary, a pencil and a bell to ring for attention. She ignored the bell and wandered along the narrow corridor. At the end was a door marked NO ENTRY.

Inside was the studio. The high-backed chair, a footstool, a tall wooden stool and a further couple of chairs were lined up. Over against the far wall was the velvet curtain on a portable rail which had served as the backdrop for the school photographs, along with a screen painted with a drab pastoral scene. In front of the curtain was a small pink *chaise longue*. There was also a further door, bearing the sign DARK ROOM – STRICTLY NO ENTRY, and Genevieve thought she could hear Alexander moving about behind this door.

It was then that she got the jitters and had to sit down on the *chaise longue* to try to regain her composure.

What do I do now?

He was whistling.

Will he be glad to see me?

There was a smudge on the toe of one of her new red Bally T-strap shoes. She licked a finger and rubbed at it.

I ought to go over and knock on that door.

But it was as though someone had glued her to the *chaise longue*. Maybe, after all, it would be better to allow him to discover her reclining on the couch. Yes, that would be rather stylish.

I'll wait here for five minutes, she thought. And if he doesn't come out by then, I'll get up and leave. Slowly, she took off her shoes and lay back.

*Flash*. Sudden lightning behind her eyelids, which flickered open with a start.

*Flash*.

'My . . .' Dazzled and bewildered, she jerked up to a sitting position. He was behind the camera, the cloth covering his head. How could she possibly have *fallen asleep*? And how long had he been watching her, *focusing* on her?

'Alexander . . . How could you!'

He lifted the cloth and straightened up.

'Waiting for my son, were we?' The face had a mocking expression. 'He had to stay home and help his mother today.'

'Mr Giles . . . I . . .' A deep flush spread across her face and down her neck.

'Oh, very pretty. Hold that.' And he disappeared under the cloth again.

*Flash*.

She reached for her shoes. 'I was just . . . waiting. I didn't want to . . . disturb him while he was working.'

'Him? Work? That's a good one.'

All her fingers were thumbs as she tried to fasten her buckles. And all the while she fumbled he was watching her.

'What's your name, schoolgirl?'

'Genevieve Samuel.' She got to her feet.

'Oh, that's right. The *Honourable*, wasn't it? I wonder what your headmistress would say about this, Miss Samuel the Honourable?'

213

'Oh, *please* don't tell, Mr Giles. I'm really sorry. It won't happen again, I promise.'

'Trespassing on my property in order to meet secretly with my son – who, by the way, will be in big trouble when I get home . . .'

'It's not his fault.'

'Isn't it?'

'I just wanted today to be different,' said Genevieve. 'I hate school. It's so boring.' The tears were building. 'I'm sick of being treated like a child all the time.'

His face softened. He looked amused.

'I wanted something to *happen*.'

'Well, well.' He stroked his chin and stared at her in a searching sort of way. His face was very precisely an older version of Alexander's.

Her mouth was uncomfortably dry. 'May I have a glass of water, please?'

'I can do better than that.' He slipped back into the dark-room, reappearing a moment later with a bottle of red wine, a corkscrew and two glasses.

'I've never tasted wine.'

'Well, it's your lucky day then, isn't it?'

He popped the cork and poured. As he passed her the glass, his fingers brushed against hers. She felt strange. Tingly.

He put his head to one side, watching her. His eyes were exactly like Alexander's. Beautiful eyes.

'So you're sick of being treated like a child, are you?'

She sipped the wine and tried not to make a face. It was nasty stuff but she was determined not to let her lack of sophistication show.

'I wonder how you'd like me to treat you.'

She'd never been alone with a boy before, let alone a *man*. What would the other girls think?

'Just how *honourable* are you, Miss Samuel?'

And suddenly he moved up close and she realized he was going to kiss her.

She wanted him to do it. She'd never wanted anything quite so much.

There were further Sundays. Eight or nine of them. Genevieve gained a subtle knowingness, lightly mocking her friends and their adolescent beaux. She was tempted, when questioned by Irene Nicholas as to where she went each week, to say that she was meeting Alexander Giles, but thought better of it. She claimed to be visiting a war-widowed aunt, and delivered the lie with the kind of smile that made it evident she was lying.

Often she lay awake at night, thinking about Mr Giles and touching herself under the blankets. Her appetite waned and she had to force herself to eat any of the bland school food at mealtimes. She lost weight, her cheeks became hollow and her eyes gleamed darkly. She looked and felt older. Her classmates seemed to sense that something was up, and began, whether consciously or unconsciously, to distance themselves from her. Genevieve didn't care. She only cared about her Sundays with Mr Giles. She wondered if this was love.

And then it happened. Or rather, it didn't happen. Her 'monthly' didn't appear on the expected day or the following day or the day after that. After five days, Matron asked her if she was 'quite the ticket' and instructed the kitchen staff to give her extra meat and greens. On the Saturday morning, in the bath, Genevieve used a razor to make a small cut in one of her shins and squeezed blood, mixed with a little bathwater, on to a few of her 'monthly' towels, putting them out with her laundry so as to fool Matron. On Saturday night she lay awake, agonizing over what to say to Mr Giles, and then on Sunday she told Matron she had a migraine and stayed in bed all day, too frightened to get up and face the world.

She never doubted for one moment that she was pregnant. They had taken no precautions – hadn't even discussed doing so. She'd trusted him to take charge of the situation. He surely knew more than her about what was risky and what wasn't. He wouldn't take a *real* risk, would he? He was a married man, after all. And she had enjoyed becoming his creature, doing what he wanted, living in the now. If ever the possibility of conception crossed her mind, it was in an unreal, almost playful way – 'What would my parents say!' She thought about her mother, crying and clutching her throat, her father rumbling and thundering and exploding with anger, his head actually blowing off his neck in a shower of blood.

What a stupid little fool she'd been.

Three weeks passed in a kind of emotional greyness. She didn't go to see Mr Giles and he didn't attempt to contact her. She imagined him eating dinner at home with the wife she'd never seen and the son she'd once desired. For some reason she always imagined roast chicken: Mr Giles tearing a leg to pieces and licking his greasy fingers; his wife – dough-faced and gap-toothed – pulling at the other; Alexander dropping scraps for the dog. She thought about the havoc she could wreak on the cosy scene. But these imaginings were no more real than her earlier fantasies of shocking her parents with the evidence of her 'ruin'. Her passion for him cooled a little more with each day. She knew now that she hadn't been in love with him, though she had certainly been under his spell. The important thing was to hide what was happening to her for as long as possible while she tried to come up with a plan. The important thing was to do her absolute best not to fall apart.

She faked a second period. Her breasts were lumpy and painful now, her stomach permanently distended and hard. Her appetite had returned with vehemence and she polished off all those extra greens and meat portions effortlessly, gnawing on biscuits in the dormitory at night as she battled with the nausea which came over her in waves, making her salivate so much that she had to keep swallowing and swallowing.

The French mistress noticed the constant gulping and told her she looked like a *poisson*. The Gym mistress castigated her in front of the other girls for being uncharacteristically lazy and sluggish. The Algebra mistress found her asleep on a desk in the middle of a lesson, gave her lines and reported her to Matron. Irene Nicholas noticed her remoteness, her incoherence and seeming inability to finish a sentence, the way she took to her bed at the slightest excuse and showed no signs of wanting to get up again. Finally Irene walked in on her in the bath when she was holding the razor, about to fake another 'monthly'.

'Genevieve, don't!' Irene slammed the door behind her and snatched the razor away. 'Nothing in this world is as bad as that.'

Genevieve, who hadn't noticed that she'd left the door unlocked, let out a squeal, and then – realizing what Irene thought was happening – began to giggle.

'I don't understand,' said the dismayed Irene. 'What's funny?'

Genevieve laughed harder, barely able to draw breath, tears of mirth streaming down her face, until she choked and coughed and the tears flowed.

'He'll have to marry you,' said Irene, as they sat together on the bathroom floor, their knees drawn up to their chests. 'Whoever he is . . . Have you told him yet?'

'No.' Genevieve was sodden and subdued in her bathrobe.

'Well, you better had.'

'You don't understand. I can't tell him.'

'What do you *mean*? You can't hide it much longer, Jenny!'

'I know.' Her face was in her hands.

'Do you have any *idea* what you've done?' Irene grabbed hold of her, dragging those hands away from her face. 'If you don't get him to marry you – and fast – this could be the end of *everything* for you.'

Genevieve pulled away. 'Leave me alone.'

'I just can't *believe* you've done this. Nobody will want to know you, Jenny. Not your parents. Not the school.' She may as well have added, 'Not me.'

'I said leave me alone! And don't you dare tell anyone!'

In spite of what she'd said to Irene, Genevieve played truant the next day and got on the bus to town.

It was only as she approached the shop that she realized he wouldn't be alone. In her head she had walked straight in, as she always did, through the empty studio and up to the darkroom. But it was a Tuesday and the shop was open. A receptionist sat behind the front desk and a woman with elaborately curled hair was reading a magazine. A similarly elaborate and beribboned poodle was seated on the floor at her feet.

'Good morning,' said the receptionist. 'What can I do for you?'

'I . . .' Genevieve cleared her throat. 'I'd like to see Mr Giles, please.'

The receptionist – an attractive woman in her early forties with blond hair and green eyes – smiled politely, glanced at the diary and said, 'Your name, please?'

'I don't have an appointment.'

'I'm sorry.' The receptionist, still smiling but more quizzically now, picked up a pencil. 'The diary's full for today. He has portraits all morning and then he's out this afternoon. I could put you in for tomorrow at about eleven?'

'Oh, I'm not here to have my photograph taken. I just need to speak to Mr Giles.'

The receptionist studied her more carefully, apparently taking in the school uniform for the first time. 'But of course – he did your school a few months back, didn't he? If your parents want some extra copies, I can help you with that. Did you want the small size or the large? We do some very nice frames, you know—'

'No.'

The curly-haired woman peered up from her magazine.

The dog looked over too, wearing precisely the same nosy expression.

'Is there something else I can do to help?' The receptionist wasn't smiling now, but her face was still kind. She had one of those rare faces that manage to be pretty and motherly at the same time.

'Please.' The nausea came on and Genevieve swallowed several times. 'I need to speak to Mr Giles urgently.'

'Anthony is busy with a client.' The voice was quiet but firm. 'Would you like to leave a message?'

Anthony . . . The sign over the shop said A. R. GILES and Genevieve had always assumed the 'A' stood for Alexander, the same as his son. She had never called him anything but 'Mr Giles'. How absurd.

Anthony . . . It was as though the receptionist was talking about an entirely different person.

'Miss?'

Genevieve felt herself pale under this woman's gentle gaze. And she knew, as she bolted out of the shop and threw up in the gutter outside (watched through the window by the curly woman and her poodle), that Mr Giles's wife was not dough-faced and gap-toothed at all. Far from it.

## 24

GENEVIEVE WALKED ALL THE WAY TO THE LUXEMBOURG Gardens in a pair of satin dancing slippers – pale turquoise, decorated with a rose in cream silk, and cream silk ribbons. The slippers were soft and insubstantial. She could almost have been walking on bare feet, and this added to her sense of her own vulnerability.

She walked so she could think. But the city was loud and alarming today. Cars, lorries and horse-drawn carts lurched out at her from every direction, determined to mow her down. Her sun-hat had a very wide brim under which she could hide her eyes, but it partly obscured her vision. On the Boulevard St-Germain, a waiter leered at her from the doorway of a café, causing her to change direction so suddenly that she almost walked into a chestnut seller. Backing away from his stream of abuse, she stepped off the pavement into the path of a bicycle. The cyclist swerved sharply and bellowed something unintelligible at her as he rode on and away.

It was a relief to enter the gardens of the Palais du

221

Luxembourg – to pass through the gate and along a cool, shady avenue, edged with geometrically perfect trees. All was carefully designed and excellently maintained – from the manicured lawns to the formal flower gardens blooming with the red, white and blue of the Tricolore. Nothing here was allowed to be wild or unruly or tempestuous.

It wasn't until she arrived at the Fontaine de Médicis that Genevieve started to question what she was doing here. She had come because she couldn't bear to be at home in the apartment, sitting about while Céline dusted and polished, and reflecting on the way the night had ended, on her fear of Monteray, her anger at Lulu and at Betterson, her dread of Robert's touch. She had come because she wanted to be here in the gardens where Nature was tamed, moulded, shaped, controlled. She had come because she wanted to see Zachari again.

But there was no sign of him.

A little way off, two old men were sitting playing chess, intent on their game. Two babies in perambulators were being pushed along the gravel path by their gossiping nannies. In the distance, under the spreading branches of a horse-chestnut tree, a game of *pétanque* was in progress. Parisian park life, slow and considered, was flowing all around her.

Ten minutes passed while Genevieve became increasingly angry with herself. I shouldn't be here. Seeing Zachari is only going to make everything worse. How can this possibly end well? But she craved his presence. She couldn't bring herself to turn around and go home.

Another ten minutes and Genevieve still stood in the shadow of the looming Cyclops statue. He's not going to come, she thought. And this seemed the worst possibility of all. But inevitably, just as she had given up hope and turned around to retreat down the tree-lined avenue and out of the gardens, there were sounds of running feet hitting the gravel; panting breath; and now here he was, red-faced and bending almost double while he recovered himself.

'You're still here,' he said, straightening up. 'I thought maybe you'd have gone. I spotted you way back there, but I couldn't see your face under that hat.'

'I was just about to leave.'

'I'm sorry,' he said. 'A shoe-fitting. It was going on for ever and it was awful and all I wanted was to get away and come here.'

'It's all right.'

'No, it isn't,' he said. 'I'm late for you, and the shoes were terrible! I hate it when they're not right.'

'What was wrong with them?'

'Nothing.' He raked a hand through his messed-up hair. 'And everything. They weren't for *her*. That's the truth of the matter. The shoes must be precisely right for the woman. That's how I work.'

'Did she take them anyway?'

A frown. 'Of course not. I would never have let her.'

'Was she angry?'

'She knows me too well for that.'

'So what will you do with the shoes? Alter them in some way?'

'As I said, they weren't right.'

She shook her head. 'My husband would think you were mad, spending so much time and effort on one pair of shoes and then just throwing them away.'

'Your husband and I are very different men. Let's walk a little, shall we?'

He offered her his arm, and after a moment's hesitation she took it.

For a time, they walked in silence. As they passed the *pétanque* game, one old man touched his cap to them. Another gave a gormless smile.

They think we're a married couple, Genevieve reflected. Or a pair of sweethearts. She looked at him sidelong.

'What you said last night – it's all true. And I want . . . you *know* what I want. But . . .'

'But?' He was smiling.

'It's all very well for you.' She pulled her arm away from him. 'You can do as you please – follow your every fancy. There are no real consequences for you. Nobody to find out. Nobody that you have to lie to.'

Zachari sucked in a breath. They began walking again.

'I'm not married, we both know that,' he said. 'But my life is complicated enough, believe me. There are plenty of lies.'

'Yes.' Violet de Frémont came, unbidden, into her head. She wondered about the others. 'Yes, I suppose there are.'

They drew up before one of the flowerbeds and looked across at the palace: classic Italian architecture for a seventeenth-century Florentine regent.

'Do you know who that is?' Zachari indicated a statue of a formidable-looking woman.

'Who?'

'It's Saint Genevieve.' He shaded his eyes from the sun. 'Patron Saint of Paris.'

224

She smiled. 'Really? St Genevieve? I always knew I was meant to be here. Can I ask you a question?'

'Go ahead.'

She wanted to ask something about the women – perhaps even probe into his relationship with Violet de Frémont. But she didn't dare. Instead, she asked about something else that had been puzzling her.

'Tell me about Olga.'

Zachari looked startled. 'What about her? Oh, I see. I suppose it all seems a bit odd.'

A half-nod.

'She was my landlady when I first came to Paris. I needed a cheap room and she was looking for a lodger. She was a Russian migrant. A widow with two children living hand to mouth. I moved in, she cooked for me and cleaned up after me and somehow we became friends. I'd only been here for a few months when my mother died. It was sudden and a great shock. My father was already dead by this time, and my mother had been everything to me. I thought about going home but I knew she'd have wanted me to stay here – to have the chance of a better life. Olga felt sorry for me, took me under her wing. She loved my shoe designs – gave me a lot of encouragement. When I was trying to get the money together to set up on my own, she told me she wouldn't take any more rent from me. She wanted my business to have the best possible chance of success.'

'That was kind of her.' Genevieve couldn't quite keep the ice out of her voice.

'I was so full of myself, I must have been unbearable. But she saw through all the swagger. She cared for me,

225

supported me. When I became successful, she told me she wanted to work with me – to be my assistant.'

'Is it useful having an assistant like her?'

'How could I refuse her? She used to scratch a living by taking in laundry and cleaning people's apartments. She had no money but still she shared the little she had with me. I owe her so much. I will always be in her debt.'

'I see.'

'I know she has her shortcomings and that people don't take to her. You're not the first woman to ask me about Olga, I can tell you that. But she's an important part of my life. I can't abandon her.'

'She will always treat your customers like dirt. She's jealous of each and every one of them. She's made it abundantly clear that she doesn't want me around you.'

Zachari shrugged. 'She's . . . possessive. And she knows there's something between us. She always knows.'

Genevieve turned to face him. 'What are we going to do, Paolo?'

'I'm going to make you another pair of shoes.' And now he smiled, with his eyes as well as his mouth. 'I have them in my head already.'

'Maybe they'll be wrong for me.'

'No. That won't happen.' Gently he lifted the sun-hat from her head and set it down on the grass beside them. 'There. I can see you now.' He touched her face, letting his hand rest against her cheek. As he leaned forward, she knew what he was about to do, and the anticipation was delicious and agonizing in equal measure. When his mouth touched hers, there came an incredible heat. Whether it emanated from him or from her was impossible to say.

It was there in both of them, in their kiss. And it was all about them too, in the vivid blue sky. His arms were around her waist now. Her eyes were closed, and a voice in her head said, This is it. I have always wanted to feel this way. I can't bear for this to end.

But even as she thought this, her eyes were already opening. Over his shoulder she saw a woman in a flowery dress walking in their direction but then veering off suddenly down another path. The woman's cheeks were very pink. Her gaze met Genevieve's and then was cast down. She was one of those women you'd call 'neat'. Small and unremarkable with thick white calves and ankles that had no definition to them – no visible ankle bone. Genevieve saw the woman looking at them. And then she knew she had seen her somewhere before.

'What's wrong?' asked Zachari.

The woman was walking away.

'Genevieve?'

'It's nothing.' Genevieve shut her eyes and opened them again, trying to collect herself. 'That woman.'

'What woman?'

'She looked at me as though she knew me. She seemed ... familiar, but I can't place her.' In spite of the heat, she shivered. 'What if she *does* know me? And what if she knows Robert?'

'I doubt it. She was probably just embarrassed because you caught her staring at us.' He reached out for her hand but she drew back.

'I have to go. I can't be . . . I mustn't do this.'

'You're nervous, that's all.'

She shook her head. 'That woman saw me. She saw me

227

and she recognized me. I have to go.' She scooped up her hat and headed off fast down the shady tree-lined avenue.

'Genevieve!'

I must not look back, she told herself. He's watching me walk away and I can't allow myself to look into his eyes again.

She wished she could lose herself in the shadows cast by those geometrically perfect trees. She wished she could close her eyes and disappear.

# V

# Tongue

## 25

MR FELPERSTONE WAS SEATED IN THE DARKEST, MOST REMOTE corner of the brasserie, beneath a squeaking ceiling fan. Robert had only been to this place once before, when he'd eaten something that purported to be beef but which he suspected was horse. There was a much better brasserie (they served excellent roast *poussin*) just next door to his office building, on the other side of the Boulevard des Batignolles. But when Robert suggested that they went there instead, Felperstone had muttered about the need for discretion and subtlety and insisted they should go some-where quieter. It was irritating, then, to find the detective sporting a large Panama hat and looking about him in a decidedly shifty way.

When Robert had finally attracted a waiter (they appeared to be giving Felperstone a wide berth) and ordered a *café espresse* for himself, he simply asked, 'Well then? What's this all about?'

With many a sideways glance, Felperstone removed the hat and set it down on the seat next to him. Then he drew a foolscap envelope from his briefcase and slid it across the table.

Robert scowled. 'What's this?'

Felperstone merely nodded, tapped the envelope with a long fingernail and raised his eyebrows.

'Now look—'

'Before you say anything,' said Felperstone, 'I suggest you open it.'

Robert had a sudden sense of the sordid all about him. The envelope, Felperstone, the brasserie even – they were infected, diseased. He could almost smell it. If he touched that envelope, he might catch it too. And then it would spread to his wife, their life together – everything he held dear.

'Go on.' Felperstone pushed the envelope closer.

He didn't have to open it. It was his decision entirely. He could pay this wretch off, get up and walk out of this place right now. Yes, that's what he'd do.

'*Café espresse*, sir?' As the waiter set his cup down, Robert snatched up the envelope and ripped it open.

Inside was a series of photographs.

*Genevieve standing by the river with a tall man in a white suit, drinking something. Her expression is bright and animated. Her party face.*

*Genevieve with the same man, dancing close, her eyes shut and a languid smile playing on her lips. They are surrounded by other dancing couples. In the background is an old boat, crowded with people.*

The ceiling fan squeaked. Robert reached up to unbutton his collar.

'What is the meaning of this?'

'Well, sir.' Felperstone drew out a notebook. 'The man's name is Guy Monteray. He's an American. A poet, apparently.' He pronounced 'poet' as though the very word was suspect. Dirty. 'And a dandy. He's not been in Paris long but his reputation runs before him. He's been involved with eight wealthy married women in the past three years, all in the States. And profited nicely from it. Go-away money. Hush money. Divorce-settlement money. Mr Shelby King, this scoundrel is dallying with your wife.'

Robert sucked in a sharp breath. '*Dallying?* There's no evidence of *dallying* in your photographs.'

'Sir, if I may . . .' The detective opened the notebook and glanced down a couple of pages. 'The photographs were taken at a party given by a pair of notorious pagan artists. *Dutch*, if you please. Your wife was in Mr Monteray's company for the better part of a long night. She remained in his company after the party decamped to a mansion on the Rue de Lille. At this further "party", guests were seen to strip naked, jump into a bath together and engage in carnal acts . . . It's all here, sir, if you'd like to see the notes.'

'No, thank you. Are you trying to tell me that *my wife* was one of the people who stripped naked and engaged in . . . ?'

Felperstone drew out his snuffbox. 'No, sir. But doesn't it worry you to think of Mrs Shelby King dabbling among these Bohemian types? Hanging about in the most notorious Montparnasse bars and cafés? Going to parties where people take all their clothes off and get in the bath together and engage in . . . ?'

Robert returned the photographs to their envelope and shoved them back across the table. 'All I see here is my wife dancing with a man at a party. Yes, my wife hangs about with artists and Bohemians. But there's nothing you've told me that suggests she's done more than talk and dance with these people. She'd do as much right in front of me.'

'And what of Mr Monteray?'

'Frankly, I don't know why I'm even discussing this with you.' He'd spoken louder than he meant to, and the waiter was looking over quizzically. He lowered his voice as he continued. 'It seems to me, Mr Felperstone, that you are going off on something of a tangent.'

Felperstone, about to start his infernal snorting, paused with the snuff pinched between his fingers. 'Perhaps so, but . . .'

'I hired you to find out what happened to my wife when she was a girl. Have you made any progress on that front? Any news of the friend – little whatshername – or anyone else from the school? I am *not* paying you to follow Mrs Shelby King around and take pictures of her and her friends.'

'I see.' Felperstone opened his fingers, so that the snuff drifted like dust on the still air, settling on the tabletop. 'I'm sorry, sir. I didn't mean to give offence.' He picked up his hat. 'But you know, in this job, one starts to get a nose for things. I've never yet been wrong in a matter such as this. Of course, I should have stuck to my original remit, but . . . Well, I just don't like to see a decent man like yourself being played for a fool.'

Fool. That most hideous of words.

'Nevertheless, I do see that I've overstepped the mark and—'

Robert felt his face go stiff. Something crumbled behind his eyes. The Englishman twitched and started. He had seen it crumble, whatever it was. Slowly he set his hat back down on the chair.

'In my experience,' said the detective, 'the fairer sex . . . Well, let's just say that ladies, however virtuous, can fall prey to an unscrupulous man, through no fault of their own. The sort of bounder who knows how to seek out the chink in their moral armour, so to speak.'

'I trust Genevieve.'

'And very commendable that is, sir. But do you trust the gentleman?' Out came the snuff again. A filthy habit. A filthy man.

Robert dabbed at his brow with his handkerchief.

'Ladies are . . . vulnerable, sir. With your permission, I should like to look a little further into this situation.' Felperstone gave three almighty sneezes and blew his nose. 'Just to be on the safe side.'

# 26

THREE DAYS HAD PASSED SINCE THE INCIDENT AT THE JARDINS du Luxembourg. The Shelby Kings were eating a tense breakfast together, a strangeness reverberating between them. Genevieve was doing her best to play the happy wife – hoping that if she acted hard enough it would cease to be an act. Robert was peering at her as one might peer through a dirty windowpane. His mood was changeable to say the least. When they'd first sat down, he'd issued another irritable diatribe about the infamous horse statue (which hospital was the bronze-cleaner in and how bad was his accident? He didn't see any reason why he shouldn't be able to ask the man where the statue was and go to fetch it). But minutes later he was clutching Genevieve by the hand, staring into her eyes and proclaiming that she was looking lovelier than he'd ever seen her look and that he must, as a matter of urgency, commission a larger-than-life portrait of her by 'the best guy in town, whoever he is' to hang above the mantel in the salon.

All in all, Genevieve was only too glad when he'd left for

work. Sitting at her desk in the study, she took out a sheet of paper and picked up her pen. But how, in all seriousness, could she even think of writing a poem after that conversation with Betterson? It was as though he'd robbed her of something – the ability to pour out her feelings and find a kind of peace for herself. Distractedly, she began doodling a figure in the margin. A long-legged figure. A man running.

No!

As soon as she realized who the figure was, Genevieve tore up the sheet of paper and threw it in the basket. She was still sitting, frozen, a few minutes later when she heard an odd sound coming from the salon.

Someone was crying.

She knew that it must be Céline. And yet there was something about those muffled, girlish sobs that made her shiver. She had cried that way, when she was a girl. The little gasps, the almost-coughs, the very pitch of the voice behind it all. This wasn't the first time she had recognized her child-self in the maid, and been unsettled by it. She'd felt it that evening when she'd found Céline trying on her Joseph Box court shoes. Fantastical though the notion was, she couldn't shake it: she was being haunted by her own lost innocence. And it was no more than she deserved.

'Céline?'

The maid was sitting hunched up on the Pirogue couch. When Genevieve entered the room she jumped to her feet, rubbing her eyes with her apron. 'Madame! I'm so sorry, madame.'

Genevieve moved further into the room. 'What's the matter?'

Céline pointed, wordlessly. Some pieces of broken glass lay on the hearth, along with a puddle of water and six strewn lilies.

'I see.'

'I don't know how it happened,' said Céline. 'I'm so clumsy today. How am I ever going to pay you back?'

'Don't cry.' Genevieve awkwardly placed a hand on her back. 'There are bigger things to worry about than broken vases. We'll just agree not to mention it again.'

The sobs died instantly away. 'Really? That's so kind of you, madame. You know I would pay you back if I could? My mother is ill and—'

'It's all right.' Embarrassed, she waved a hand to stop the outburst. Walking gingerly across to the hearth, she stooped and began to collect up the broken glass.

'No, madame! You'll cut yourself! I'll fetch the dustpan and brush.'

Genevieve picked up one of the lilies. The vase was Lalique. One of her favourites. But she was glad this had happened. They had lots of vases and glassware. The act of comforting the maid – of being able to make someone else's problem vanish in an instant – was more unusual. And there was something about this girl.

'Madame.' Céline hovered at the door. 'You're very kind. You and Mr Shelby King. You're good people.'

'I wish that were true.' She plucked at one of the petals.

While Céline was busy cleaning up the mess, she went to the cashbox in the study and unfolded two hundred dollars from the roll. These she placed in an envelope. She took the envelope to the maid's little room and pushed it under the door.

It was then that the telephone rang.

'Madame. It is someone calling himself Monsieur Renard.'

'Monsieur Renard? I don't know any Monsieur—' She stopped herself. *Le renard* – the fox ... An obvious pseudonym, as even Céline had realized. Guy Monteray, perhaps? Who else would do something like this?

'Madame?'

Clutching at her throat, she took the receiver.

'Hello, Genevieve. I had to know that you're all right.'

A breath. 'I am now.'

The workshop smelled of rich leather, wood and dust. Genevieve saw a low table, its surface barely visible beneath a chaos of sheets of paper on which were pencil sketches of shoes – ribboned pumps, jewelled dancing slippers, shoes with odd jagged shapes cut into them, shoes with laces twining all the way up to the knee of an invisible leg, shoes with toes tapering to a fine point and others with toes squared off in the most brutal manner. Shoes with spikes and others with tiny globes for heels, shoes that looked oriental, shoes that looked like old workmen's clogs. Some of these sketches were no more than a few lines, others were intricate and with dashes of paint here and there – bold yellows and oranges, subtle creams, deepest blues. Some sketches had notes scribbled at the side in a minute, illegible hand.

Stubby pencils with their ends chewed and wood shavings lay scattered among the debris, along with an old, messed-up tray of watercolour paints, some mangled brushes and paint-splattered rags. There were little squares of fabric – gold satin, green silk, a deep red velvet which she recognized as the material he'd used for her own shoes. Fragments of antique lace, scraps of something that might be black antelope and something else that might be ostrich skin. Gold-handled scissors with long pointed blades.

'What do you think?' asked Zachari. 'Is it what you expected?'

'I feel like I've stepped inside your head.'

He laughed. 'Is it a nice head?'

'It's a mess. A nice mess, though.'

'I don't let people in here, you know.'

'Thank you,' said Genevieve. 'For letting me in.'

The walls were full of shelves and the shelves were full of jumble. A jar of downy white goose feathers, some long grey feathers that could be seagull, a cardboard box with little yellow duck feathers glued on to the sides and one languid peacock plume. A tiny bottle of gemstones – diamonds or glass? Another full of pink crystals, and a box of delicate gold leaves. A bottle of little white pebbles that might have come from a beach. Brightly coloured dyes, in every colour of the rainbow. A glass tube of what looked like mercury.

'I'm sorry about what happened the other day,' said Zachari. 'I took a liberty and I shouldn't have. Not in public, at any rate.'

'You're forgiven,' said Genevieve. 'As long as you make me those shoes.'

His tools hung from hooks: a row of awls in varying sizes; pincers; something resembling a poker; tape measures; some evil leather-cutting knives. Sheets of leather lay in a pile – brown, black and red. A workbench with vice sat beneath the window, its heavy wood scarred and stained. A low bench had several hooks lying on it, along with some reels of thread and large needles.

'Is it *only* the shoes you want?' That familiar teasing note was back in his voice.

'Where do you keep them?' She glanced around. 'The shoes, I mean? The pairs waiting for collection. The pairs you're working on.'

He pointed at a padlocked cupboard. 'I don't leave them lying around.'

'Can I see?'

He gave her a withering look.

Her gaze moved on to the row of wooden lasts arranged along a shelf. She wandered over and picked one up at random. A name was pencilled on the side in the tiny hand, just about readable as *Coco Chanel*.

'They're all unique,' said Zachari. 'A pair of lasts for each of my customers. They're made of beech.'

'Are mine here?'

He pointed to a pair that were almost at the end of the row, and Genevieve bent to look at her own name – noticing as she did so another name on the next pair along. *Violet de Frémont*.

'Look at this.' He indicated an old woodcut hanging from the wall. It showed two men in Roman robes, barefoot and carrying hammers, their arms around each other.

'Saint Crispin and his twin brother, Saint Crispianus. Patron saints of shoemakers.'

'What's their story?'

'Well, that depends. In the English version, the brothers, who were sons of the Queen of Kent at the time of the

241

Roman Emperor Diocletian, had to flee from his forces, in disguise. Crispin became an apprentice shoemaker and was sent to Canterbury by his master with shoes for the Emperor's daughter, Ursula. The two fell in love and secretly married. Meanwhile, Crispianus had actually become a Roman soldier, heaped with honours, and he was able to convince the Emperor that this was really all right as the brothers were born into nobility. The marriage was confirmed on 25 October, which became the traditional shoemakers' holiday.'

'That's sweet.'

'But then there's the French version. In this story the brothers were from Rome. They got into some trouble and had to run away. The Emperor's military commander, Maximus, caught up with them in Soissons, where he tried to drown them, plunged them in boiling oil and smothered them in white-hot lead, but still couldn't kill them. In the end he beheaded them. Their bones were divided up and placed in two churches in northern France. Sick people went there to touch the remains, believing they had magical healing powers.'

'I prefer the English version.'

'So do I. What kind of shoes do you want?'

'I thought you never asked that question. I thought you already had them in your head.' She reached up and touched his face. His skin was smooth. She wanted to put her face close to his so that she could smell that skin again.

'What are you doing to me?' His voice was low and uncertain.

'Nothing.' She withdrew her hand – aware, as she did so, that she was taunting him, and that she wanted to.

'Don't say that.'

'All right then, I won't.' The day had taken on a dream-like quality. Whatever they did here, in the safety of his workroom, it didn't matter. Nobody need ever know but them. 'I want you to touch me.'

'Where?'

'Everywhere.'

He put his hands on her waist, guiding her through the chaos of the room, and half lifted her to sit her up on the edge of the work-table. She reclined slowly among his sketches, the paper crackling beneath her back.

He was looking down at her, smiling, and she was aching for more – when suddenly the ceiling creaked loudly. Someone was walking about in the shop directly above their heads.

'Damn!' He moved away from her. Turned his back. 'She said she wasn't coming in.'

Reluctantly Genevieve sat up. 'Does it matter? She can't see us. She doesn't know I'm here.'

The ceiling was creaking rhythmically now. Olga must be pacing back and forth.

'I'm sorry.' His face was troubled.

'Why are you afraid of her?'

He shook his head, denying it. 'She deserves to be treated with respect, that's all.'

'She's in love with you.' Genevieve slid off the table. 'Anyone can see that.'

Again he shook his head. 'Can I telephone you tomorrow?'

'I suppose so, *Monsieur Renard*.' She was still despondent.

'Genevieve.' He took her firmly by the shoulders. 'We'll

meet tomorrow. Somewhere away from here. Somewhere we can be properly alone.'

'I don't know, Paolo.'

She could smell his skin. That lemon scent.

'Say yes,' he said. ' "Yes, Paolo, I'll meet you." '

Upstairs, in the shop, Olga was seated at the reception desk, her back poker-straight.

Genevieve mumbled a cursory greeting as she hurried by, but Olga said nothing in return, and neither did she get up to open the door. As Genevieve stepped out on to the street, she turned to look back. The Russian woman was absolutely still, at the desk. There was an emptiness about her. Her face was a dead person's, devoid of expression.

## 27

THE SHELBY KINGS WERE AT THE THEATRE THAT EVENING, with some Boston acquaintances of Robert's who were visiting Paris as part of a European excursion. The Fanshaws were, of course, quite dreadful. On meeting them for the first time in the foyer – Druscilla fussing with a ridiculously heavy coat, Charles polishing his spectacles obsessively until they shone almost as much as his bald head – Genevieve knew she should have persuaded Robert to stick with Folies. At Folies you were guaranteed brevity. You could hide yourself in the noise, the laughter, the champagne. It was always a great show and American tourists like this pair always loved it. But Robert was keen to show off his 'Parisian sophistication', and instead picked up tickets for a play that he'd heard was receiving rave reviews (not that he'd actually read any of them). A play which turned out to comprise two men and a woman dressed as circus clowns, talking to each other rapidly and ardently in French (it was so typical of Robert to have assumed the play would be in English)

as they rode back and forth across the stage on bicycles.

They had a box, something Genevieve usually enjoyed for the opportunity it gave to people-spot with her opera glasses, but the drag of it, on this occasion, was that Druscilla took advantage of their not being surrounded by strangers to talk loudly in her ear.

'What are they saying now?' Druscilla bent towards Genevieve and enveloped her in a cloud of cloying cologne.

Genevieve's head was full of Paolo Zachari. I am hungry for him, she said to herself. I am ravenous. *Why* must I wait until tomorrow?

'What are they saying?' Druscilla hissed again.

'Oh.' Genevieve shifted her attention to the stage just long enough to catch a snippet of dialogue. 'The tall one told the woman she looks like a fish. She replied that his mother is a prostitute.'

Druscilla blanched – you knew she had blanched even in the darkness of the auditorium and even through her thick rouge.

'Then the short one said he'd known the tall one's mother for years and could vouch for her – she was really very good in bed and he wouldn't hear a word said against her.'

'Mercy!' Druscilla fanned herself with her programme. 'Are you *sure* that's what they're saying?'

'Quite sure.' Genevieve was peering down at the stalls. There were plenty of diamonds here tonight, much cleavage and a lot of bad toupées. Not many faces she recognized.

Druscilla scrutinized her programme. 'I thought it must

be nearly over but there's another interval and a whole other act to come.'

Genevieve tried to smile. Someone in a box on the other side of the auditorium was looking at her through opera glasses. A woman. She couldn't make out who it was but she had her suspicions.

During the interval, Genevieve detached herself from Robert and the Fanshaws on the pretext of needing to powder her nose, and went wafting through the bar looking for people she knew, catching her reflection in the long mirrors with a certain pleasure. The daringly backless Myrbor dress was the kind that emphasizes your nakedness rather than hiding it. She wanted Zachari to see her wearing that dress with his red velvet shoes. Shoes like mouths, the tongues licking high up her feet as she walked. She could still smell his skin.

There was a tap on her shoulder. Violet de Frémont in a dress that shimmered like the inside of an oyster shell, with a great rope of pearls around her neck, and delicate dove-grey pumps with tiny globe-shaped heels, inlaid with mother-of-pearl.

'Genevieve, darling. So good to see you.'

'Hello, Violet.' Genevieve wondered if her own smile was as strained as the countess's.

'I've been thinking about you lately. We should have lunch, we really should.' She glanced down at Genevieve's feet. 'My, but that's a lovely colour of velvet. Zachari?'

The tiniest nod. 'Yours too, I see.'

Her smile stretched wider. 'You know, I do believe I saw

247

a piece of that velvet down in Paolo's workshop just the other day.'

'Oh, really?' Genevieve struggled not to show the hit. 'Have you noticed that Paolo keeps your lasts and mine next to each other on his shelf?'

'Well, fancy that.' Violet's smile was like a piece of elastic pulled to snapping point. 'Goodness, darling, I've just seen . . . If you'll excuse me, I must go over and say hello.'

A moment of cool satisfaction, but only a moment. She'd thought she was the first to see his workshop . . . He'd said so, hadn't he? *Hadn't* he? She'd have liked to gather all the countess's shoes in a big pile, pour petrol over them and set them alight.

Five minutes or so into the final act, in which the three actors continued to move back and forth while conversing (but now on stilts), a man climbed up on to the stage and started reading, seemingly at random, from a newspaper while the actors whispered to each other, shrugged and wobbled.

'Is this part of the play?' Druscilla asked, when the theatre manager appeared and two burly doormen mounted the stage.

Another man in the upper circle got up and started shouting, 'Dada is dead! Dada is dead!' And someone else, who might have been Tristan Tzara, yelled, 'Dada is reborn!' and began hurling cabbages at the doormen, who were still struggling with the man at the front of the stage.

Across the auditorium, Genevieve saw Violet de Frémont kissing her friends goodbye and leaving her box. Her husband wasn't with her tonight.

'Where did you say we're having dinner?' asked Druscilla. 'I do hope French food is not so experimental as French theatre.'

They dined at Michaud's. While Genevieve ate her oysters, her head tipped right back, she could almost feel Druscilla staring bug-eyed at her long, white neck.

'How can you swallow them whole like that?' asked Druscilla. 'Doesn't it make you want to gag?'

'I love oysters,' said Genevieve. 'It's like swallowing a whole ocean.'

'Foul slimy things.' With a shudder, Mrs Fanshaw returned to her *bien cuit* steak and began prattling about her pugs (she had eight, apparently. Two had won prizes).

Robert and Charles had been deep in conversation ever since they'd sat down, but now Robert broke off to ask, 'Say, honey, is that Joyce over there? Over by the wall?'

'Joyce?' said Charles. 'Who's she?'

'He's talking about *James* Joyce,' Genevieve said quietly. 'That's him with the round spectacles and the moustache. The two women are his wife and daughter. They eat here practically every day.'

'Oh, my! The famous writer!' Druscilla twisted round to gawp in a manner so obvious that Genevieve cringed.

At that moment Joyce was tasting some wine, rolling it around his glass and sniffing it while the waiter fawned. He and his wife were speaking Italian together. The dark-haired daughter was hiding behind a curtain of hair.

I wish I was sitting with them, Genevieve thought to herself.

'Quit staring, Drusy,' said Charles. 'So the man wrote a

249

big fat book. So what? They're just a family eating dinner.'

'I couldn't get on with *Ulysses*.' Robert's chest was all puffed out and his manner puffed up. 'Everyone *says* they've read it, but I bet almost nobody actually has. If you ask me, it's utterly incomprehensible.'

'You're talking about the greatest book of this century.' Genevieve looked longingly over at the Joyces.

'Come on,' said Robert. 'You haven't read it any more than I have.'

'Haven't I?' But she couldn't look him in the eye.

'Well, I do declare!' said Druscilla. 'I had better buy a copy. Though whether I'll read it or just press flowers between the pages remains to be seen.'

'I should think it would press flowers very nicely.' Robert nudged Charles in the ribs and they both started laughing.

Genevieve shook her head and muttered to herself.

'What was that, honey?' Robert turned back to Charles. 'My wife is a poet, don't you know.'

'Can't she find a more useful pastime?'

'Oh, it has its uses.' Robert's face was flushed with alcohol and merriment.

'Like what, for example?'

'Well, occasionally we run out of paper for the fire,' said Robert – and the two of them were off again.

'Pay no attention.' Druscilla put a hand on Genevieve's arm. 'Men!'

But Genevieve had already stopped listening. She was thinking about Violet de Frémont. She could see her walking around Zachari's workroom. Touching things.

'I'm not feeling well,' she announced. 'I shall have to go home. You don't mind if I take the car, do you, darling?'

'Oh, come now, honey.' The smile vanished from Robert's face. 'We were only having a little joke.'

'I couldn't care less about that.' Genevieve got to her feet. 'I have a migraine coming on. You're all floating about in a sea of coloured dots.'

'I'll come with you,' Robert began.

'Don't worry, I shall be quite all right. You stay here and look after our guests. Now, if you don't mind, I'd like to get home before the headache starts. It's been . . . a delightful evening.'

The Bentley crossed to the Right Bank by the Pont de la Concorde, weaving its way through the *place* of that same name, and then along the Rue de Rivoli and up the Rue de Castiglione to Place Vendôme. The column looked dark and sinister tonight. One might not be surprised to find a coven of witches dancing about before it, brandishing daggers and sheep's heads.

Genevieve's head was whirring with crazy jealousy but she did her best to breathe deeply and stay calm.

'I just need to go and speak to someone,' she said, as they swung round on to the Rue de la Paix. 'I'll only be a few minutes.'

'Where would you like me to stop, madame?' asked Pierre.

'Anywhere along here.' She leaned forward and peered out of the window. 'No! Wait.' She dug her nails into the soft leather of the seat in front of her. 'Drive on.'

'But madame—'

'I said drive on!'

There it was, just as she'd dreaded. It was parked out on

the Rue de la Paix, near the opening to the passageway which led to Zachari's shop.

A long black car. The chauffeur napping in the driving seat, his cap pulled down over his eyes.

A Lea Francis, with silver figurine.

# 28

LULU WAS DRESSED ALL IN WHITE LACE TONIGHT, WITH A veil. The dress must have started out as a bridal gown, but the skirt had been altered and cut short, way above the knee. The rowdy audience were in love with her, and she was in love with them too. As Genevieve arrived, she was starting on a new song-and-dance number, for which she was joined by a lithe girl dressed in a black catsuit – perhaps a dancer from the Ballets Russes or Suedos. She danced up very close behind Lulu, echoing her every movement in a perfectly timed and executed routine. When Lulu high-kicked, the girl in black high-kicked too, just inches behind her. When Lulu bent like a reed, so did the ballet dancer.

The song was about a girl whose shadow starts to misbehave, refusing to follow the girl about as shadows are supposed to, and instead dragging her off to wild parties where it dances all night, forcing its owner to dance too, and wearing her out.

Genevieve, still knotted up with jealousy and needing a

drink, ordered a cherry, and spotting Norman Betterson went to perch on the empty stool next to him.

'I didn't know Lulu was collaborating with a dancer,' she whispered. 'They've obviously rehearsed pretty thoroughly but she's never once mentioned it.'

'You make it sound as though she's been fraternizing with the enemy.' Betterson was wearing a formal black suit. He had oiled his moustache to make it curl at the tips.

'We're supposed to be best friends. We tell each other everything.'

'Do you now?' Betterson gave her an odd look.

On stage, the shadow was gaining the upper hand. Lulu sang of how, in the last days before the girl's wedding, she becomes wan and exhausted – shadowy, in fact – while the shadow grows more vivid and real.

'The story's vaguely familiar,' said Genevieve. 'I think it must be based on a folk tale.'

'It comes straight from the heart,' said Betterson. 'That's the kind of girl she is, our Lulu.'

Genevieve shot him a daggers glance. *Our* Lulu, indeed!

Someone at the back of the room started heckling. His voice was so slurred with drink that you couldn't make out the words. Another man shouted, in English, that he should shut up if he wanted to keep his teeth. Genevieve couldn't see either of the men over the sea of heads but she recognized the voices. The heckler was Joseph Lazarus, Lulu's penguinesque admirer. The second man was Frederick Camby, her on-again-off-again true love.

'Everybody loves her,' whispered Betterson. '*Everybody*.'

Genevieve, irritated for some reason she didn't entirely understand, was about to bring up the subject of the magazine when Betterson piped up again. 'Did you hear about your friend Guy Monteray?'

'My friend?'

'It happened earlier this evening. He punched the owner of La Rotonde. Clean knocked him out. I saw the whole thing. Someone called the gendarmes and they took him away. That girl of his – Whisper – she was shouting and cussing at them and flashing her money for all she was worth, but they weren't having any of it. She'll have to wait till morning to bail him out.'

Genevieve rolled her eyes. 'Sooner her than me. That man is Trouble.'

'Have a heart, Vivi. Poor Guy's locked in the pen for the night. That sleazebag from La Rotonde has the police eating out of his hand. Haven't you heard, he once reported on a conversation Lenin was having at one of his tables? He's an informer – has been for years. We good guys have to stick together.'

'Do we really? Well, I've had quite enough of Guy Monteray. I want his poems taken out of the magazine.'

But Betterson was glued to the performance.

The wedding day has arrived. The girl, desperate to rid herself of her shadow once and for all, takes up a pair of scissors and brandishes them threateningly. Ignoring the shadow's pleas, she reaches down to her feet and hacks at the place where they are joined.

'Are you listening to me, Norman?'

'What?'

It is the girl, not the shadow, that starts to totter, one hand to her head. Blood is flowing from her feet, pooling on the floor. The shadow rushes to support her, to catch her as she falls. And now the girl lies lifeless, while the shadow gently lowers the veil – a shroud – over her face, and weeps.

'I said I want Monteray out of the magazine.' Genevieve could hear the bitterness, the vitriol in her voice. She was aware, as she spoke, that it wasn't really Monteray she was angry with – or even Betterson. But it felt good to do this – to throw her monetary weight about. Here was a situation over which she had control. Oh yes, this felt good.

Betterson appeared unperturbed. Perhaps he still hadn't heard. 'Sorry, doll.' He slipped down off the stool and twiddled with the curled ends of his moustache. 'I'm on.'

'What are you—' But before she could get the words out, he'd darted across the room and into the performance.

The girl's fiancé has arrived at the tragic scene. Hands pressed to his heart, he gazes in anguish at his dead love, and then at the shadow. After a moment he moves closer to the shadow. His face is unreadable, and the shadow cowers away from him.

The fiancé reaches down to the dead girl. Gently he lifts the veil from her face and then detaches it altogether. Then he straightens, approaches the shadow, bearing the veil in his arms. The shadow backs away in fear but there is no escape, nowhere to go. The man reaches out, sets his dead lover's headdress on the shadow's head and lowers the veil.

Throughout the bar, everyone was still. Barely a breath could be heard, as the audience waited.

Now the fiancé puts his arms around the shadow and draws her close to him. He lifts the veil, touches the shadow under her chin to raise her head, and kisses her full on the mouth.

The show is over.

256

*

'So, chérie.' Lulu was wiping off the stage blood with a bar towel. 'What did you think?'

'It was a great performance. But you know that already.' She handed over a glass of beer, which Lulu gulped back thirstily. 'Why didn't you tell me you were working with that dancer?'

Lulu drank again. 'I'm so happy, chérie. There was a time, a few months ago, when I had fallen out with Camby, and you said that I should try to put my emotions into my art. Into my singing. Do you remember that?'

Genevieve shrugged.

'At the time, I didn't listen to you. But then I thought about it, and you were right. And now that's what I'm doing. I'm writing more and more songs. And dances too – I choreographed this one myself. Everything I write is true to my feelings. And consequently I feel great. Violetta's a marvellous dancer, don't you think?'

'What about him?' Genevieve indicated Norman Betterson, who was talking with Violetta at the piano. 'Since when did you get so friendly with him?'

'Ah, yes.' Lulu giggled. 'Well, that was just the other night at that party. The one where you marched off with your nose in the air. Some of us stayed on to have some fun.'

'Are you saying you *slept* with Betterson?'

Lulu narrowed her eyes. 'So what if I did? Why should that matter to you?'

Why, indeed? But it did. Betterson was *her* creature, not Lulu's. She had known him first. He was part of *her* world. 'You used him,' she blurted out. 'To get at me.'

'Hey.' Lulu smacked her beer glass down on the bar. 'Do you remember *fun*, Vivi?'

'It suits you to drag me around Paris like some stage prop for your act. Telling me what to do and who to be. But you're jealous of me too.'

'You're drunk, chérie. Go home to bed. Right now. Before you say anything more.'

'That's why you kept on at me to sleep with other men.' Now she'd started, Genevieve couldn't stop herself. 'You were jealous of my marriage and you wanted to wreck it. I was happy with Robert until you started on at me!'

'You think *I* am jealous of *your marriage*?' Lulu put her hands on her hips. 'Of *him*!'

But Genevieve was not to be stopped. 'You just kept on and on at me to cheat on Robert. Until finally I did it. And where has it got me, this *fun* of yours? I can't so much as *look* at Guy Monteray – can't even bear the sound of his name. And as for Paolo Zachari . . .'

'So you *did* sleep with Monteray. Why did you lie about it?'

'I was ashamed of what I'd done. And now I've got myself in very deep water with Paolo Zachari, and I'm absolutely *desperate*, and it's all your fault!'

Lulu's face was dark. 'My fault? Ah, but of course. Because nothing is ever the fault of a spoilt little princess like you! And *you're* a one to talk about using people, my so-called friend. You used me to get you introductions. And now you don't need me so you hardly ever bother to see me. You look down on me, like all your sort do. You always have – I just didn't see it until now.'

'Maybe I don't see you so much because I've finally

realized what sort of a "friend" you are. Bitter, faithless and false, eaten up with jealousy and determined that everyone else should be just as miserable as you. Well congratulations, Lulu. I *am* thoroughly miserable. And it's all thanks to you!' Genevieve was shouting at the top of her voice, and yet nobody so much as turned to look. Because at that moment, something louder and more explosive was happening right behind them.

Joseph Lazarus had come up behind Norman Betterson and tapped him on the shoulder. Betterson, who was deep in conversation with Violetta, flapped a dismissive hand at him. Lazarus grabbed Betterson by the shoulder and tried to yank him around – at which point Frederick Camby stepped forward and threw a fist in his beaky face. Lazarus fell, knocking over a table laden with drinks and almost dragging Betterson down with him. Violetta shrieked. Lazarus, now back on his feet, struck Camby across the head with a bottle. Lulu shrieked. Laurent, the one-eyed barman with the Croix de Guerre (two palms), vaulted over the bar brandishing a cosh. Betterson got down on his hands and knees and started crawling away fast, heading for the WC. Someone threw a glass, which smashed through a window. Someone else picked up a table, aiming to bring it down on Lazarus's head but misaiming and hitting Laurent, who fell to the floor in a dead faint. Janine, the hard-as-nails waitress with the scar, kicked the balls of the man who'd hit her beloved Laurent. Lazarus went charging across the room, squealing like a pig and heading right for Lulu and Genevieve, but skidded on something, tripped up Janine and dragged her down by the hair. Genevieve and Lulu both shrieked. Betterson emerged from the WC and shrieked, biting his lip with the sheer excitement of it all. With a towel clutched to his bleeding face, and leaning heavily on Violetta, Camby made it to the back door. As the gendarmes came in through the front, the pair slipped quietly away into the night. Laurent's poodle lapped at the puddles on the floor: spilt drink, stage blood and real blood. Marcel's spindly yellow fingers gentled over the piano keys.

## 29

SHE ENTERED THE APARTMENT IN HER STOCKING FEET, HER blood-red Zacharis dangling from one hand.

'I knew there was no migraine.' He was standing in the doorway to the salon, his collar undone.

'Robert! You startled me. I thought you'd have gone to bed.'

'How could I go to bed? My wife is taken ill and goes home in the middle of a restaurant meal, but over two hours later there's still no sign of her. Where the hell have you been?'

'Darling, let's go into the salon and sit down.' She took him by the arm but he pulled away.

'Don't take that tone of voice with me. It's you that's in the wrong here. You promised me you wouldn't do this any more. It was just a few nights ago – you promised!'

'Please, Robert. We don't want to wake Céline, do we?'

He sighed – and with that sigh, she knew she had him. He might be furious, he might be frantic with worry, but his relief that she was safe was stronger than all his vehemence. And so she had him.

She switched on the ostrich-egg lamp, and they sat together in the canoe-shaped couch. He put his arm around her and drew her close, so that her head rested on his chest.

'I'm sorry, Robert.' She listened to the beating of his heart, its slow, comforting rhythm. 'I went to see Lulu at the Coyote. I had to talk to her.'

His arm stiffened. 'You made a promise. Why did you break it?'

'You hurt my feelings.' Her voice was thin and she gave a little sniff. 'Badly.'

'I did?'

'You ridiculed my poetry.'

'But that was just a joke. I thought you knew that.'

'A joke at my expense. You wanted to look big in front of your friends by making me look small. And you expected me to smile sweetly and put up with it, like a sweet little fool.'

'Now, honey. You know I didn't mean to—'

'I invented the migraine because I didn't want to make a scene. Think about who you're married to, Robert, and count yourself lucky. A harpie like Druscilla Fanshaw would have shouted the restaurant down.'

'My love.' Robert wrapped his arms around her and held her so close that she could hardly breathe. 'Please forgive me. It'll never happen again.'

'Of course, darling.' She tried to pull away but his arms tightened.

'I don't deserve you, I really don't.' He spoke the words into her hair, and showered kisses on her head. 'I haven't trusted you as I should. If you only knew about . . . But never mind that.'

'Never mind what?'

His heartbeat remained steady but its rhythm had ceased to comfort her. She felt trapped by it. This was all too much.

'Nothing, my love. Let's go to bed.'

'Oh yes, let's. I'm so tired, and we can talk more at breakfast tomorrow.'

He swallowed heavily. 'What I meant was that we should go to bed *together*.'

That heartbeat of his – one light beat, one heavy. Boo-boom, boo-boom. His knock was just the same.

'. . . I want to *feel* . . . to really *experience* your forgiveness.'

Boo-boom, boo-boom. That was how he'd knocked the other night. It had begun with the knocking and the shouting and ended with that hideous, suffocating love of his.

'Genevieve, you're shaking.'

She was free of his arms. She'd jumped up without even being conscious of doing so. She was standing in the middle of the room, hugging herself – looking down at her red shoes, which sat tidily before the couch. She'd been thinking of Paolo tonight when she put those shoes on – and when she'd chosen the backless Myrbor dress. She'd imagined him kissing his way down her back . . . But instead it was Robert who sat there admiring her. It was Robert who was getting to his feet with that amorous look on his face.

'Honey, why are you backing away from me? It's as if you don't even want me to touch you.'

263

'I'm fine. Really.'

She had to keep him off her. *Had* to.

'Something's wrong. What is it?'

'I'm pregnant.' She didn't know where the words came from, but before she could stop them they were out there. The words were so much bigger than her. They made her want to pick up the red shoes and hug them close, like a frightened child hugging her teddy bear.

# VI

# *Insole*

## 30

IT WAS SURELY THE FINEST OF FINE MORNINGS. THE SKY HAD never been more bright, the air more fresh, the croissants more sweet and light. The women of Paris had never looked more beautiful and the babies – ah, the darling little cherubs all bonny in their bonnets, enthroned in their jouncy perambulators and pushed along by their lovely English nannies. (Could you get them in Paris – those English nannies? Would he have to go to London to purchase one?)

It was not Robert's habit to walk to work, but today he just couldn't keep still. He was whistling as he strode down the Champs Elysées, and he had to stop himself tapdancing his way along. Pierre (who was trailing him in the car at a snail's pace) must be wondering what on earth was up with him. And indeed it was all Robert could do to prevent himself from running up to the Bentley and bellowing his news through the window. Would it *really* hurt to tell just one person? How on earth could she expect him to contain his happiness so completely? But contain it he must. He had promised Genevieve. Poor little Genevieve. She had been so frightened to tell him. She still seemed frightened this morning. Well, he would comfort her and reassure her. He would wrap her up in a blanket of his love and keep her warm and safe all through the nine months of her pregnancy, and beyond.

An old woman was sitting on a street corner selling roses. Red, yellow, peach, white and pink. Robert paused in front of her and took a sniff of the nearest bunch. These roses, he decided, had a scent more divine than anything he'd ever smelled. Passing a random banknote of a high denomination to the delighted hag, he took a bunch in each colour and tossed them into the back of the Bentley.

'Drive the red and white roses to the Rue de Lota for Mrs Shelby King,' he told Pierre. 'The peach bunch can be for Céline, the maid. The pink could go to Marie-Claire, my secretary, if you'd bring them to the office.'

'What about the yellow?' asked Pierre.

'Take them home to your good lady wife. She's an excellent woman, and thoroughly deserves some flowers.'

'Thank you, monsieur!'

'My pleasure. This morning – any morning, in fact – has a lesson to teach us, Pierre. Whatever has taken place in the night, in the darkness – there is always a new beginning when the sun comes up. The slate can be wiped clean, my friend, if that is what we want most. New life, new start, new man. It's up to us to make it happen.'

As soon as he'd got away from his grateful, blushing secretary and settled himself at his desk, he picked up the phone and asked the operator to connect him to Mr Felperstone's office.

'Mr Shelby King. The very man,' came Felperstone's voice, before Robert had a chance to get beyond the most basic hello. 'I must tell you, sir, that my colleague Monsieur Cannes has been rather – how shall I put it? – active in the field. I think we shall have some news shortly.'

'Forget it, Mr Felperstone.' Robert shut his eyes and kept them shut. 'Whatever it is. I don't want to know any more.'

A nervous laugh at the other end of the line and a strange snuffling noise (that foul habit of his, no doubt). 'I beg your pardon, sir, but are you saying—'

'I'm saying . . .' Robert opened his eyes again and gazed at the framed photo of his wife in her wedding dress. Look at that face – the perfect English-rose complexion. The fine, straight nose. She was mighty aristocratic, his Genevieve. Yes, sir, mighty aristocratic. 'I'm saying that I love and trust my wife. I don't know what possessed me to hire you in the first place.'

'Mr Shelby King. I beg of you to reconsider. Monsieur Cannes is a man of his word. If he tells me something big is coming in, then you can be sure something big is coming in.'

'I'll settle your fee in full, of course,' said Robert. 'Please send the invoice to me here at the office and mark the envelope "private and personal".'

'But the net is closing, sir!'

'Aren't you listening? I'm not interested.' As if to prove the point to himself, he started riffling impatiently through his in-tray.

'We'll be hauling it in very shortly, I'm certain of it. If you could only wait a little longer . . .'

'Give up your fishing, Felperstone. Your net is empty and it always will be.' And now Robert's eye lit on a small lilac envelope with his name and the office address inscribed on it in a slanting, feminine hand. Marie-Claire had neglected to open it, perhaps because it had the look of personal correspondence. He picked up his letter knife and slid the blade under the flap.

'I swear to you, sir, Cannes doesn't make mistakes, and—'

But Robert had stopped listening.

*Dear Sir,*
    *Your wife is making a fool of you. That hobby of hers is not so harmless as you might think.*
    *A Well-Wisher*

*

Aristocratic Genevieve was at that moment tying the low sash-waist of her softly flowered rose chiffon dress with beaded banding worn over a pink satin slip. Shortly she would go to her shoe room and look out an as yet unworn pair of slippers by Michael Veil in an unusual tapestry cloth. Narrow straps with a pearl-button fastening and pink astrolac kid heel and trim. The overall effect would be elegant but suitably low-key. An outfit that would be conducive to inner calm and steadiness.

She had told Robert she would be seeing the doctor this morning. In fact, she was off to visit Norman Betterson.

The door was opened by Mrs Betterson. Or was it the secretary? Genevieve wasn't entirely sure. Both were tall and dark with shadows under their eyes.

'I was hoping to see Norman.'

270

The woman who might have been Mrs Betterson smiled. 'So kind of you to call by, Genevieve. It'll quite cheer him up.'

Confused, Genevieve followed her inside. One room served as living room, kitchen and study. But, perhaps surprisingly, its smallness was attractive. Some of the walls were filled with gaudy paintings – one, hanging above the table, was simply a red gash against a white background. Other walls were floor-to-ceiling shelves, each shelf stuffed with books. And every row of books had yet more stacked on top of it so that the shelves were bowed almost to breaking point under their weight. The floor was just bare boards, but with an intricate swirling pattern painted on it in three shades of green. There was something organic about this pattern. It only came to halfway across the floor but it looked as though it was growing, spreading all on its own, the way ivy sprawls and climbs over buildings.

'She likes the floor.' A second woman, who might also be Mrs Betterson, was sitting at the dining table.

'More fool her,' said the first Mrs Betterson, but with good humour.

The whole place seemed alive. The profusion of books and paintings. The papers spread all over the table – some typed, some scrawled on in large, sloping handwriting. It was like entering a weird literary garden.

'I've interrupted your work,' said Genevieve, apologetically, gesturing at the typewriter and the mass of papers.

'Oh, that's quite all right,' said the first Mrs Betterson.

Genevieve was straining for a glimpse at the words on the papers nearest her. 'Is that the material for the magazine?'

'Some of it,' said the second Mrs Betterson. 'But Norman's got it all mixed up with some other work of his. It's quite a job unscrambling it all.'

'I see.' Genevieve gave a half-nod. 'It must be nice to have a project to work on. Something to really concentrate the mind.' As soon as she said it, her cheeks went hot. How must she seem to these women? A spoilt little rich girl come over to peer down her nose at them and make vacuous, insincere comments. Only it wasn't insincere. She felt embarrassed, suddenly, of her flowery dress, the tapestry shoes. The obvious time and care she'd taken over dressing seemed to expose her as shallow and frivolous. They were beautiful, these women, in a way which was honest, direct, and disarmingly naked. And yet there was also a quality of deep water about them. Intellectuals, the pair of them. Women to be taken seriously. Their plain blue dresses and scraped-back hair suggested a disregard – possibly even a contempt – for high fashion and all its fripperies. You would need to take time to discover them, to really know them, and it would be worth taking that time.

She felt as though her every thought and emotion could be read on her face, and she wanted to turn and run. And yet the women's expressions were unchanged. Both appeared interested and alert. Neither looked at all contemptuous or disapproving.

'We're a bit of everything,' the second Mrs Betterson was saying. 'Editors, typists, experts on modern American hieroglyphics.' She held up a page with some particularly spidery handwriting. 'Occasionally we even have time to do a little writing of our own.'

And now Genevieve realized something.

I want what these women have. I want the deep water. But how do I get it?

'Norman's just through there.' The first Mrs Betterson pointed in the direction of the only other door, which was closed. 'In bed.'

'Is he . . . unwell, Mrs Betterson?' asked Genevieve.

'Actually I'm Mrs Betterson,' said the woman at the table. 'Augusta.'

'I beg your pardon.' Genevieve tried to smile but the error was somehow doubly embarrassing since everyone knew Betterson slept with both women, and rumour had it they slept with each other too.

'Don't worry about it.' Augusta smiled brightly and went back to her typing.

'I'm Marianne,' said the not-Mrs-Betterson. 'Would you like some tea? I'm making some for Norman anyway.'

'No, thank you. Norman . . . Is he ill? I mean, I know he's ill, in general, but . . .'

Marianne went across to the stove where a pot was boiling. 'He had a bit of a turn last night.'

'His own fault, really,' said Augusta. 'He completely over-did it. He got himself involved in some sort of performance at the Coyote. With that cabaret artiste, Lulu of Montparnasse. Friend of yours, isn't she?'

Genevieve looked down at the swirling pattern in the floorboards. 'We've had a bit of a falling-out, actually.'

'I gather there was something of a party atmosphere in the Quarter last night,' said Augusta. 'A poet friend of Norman's hit the proprietor of La Rotonde. And everyone hates that man, of course, so they were all celebrating. But perhaps you were there?'

273

Genevieve swallowed heavily. 'Is Norman all right?'

'On this occasion, yes,' said Augusta. 'He really needs to be careful with his health. But that's not his idea of living.'

'One of these days . . .' Marianne shivered.

And now there was a sound of coughing from behind the closed door. Awful coughing.

Betterson was sitting up in bed with *The Great Gatsby*. He had a high colour in his cheeks and his eyes were glittering fiercely.

'Genevieve! How marvellous to see you. Won't you get in?' He made as though to move across the bed and pull back the sheets.

'Norman, honestly.' She sat down at the very edge of the bed. 'How are you feeling?'

'Well, either the world has acquired a wonderful glistening sheen or it's just this book,' said Betterson. 'Between you and me, I think the big D is advancing a little closer. My markings are a tad clearer. But you know, there's nothing like the awareness of one's own impending doom to fire the imagination! I've been writing a marvellous new poem this morning. My best yet, I think. And there are lots more in my head.'

'I'm glad. About the poems, I mean.'

'So.' His face clouded over a little. 'What can I do for you? You haven't come here to issue more orders about who's in and out of the magazine, have you?'

'No.' She stared down at the counterpane. 'In fact, I wanted to apologize for what I said last night. About Guy Monteray, I mean. You're the editor. You decide what goes in the magazine and what doesn't, not me.'

'Splendid!' He clapped his hands. 'In that case, it really *is* marvellous to see you.'

'Oh, Norman.' She rubbed at her head. 'I was angry with you because you didn't like my poems. But you were just being honest with me.'

'Think nothing of it, honey.' He put his head to one side and appeared to be sizing her up.

'It's all a bit of a mess.' Her voice was flat and tired. 'I've made bad decisions, put my faith in wrong notions and the wrong people . . .'

'Are you talking about Lulu? That fight you had last night?'

Genevieve shrugged. 'She's not the person I thought she was. It's complicated.'

'I dare say.' He pulled himself up against his pillows. 'But I reckon she's worth a deal of trouble.'

'You can't see it because you're a man.' Genevieve thought about the two women in the other room, and wondered how much they knew. 'Are you in love with Lulu?'

'Me? No.' A chuckle from the bed, turning into a deeper laugh and then an alarming kind of coughing in which his whole body seemed to heave and judder. Genevieve wondered if she should fetch one of the Mrs Bettersons. But as she dithered, the coughing began to subside. He pressed a handkerchief to his mouth. 'She's fun though.' Then the subject was closed and he started talking about the magazine. 'We can't use the title *Fiesta* after all. Seems Hemingway wants it for his novel. Greedy of him, I'd say. He already had a title but *Fiesta* is to be the "alternative" title. McAlmon's furious but he's given way. I gather they boxed for it.'

Marianne brought in two cups of tea on a tray and retreated with a wink. Betterson swallowed a couple of pills with his, draining his cup in just a few gulps.

'Ask Augusta to look out your notebook,' he said, sleepily, after a time. 'It's out there on the shelves somewhere. She'll know where to find it.'

'What do I need a notebook for?' Genevieve took up the tray with the empty cups. 'I'm not going to write any more poetry.'

'Your caricatures.' He was struggling to keep his eyes open now. 'I told you before – they're very good.'

'Do you really think so?'

But the only reply from the bed was a snore.

Back in the other room, Augusta and Marianne were sitting at the table. Augusta was puzzling over a difficult bit of scrawl, trying to decipher it. She held the page out to Marianne, who peered closely and shrugged her shoulders. Genevieve felt an urge to go over there and help. Maybe she'd be able to make out the mystery words. But something held her back.

The street outside was empty. The drains smelled bad. She thought, as she walked away, of her worthless poetry notebook, hidden somewhere among the chaos of the tiny apartment. She thought about Lulu's mocking smile; about the dreadful lie she'd told her husband and the way it had made his face light up. That heaviness was still there in her body. It ached in every bone, muscle and fibre.

She thought about the freckle at the base of Paolo Zachari's neck. The lemon scent of his skin. The heat in his

276

mouth. She tried to send the thoughts away but they kept on coming.

When she arrived home, she waited for Céline to be out of earshot and then went to the telephone.

The lilac notelet lay in tiny pieces in the waste-basket. Robert was having none of it. His wife was beautiful and sharp-tongued, and consequently she had rivals among her circle. Enemies. The letter had 'jealous woman' stamped all over it.

If only he could put it from his mind and concentrate on his work.

'Mr Shelby King, I—' Marie-Claire was poking her head around the door.

'Haven't I told you always to knock?'

The secretary looked crushed. 'But I did, sir.'

'Did you? Oh.' Robert fussed with his pen and tried to appear as though he had been concentrating hard on the paperwork in front of him.

'Three times.'

'Well, knock a little louder in future.'

'Yes, sir. Would you like some coffee?'

'No thank you. Marie-Claire?'

'Yes?' That look of hope. Hope of what? Perhaps he'd made a mistake, giving her those flowers.

'I'm sorry. For snapping at you, I mean. I'm a little distracted this morning. Would you open the window before you go, please? It's rather stuffy in here.'

'Yes, sir.' She was happy again. He gazed absently at her round bottom as she struggled with the window catch. How marvellous it was to be able to make a woman happy in an

277

instant with the simplest of gestures. A bunch of roses, a mumbled apology. If only it were always so simple . . .

The phone rang.

'Don't hang up, Mr Shelby King,' came the hated voice at the end of the line. 'Not until you've heard what I have to tell you.'

# 31

ROBERT MADE HIM WAIT UNTIL MARIE-CLAIRE HAD LEFT the room. 'Felperstone, I thought I'd made myself abundantly clear.'

'Indeed, sir. But I consider it my duty to inform you of a situation requiring your urgent attention. Your wife is at a hotel, right now, with her lover.'

'I knew you were a slimeball, but I didn't think you'd resort to flagrant invention.'

'This is no invention. I only wish it was.'

Robert took out his handkerchief and mopped the sweat from his forehead and neck.

'Sir, my associate, Monsieur Cannes, called me just moments ago. He saw them go in. And they haven't come out.'

'Mr Felperstone, this is – at the very least – a mistake.'

'There can be no mistake, sir. I'd be prepared to stake my fee on it.'

'My wife is at home!'

A scratching sound on the line, like a mouse behind a

wainscot. He must be at the end of his snuff, scraping out the last vestiges of powder from his little box. 'Are you quite sure, sir? You had better be absolutely certain, don't you think?'

'Genevieve is resting in bed.' Robert's mouth was so dry he could hardly speak. 'My wife is pregnant.'

'Congratulations, sir. Why don't you give her a little tinkle on the telephone? Tell her how much you love her, or whatever else you happily married types like saying to each other. That way you can show me just how wrong I am.'

They were the only two customers in the grand, heavily gilded and rose-damask-covered hotel bar, at a round, alabaster-topped corner table with a solid gold ashtray, beside a statue of a horse with a fish's tail atop a grey stone plinth.

'I nearly didn't come today,' said Genevieve.

'Why?' Zachari added a spoonful of sugar to his coffee and stirred it with a delicate silver teaspoon. 'I thought we understood each other.'

'So did I.'

Zachari added two more sugars.

'I came to the shop last night. Violet de Frémont's car was outside.'

'I didn't ask her to come.' He was still stirring the coffee. 'She just turned up.'

Genevieve took a breath to steady herself. 'Did you sleep with her last night?'

'No.' Finally he set down the spoon. 'She came to the shop. We talked. That's all. She went away again.'

'I want to believe you. I really do. But I'm starting to think that nothing you say is true. You told me nobody had ever been in your workroom, but—'

'No.' He shook his head. 'I wouldn't have said that. I don't generally let people in there. But of course one or two have been in.'

'Women?'

He frowned. 'I have a past. So do you.'

She put a cigarette in her long ebony holder and placed it between her lips. Zachari reached over to light it for her.

'Paolo, I've risked a lot by coming here to meet you. And perhaps I'm about to risk a great deal more.'

Yet another sugar was added to the coffee.

She looked nervously around, dragged on the cigarette. The barman was polishing glasses. A man sitting out in the foyer was watching them over his newspaper. 'It's this. You spend your life skulking about in a basement behind a big, crass sign, with that crazy woman guarding the door. Distancing yourself from the world. Hiding behind all those rumours – you probably start them off yourself! Sleeping with your clients. I don't know what's real and what's not. I want to trust you but I don't know if I can.'

'Trust me.' His eyes were black. Too black to be readable.

'If I sleep with you again, I'll be giving you such power over me. Do you understand?'

He reached for her hand. 'Genevieve.' Just her name, softly spoken, and her hand held in his. Nothing more.

After a moment, he tasted his coffee and grimaced.

'How many sugars do you usually take?' she asked.

'None. I hate sweet drinks. Let's get a room.'

The man with the newspaper was still watching as they got up from the table.

Robert stared out of the window of the Bentley at shops, newspaper stands, traffic, people walking. The smallest glimpses into worlds which must surely be far more simple than his. That girl with the short blond hair and the summer dress – the way she swung her bag as she strolled along: there was something so carefree about it. So child-like. It was impossible to imagine her as anything other than innocent, angelic even. Would Genevieve look like that, if you glimpsed her walking down the street?

And now here was Felperstone, lurking about near the Brasserie Lipp, just where he said he'd be, getting stared at by a couple of waiters who probably thought he was up to no good. Robert recognized the round, sloping shoulders, the curved back, the bad suit, long before he could see the professionally concerned face. He'd like to land a good punch square in the middle of that face. He'd like to break the long, delicate nose.

'Pull over,' he said to Pierre. 'This gentleman's getting in.'

'I grew up in Sicily.' He was lying on his back, gazing up at the canopy over the bed – russet velvet, heavily tasselled. She lay beside him, breathing in the scent of his skin. The sheets were a tangled ball on the floor.

'My father was a shoemaker. His customers were poor farmers. They would have one pair of heavy boots, and they would wear them to work in the fields, to dance in the village festivals, to woo their sweethearts, to go to church. The boots were made of stiff leather and they had metal caps on the toes and heels like horseshoes. When they were new, they would rub the feet raw. But then, over time, they became like a second skin. They had to last practically for ever, so my father's main work was repairs to boots he'd made years before. I used to help him. That's where I learned my trade.'

She looked at his throat as he spoke. At his chest. She loved the sound of his voice. Being here with him, this intimacy – it was intoxicating.

'My mother was the one with the real talent. She could draw beautifully, and she had such ideas . . . She should have been a designer. In another place, at another time, she would have been Coco Chanel. We would sit and dream dreams together, she and I. My father hated it. He thought she was filling my head with rubbish, giving me ideas above my station. But my mother – she had plans for me. She had a brother with . . . let us say, connections. We talked about how I could come to Paris and learn to design costumes for the theatre. This brother had been in Paris and he knew a theatre owner. He was willing to pay my fare and speak to this acquaintance for me. After that I would be on my own to make my fortune or lose it.'

She took one of his hands in hers. His fingers had tiny cuts on them – some scabbing over, some fresh. Little bits of dead skin. Hard calluses. She wanted to massage his fingers with rich D'Orsay cream to make them smooth and soft again. She wanted to put his fingers in her mouth one by one.

'My father wouldn't hear of it, any of it. I think he resented my uncle, the power he had. The sway. He hated my uncle's visits – the sharp suits he wore, the fancy patent-leather shoes – and what it all meant. He felt unmanned, I think. But my father was ill. We all knew it. We could see him wasting away into nothing. It's not a nice thing to wish your father dead, Genevieve.'

'I know.'

He hadn't been looking at her at all while he was speaking, but now he did. There was recognition in that look.

'I knew my life wouldn't really begin until his was over. He went on and on, like one of his pairs of boots. But then, one day, he was gone. And so I came to Paris. I was twenty-four, and so hungry for life, you can't imagine.'

'Can't I?'

Again he looked at her. And this time he smiled. A smile which utterly transformed his face, made it soft and golden, like butter.

'At first I did well at the theatre. I worked on other people's costumes, cutting and stitching and dyeing, and then they let me make some of my own designs. My costumes were good. But I ruined everything with the shoes. My career as a theatrical costumier was over almost before it began.'

'Your shoes were no good?'

'My shoes were *too* good. They distracted the audience from the action on stage. Sometimes my shoes were getting more review space than the shows. They asked me to tone them down, make them inconspicuous. And when I wouldn't, they fired me.'

'So, what then?'

'I knew what I wanted – a place to make shoes. A business of my own. I wrote to my uncle and he loaned me some money. I borrowed some more money from a couple of rich theatre people who had liked my shoes so much that I'd taken private commissions from them. And Olga helped me, of course.'

Olga – sitting behind that desk in the shop, with her dead person's expression . . .

'At first I shared space in a tiny workshop with three other designers. It was hard to see how I was ever going to establish myself and progress was slow, but gradually people began to talk about my shoes; the customers started dribbling in. Eventually I was able to get my own premises. That's it, really. Business got better and better and I had some commissions from one or two prominent society women . . .'

A black Lea Francis car slid across Genevieve's thoughts.

'My shoes became famous and I moved to the fashion quarter.' Zachari turned on to his side to face her. 'So now you know. No Calabrian wolves. No baby in a basket. No blood feud.'

'Paolo.'

'I don't tell these things to people, Genevieve.' He moved closer to her – brushed his lips against her face. 'You and Olga – you're the only people who know my story. That's the truth.'

'There's something I want to tell you too. Something I've never told my husband.'

'Is that why you want to tell me? Because you've never told him?'

For answer she kissed the freckle at the base of his neck. And then she began to tell him about the day of the school photographs and what followed.

\*

The Bentley had been parked outside the hotel for almost twenty minutes now. Robert was sitting with his face in his hands.

'Robert?' came Felperstone's calm, even voice. 'May I call you Robert?'

'You may not.'

'In situations such as this, it's sometimes the best policy to take the bull by the horns, so to speak.'

'She's not in there. I can't believe it.'

'Well, where is she then? And why did you agree to come here?'

'Sir,' called Pierre, from the front. 'We're going to have to move the car.'

'Do you get a kick out of this?' Robert had his fists pressed hard into his eyes now. 'You must have seen so many poor saps catching their wives *en flagrante*! Ever thought of selling tickets?'

'Robert, I do think . . .' the detective began.

'Sir,' said Pierre. 'There's a porter coming over.'

'All right!' Robert uncovered his eyes. 'All right. We're going in. Pierre, please park the car as near by as possible, and wait for us. I'm afraid I don't know how long we'll be.'

## 32

GENEVIEVE SAMUEL WATCHED, THROUGH HER BEDROOM window, the frost on the grass, the crocuses blooming and dying, then the daffodils, and then the roses coming into flower in her mother's rose garden. She read Henry James, D. H. Lawrence, Emile Zola (her parents, who had no idea about literature, thought it would help improve her French). And *Vogue* of course. She scribbled furiously and candidly in her diary and then burned it in her grate, one night, out of fear of discovery. She longed for communications from the outside world, but the only person she could think of writing to was Irene Nicholas, and the prospect of receiving detailed accounts of her school life and the latest romances filled her with despond.

She thought about Mr Giles, wondering if he'd taken up with another girl too young and naïve to know better. Then she chased him from her mind – unable to bear, any more, the thought of his hands on her body, his mouth finding hers. It made her sick to think of how he'd used her. It made her hate herself.

She saw nobody. The servants were told to bring her food up on a tray, knock on the door and then leave it outside for her to take in. Her room was tidied and her bed made each morning while she was in her bath. A story was put about that Genevieve was 'ill' – non-specifically but seriously. Many of the household, family friends and gossipy locals assumed it was tuberculosis. She'd always been prone to coughs. Others thought it might be a 'nervous disorder'.

'Cheer up.' Dr Peters made a note of her blood pressure, and began putting his instruments away in his black bag. 'Only a few more months to go.'

'You really have no idea, do you?' said Genevieve, propped up on her pillows.

Dr Peters sighed. 'You're an extremely lucky girl.'

'Lucky?' She spread her hands over her bump. 'That's rich. And as for the poor little thing growing in here—'

The doctor sat down on the edge of the bed, took one of Genevieve's hands and gave it a squeeze. 'We've been over this time and again. Who's going to want to marry you with another man's baby in tow?'

'I don't care about that.' She pulled her hand away, unable to tolerate his limp, damp grip.

'They're a very nice couple,' said Dr Peters. 'Perhaps it would help if you met them. I could bring them here next time I come to see you, and—'

'No!'

The doctor shrugged. 'As you wish.'

'I dream about dying,' said Genevieve. 'I think it's the only way I'll ever get out of here.'

288

'Don't be silly.' He snapped his bag shut. 'Get plenty of rest. Your blood pressure is a little high.'

'It's mine, Dr Peters.'

'Eh?' He got to his feet.

'The baby. I won't give it away.'

He was putting his coat on now. 'There'll be other babies, Genevieve.'

Her mother came to sit with her for an hour or two each day, chatting inanely about people from the village whom Genevieve didn't know. She tried, for a while, to remember the names so that the dull stories would at least make sense, and then gave up – just let Mummy's voice wash over her like muddy, tepid water. She watched her mother – that hand forever clawing at the throat, the feet twitching and tapping, the eyes bulbous, restless and empty.

I will do whatever is necessary to ensure my life doesn't turn out like hers, she told herself. And then realized that she already had.

Her father never came.

The bump grew enormous. She ached under her ribs and in the small of her back. Her throat burned with bile. The baby somersaulted, padded, prodded, thumped, and then started pressing on nerves, sending sharp pains shooting all through her like electricity, making her wince and catch her breath. The frenzied activity inside her body compensated in part for her total lack of activity in the outside world. She loved every soft patter from within, every kick, every twinge. She longed to hold her child, to feed it, watch it sleep, hear it cry. Keep it safe. She had never before experienced a love like this. Physical, passionate, all-consuming. She would give up everything for this tiny being if she had to. She would lay down her life for her baby without a moment's hesitation.

In spite of all the vehemence and teeth-gnashing, it didn't occur to Genevieve to try to run away. All of her dreams of keeping the baby relied on the co-operation of her father. Life without Daddy's financial support was inconceivable. And so she had to believe she could find a way of changing his mind about what should happen when her child was born.

Dr Peters came each week. He was a key figure in the whole baby-snatching conspiracy, but she sensed moments of sympathy from him. Chinks of light. Each time she saw him she wept and raged in front of him, threatening to throw herself from the window, appealing to him as a doctor, a God-fearer and a father. How could it be right and humane, she implored him, to shut a pregnant woman in a room for six months and then steal her baby?

'You agreed to this plan,' the doctor insisted. 'I was there in the room when you said it was what you wanted.'

'I didn't know what I was agreeing to. I was frightened.'

'You're not being rational.'

'No, I'm not.'

The best she could get from Dr Peters (secure in her father's pay) was a promise to speak to Daddy about letting her walk in the gardens when the servants weren't around. Permission was granted, and for a few short weeks she paced the grounds, taking huge lungfuls of fresh air, sighing her frustration into the breeze – before her ankles started swelling and her blood pressure rising, at which time complete bed rest was prescribed, and the outside world shrank back to the view through her window; the broken, labyrinthine trivia related by her mother; the dewy eyes of the family doctor.

Two weeks early, Genevieve's waters began slowly to seep. Every now and again she felt a gentle twist in her womb which made her want to stop whatever she was doing and breathe deeply. She knew it had started, but tried to pretend to herself that nothing was happening. As long as the baby stayed inside, it remained hers.

After a few hours the twists became more of a wringing-out, lasting for around a minute, during which she panted shallow little breaths. It was late in the evening. Her mother would have gone to bed by now. Her father would be sitting in the drawing room in his dressing gown, reading. In times past she would have sat on the other side of the fire and they would occasionally have looked up at each other and smiled. Not now.

She dragged herself out of her room, down the corridor and across the landing, gripping the banisters for support as a contraction, the strongest so far, wrenched at her insides – and then descended the stairs as quickly as she could, before the next could come. She could see the light under the drawing-room door. She yanked it open.

She was already in the middle of the Turkish rug, breathless, her hair and face drenched with sweat, when he looked up over his half-moon spectacles.

'Jenny, what are you thinking of, coming down here? Has anyone seen you? Look at the state of you.'

'You won't take my baby!'

He rose from his chair but didn't move towards her. 'Do you have a fever? You should be in bed.'

'I will not give my baby away.' She shrieked with panic as a giant contraction swept over her like a wave and sent her floundering.

Lord Ticksted scrambled for the telephone. 'Dr Peters, please. Southminster 223.' Turning to Genevieve: 'Sit down, for goodness' sake. And try to be quiet.' Back to the telephone – 'Nigel, I need you to come at once. She's . . . yes.'

'Daddy.'

He covered the receiver. 'Go back to bed and I'll fetch your mother. Why on earth did you come to me?'

She was near exhaustion. A woman she didn't know was mopping her head with a cloth which smelled of ammonia. They kept trying to get her to lie down. But lying down made it worse. It made her feel she would go under the waves instead of staying on top of them. She wanted to lean forward and grip the bedposts but they just kept on coaxing her back down, the woman with the stinking cloth and Dr Peters with his pathetic eyes. Sometimes she saw the door opening and her mother hovering there, knitting her hands together. But she never came right into the room. She kept disappearing and reappearing again like an apparition.

'Drink some water,' said the doctor. But when Genevieve tried to take hold of the glass, another contraction reared up and she threw it across the room in her haste to grab the bedposts.

'Charming,' she heard the woman mutter.

'Get out, bitch! I don't want you here!'

'Delightful,' said the woman, louder.

They were trying to prise her off the bedposts again as a

whole bunch of fireworks crackled through her and she grasped hard on to a hand.

There was a yelp that wasn't hers, and someone slapped her in the face – slapped her again and again until the fireworks had gone and she let go and fell back against the pillows.

'That little madam has broken my fingers!'

She watched the woman holding out one of her hands to the doctor, who was examining it. The hand was becoming strangely elongated – stretching out as though it were made of molten toffee.

'Dr Peters.' She tried to shout but her voice wasn't working properly. The doctor was still busy with the woman's hand. His head grew and shrank, pulsing and becoming liquid. The walls came towards her. Something gushed between her legs.

'Help me.'

Her eyes opened and she saw clouds through the window. She tried to lift her head off the pillows but it was too heavy. Her eyelids were leaden and she struggled to keep them open. She could hear her mother buzzing ceaselessly, like a large fly.

'So I said to Audrey, "Why ever not?" And she said, "Dorothea," she said, "I can't. Just can't." And there was no—'

The scene faded.

Now her father was in the chair beside the bed, reading *The Times*. No, that couldn't be right, could it? She closed her eyes and opened them again. He was still there, his lips moving slightly as he read.

'Daddy?'

He laid the paper down. 'Genevieve. How are you?'

She moved her arms with an effort, reaching under the sheets to run her hands over her stomach. It felt like a partially deflated balloon. Inside her, all was still.

'Where's my baby?'

Her father stood up and headed over to the door, calling out, 'Dorothea? She's awake.'

She heard her mother bustling starchily up the stairs. Lord Ticksted sat down again, folding his hands in front of him, frowning.

'So you've decided to join us again.' He crossed one leg over the other. He was wearing beige slippers. Genevieve hated them.

'I want to see my baby.'

'Your blood pressure went through the roof, girl! You're damned lucky you're still here.'

'I don't . . . remember . . .'

'That'll be the morphine.'

'Daddy . . .'

He made an odd whistling sound and then sucked his cheeks in. It was something he did at difficult moments.

'It's dead, Genevieve. Probably for the best, all things considered.'

Her mother wanted to hug her, now. But it was too late for all that.

She was told the baby was a girl. When she asked to see it, they said it had already been buried. Already! The grave was unmarked because of the need for secrecy. She named

294

the baby Josephine but told nobody. She cut the name into the trunk of an oak in the graveyard.

Her education was completed at home by a governess. Her headmistress would never have allowed her back after what had happened, and it was felt that it would not be in her best interests to go elsewhere. They wanted her where they could keep an eye on her.

The stories about tuberculosis and nervous disorders persisted. Genevieve went out and about in the village now, but quietly and rarely. Mostly she stayed within the grounds. Everyone – her parents included – treated her as though she was an invalid: questioning the wisdom of long walks or cycle rides, urging her to cover her legs with blankets when she sat out of doors, speaking in hushed voices of her 'delicate health'. They had come to believe their own cover story. She almost believed it herself.

She spent her days reading books and magazines and writing poetry. Literature stood in for a life. Increasingly she read about Paris and the Bohemian scene in Montparnasse. The French didn't care for strait-laced English morality. You could be whoever you wanted to be in Paris.

She began collecting shoes, ordered from catalogues and delivered from Harrods. Shoes were beautiful, sensual objects. They provoked, subtly – drawing attention to the delicate arch, the slender ankle, and prompting a glimpse further up the leg. Shoes connected a person to their world – you walked in them, you danced in them. Without your shoes, you could barely step out of the house. The marks on their soles were the outward signs of a lived life.

Genevieve's shoes were unworn.

At the dinner table, she watched her mother nibbling tiny mouthfuls, her father munching methodically. She hated the movements of their respective jawbones. The way her father would clear his throat before speaking loudly about something he thought would make him sound knowledgeable. The way her mother would fiddle ceaselessly with her napkin or her hair or the stitching on her sleeve, murmuring occasionally to show that she was listening even though she wasn't. Topping up her glass when she thought nobody was looking. She hated her father for his pointless bluster and for the way he let himself believe anyone was paying attention to him. She hated them both for what they'd done to her, and for what they'd been doing to each other for as long as she could remember. She ate her food in silence, looking down at her wrists and hands – pale and brittle.

So many dinners, so much hate. Years of it. Until the day when Lord Ticksted brought home a young American he'd met at his club, and Genevieve saw her chance.

## 33

ROBERT MADE A BOGUS ENQUIRY ABOUT VACANCIES AND prices to distract the receptionist while Felperstone snuck a look at the occupancy list to get the room number.

'They've used a false name,' said Felperstone as they crossed the polished floor through the oval atrium. The hotel's twenty bedrooms were arranged around this open oval, on six floors. You could stand here, where Robert now stood, and look all the way up those six levels to the glass roof at the top and through it to the sky above.

Robert stopped. 'Then how do you know it's them?'

'Easy.' Felperstone looked so pleased with himself. 'The list was clearly written in advance by last night's receptionist. There was just one entry in another hand, in ink of a subtly different blue – presumably made by this morning's receptionist when they arrived without a reservation. And there's a note that the room's been paid for up front in cash. It has to be them.' He was absolutely in his element. Standing taller now, and with a hungry look about him like a wild beast about to spring for the kill.

Robert, on the other hand, was weak-kneed and sick to his stomach as they entered the elevator. Felperstone asked for the third floor and then firmly turned his back, leaving Robert fumbling in his pocket for a tip and wishing he was anywhere but here.

Zachari was playing with a few strands of Genevieve's hair, running them across his hand, tightening them so they became a single thread, combing his fingers through.

'I never saw her. They said they'd buried her in an unmarked grave. I didn't even see a mound of earth. It eats away at me, wondering what really happened.'

'You think she's still alive?'

'Maybe. They might have told me she was dead so that I wouldn't stop them giving her away.'

'You could try to find her.' He was still playing with the hair.

'How?'

'You could ask your father.'

'He'd never tell me the truth.'

He kissed her bare shoulder. 'The doctor, then.'

'I won't get anything out of him. He's been paid well.'

'Your father's not the only one with money.'

'No.'

He let go her hair. 'It doesn't seem like you, to be afraid to go after the truth.'

'But I *am* afraid. Afraid of finding out for sure that she's dead. As long as I don't know for certain, there's a chance that she's alive.' She gazed past him, out the window at the clear sky. 'There's something else. Maybe she didn't die the way they told me.'

His eyes narrowed. 'You think they could have done that?'

'I don't know. It tortures me.'

A *thunk* from outside made them both jump. It seemed someone had banged suddenly on the window, but looking up, they saw a stream of bird shit had just landed on the glass.

'You hate me now.' She pulled her knees up to her chest and lay in a ball. 'I should never have told you.'

But his hand was on the back of her neck, stroking. 'I don't hate you. You were a young girl having an adventure, and it ruined your life.'

Slowly she uncurled. 'What are we going to do, Paolo?'

'Us? I think we should meet as often as we can. Make love as often as we can.'

'And what then? What will happen to us?'

'I don't know.' He put his mouth to her palm. 'We can't ever know, can we?'

'I told you my secret,' said Genevieve in a whisper. 'I wanted to draw you deep into my world. I wanted to lay myself open to you, and now I've done it. I've made myself utterly vulnerable.'

'You want me to do something in return?'

She thought about the rows of lasts in his workroom. 'I want you to give up the other women. I want you all to myself.'

He laughed. 'But what about you? What about your husband?'

'I'll make sure he never finds out.'

He raised his eyebrows. 'So I have to promise not to see other women but you can continue sleeping with your husband?'

'Absolutely not. I'm ending that side of my marriage. I have no intention of ever sleeping with him again.'

Sounds from the corridor outside. Muffled voices.

And now another bang – this time on the door.

Robert was standing before the door of Room 32, trying not to imagine the scene taking place on the other side of it. Shaking all over.

'Go on,' urged Felperstone.

'I can't.'

'For God's sake.' The detective grabbed his shoulder. 'Be a man. Go in there and give the fellow what-for.'

'Are you married, Mr Felperstone?'

Felperstone gave a snort. 'I've seen too much, my friend. I could never trust a woman.'

Robert's hand hovered above the doorknob. 'Then you can't possibly understand what I'm going through.' And he clenched his fist and thumped once on the door.

'There's someone out there,' said Genevieve. 'What do you think they want?'

'Ignore them. They must have the wrong room.'

'Will you do it, Paolo? Will you give up the other women?'

'Enough talking. Save it for later.' And he took her by the shoulders and pressed her back against the pillows.

'What did you go and do that for?' Felperstone was beside himself. 'You've given them a warning. They'll cover up.'

Robert's fists were still clenched. 'I *want* them to cover up.' And he banged again.

'They're not going away,' said Genevieve, when the second thump came. But he was on top of her now. He was pinning her down and she didn't want him to stop.

The door handle rattled.

'Is it locked?' she whispered.

'I can't remember. I don't care.'

'It's locked.' Robert couldn't help feeling relieved. Maybe it was all a big mistake and there was nobody in the room after all.

'Stand away, sir.' Felperstone shoved him aside.

'What are you going to do?'

'You have to kick it hard, just below the knob.' Felperstone was taking a couple of steps back, limbering up . . . 'People barge at doors with their shoulders, but you just end up bruised and the door's still shut.'

'Don't,' said Robert, quietly.

The detective kicked, swiftly and accurately.

The door flew open.

## 34

THEY LAY SIDE BY SIDE ON THE BED, FULLY CLOTHED. THE tiny woman had a bullet hole in her left temple. The man had an identical hole in his right temple. A .25-calibre Belgian pistol lay on the floor, where it must have dropped. They were holding hands and their feet were bare. A tattooed skull was clearly visible on the man's forearm. The woman had an identical tattoo on the sole of her left foot. Their shoes were placed neatly on the floor in front of the bed.

Hart Crane would later write an elegy to Guy Monteray called 'The Cloud Juggler'. It was his last published work before his own suicide.

E. E. Cummings would write the epitaph:

> 2 boston
> Dolls; found
> with
> Holes in each other
>
> 's lullaby.

'Thank God.' Robert couldn't help himself. In spite of this carnage, he was relieved. Genevieve wasn't here. He reached to loosen his collar.

Felperstone was over by the broken door, wiping the handle clean with a large, white handkerchief, but then, seeing Robert about to sit down on a chair, he came rushing forward, shouting, 'Don't touch anything!'

Robert swallowed heavily. 'I'd better get down to reception and have someone call the police.'

'No!' The detective wiped sweat from his brow and thrust the handkerchief back in his pocket.

'So what do you suggest we do?'

'We get out of here. Fast.'

Robert looked down at the bodies. There was very little blood. In spite of the obvious violence of their deaths, the couple looked peaceful. More peaceful – or at least, more real, more *human* – than his father had looked in his coffin, once the funeral directors had prettied him up.

'Sir.' Felperstone grabbed him by the arm. 'You don't want to be dragged into a mess like this. A man of your standing.'

'These poor people,' said Robert.

'I'll kill that bloody Cannes,' said Felperstone.

The bodies of Guy Monteray and Elizabeth Leicester (known as Whisper) were officially discovered just before noon by a fourteen-year-old chambermaid, who'd never seen a dead body before. Her shriek reverberated around the glass-topped oval atrium and out on to the Rue des Beaux Arts, where people stopped and stared up at the smart stone façade of the Hôtel d'Alsace, and at the

303

sculpted ram's head above the main entrance, and then shrugged and carried on their way.

The shriek was almost – but not quite – loud enough to reach the Hôtel Lutétia on the nearby Boulevard Raspail, where Genevieve Shelby King and Paolo Zachari were making love for the second time that morning behind a locked door.

# VII

## Heel

## 35

*Dear Sir,*

*Don't you think your wife has spent more than enough time at the shoe shop lately?*

*A Well-Wisher*

'Let's go away for a couple of weeks.' Robert set Genevieve's breakfast tray down on her bedside table and pulled up a chair. 'We could motor down to St Tropez.'

'Must we?' Genevieve adjusted her nightdress and did her best to look wan.

'The city's stifling, darling. It can't be good for the baby. Who'd ever have thought such a damp, grey place could get so damned hot in August?'

'I can't bear the thought of the journey.'

'Well, how about Deauville, then? You could manage that little trip, couldn't you? I'm sure the sea air would do you the power of good.' He picked up his newspaper and started rustling his way through it.

'If only you knew how terribly sick I'm feeling.' She

leaned back against her pillows and closed her eyes. 'I just want the comforts of home. Can you understand that?'

'Of course, my love.'

'And please take that tray away. Even the smell of bacon is enough to make me heave.' In fact it smelled delicious. She could cheerfully devour it in one mouthful but this didn't exactly accord with the story she was spinning.

'Won't you have even a little?' Reluctantly he got up and picked up the tray. 'You really must eat.'

'I'll have something later. When my stomach settles down a bit.'

He was over by the door with the tray. 'Perhaps I should ask the doctor to look in on you.'

'*No!*'

It came out much too loudly. He was staring at her, perplexed.

'That won't be necessary, thank you, darling. The sickness is normal at this stage.'

When Robert returned with his coffee, Genevieve had taken up his newspaper.

'Goodness!'

'What is it, honey?'

'He's really done it!'

'Who's done what?' But as he took his seat again, he knew exactly what she was talking about. He'd already seen the story himself.

'Guy Monteray and Whisper – it says here that they killed themselves at the Hôtel d'Alsace two days ago! Oh gosh, that's where Oscar Wilde died. He was going on and on about Oscar Wilde at that party.'

'So you know him, then? The dead guy?'

'Well, yes, a little.' She was still scanning the paper. 'He's a friend of Lulu's and a contributor to the magazine. He once said he had a death pact – ah yes, see here? He had a tattoo of a skull. And *she* had one too, it seems.'

Please let her stop talking about those tattoos . . . He couldn't look at her. Just couldn't.

'He always made me nervous. There was something about him . . . People found it amusing. You know – eccentric poet, and all that. They thought he said these things for the drama of it. To make himself seem more interesting or funny or something. But I was afraid of him. He had a skeleton in a raincoat hanging above his staircase. It had a contraceptive in its mouth. Does that sound normal to you, Robert? . . . Robert?'

'I'm sorry. I have to be off to work. Do please think some more about us going away. I understand that it's difficult for you, but . . .'

'Oh my!' She was clutching at her throat. 'They must have gone straight from the police station to the hotel and done it! Really, I'm surprised it was *such* a momentous thing for him – hitting the owner of La Rotonde, I mean. Of all the things that would push a person over the edge, it seems rather trivial. I wonder – did they both commit suicide? Or did one murder the other and then turn the gun around? How does a death pact work?'

'Only . . . Genevieve . . . I've been under quite a bit of strain lately, and I really feel . . .'

'Strain?' She put down the paper. There was an odd look on her face. He had the sense that he wasn't the only one of them who was hiding something. But that was how he'd

309

got himself into this mess, wasn't it? Groundless suspicions about his wife. He closed his eyes, but the bodies were there, lying neatly, each with a hole in its head.

'What's the matter?' she said.

'Nothing in particular.'

'Well, do buck up then, there's a good chap. Oh, I know what it is!'

He gulped. And twitched.

'It's to do with that letter, isn't it?' she said.

'What letter?'

'The postman brought it half an hour ago. I saw it on the hall table. The one in the lilac envelope.' A mischievous smile had crept across her face. 'It was from a woman, wasn't it? What woman is writing to you, Robert?'

What could he say to that? He could hardly expound his latest theory: that it was Felperstone – bitter and desperate to get back on the job.

'Do you have a secret admirer, darling? Come on, you can tell me. I shan't be all mad and jealous, I promise.'

'It was from my sister,' said Robert.

'Your sister?' She frowned. 'But it was posted in Paris, surely?'

'It was damaged in transit. Some kind person put it in a new envelope and reposted it.' How ridiculous this sounded, even to him. He had to steer the conversation away from the damned letter. 'Genevieve, remember what you were saying just now about the comforts of home? I'm so homesick, I can't begin to tell you. I want this baby to be born in Boston, in the heart of my family.'

He'd said it to change the subject, but as he spoke the words, he knew he'd never been more in earnest.

'Well,' she said, and picked up the newspaper again. 'Well . . . Aren't you in a hurry to get off to work?'

'Genevieve?'

'Look at the time, Robert!'

Paolo Zachari was busy at work on a pair of shoes for Sissi de Marco Thessaly, a long-standing client. She was an Italian patron of the arts and one-time society beauty with a rich American husband, who bought all her shoes from him and had done ever since he'd first started. This latest pair were almost finished. He was painting a design on the silk uppers with a steady hand and a very fine brush: a pattern resembling the wings of a Red Admiral butterfly. She liked butterflies. She and the husband would go out together with big nets, catching them. It was about the only thing they still did together after thirty years of marriage. The rare breeds would be impaled on pins in glass cases and labelled in Sissi's tiny italic handwriting. Zachari had stopped sleeping with Sissi de Marco Thessaly about three years ago. He'd kept on long after his interest had faded, principally because he liked her and didn't want to offend her. Theirs was a leisurely, friendly affair. She had still been very beautiful when he first met her, though she claimed she was already well past her prime.

He had enjoyed sleeping with Sissi. He laughed more with her than he'd ever laughed, and fucked more than he'd ever fucked. She dribbled champagne into his mouth and buried his face in her luxuriant golden hair. She inspired him to make pair after pair of shoes for her tiny, white feet. It was due to Sissi that he'd landed the

Marchesa Casati as a client. And Mistinguett, and Coco Chanel. And the Countess de Frémont.

Sissi had been the one to end the sexual side of their relationship, one day in bed, with a light slap on the buttocks and a friendly 'I think we'd better call it a day, don't you, sweetie? Undressing in the dark can be sexy but it's becoming something of a necessity for me.'

He'd begun sleeping with Violet de Frémont on almost the very day he stopped sleeping with Sissi. It was almost as though the older woman had passed him on to the younger. Secretly, he rather liked that idea. And then there were the others: Madeleine Duffrey, with the highest insteps he'd ever seen; Ana Markova, the ballerina (feet in a terrible mess, of course, but what a joy to watch her walk); the Princess Meurier Bernard, with her long toes (she used them like fingers – could even hold a pencil between them and write). He didn't sleep with all his clients – not quite. But he did seem to make better shoes for those who were his lovers. It was as if the sex allowed him to divine each woman's essence. Somehow he was able to absorb their physical secrets, translating them and shaping them as shoes.

Choosing his clients – and indeed, his lovers – became something of a hobby for Zachari. He'd go to the grandest parties (Sissi or Violet could always get him an invitation) and stand quietly at the side of the room, watching the women walking about and dancing. It wasn't enough for them to be rich or beautiful. Rather like Sissi and her husband out in the meadows with their butterfly nets, he'd be waiting to spot the rare breeds. He had no fear of rebuffing the commonplace, however wealthy and influential they might be. He'd look for someone with music in her feet.

His life was so easy. They came and went, the fine ladies, and they smiled as they left. He'd had a good fifteen years of pure effortless pleasure, with nothing to bother him or challenge him unduly. Until Genevieve Shelby King mistook him for a footman at Violet's party and bludgeoned her way through his shop door and into his life.

A banging from above made Zachari jump. Somehow – the result of long years of practice, no doubt – he kept his hands steady. The perfect golden brush-stroke was concluded without even the slightest smear. Quite a relief – one tiny mistake would be enough for him to throw out the shoes and return to the drawing board. This was one of the reasons why his shoes were the best, the most expensive, of any in the world.

The banging came again. It was the door knocker. But he wasn't expecting anyone. And anyway, where was Olga? Why hadn't she answered it?

He would ignore it. They would go away eventually, whoever they were. He looked down at the book on the table – the full-colour illustration of the Red Admiral butterfly – and back at the shoe in his hand. There was something not quite right about his design, but what was it? He set the shoe down and bent to peer at it from the side. Why could he not concentrate properly this morning? His focus – usually crystal-clear – was fuzzy. Damn Genevieve! It was she who'd done this to him. Genevieve with her demands and her secrets. Genevieve with her wild eyes and her rage and those most surprising moments of softest vulnerability.

He should phone her. Straight away. Nip this thing in the bud. Tell her that he would not be dictated to by any woman. Tell her he liked his affairs to be casual and amusing, and this was neither. Tell her he'd never be making her that second pair of shoes. Yes, he'd get on the phone and tell her, and it would all be over between them.

Trouble was she'd got to him. Wriggled inside his head, inside his ribcage. That was why he hadn't slept with any other woman since that first evening with her (not that he would tell her that. She had quite enough of a hold on him already). He wished he could feel less for her. Life was becoming messy and complicated. That was why he had to end it. Go back to his old ways.

The shoes were ready, of course. They were safe in his locked cupboard, waiting for her. Probably the most amazing pair he'd ever made. Shame they would never see the light of day.

Setting down his brush, he started up the stairs. But as he reached the telephone, the banging came again. Someone was practically ripping the knocker off. Angered, he started for the door, but then paused, his hand outstretched. What if it was Genevieve? What if she'd come to make more demands?

No, it wouldn't be her. He was being silly. It was surely Olga, having forgotten her key. It had to be. Nobody else would dare to knock so insolently and insistently.

'Paolo. And about time too.' Violet de Frémont shoved right past him into the shop, almost knocking him off his feet.

'Violet! What a surprise. I—'

She whipped round, scowling. 'It *shouldn't* be a surprise.

I'm right there in the book.' She pointed a sharp talon at the open diary.

Zachari leaned over and peered at the day's page. 'Actually, you're not.'

The countess swiped the book. 'Well, I certainly should be. I spoke to Olga last week. My, but it's hot.' She took a couple of pins out of her hair and ran her hands through it, freeing its curls, and then undid the top two buttons of her white blouse. 'Where is Olga, anyway?'

'I'm sorry, but there seems to have been a mistake. I'm busy this morning.'

'Not according to your diary.' Violet stooped to unlace her sporty spectators.

'I'm working on some shoes.'

'You can do that later. You're not exactly wall-to-wall clients today, are you?' She was wandering around the shop in her bare feet, picking up the latest *La Vie Parisienne* and flicking idly through it.

Zachari's lips tightened. 'I said, I'm working this morning.'

She rolled her eyes. 'Come on, Paolo, don't be a spoilsport.' And now she wandered barefoot across to the stairs. 'In some ways, it's rather handy that Olga's not here, don't you think?'

'I'm sorry, but it's quite impossible for me today. Let's put another appointment in the diary.' He took up the book and started looking for a suitable slot.

Violet stopped, her smile gone. 'Really, this isn't on. I cancelled my tennis lesson to come to see you.'

'I've said I'm sorry.' An image flashed through his head of Violet holding a tennis racquet, and of her grip being corrected by a tanned, burly man who stood very close to her.

'You can do better than sorry.' Her best flirtatious smile. A toss of the head.

And quite suddenly, watching the Countess de Frémont turn and begin to climb the stairs to his apartment, her hand trailing suggestively down the banister, Paolo Zachari realized that he was not the butterfly catcher. Never had been. He was the butterfly.

Genevieve was too restless to remain in the apartment for long after Robert left. Her insides were tangled up, and she didn't know how to untangle them. Lingering in front of a display of Cubist origami in a window of the Galeries Lafayette, she caught sight of her reflection. An enormous head on a tiny body, like something out of a fairground freak show. It was all down to distortions in the glass, of course, but at this moment Genevieve felt the reflection to be true. Her head might really be bulbous and swollen. Perhaps it would burst.

Outside Rumpelmayer's, she gazed wistfully at the cakes under the long glass counter. Cakes in all colours of the rainbow. Two fashionable girls (clothes and shoes from the Atelier Martine) were gossiping and laughing over their coffees and desserts at a table near the window. Genevieve could almost be watching herself. She'd be spilling out her troubles to her friend, waiting for that raised eyebrow, the half-smile. *Don't worry, chérie. Stick with Lulu and everything will be all right.* They'd make a special toast in cake to whichever lover Lulu had just dumped. Lulu would tip brandy into their coffees and relate her latest wild escapade, and they'd giggle the morning away – and somehow, everything *would* turn out all right.

Down by the river, she watched the men fishing. They sat close together in a long line on the bank, but each was essentially alone.

*You have only two options.* The voice in her head was still Lulu's. One: get yourself pregnant and go back to Boston with Robert. Two: fake a miscarriage and persuade him to stay in Paris. Tend to your marriage with the diligence your mother used in caring for her rose garden, but continue the affair with Paolo – *quietly*. Gazing out over the water, Genevieve tasted those options on her tongue, rolling them around her mouth like wine. The first was totally unpalatable. The second was all wrong too – quite off.

On the Ile St-Louis, soft voices were murmuring from within a walled courtyard. A cat basked in the sunshine. An attractive young man lounged on a first-floor window-seat, reading. As she looked up, he smiled and waved, as though he knew her. As though they were old friends. She raised a hand to wave back, without quite knowing why. It was only after she'd already left the island that she realized she did know the boy a little. He was a barman from the Ritz.

Thinking about the Ritz made Genevieve nostalgic for the early days of her marriage. The fledgling relationship had seemed good raw material. She'd believed, then, that she could shape something interesting from it. She would have to work hard to convince herself that this could still be true.

Crossing to the Ile de la Cité, she entered Notre Dame by the south transept, beneath the carving of the life and martyrdom of St Stephen. Saul, a coldly isolated figure, stands and watches Stephen being stoned.

Notre Dame had always frightened Genevieve. So dark and cavernous. It was a haunted place. But there was nowhere better to be quiet and still. To sit so long that you'd lose all sense of time and wouldn't even know if it was day or night outside. To try to isolate one voice from the cacophony inside yourself.

Today, though, Genevieve would not have time for contemplation. Shortly after she'd sat down, she found herself watching two women in black.

They made their way slowly up the aisle, their arms linked. They seemed to be leaning on each other. Certainly you had the sense that each could not have remained upright without the support of the other, though they weren't old and didn't appear frail. One wore a hat with a wide brim which obscured her eyes, and the other had a scarf wrapped around her head. Something weighed them down. A shared sadness. They stopped near Genevieve to light a candle. The woman with the hat dropped a coin in the box while her companion took up the candle, lit it and placed it with the others. Then she lifted her headscarf and laid it about her shoulders, and Genevieve suddenly realized who they were.

'Augusta!' The name echoed all about them, loud and shrill through the hubbub of prayer and tourist-babble.

The women turned, startled, showing pale faces, red eyes. Somewhere far off, a child was crying.

'What's wrong?' But she felt foolish as soon as she'd said it. 'Oh, no. Norman . . .'

'Stupid man.' Augusta rubbed at her eyes. 'He kept saying he had five years to live. He said it so often that we believed him.'

'Come and sit down,' said Genevieve. But the women remained standing.

'We didn't realize how ill he was,' Augusta continued. 'It's ridiculous. Any stranger could have seen in an instant that he was dying. You only had to look at him. But we were used to it, you see. The coughing. Even the haemorrhages. He always bounced back.' She buried her face in her friend's shoulder.

'It happened yesterday,' said Marianne. 'He'd just finished reading *The Great Gatsby*. He was absolutely raving about it. Kept saying Scott was a genius – that he'd turn out to be the biggest star of the century if he could only keep his wife and his drinking under control. He was so high.'

'Bob came over,' said Augusta. 'Bob McAlmon, I mean. They were laughing together. And then all of a sudden Norman just folded up like an umbrella and I tried to catch him as he fell, and there was blood everywhere. I . . .' She dabbed at her face with a handkerchief. 'I'm sorry, I have to get out of here.' And she broke off and walked quickly away, heading out of the cathedral.

'She's known him practically all her life,' said Marianne. 'They were childhood sweethearts. He had so much poetry in his head. And now it's all gone. It's not real until it's on the page, is it?'

Genevieve remembered the tiny apartment with its squirling green floor and its book-lined walls. That place was so alive . . . 'He must have left notebooks?'

Marianne shook her head. 'It would be wrong. We'd be ransacking his private world.'

She tried to think about what Betterson had said, the day

319

he'd snatched up her own poetry notebook. The day they'd visited Natalie Barney's salon. What was it? If there was anything of worth in that book, he'd find it. Something like that. 'I don't think Norman was precious in that way,' she said. 'I think he'd want you to salvage what you could.'

'I loved him too.' Marianne gazed out the door, after Augusta.

Genevieve reached across and touched her hand. 'I'm so sorry. I'll miss him. Lots of people will.'

'I should go after her.' Her voice was small.

'Telephone me,' said Genevieve. 'Perhaps I can help. With the notebooks, I mean. When you're ready. And then there's the magazine . . .'

'I can't think about this.'

'I know. But don't go throwing anything away, will you? It's not real until it's on the page. But maybe some of it *is* on the page. It's important.'

'Excuse me.' Marianne smiled politely, but there was a tremor of anger in her cheek. 'I should go after her.'

Alone again, Genevieve resumed her pew and sat for a while, thinking about Betterson and his work – about the waste of it all. Time and life and poetry. And suddenly something seized her: she was horribly aware of her own life trickling away, and she didn't want to sit there any longer.

# 36

THE PACKAGE WAS DELIVERED IN THE EARLY AFTERNOON, NOT long after Genevieve's return, by a boy with a pale face and dirty knees. Semi-hidden behind her bedroom door, she got a look at him when Céline went searching for a tip. And the boy, gaping at the gold and grey hallway, the gleaming ebony and glinting lacquer of the furniture, happened to catch her eye.

The box was wrapped in white tissue paper and tied with a pink silk ribbon. Genevieve carried it into the salon. It was probably a gift from baby-besotted Robert, but for some reason her breath was quickening as she closed the door, sat down in a Bibendum chair and placed it on her lap. Something made her close her eyes when she pulled at the ribbon and let that pink bow slip away.

The box was lined with crushed velvet in deep red. And sitting in the centre of the velvet lining were the most staggeringly beautiful evening shoes she'd ever laid eyes on.

The gold satin uppers were covered in intricate bas-relief embroidery in gold thread. A pair of magical creatures faced each other on the slender toe of each shoe. Winged, taloned and fierce, they weren't eagles, weren't lions, weren't unicorns, but were somehow all three. They were almost identical to each other – almost mirror images, but if you looked carefully you could discern subtle differences between them. They were rearing up in such an intense manner that you couldn't tell whether this was the prelude to fighting or mating.

The monsters were surrounded by spirals and swirls, hearts, flowers and snakes, which spread, burgeoning, all over the gently curving T-straps and the counters at their backs. Genevieve had never seen embroidery like it. The patterning was so densely detailed that from a distance it was a mere golden shimmer. It was only when you got close up that you saw the design in its full glory and perfection.

The four-inch narrow heels were made from what looked like solid gold, and they were embossed with a simple design – some intersecting curves inside a circle. The tiny ball-shaped buttons were also of gold, and wore the same embossed design in miniature.

For a while she sat and gazed at the shoes, butterfly-fragile and dreading the possibility that this might be a dream she was about to wake up from. When she felt strong enough to move, she tiptoed across the hall, hugging the box to her chest.

In her shoe room, she slipped the shoes on to her feet. The perfect fit, of course. Admiring them in the long mirror, she finally made sense of the embossed design on the heels and buttons. An intertwined and reversed G and P, reflected back to her the right way around.

Now Genevieve allowed herself, gradually, to begin to

feel and know that these were more than simply the world's most beautiful shoes. He wanted her, and he was prepared to accept her terms. He would give up the other women, she knew it. These shoes were a declaration, a love letter. The embodiment of all her deepest hopes and yearnings. Alone in front of the mirror, Genevieve began to dance.

Paolo Zachari was woken by the unsettling feeling that someone was watching him. It was not unusual for him to wake in this way – he'd long been paranoid about intruders breaking into his apartment, stealing up on him in the dark. He suspected the fear stemmed from a real incident that took place in his childhood, an event only hazily remembered but which had haunted him for many years.

He must have been six or seven – no older, certainly. His father had gone away, which was odd, since he didn't have the kind of business that took him away from home. Zachari had no idea, looking back, where he'd gone or why, but his father must have been away because he was sleeping in the big bed with his mother when it happened.

It was a hot night. Paolo lay at the very edge of the bed in his pyjamas, curled on his side. His mother was tucked behind him, one arm flopped limp across his body, her sleep-breathing warm and even, tickling the back of his neck. He lay with his eyes open, gazing out through the open window at the big half-moon, centre-stage in a clear starlit sky. Odd that the shutters weren't closed – it must have been because of the heat. His mother must have wanted the breeze.

There was some sort of plant growing all up the back of the house. He couldn't remember now if it was a kind of vine or ivy, but curling green tendrils hung down outside the window, moving very slightly in the night air. What time was it? Felt like utter dead of night – maybe 3 a.m., when all is so still and quiet that you feel time itself has stopped. He thought he could see the plant growing, uncurling. He stared at it, wide-eyed, not the tiniest bit sleepy.

Someone was watching him – him and his mother. He felt an odd creeping sensation, like a shadow falling across him. The darkest kind of shadow. He began to sweat and his heart beat hard in his head. He couldn't move. Just kept on staring out that window. Maybe the watcher was out there, hiding in the moon or hanging from the windowsill, trying to climb up.

There was a muffled noise from behind him. His mother. Her arm pulled suddenly back and her body jerked away from him. The bed shook violently. He lay rigid, unable to turn his head to look back at her. Unable to move at all. And then someone shoved him hard so that he fell out on to the cold wooden floor, while above him the bed continued to shake. He didn't dare look but he heard things. The bed creaking. The slap of an open palm against a face. Some male grunts and something from his mother that was not quite a scream, not quite a moan. How long did it go on for? He lay on the floor, staring at his mother's dancing slippers, which sat on the rug below the window. They were made of red silk with little white flowers embroidered across the round toes, and they had long red ribbons which you'd wind up the leg to secure them. They were her pride and joy but he'd never seen her wear them. He imagined his mother's feet dancing in the shoes, hopping and

324

pointing and skipping. Happy feet. He imagined white flowers, like those stitched on the shoes, raining down from the sky and gathering in a thick, soft carpet on the ground.

Eventually the bed became still again and there was an odd rasping sound – perhaps the sound of his mother attempting to stifle her sobs.

He stayed there, on the floor, until morning. He must have slept. When daylight finally came, his mother had already risen and left the room. The bedsheets were rumpled, but no more than usual.

She told him he must have dreamed it.

Years later, just before he was due to leave for Paris, he asked her about what had happened that night – tried to press for an explanation. She insisted she didn't know what he was talking about.

Now and then, in dead of night, that feeling would come over him again – a nasty creeping sensation, like the darkest shadow falling across his body – and he would wake with a gasp, clutching the sheets, soaked in sweat. Sometimes, when he fell asleep again, he would dream of red dancing slippers or flurries of white flowers.

There was never anyone there watching him. There was never anyone beside him in the bed. Until now.

She was propped up on one elbow in his big, squeaky bed in the apartment above the shop, her eyes wide open and staring at him, her hair sticking up, her neck pink and flushed.

'What . . . Where . . . ?'

'Is it that bad, waking up with me?' she said.

His eyes adjusted to the almost-dark. The unfamiliar,

325

shadowy shapes consolidated themselves into his wardrobe and chest of drawers.

'Shh.' She reached out to touch his face. 'You're safe.'

'Am I?' He'd jerked away from her. A reflex. He tried to force himself to relax.

'Do you remember what you were dreaming?'

'No.' Deep breaths. 'I'm not used to this.'

'Me neither.' She touched his shoulder now, running her finger along the scar. 'How did you get this?'

'An accident in my father's workshop.'

This seemed to satisfy her. She trailed her finger slowly down his body to the wider scar on his side. 'What about this one?'

'An accident in my father's workshop.'

'It seems you had a lot of accidents back then.'

'What time is it?'

'I don't care.'

'Don't you?' He pulled himself up in the bed and fumbled about for the lamp switch so he could see his watch-face properly. *Click*, and the room was bathed in orange. Genevieve squeaked and hid under the sheets.

'My God, it's almost ten!'

An audible sigh from under the eiderdown.

'We've been asleep for *hours*.' Irritated, he grabbed the sheets and yanked them off her. Exposed, she squealed again but then giggled and stretched her arms out for him. Her skin was beautifully creamy in the lamplight. He was tempted to let himself be drawn back in. But as she reached for him, an image from his dream flickered back. The plant outside his mother's window; the green, curling tendrils . . . He pulled away from her and got up.

'It's your dream, isn't it?' she said softly.

'No.' It was as though she had found a way under his skin to the raw flesh. You couldn't have someone under your skin like that. 'It's nothing to do with the dream. You should get back.'

'Back to Robert?' She rolled on to her back. 'I don't ever want to go back.'

'Don't be silly.' He began searching about on the floor for his clothes. They were all intertwined with hers, as if even their clothing had been making love. Again he thought of that climbing plant, and shuddered. Picked up his shirt.

'He thinks I'm pregnant.'

He dropped his shirt where he'd found it. 'You're not, are you?'

'Of course not. I said it to keep him off me.'

'That was silly.'

'I know.' She started to cry. 'I just can't stand for him to touch me. Not any more. I meant it, you know – when I told you I was going to end that side of my marriage.'

What to do now? They didn't cry, his lovers. His encounters were civilized and witty. One fucked and chatted and then got dressed again. Simple and pleasurable. One might sip wine or eat fruit with one's lover. One did not lose all track of time and then wake with a shock to an unruly emotional scene. It simply wasn't the Parisian way. Or his. Until now.

'Hold me.' Her voice was thin. She had scrunched herself up with her arms wrapped tight around her knees. She looked tiny and helpless.

Hesitantly, he returned to the bed, sat in beside her, and, after a moment, drew her close. He patted her back

327

clumsily, painfully aware of his own awkwardness – frustrated with himself for his inability to act decisively. To either walk out of that door or comfort her in the way she wanted to be comforted.

'Tell me something,' she said, her sobs dying down.

'What do you want to know?'

'Anything. Just talk to me.'

'All right.' He put his mouth against her hair and breathed in its sweet, earthy scent. 'Yesterday I drew your feet from memory. I have the drawing back at my workroom.' As he spoke, he could feel her body begin to loosen up again. The warmth was returning. 'I got them just right. The shapes of the bones in your toes, the curve of the arches, the veins running under your skin like rivers on a map.'

'Can I see the drawing?'

'If you like.' Their voices were low whispers. The warmth was spreading from her body to his. He felt himself begin to curve around her, subtly – a very slight movement. His body wanting to fit itself to hers. 'I could draw the Marchesa Casati's feet too. Or Mistinguett's. It's what makes my shoes special. The fact that I know the feet so well. The way I can remember them.' He was starting to want her again.

'But it was my feet you drew yesterday. Mine.'

'Yes.'

She had forced her way into his life just as she'd forced her way into his shop. She had imposed herself on his imagination and now there was no getting rid of her.

She shifted in his arms and pressed her wet face against his neck. He wasn't repelled by the tears now. He wanted to lick them away.

328

'Tell me something else.'

'I love your back,' he said. 'Your lovely, long back. Your skin has a translucent quality, like pearls.' She was shifting her position. Kissing his chest. Kissing her way down. In a moment or two she would take him into her mouth and it would be heaven. 'I want to make a pair of shoes which have the curve of your back and the pearly quality of your skin. If only I could make shoes from cream. If only I could melt a fistful of pearls and mould them into the shape of a shoe.'

'You can,' she said, dreamily. 'You can do anything you want.'

The poker game was over. It had been Maurice Henier's night. Flush after straight after flush after full house. Henier, who'd only started playing recently, was a bluffer, and a bad one at that. The boys were usually able to separate him from his cash in the early stages. It made for a nice hors d'oeuvre. But tonight, they wouldn't move beyond that first course. It seemed inconceivable that Henier could be dealt so many good cards. Surely his luck would run out soon and he'd fall back on his habitual wild bluffing. They watched him closely – his nervous blinking, his nail-biting, the usual tells – and piled in their chips. But he just kept winning and winning until suddenly – *far* too early (it was barely ten, for goodness' sake!) – nobody had any chips left, and Henier was whistling his way up to one of the back rooms with two whores and a bulging wallet.

'We could play another game,' suggested Cabbott. But the boys were feeling too bruised and grumpy to go on. Even Cabbott spoke without enthusiasm. The occasional giggle or thump from somewhere above their heads served to make matters worse still. One by one they finished their drinks and slipped off home to their wives.

'What's got into you, Robert?' Harry Mortimer asked, practically the moment the two men were left alone in the cards room.

'I guess I don't like to lose any more than you do, Harry. Particularly to Henier.'

'That's a lot of crap, friend.' Harry leaned back in his creaking chair and folded his arms. 'You don't give a damn about the game, never have done. You're in it for the company. Now, what's wrong?'

Robert nursed his glass. 'Nothing. In fact, life is good. Genevieve's in the family way.'

'Well, well, you old dog!' Harry gave him a big-handed slap on the arm. 'So we'll be fathers together. Perhaps we should order some champagne?'

'It's too early for that. I shouldn't have told you. She made me promise.'

'Oh, don't you worry about that. She'll never know. And you can't keep a secret like that all to yourself, can you?' Harry's face, in the dim red light, was demonic.

'I suppose not.' Robert stared down into his drink.

'Now,' said Harry. 'If you'll let me give you some advice—'

'I'll have no more of that, if you please.'

A creak of the chair. 'Bob? What the devil is going on?'

Robert drained his glass and grabbed the bottle to pour another couple of fingers' worth. He'd been drinking heavily all evening.

'Robert?'

330

'Well, it's like this. I took your . . . *advice*. I hired your "friend" Mr Felperstone. And he proceeded to stir up a whole heap of trouble for me.' Robert forced himself to look at Harry's face, open and creased with concern, as a volley of high-pitched giggles broke out somewhere above them, along with the deeper laugh of the victorious Maurice Henier. 'My wife has done nothing wrong, Harry. Nothing! She's having my baby, and she's suffering for it. She's sick as a dog, poor girl.' He gulped again at the bourbon. 'Harry, I've had that low-life snoop into her past and follow her about and fill my head with the worst lies you can think of. I've allowed my trust in my wife to be utterly eroded. Your "friend" dragged me into a scene that will haunt me for the rest of my life – no, don't ask what it was, I don't wish to rehearse it again – but suffice to say it had nothing to do with my Genevieve. Thanks for your advice, Harry. Thanks a lot.'

Robert's ragged breathing. A creak of Harry's chair as he shifted uncomfortably. A waitress bobbed cheerfully into the room, but when she saw their faces she retreated without a word.

Harry gave a long, low whistle. 'Robert, I'm truly sorry. All I can say is that I was trying to help you. I *am* your friend. Come on, let's have another drink.' He refilled both their glasses. 'I guess I made a mistake putting you on to Felperstone, but I do know a thing or two. Believe me. I've met girls like your wife. I've lost my head over a few. Did I ever tell you about my first wife?' He seemed to notice the contemptuous expression on Robert's face. 'But let's not get into that now.' He brought out his cigar case, took one for himself and offered one across. Robert accepted out of a

331

kind of numbness – an inability to move. Maybe it was down to the bourbon or maybe it was the strangely hypnotic quality in Harry's voice. Either way, he stayed where he was.

'Suffice to say –' Harry lit both cigars and took a puff – 'that Genevieve is one of those girls who are pretty enough to have men falling all over them, and who are in love with drama. They have sufficient brain to know how to work a situation – how to manipulate a man's feelings. And they don't care how it ends. They're in it for the ride, if you'll excuse the expression. And that's an irresistible but lethal cocktail in a woman. I can smell it a mile off, Robert. I've tasted it too often. Now, I'm not saying these girls are irredeemable – not altogether. But they don't have a sense of responsibility. They don't care about getting hurt or about hurting other people – and that is how good men like you and me end up with broken hearts.'

The cigar was blending evilly with the bourbon. The room was drifting about. Harry's face loomed larger and larger.

'They have to grow up and *learn* responsibility, these girls, before it's too late. Now, I suggested you hire Felperstone because I thought to myself, The sooner that boy sees it how it is, the sooner he can take action. You catch the lady before she falls, so to speak, and you can save her. You can save yourselves, both.'

That creak of the chair. How it taunted. A squealing from the upper room. Robert closed his eyes and all he could see were the two bodies, side by side, like dolls. The holes in their heads.

'I'm mighty glad that she's having a baby, Robert. *Mighty*

glad. Now, if I were you, I'd get her on the first boat home you can manage.'

Robert was shaking his head. The movement was bigger than he wanted it to be, so that he almost lost balance on his chair. 'What are you talking about, Harry? *What?* This is all your fantasy, don't you see that? All this stuff about "these girls". It has nothing to do with me and my wife. Why, I could almost feel sorry for you.'

'Don't feel sorry for me. *Listen* to me.'

'I should go home,' said Robert, stubbing out the cigar. 'Or I'll end up knocking you out. You know what? I think perhaps we shouldn't meet any more.'

He made to get up but Harry put a hand on his arm.

'I wasn't going to tell you this, Robert. But it's the only way I'll get through to you.'

'Tell me what?'

Harry sighed. 'It was about a week ago. Maud saw Genevieve in the Jardins du Luxembourg. She was with a man.'

'What man?'

'They were kissing.'

'Friends kiss, don't they? This is Paris.'

'Maud said it was obvious they were lovers. I'm sorry, friend.'

'What are you thinking?' Zachari asked. They'd just made love again and Genevieve was lying in his arms.

'I'm thinking the yellow stain on your ceiling looks like a map of France.'

'That's exactly what it is. What else?'

'I'm thinking the squeaking of your bed sounds like a really old person laughing.'

'You're exactly right. There are five old people trapped inside this mattress, holding the bed up. They're laughing because they're permanently drunk. What else?'

'I'm thinking . . .' She gazed around the bedroom. Good antique French furniture but mismatched and not well maintained. Faded curtains. Décor that needed to be rethought and refreshed. 'I'm thinking, why does the world's most expensive shoemaker live in such a creaky old apartment?'

He was silent for a moment, as though he was trying to figure out how to answer the question. And then, 'What else are you thinking?'

She couldn't read the expression in his eyes. Pulling free of his arms, she sat up. 'I'm not sure you want to know.' She took up the shirt he'd thrown on the floor and put it on, loving the fact that she could do so – loving the fact that it smelled of his skin. Then she slipped on her beautiful gold shoes and wandered through to the kitchen.

She was filling a glass with water when he came up behind her, put his arms around her waist and rested his chin on her shoulder. They stood that way for a while, and she leaned back against his naked body.

'Why do you want to punish yourself?' she asked.

'Punish myself? What do you mean?' And he kissed her neck.

'You deny yourself luxuries you can obviously afford. This place is . . . well, it's not what it should be. It certainly lacks a woman's touch.'

'It's just my way.' He was still holding her close. 'My time is valuable. Why should I spend it decorating apartments?'

'But it's your *home*.'

'Home?' He sniffed. 'I'd be happy to live in a cardboard box as long as I can go on making shoes.'

'Well, I think there's something odd about that.' She pulled away from him to sit down at the kitchen table. 'I don't want us to have secrets from each other, Paolo.'

He sat down opposite her. 'If you don't like it here, we can meet at the hotel in future.'

Frustrated, she balled her hands into fists and banged at her own head. 'There's something you haven't told me. Maybe you don't even fully understand it yourself. Think about it. You are the best shoemaker alive. So why aren't you also the world's most *rich* and *famous* shoemaker? You should be making shoes for Coco Chanel's new fashion lines and they'd end up on the front of *Vogue*. You could work with anyone you wanted to. Paul Poiret, Jean Patou, Madeleine Vionnet – anyone! You're so much better than Ferragamo or Perugia. They'd all want to have your shoes. You must know this is all within your reach.'

'So you want to tell me how to run my business now?' His face was dark.

'I want to know why you're so determined to spend your life hiding in this shop when you could have the whole world!' She tried to calm herself. 'Look, I'm sorry. Maybe I'm not quite myself. I found out this morning that a friend of mine died yesterday.'

'I'm sorry to hear that.'

'He was a poet. A good one. I bumped into his wife at Notre Dame. His girlfriend too. They were grieving together. Helping each other.'

335

'Cosy,' muttered Zachari.

'It made me think about how short life is. It made me realize that you have to do everything you can to find true happiness and make your life mean something. And you have to do it today because maybe there won't *be* any more days. You can't afford to be complacent.'

He smiled now. 'I wish I could make you understand that I *am* living my life to the full. My work is my whole world. It's exciting and beautiful and colourful. It changes all the time. Every hour and every minute. It's right here.' He tapped his forehead. 'And here.' He held out his hands, showing her the palms.

'Well, I haven't been living *my* life to the full,' said Genevieve. 'Something important happened to me today. I've made a decision. I'm not prepared to go on being Robert's wife.'

'What are you saying?'

'You know what I'm saying.' She was watching him closely. Could there be softer feelings behind that brusque expression? She needed to know that there were.

'Go home and sleep on it,' he said, eventually.

'Why? What will that achieve?' She got up, and went back to the bedroom to find her clothes. He followed her.

'You haven't remotely thought this through.'

'And nor,' she said, 'have you.'

She unbuttoned his shirt and picked up her slip. 'Is this about Violet de Frémont? You still don't want to give up the other women, do you?'

'Oh, for God's sake!' He bashed his hands down on the brass bedhead. 'There *are* no other women. Not since you.'

She felt herself smile. 'Do you love me, Paolo?'

'I need my freedom.' He kept his back to her. 'As things are, I'm free to wander in my own imagination. I work whenever I want to. Sometimes I work all night and all day. My shoes come first. I can't allow any woman to get in the way.'

'I love you,' said Genevieve. 'I *love* you, Paolo.'

Silence from Zachari. She could see the tension in his back and his neck.

'Has it occurred to you,' she said, 'that I might be happy to let you put your work first? It's just possible, you know, that your designs might be *better* if you lived with a woman you loved. You'd have everything you have now but you'd have me too. I could help you. I'm not an artist, Paolo, but I *understand* art. I could be your strongest champion – your partner even. Who knows more about shoes than me? I'd even make friends with Olga.'

He shook his head. 'It's not possible.'

She began to gnaw on an expensively manicured nail. 'There's a whole room full of shoes at my apartment, Paolo. Floor to ceiling. They've been my passion. I hold them close to my heart. Every box in that room contains an unfulfilled desire, a dream, a fantasy.' She closed her eyes for a moment. 'I love my shoe collection but I've let it stand in for a life. I'm not going to do that any more.'

'Genevieve.' He turned to face her again and his eyes were sad now. 'It wouldn't work. The two of us living here ... *Here*. Your damn shoe collection alone would take up my entire apartment! You really should go home now.'

'I know you love me, Paolo. This one pair of shoes –' she looked down at her feet again – 'they mean more to me than the rest of the collection put together.'

'You make me want to punch walls.'

She stooped to pick up her dress, fussed with buttons. Zachari stood and watched her.

'I'm serious,' she said. 'About leaving Robert. Say the word and I'll walk out on him right now.'

'You haven't even begun to think of the consequences.'

'Yes, yes – your work, your freedom . . .'

Zachari smiled sadly. 'I'm talking about the consequences for *you*, Genevieve.'

## 37

ROBERT WOKE WITH THUMPING HEAD, A FOUL TASTE IN his mouth and no idea of where he was. The bed was tiny – child-size – and his feet stuck over the edge. The room was completely dark. As he blundered to open the shutters, he trod on a sharp object and almost tripped over something else.

Sunlight flooded in. It was a boy's bedroom. The floor was scattered with toys – a tin car, a spinning top, a stuffed bear, some books. The walls were painted sky-blue. He was wearing a pair of blue cotton pyjamas, not his own.

Where the devil . . . ?

Sitting down on the bed, throbbing head in hands, he attempted to piece together the events of the night before. He remembered the poker game, of course, and then drinking with Harry. Reluctantly, heavily, he remembered what Harry had told him. And then all he wanted to do was to go back to sleep in this little boy's bed and stay there.

From somewhere outside the room came clattering sounds. Dishes, perhaps. The muted thumping of cupboard doors being closed. The trill of a young child speaking French.

He'd gone home, hadn't he? In a taxi? He was angry. He'd wanted to talk to her, even if it meant waking her up. But her bed was empty. There was no sign of her anywhere in the apartment.

More chatter from the child in the other room. An answering voice – deep and soft. A woman's voice.

He'd taken another taxi back to the club, looking for Harry. He had a horrible feeling, thinking back, that he was crying when he arrived. Mme Hubert, the owner, was friendly enough, but told him his friend had left. She asked him if he wanted to come in. And he'd said . . . Oh dear, he'd said yes.

Was that where he was now? In some back room of the club?

'Please *God*, no.'

The scraping of a chair against a wooden floor. The woman telling the child that he should get on and finish his breakfast. It was almost time to leave for school.

It was coming back to him bit by dreadful bit. A brass bed with a dirty yellow counterpane. A girl in a corset who smelled of cheap perfume. He'd just wanted to sleep on his own but she'd got in too. He'd been so tired but she'd kept prodding and whispering and sidling up to him. Getting in his face.

'Mr Shelby King?' The woman again. 'Are you awake?'

'Yes.'

This surely wasn't the club. He distinctly remembered the brass bed; that yellow bedding. The room was wrong

340

for the club. And that back-alley view out the window –
this wasn't Montmartre.

'Mr Shelby King? I don't mean to disturb you, but . . . I'm
leaving a dressing gown for you. You'll find it just outside
the door.'

He knew the voice. He knew it well.

'Thank you, Marie-Claire. I shall be out directly.'

She was sitting at the kitchen table with her son, who must
have been seven or eight years old. They were eating bread
and jam and drinking milky coffee out of bowls. The boy
was prattling away but Marie-Claire told him to hush when
she became aware of Robert standing in the doorway.

The kitchen – the apartment generally – was basic but
homely. They lived here alone, mother and son. The
husband had been killed in the war. Robert had always
known this, of course, but he'd never really thought about
his secretary's home life. It must be the dead husband's
pyjamas and gown that he was wearing.

'Do sit down and have some breakfast.' Marie-Claire was
avoiding his gaze. Oh God, had she undressed him last
night?

'Thank you.' But there was nowhere to sit. There were
only two chairs at the small table.

Marie-Claire barked at the boy to give up his seat. She
must have done something similar when he had arrived
during the night – simply instructed the child to surrender
his room. Robert did his best to overcome his awkwardness
and his hangover and smile warmly as the boy (now, what
was his name?) slipped past. He received only a sullen look
in return.

341

'I'll make you some coffee.' She was up at the stove before he could speak and was bashing about with pots. 'Would you like some bread? It's yesterday's, I'm afraid, but if you're prepared to wait ten minutes or so until Charles leaves, I'll go out for some fresh.' The words came rushing out. She was as nervous as he was.

'Please don't trouble yourself. I'm not at all hungry.' He wiped the sweat from his forehead. 'The coffee would be nice though. I'll take it black.' Though she knew how he liked his coffee, of course.

'Certainly.' She kept her back firmly turned. There was a bunch of pink roses hanging upside-down to dry from a hook just beside the kitchen window. It was one of the bunches he'd bought the morning after Genevieve announced she was pregnant.

Someone was whistling in the street, and Marie-Claire started humming to herself as she made the coffee. The kitchen smelled of good cooking. The boy called out, 'Maman, where's my schoolbag?' and was told, 'In the hallway, with the shoes.' It was an everyday singsong exchange. A ritual. There was a cosiness to this scene: the woman making coffee, the man still in his pyjamas, the boy getting ready for school . . . For a moment, Robert indulged in a fantasy that this was *his* life, these were *his* pyjamas.

'It's very kind of you to have let me stay.'

'Well, I could hardly turn you away, now, could I?'

Was her implication that she would have liked to, if she'd felt able?

'It *was* kind of you.' He stared at the table. 'I realize I must have put you in a rather awkward position. I'm very grateful, and very sorry.'

342

'Oh, Robert.' The emotion broke through in those two little words and then was quickly suppressed. She put the coffee down in front of him and went out into the hall to chivvy her son along.

The coffee was thick and bitter. The first sip made him dizzy but the second steadied him. He closed his eyes and went back under the yellow counterpane at the club. The girl had invited him to unlace her corset. And he had tried to oblige her (horrors!) but the drink had turned his hands into useless paws, and she'd had to take over the job. Then she'd got on top of him in the bed and started undoing his shirt buttons. He could see her fingers working away at them, and her white face coming down close to his. She'd kissed him, or tried to. It was when she'd pushed her breasts into his face that the cloying perfume became overpowering. He'd vomited.

The front door banged shut and Marie-Claire came back into the kitchen and sat down at the table. The boy had gone.

He'd vomited everywhere. On the yellow bedding, on himself, on the girl. And then Mme Hubert had come into the room with a look of utter disdain and disgust on her face, and started shouting at him.

'My clothes . . .' He couldn't get any further.

'I've given them a good wash. But they're still wet, I'm afraid. I'll fetch you some of Gaston's. He was about the same height as you.'

'Thank you.' He swallowed another mouthful of coffee. 'Last night . . . I hope I wasn't . . . I hope I didn't . . .'

'No, no!' But did she say it too quickly? Too adamantly? 'You were rather the worse for wear. Gaston used to get like that sometimes. I suppose all men do.'

'I never have before,' he said. 'And never will again.'
Their eyes met. Hers were a soft squirrelly brown. She was
attractive, in a quiet sort of way. Slightly plump, but in the
right places. And thoroughly decent.

'I don't know why I came here,' he said. 'Frankly, I'm
surprised I even remembered your address. It's not as if
I've been here before. I don't know how to apologize for all
the trouble I've given you.'

'I'm glad you came here,' she said. 'Perhaps you knew I'd
take care of you. I'd always take care of you, Robert.'

'Would you?' There was an ache in his chest.

She got up and went over to the sink, brusque again.
'Better here than lying in some alleyway with your watch
and your wallet missing.'

'I'm so tired.' As he said it, he felt overwhelmed with
exhaustion. 'I don't know what to do.'

'Why don't you go back to bed for a while? I'll leave
Gaston's suit outside the door for you and I'll bring your
clothes back to work tomorrow. I have to get along to the
office now, but you can let yourself out.'

'*You* have to get to the office?' A dry chuckle.

'That's right.' She stacked the breakfast dishes up on the
draining board. 'I have lots to do. You can come and go as
you please, but I can't.'

'Marie-Claire—' He was looking at those roses again.

'It's for the best.' She dried her hands on her apron.
'Don't worry. This shan't go further than ourselves. We
won't mention it again.'

## 38

ROBERT, I'M LEAVING YOU.

Such a simple phrase. Four little words. Three, really. That was all it took to destroy a marriage. Two carefully constructed and intertwined lives. Her world, and his.

Genevieve had slept heavily. Sleep like the deepest ocean. Dreamless, dense. It washed over the boundaries of night and beyond. Once or twice she struggled to wake up, aware of the strong rays of sun creeping through the gaps at the edges of the shutters, peeping between the curtains. But the house was quiet and her eyelids were heavy and the sleep came and swept her away again – until finally it beached her well into the morning. Still she lay on, eyes open now, listening to the sound of the blood in her head. Toying with four little words and what they would mean.

Robert, I'm leaving you.

Thinking about what Paolo had said. The consequences.

There would be a nasty scene when she told him. Perhaps many nasty scenes. He would be devastated. Would he become violent? She didn't think of him as a violent man, and yet . . . And yet she'd seen another side of him on that recent awful night.

There were other ways he could hurt her. She'd lose this place, of course. Her bespoke Rue de Lota apartment with all its trimmings: the silver and gold veneer, the Pirogue couch and ostrich-egg lightshades, her bedroom with its silk walls in cornflower-blue, the delicate amboyna and *acajou* desk. Robert wouldn't want to stay here. He'd hot-foot it back to Boston to be clasped to his mother's breast. But he'd make damn sure she didn't stay here either.

What else? He could go to see her father. Daddy would of course take his side. The poor wronged husband. When had he *ever* taken her side? Robert could see to it that she was disowned and disinherited if he really wanted that kind of revenge. Oh yes, he could surely accomplish that.

What else? He could drag her through the courts and across the society pages. He could make sure she was publicly humiliated and left without two francs to rub together. By the time he was done, she wouldn't be received in any respectable household either side of the English Channel.

*But who cares about respectability, chérie? What could be more boring than to live a respectable life?*

What else?

He'd take her shoe collection! The most obvious and the cruellest revenge. That was something she absolutely couldn't bear.

She was out of bed and rushing through to the shoe room. Here they all were, all 523 pairs, safe in their boxes. She couldn't possibly leave her collection behind. They would all come with her to her new life – *all* of them. From the Zacharis, the Ferragamos and the Perugias to the Mary

Janes of her girlhood. Every pair of court shoes, long boots, dancing slippers, pumps, spectators, lace-ups and slip-ons. High heels, low heels, Louis heels. Every buckle and button. Every square inch of leather, silk, suede, satin and velvet. The entire collection would need to be moved out of the apartment to a place of safety while Robert was off the premises. This was a delicate situation requiring careful planning. She must not allow herself to get carried away and act in haste.

The new gold Zacharis were still lying on the floor from last night. The intertwined G and P on the heels were enough to make her melt.

By the time she'd bathed and dressed it was mid-morning. Putting her head around the kitchen door, she asked Céline for a late breakfast to be laid out. A mushroom omelette would be nice. Some freshly squeezed orange juice and some coffee.

The maid stood gaping at her.

'What is it? Is it so strange to want an omelette?'

'Well, madame. I don't know, I'm sure.' Céline's face still wore that expression: sheer disbelief.

'What on earth is the matter?'

'It's not my place, madame.'

'Either tell me what's wrong or pull yourself together.'

A vague mumbling.

'Céline!'

'Well, aren't you worried?' It was blurted out. 'Doesn't it matter to you?'

Genevieve shook her head. 'I haven't the slightest idea what you're talking about.'

'It's not natural! Your husband hasn't come home and you're talking about mushroom omelettes!' Her face was flushed. 'Something must have happened to him, madame. He's not the sort of man to ... He's such a gentleman!'

'Hasn't come home ...' She repeated the words, frowning. 'Don't be silly. He'll be at the office as usual. He often leaves me to sleep in when I've had a late night. You know that.'

'He didn't come back last night.' The maid spoke more slowly. 'Didn't you notice?'

Genevieve's lips tightened. 'Make me that omelette. Right away. And the coffee. And the orange juice.'

She went straight to the telephone, queasy in the stomach.

This is your punishment, said a voice in her head. Robert's dead or in hospital and it's *all your fault*.

How had she allowed herself to even contemplate moving out? She couldn't possibly manage without Robert. Zachari was right – her dream of the future was nothing but the fantasy of a spoilt child. Robert was reality. Solid, steady reality. Paolo Zachari, on the other hand, was something slippery and elusive. What did she know about him, really?

As she reached out to pick up the receiver, her hand shook.

Let him be all right, she told herself. Let him be there at his desk, telling me the maid has lost her marbles.

Her voice was small as she spoke to the operator. She seemed to wait for ever to be connected to Robert's office. And as she waited, she could sense the presence of the maid on the other side of the kitchen door. Listening in. Waiting with her.

She shut her eyes. *If he's there, I will give up Paolo once and for all.*

'Good-morning, Mrs Shelby King.' It was the secretary.

'I'd like to speak to my husband, please.'

There was a pause at the end of the line – a pause that went on slightly too long. 'He's not able to speak to you just at the moment.'

'What do you mean?' She caught sight of her reflection in the hall mirror. Her face looked drawn and anxious. And guilty – her face looked guilty.

Another pause. 'He's not here.'

'Well, where is he then?'

'He's out at a meeting. I'll get him to telephone you when he gets back.'

A rush of giddy relief. The reflection in the mirror was transformed in an instant. The guilt ebbed away.

Sitting in the dining room, waiting for her breakfast, Genevieve tried to get her head straight.

She thought about what had happened to her this morning – the way her emotions had rocked violently back and forth. She was like a set of scales tipping one way and then the other and failing to balance. She loved Paolo but she couldn't rely on him. She could rely on Robert but she didn't love him.

How she missed Lulu! How she needed to talk to her friend.

What had her fight with Lulu been about, really? Everything and nothing. In the immediate aftermath of the argument, she had felt it was everything. But now she inclined towards the nothing. Nothing but a bit of jealousy on both sides. And too much alcohol. She would have to do something about it. Today.

'Here. Your omelette.' The maid smacked the plate down on the table in front of her and walked straight out of the room.

The omelette was grey. It sat in a pool of dark oil on a chipped blue plate.

Genevieve's queasiness returned, along with an odd agitation. The omelette was clearly inedible. And yet it still bothered her that Céline had not brought in a knife and fork or a napkin.

'Céline?'

No orange juice or coffee either. Genevieve eyed the grey mass in front of her. It had a nasty rancid smell.

'Céline?'

The sound of the front door being shut quietly. That damn girl had walked out!

Genevieve sat for a minute or two, drumming her fingers on the table. She had a strong urge to hurl the omelette at the wall, but with the maid gone she would be left to clear up the mess herself. She was about to pick up the plate and return it to the kitchen when the doorbell sounded. Céline, no doubt, having got as far as the lift before calming down and realizing how daft she'd been. Good. Genevieve was ready to hear her apology. Perhaps.

But it wasn't the maid.

## 39

OLGA WAS BENDING TO EXAMINE THE ROCK-CRYSTAL sculpture by Gustave Miklos. It had a phallic thrust to it but was also angular like a skyscraper.

'This is nice,' she said.

'Thank you.' The smell of that omelette lingered on in Genevieve's nostrils. A nasty, grey, eggy odour. 'Would you like some tea?'

Olga was wandering around the salon. Running her hand along the fine leather upholstery of one of the Bibendum chairs, peering at the walls – the silver geometrical landscape on shining black background. Taking the stopper out of the Lalique crystal sherry decanter to weigh it in her hand.

'You have very nice things.' There was a silvery quality about her. Her eyes and hair carried the same colour as the shimmering salon walls.

'Excuse me a moment. I'll order that tea.' Genevieve went out to the hall to call Céline, only to remember that she'd gone. Damn that girl! Uneasy about leaving Olga alone, she returned to the salon.

Olga was now perched on the Pirogue couch. 'That doesn't give out much light.' She pointed at one of the lacquered-wood and painted-parchment standard lamps. 'So what is it for?'

Genevieve tried to imagine what Olga's own apartment must be like. Paolo's stories and something in Olga's manner had conjured in her mind a poky, dark interior – wet laundry and mouldy walls and children with a look of hunger about them.

Olga was clearly not well today. She looked thinner than when Genevieve had last seen her, a mere four days ago at the shop. Her cream shift-dress emphasized her paleness. She coughed frequently into a handkerchief, and seemed slightly breathless.

'Does Paolo know you're here?' She took a seat on one of the Bibendum chairs. 'Has he sent you with a message for me?'

'Don't be ridiculous.'

'Then why have you come? This surely isn't a social call.'

'Where do you keep your shoe collection?' This was spoken with a false brightness.

'Why do you want to know?'

'Just interested. Shoes are my life, you know.'

'Really?' Genevieve took a cigarette from the ivory box before her and offered one across. Olga accepted.

'Of course. I've been working with the world's greatest shoe designer for some years now.'

Genevieve took up her lighter and lit both cigarettes. 'I didn't think it was the shoes you cared about.'

'Didn't you?' Olga raised one arched eyebrow and drew on her cigarette, bursting into a coughing fit as soon as she'd inhaled.

'No.' Genevieve let the word hang in the air between them, and for a moment they were both silent.

'You were with Paolo yesterday, weren't you?' Olga said eventually. 'He sent me home early. It was because of you, I know it.'

'That's none of your business.'

'What is this smooth stuff?' She was touching the inside of the couch. 'It's not wood, is it?'

'It's tortoiseshell.' For a horrible moment, Genevieve thought she might grind her lit cigarette against the couch-frame. There was always an undercurrent with this woman, and never more so than today. But then Olga tapped ash sedately into the ashtray and the moment passed.

'So are you going to show me your shoe collection? I hear you have a whole room full of shoes.'

'It's not open to the public,' said Genevieve, curtly. 'I wish you'd get to the point.'

'All right. You are bad for Paolo. I want you out of his life.'

Genevieve folded her arms defensively. 'This has nothing to do with you.'

'I want you to promise me that you'll stay away from him. For good.'

'I'm sorry but I won't do that. I *can't* do that.'

A hateful look. She seemed to be building up to something. 'This couch is not comfortable. That lamp is not bright. Your world is full of stupid, useless, expensive things.' She hit the cushion with her fist. 'Stay away from Paolo!'

'No.'

And now she did it. She stubbed out that cigarette of hers against the gleaming tortoiseshell couch-frame and dropped the butt in the tray. 'I have known him a long time, Mrs Shelby King. I have seen him with many women. He will flick you away –' she reached across the space between them and flicked her thumb and forefinger – 'like you are an insect. And if he doesn't, I will.'

Genevieve pushed Olga's outstretched arm away and got to her feet, her anger rising. 'Who the hell do you think you are – threatening me in my own home! Damaging my property! I've been making an effort with you for Paolo's sake. Because he cares about you. But frankly, you're nothing but a pain and I shall tell him exactly how you've treated me.'

'You do that.' Olga stood up and brushed invisible dust off her dress.

'Look.' Genevieve made an effort to calm herself. 'If you carry on like this, you're going to force Paolo to choose between us, and that's something you might live to regret. I know he's fond of you, Olga, but do you really think that he's going to choose a friend over his lover?'

An unpleasant smile spread across Olga's face. 'Is that what he said I am? Just a friend?'

Something turned over in Genevieve's stomach. She had the urge to start running, but she could hardly run away from her own home. It took an effort to speak again. 'Get out of my apartment.'

'He's not something you can collect,' said Olga. 'You don't know him like I do. He has to be free. That's what I've given him for all these years. His freedom.'

'Did you hear me?'

At last she walked slowly to the door, but then turned and cast a look back at Genevieve. 'If you see Paolo again, I will tell your husband.'

'Tell him what you like.'

Olga's mouth opened very slightly and her tongue showed between her teeth. 'I think Mr Shelby King would be very interested to know about baby Josephine, don't you?'

'*What?*'

'Goodbye, Mrs Shelby King.' Olga gave a little wave, that tongue still showing between her teeth. Just the tip.

# 40

'I'VE BEEN MAKING SOME SHOES THAT ARE SUPPOSED TO LOOK like Red Admiral butterflies.' The phone line was crackly and Zachari's voice was indistinct. 'Did I tell you? I couldn't get them right, no matter how hard I tried. And this morning I realized why. It was my worst idea ever. Shoes are not butterflies and they shouldn't try to be. They don't flit about in the air. They connect you firmly to the ground. It's been an interesting morning, all in all. How about you?'

'I've had an interesting morning too,' said Genevieve. 'Olga came to see me. I want you to tell me the truth, Paolo. About you and Olga. The whole truth this time.'

Silence.

'I used to have nightmares,' came Zachari's voice. 'Terrible nightmares about something that happened to my mother years ago. Someone coming into her room, and . . . well, they were such frightening dreams. I used to wake up screaming. Olga heard me, one night. She came into my room in the dark. Got into bed beside me. At first she just cradled my head. Stroked my temples. It soothed me.

356

'Helped me to fall asleep again. When I woke up, she was gone.'

'How touching.'

'She came back the next night, and the next. I was just a boy. I was . . . I had no experience. She taught me.'

Genevieve could still see that tongue showing between the teeth. Just the tip.

'I was young. Hot-blooded. With no outlet. And she was younger too. She was softer then.'

Another silence. The sound of his breath. Or was it merely a fuzzing on the line?

'It's been over between us for years. It ended when I moved out of her apartment. We never talk about it. Never *did* talk about it. Nobody knew, not even her children. She would always go back to her room afterwards. We never spent the whole night together.'

Genevieve closed her eyes. Her grip on the receiver slackened slightly.

'You have to forgive me!' His voice was louder now. 'It's like you and your photographer. It was an adventure. And it's all in the past.'

'How *could* you?'

'Don't judge me, Genevieve. I didn't judge you.'

'You betrayed me.'

'What?'

'I told you my secret. And you told Olga.'

## 41

EVERY SURFACE WAS COVERED IN CLUTTER. THE BED WAS A disaster area of grubby nighties and patchwork quilt. The only chair was barely recognizable as a chair beneath the heap of clothes – silk dresses, tatty furs, a pair of men's long-johns. Stray black stockings lay about the floor like skins that had been shrugged off, among brightly coloured scarves, old newspapers and brown apple cores. The sink in the corner was stacked high with dirty crockery, the tap dripping steadily. The counter was a sea of empty bottles and wineglasses smeared with sediment. The dressing table was a mess of open jars of cream and pots of powder, several odd earrings, a necklace of fake pearls, a heavy turquoise ring, saucers of cigarette ash. Someone had written LE CHAT NOIR in red lipstick on the mirror. The walls were covered in sketches and photographs: Lulu in top hat and tails, Lulu naked with a wicked smile, Lulu dancing in a tutu, Lulu in a wedding dress with a donkey and a bunch of violets, Lulu under a shroud, Lulu with wings flying above Paris, Lulu as a cat, five Lulu faces – smiling, frowning, laughing, crying and just deadpan – a violin that was unmistakably Lulu, a series of triangles with a Luluness about them, Lulu's beauty spot on a plain white page. Lulu – the most painted and photographed woman in Paris. Lulu by Picasso, Chagall, Matisse, Léger, Miró, Brancusi, Man Ray. And of course, the real thing. Lulu of Montparnasse, commonly attributed to Frederick Camby.

She was wearing an orange kimono and smoking a cigarette in a long ebony holder. Her drawn-on beauty spot, larger than ever, was on the wrong side, the right instead of the left. She had an odd air about her – was it nerves or hostility?

'About the other night—' Genevieve began.

'You know,' said Lulu, 'Camby went off with that whore, Violetta. Can you believe it? I should be raging, but actually I'm worried. He's not himself at the moment and she took advantage of that. He got like this a couple of years ago and ended up in Malmaison. You know, the asylum.'

'My darling!' Genevieve opened her arms. They stood for a time amongst the mess of Lulu's room, holding each other tightly.

When they let go, Lulu was wiping her eyes with the back of her hand, smearing kohl across her face. 'I'm telling myself he'll be back,' she said. 'He always comes back. But still I worry. When I see Violetta I'm going to gouge her eyes out and set fire to her hair.'

'Got anything to drink?' Genevieve sat down on the bed.

'Somewhere.' Lulu knelt and peered under the bed, recovering a half-bottle of cheap Scotch. 'Will this do?'

'Pass it here.' Genevieve unscrewed the cap and drank straight from the bottle, craving that fire in her throat.

'Oh, chérie.' Lulu shook her head sadly and came to sit beside Genevieve. 'We are a stupid pair. We get so carried away with the moment, both of us. And then we let our mouths get in front of our brains and all hell breaks out.'

'I don't ever want to fight with you again,' said Genevieve. 'You're the only person I can really talk to. There's never been anyone in my life who understands me like you do.'

'I feel the same. I've missed you, Vivi.' She took the bottle and swigged from it, and for a while they sat in silence. It was Genevieve who eventually spoke.

'Did you hear about Norman Betterson?'

'I heard last night. Edward Hausen came rushing into the Coyote to tell everyone. They gave free drinks away for half an hour in Betterson's memory. When they started charging for the drinks again, Hausen went off to break the news at the Jockey Club. I should think he had quite a night of it.'

'To Norman.' Genevieve raised the bottle, drank and handed it to Lulu, who did the same.

'It's Guy Monteray's funeral today,' said Lulu. 'Did you know?'

'No, I didn't. What about Whisper? Are they being buried together?'

Lulu shook her head. 'She was married, apparently. To an American. He's shipping her back there.'

'He can't do that!'

'Apparently he can.'

'But they were in love.' Genevieve flopped back on the

bed and lay there, staring up at the mottled ceiling. 'A strange kind of love, but love all the same. They died together, holding hands. They should be together in the ground.'

'Chérie.' Lulu reached over and stroked her cheek. 'This isn't about Guy Monteray and Whisper, is it? What's going on?'

Genevieve sat up again. 'I was going to leave Robert to be with Paolo. But I've just found that he's betrayed me and now I don't know what I'm going to do.'

Lulu got up and set her cigarette holder down on the dressing table. At the sink, she filled a glass with cloudy water and stood with her back to Genevieve, gulping it down. When she spoke again, she still had her back turned and was leaning on the sink. 'What do you mean, he betrayed you?'

'He told that witch Olga about baby Josephine. Can you believe it?'

'Has he admitted it?'

'No, of course not. But how else could she have found out?'

There was an acrid smell. Something was burning.

'Shit!' Lulu lunged for her cigarette, scratching ineffectually at the fresh black scorch mark on her dressing table.

'He's broken my heart, Lulu.' Genevieve began to cry. 'Why did he do that?'

'Oh, chérie.' Lulu reached out for her hand. 'This is all very bad.'

The Coyote was a mess of broken glass, spilt drink and spilt blood. Marcel and a few others had stayed on to help

Laurent and Janine clean up, but Lulu needed to get out of there. She was in a blue mood. Too blue to hang around. She'd argued with Genevieve and then watched Camby and Violetta leave together through the back door. Enough was enough. She had to be alone – to walk a little. To drink a little.

She didn't know quite how she came to be back at that godforsaken bar again, but here she was. The barman with the tattooed arms was breathing on a glass and rubbing it with a cloth. The two old men on their barstools were smoking and talking in low murmurs. The three whores in the far corner could well have been the same ones as before. Though one whore could look much like another. The matted dog snoring away on the floor was definitely the same one.

'A cherry, please.'

The barman looked at Lulu with a face devoid of expression. She sighed. 'All right, make it a beer.'

She leaned on the bar while he fixed her drink. She was tired of this way of life – the effort required of her to be Lulu of Montparnasse twenty-four hours a day. Lulu, the life and soul of the party. Lulu, that funny little thing the artists love to paint. Lulu, the cabaret singer with the ashtray voice, the spooky accompanist and the heart stitched on her sleeve. Good for a giggle, for a party, for a night. She's yours for the price of a drink and a sandwich.

How easy it was for Genevieve. All that money. The clothes, the shoes, the indulgences. The games that money lets you play. The superior attitude that comes free with the cash. God, she was so angry with that woman. The things she'd said back there at the Coyote . . . Cheating on her husband with two men and then trying to put the blame on Lulu! Well, Lulu might have done a few low-down things in her time, but she would never have stooped so low as to marry a man she didn't love. Lulu was worth more than that.

Taking her glass of beer she turned to find a place to sit, and . . . Could it be? She was almost sure . . . Yes, it *was*.

Olga was sitting alone at a table, staring into her empty glass.

'You know, chérie,' said Lulu, 'I love you more than anyone in the world.'

'Except Camby,' said Genevieve.

'*Including* Camby.' She lit a fresh cigarette and passed one to Genevieve. They'd finished the Scotch. 'Men, they come and go. But your best friend is for ever.'

'Got anything else to drink?'

'You have a lot of power over me,' continued Lulu. 'Power to make me happy. Power to hurt me badly.'

'I want to get tight,' said Genevieve. 'Tighter than I've ever been.' And she got down on her hands and knees and started groping around under the bed, searching for more bottles.

'Sometimes,' Lulu's voice had gone vague and dreamy, 'I am wounded so deeply by the people I love that I go crazy-mad. And then I get drunk and do stupid things.'

Genevieve tried to come out from under the bed and bashed her head hard on the metal frame.

'I do these stupid things out of love,' said Lulu. 'Not out of hate.'

'What are you talking about?' Genevieve rubbed at her sore head.

'I went and put my mouth before my brain,' said Lulu. 'The way we both do sometimes. Because we are hurting in our hearts. We have terrible tempers, the pair of us. We go off like fireworks and say things we regret.' She reached out to stroke Genevieve's face again. 'Vivi, I am truly, deeply sorry.'

Camby and Violetta had gone off together and Genevieve had let her down unforgivably. Lulu was drinking to forget her woes but with every drink, they grew. At least she didn't have to drink alone. Olga, as it turned out, was surprisingly sympathetic, as well as being morbidly fascinating. She was talking about how she'd first fallen in love with Paolo Zachari.

'He was so full of ideas,' she was saying. 'So beautiful and clever. There was an energy about him – a magnetism. And there I was – an empty husk in comparison. I'd used up all my youth and my strength on just surviving.'

'I certainly know how that feels,' muttered Lulu.

'In the beginning I envied him,' said Olga. 'I wanted his energy for myself. If I could have extracted it, somehow – if I could have bottled it and drunk it – I would have done. And then it changed and evolved. It wasn't just the energy I wanted any more. It was him. I wanted to possess him. *All* of him. And I started to see that he needed something from me too.'

'What?' Lulu asked. 'What did he need from you?'

'It was very simple. He was alone in Paris, and afraid. He needed to belong somewhere. He needed to be cared for. I built him up and made him strong. I made him into the person he is today. My love for him.' She stared down into her drink. 'He thinks he doesn't need me any more. But he's wrong. One day soon he will understand that.'

Then she started talking about her children. Lulu wasn't sure how many there were. She became confused as the story progressed. By the end of the tale she was imagining a whole sea of hungry little faces, with Olga dropping crumbs in their mouths like a big mother-bird. When the barman brought more drinks over, Olga started coughing hard into a handkerchief. She was trying to hide the blood, but Lulu had seen it.

'Does Zachari know how ill you are?'

'Not really. Not the full extent of it.'

'Don't you think you should tell him?'

Olga buried the handkerchief away. 'What for?'

Lulu toyed with her glass, looked sidelong at her. 'My friend Genevieve – she's in love with him. Did you know that?'

Olga laughed. At least, the sound resembled a laugh, but the expression on the face was far from happy. 'There are always women like her around Paolo. They come and they go.'

'What do you mean – "women like her"?'

'Rich women.' Olga spoke the word 'rich' like it was the worst kind of insult. 'Women who buy his shoes. They think they can buy Paolo too. But in the end I am the one who stays. He tires of them. He always does.'

'What if Genevieve is the exception to that rule?' Lulu drank deeply.

Olga shook her head firmly. 'He will reject her.'

'You seem awfully confident. You think you know him that well?'

'I am the only person in the world who really knows him. He is everything to me.' Suddenly Olga started quivering, her hands barely able to grab her drink.

'Are you all right? Do you need to go home?'

'She doesn't know how to love.' Olga was shaking violently. 'She's cold like a stone.'

'It's getting late.' Lulu was suddenly aware of how drunk she was. 'I'd better go.'

But Olga had seized her hand. 'Have another drink with me. I'm afraid to be alone.'

Lulu was calling after Genevieve as she ran down seven flights of stairs to get out of the apartment building, tick-tacking stupidly downward on spindly heels and almost twisting her ankles. Gagging at the stench of the shared squat toilets on the landings, and with the sheer physical effort of holding herself together. She could still hear Lulu's voice as she hit the street outside.

It was a different city here. The flashy boutiques of the Rue de la Paix with their huge windows and opulent foyers; the flamboyance of the bars and cafés of Montparnasse; the genteel elegance of the Rue de Lota – they could have been a million miles away. There were no taxis – no cars at all in evidence – so she was forced to walk back to civilization.

The air was heavy. Summer was bulging and overripe – rotting, almost. Genevieve passed through alleyways between towering buildings that seemed precarious, on the verge of crumbling. Beneath lines of washing strung back and forth like some crazy cat's-cradle game. Bare-armed women leaned out of high windows, smoking and chatting to each other. Children in outsize knitted clothing hung about in the dirty doorways, playing with marbles and stones and dice. Dogs without collars dabbled in the gutters.

She'd been here once or twice before. Pierre had waited for her in the Bentley outside Lulu's building, while the local children looked on and whispered to each other. But she'd never walked through these streets and looked at them close-up. She'd never given much thought to the way Lulu lived – assuming, perhaps, that her circumstances were a deliberate Bohemian choice: colourful, artistic, kimono-wearing poverty rather than mere drab penury. Now it struck her that her assumptions and complacency may have weighed heavily on Lulu. She thought about Lulu and Olga, drinking together in the little bar, sharing secrets, and perhaps sharing more than that, implicitly, without words. But was it her fault that she was rich while Lulu and Olga were poor? It was no excuse for such a betrayal.

Finally she was out of the squalor and nearing the river. A pair of young lovers stood kissing in the street, their bicycles leaning against a lamppost. The boy had a soft downy look to his face. The girl was pink and glowing and tiny. Genevieve couldn't look at them without crying. At last she spotted a taxi.

## 42

IT WOULD BE LIKE A WOUND CLOSING AND DISAPPEARING, like a bruise yellowing and fading to nothing. You can recover from anything if you really have to. You grow new skin and it stretches across the hurt, thin and taut. You might be scarred but you hide the scar. You have to. Genevieve had done it before, when she lost her baby. She could do it again now. You take each day as it comes, making yourself go through the motions of living a life. And with each day that passes, you feel a little less. Until eventually you feel almost nothing.

Robert was in the salon, pouring himself a drink.

'What's happened to the stopper from the sherry bottle?' There was an edge to his voice.

'I don't know.' It was an unwelcome surprise to find him home so early. She wasn't sure she could face being around him just yet. It felt rather too much like the start of a life sentence.

'Odd thing to have gone missing, don't you think?'

'I suppose so.' She slumped on a chair, watching him. He had a certain way of standing – poker-stiff like a soldier, with his feet slightly apart. Paolo, on the other hand, would lean against things – walls, doorframes – slouching casually. There was a relaxed quality about his body. A natural ease.

But she had to stop thinking about Paolo.

'It was probably Céline.' Her voice was empty. She had swung a wrecking ball at the only true love she'd ever known. He'd never take her back. Not after the things she'd said to him on the telephone. Not after the way she'd behaved.

'You think she broke it?'

'Or stole it. She walked out today. I suppose we'll have to find a new maid.'

How she hated Lulu. Enough to find a source of strength in her hatred.

'Why did she leave?' He sipped his drink.

'How should I know?'

She would run into Paolo around town. At parties, on the street, in shops. Lulu too. It would happen all the time. It would be unbearable. They would have to leave Paris, she and Robert. They'd have to start again somewhere else. It was the only way forward.

'Well, you must know something about it. She wouldn't have walked out for no reason at all, would she?' He handed her a glass of sherry. 'What happened?'

'Oh, I don't like to bother you with these little domestic matters, darling. I'm sure you're not really interested.'

'Yes, I am.'

'No, you're not.' She tried to laugh.

There was definitely something strange about him. It

wasn't just the way he was speaking to her. He was glancing at her and then looking away again. His appearance was rather rough. His hair was tousled and he hadn't shaved. Even his clothes – well, they simply didn't fit him properly. Were they actually *his*?

'She broke the stopper of the sherry bottle. Deliberately. She smashed it down in the hearth. She'd have broken more things if I hadn't stopped her. You remember that Lalique vase we used to have on the mantelpiece? She broke that too, a while back.'

'But I thought you didn't know what happened to that stopper.'

'I didn't want to talk about it. I'm still feeling shaken. She stubbed out a cigarette on the couch too. Look.' She pointed.

'I've never seen her smoking.' Robert walked across to the couch and touched the black scorch mark.

'You've never seen her eat either. That doesn't mean she doesn't do it.'

He went to the fireplace and started peering, as though looking for shards of glass. Evidence.

'I think I'll go to my shoe room. I'd like to be alone for a while.'

'You're lying to me.' His voice was flat. Resigned. 'You've been lying to me for a long time.'

Genevieve swallowed. 'Why should I lie? She was a silly girl, prone to hysteria. Good riddance, I say. I'll find a replacement soon enough.'

'I'm not just talking about the maid!' His fist crashed down on the mantelpiece.

'Darling . . .'

'Tell me the truth for once. Are you having an affair?'

'No.' She could barely get the word out.

'You were seen, damn it! Harry's wife saw you!'

The Luxembourg Gardens . . . That woman . . .

He sat down and put his head in his hands.

'I was, but it's over,' she said quietly. 'I won't be seeing him again.'

'I loved you so much.' He rubbed at his face. 'But how can I go on loving you? I can't believe anything you're saying to me.'

Genevieve sat alone in her shoe room, her eyes red, sore and dry as sandpaper. She was thinking about a game that the little boy downstairs played, if he saw you in the lift or the hallway. He thought that if he covered his eyes with his hands, he was hidden. He couldn't see you and therefore you couldn't see him. He was invisible.

She wished she too could cover her eyes and vanish.

She was sitting on the floor, barefoot, her back to the wall. In front of her were two pairs of shoes. Red Genoese velvet, the buckles set with tiny diamonds. And two beasts facing each other to fight or mate. Gold heels with a G and a P intertwined in mirror-writing.

The door opened. Genevieve kept her eyes on the shoes.

'Genevieve . . .'

'These are fiddly to clean.' She picked up one of the red shoes. 'One should tease the velvet with the softest of brushes and polish the glass with a little newspaper, taking care not to smear newsprint on the fabric. The diamonds should be left well alone or one might loosen their settings.'

'There's something I need to know.'

'When you slide your feet into these shoes . . .' and now she did just that, 'it's like having your feet taken into a warm, silken mouth.'

'Is it mine? The baby, I mean.'

A breath. 'There is no baby.'

'I see.' He cracked his knuckles one by one. 'I'm going out for a walk.' As he turned away, he looked smaller, somehow. Like he'd shrunk. Like he was an old man. 'Wait here. We'll talk when I get back.'

# VIII

## *Facings*

## 43

GENEVIEVE SHELBY KING SAT ALONE IN THE CLOSERIE DES Lilas at a corner table, a small suitcase by her side, a cognac in front of her, a cigarette pinched between two fingers of her right hand. She was wearing a Chanel day ensemble in black wool jersey and silk: round-necked with long loose sleeves, a wide low belt and a pleated skirt. Around her throat were her mother's pearls. On her feet were Zachari's gold-embroidered shoes. On her head a cloche hat with a diamond pin and a black ostrich plume. She'd been here a while now and her clothing was considerably more sober than she was.

The case contained her red velvet Zacharis and her Mary Janes. She'd packed (in some haste) the diamond tiara she'd worn on her wedding day and her sapphire-and-diamond cluster ring, thinking they'd fetch quite a bit of money if necessary. These pieces were family heirlooms. She didn't want to take anything that had been a gift from Robert. She was also carrying the contents of her cash box – five hundred dollars, a couple of thousand francs – and her passport.

A lot of Hemingway and McAlmon soundalikes were trooping through this place today, sitting down with their clever women with fashionably waved hair, Luluesque beauty spots, short V-necked dresses and hard laughter that came out like rounds of artillery. Snippets of conversation drifted across to Genevieve through the smoke haze.

'Oh really? A novelist, you say? I thought it was the name of a racehorse. Or a small town in Brittany . . .'

'But you don't understand. When I'm alone with her I feel I'm lost in a vast, damp cave, calling out for help and hearing my own voice echoed back for ever and ever . . .'

'*Trois Filles Nues*, at the Bouffes-Parisiennes. Marvellous dancing. They dress as shrimps. Yes, I did say shrimps . . .'

They were all chasing it, these would-bes. The buzz – the jazz buzz, the crazy buzz – that lit Paris far more brightly than the streetlamps, and flowed, electric, from person to person. Genevieve had craved so much to be a part of it, and lately she'd come close. She'd felt it sparking when she was with Paolo Zachari. The air around Lulu crackled constantly. She'd glimpsed it in Norman Betterson's home. Even when she ran from Guy Monteray.

But ultimately she had failed. The buzz – Paris – had eluded her. She'd lost her lover and she'd smashed her life here to pieces. It was time to give up and leave.

Trouble was, she had no idea where she was going.

She'd left a note:

*Dear Robert,*
   *I'm sorry for the way I've treated you. One lie led to another and yet another. I've built a path of lies and*

*followed it all the way out of our marriage. I had thought
I could turn back, but now I see I can't.*

*I hope you'll find happiness. You deserve to be happy. If
it's any consolation, I'm not.*

*Vivi*

*PS The horse is in the cellar.*

\*

She stubbed out her cigarette and lit a fresh one. She put
her left elbow on the table and used it to prop up her heavy
head.

'Genevieve?'

She looked up.

Two women in black were standing in front of her.

'Marianne spotted you from outside,' said Augusta
Betterson.

'Norman used to come here, didn't he?' Marianne had a
clear, intelligent face. Her nose was rather horsey but her
eyes were huge and lovely and dewy. Full of compassion.

'They all come here,' said Genevieve.

'Did you ever meet up with him here to talk about the
magazine?'

'Once or twice.'

The two women glanced at each other.

'Did you sit at this table? With Norman, I mean?' asked
Augusta.

'Perhaps. I don't remember.'

'May we?' Augusta pulled out a chair and sat down.
Marianne followed suit.

'We've been thinking,' said Marianne. 'About what you
said yesterday.'

'What did I say?'

'I told you his poetry was lost – that it's not real until it's on the page. But you said that maybe some of it *is* on the page. That it's up to us to salvage it.'

Genevieve shrugged.

'Norman worked so hard on the magazine.' Augusta was softer than Marianne. She was older and her face had a certain fleshiness to it. But something steely showed beneath. 'And McAlmon too, and all those writers. It would be such a shame for all that work to go to waste.'

'Ah.' Genevieve looked from one to the other. 'You want my help. I'm sorry, but—'

'Think about it.' You could still see tear-tracks on Augusta's cheeks. 'The poems and stories have all been delivered. And from some big names too. The editing is pretty much done.'

'It's just the one issue,' said Marianne. 'For now.'

Genevieve opened her mouth to speak but Augusta cut in.

'This was your project as well as Norman's. We'd appreciate any expertise you can offer.'

'Expertise . . .' She tried the word out on her tongue. It felt alien there. 'That's funny. Really, it's very funny.'

But neither of them was laughing.

'I'm talentless,' said Genevieve. 'My poetry is worthless. If you don't believe me, look for yourselves. My notebook is still there, in your apartment.'

'We didn't just run into you by accident yesterday,' said Marianne. 'It was a sign. And now, finding you here – that's another sign. We have to save the magazine. For Norman.'

'We need money,' said Augusta.

Genevieve called out for three more cognacs. 'Have a

drink on me, ladies. I'm afraid it's about the best I can do for you now. You see, I've just walked out on my husband.'

'Walked out?' Marianne frowned.

She held up her little case. 'I travel impressively lightly, wouldn't you say?'

'So the money . . .' began Augusta.

'Was all his. I have none of my own. You could go and speak to Robert if you like, but I can't imagine he'll be very well disposed towards the magazine. Not after everything I've put him through.'

The waiter brought the three cognacs. Genevieve toyed with her glass and Marianne looked crestfallen, but Augusta smiled and downed her drink in one.

'Oh well. We'll just have to find a new backer. There'll be someone out there. This magazine *will* happen. Some things are *meant*, and this is one of them.'

Something passed between the two women. A kind of energy. Only twenty-four hours ago, at Notre Dame, they had seemed spent. Empty. But today they were full of resolve.

'Do you really think it's true?' asked Genevieve. 'That things are "meant"?'

Augusta shrugged. 'I don't know. Maybe a little. But it's more about attitude. If something is worth fighting for, then you'd better fight for it. You'd better make it happen.'

'Yes.' Something was igniting in Genevieve.

'That was how Norman lived his life,' said Augusta. 'People who didn't really know him thought he was "just another of those poets" – drinking and spinning yarns at the bars in the Quarter. But there was so much more to Norman. He worked harder than anyone I know. He didn't waste a single day. For a long time, his illness made him stronger. Does that make sense? It made him stronger because it made him more purposeful and determined.'

A fire was spreading through Genevieve. What had she been thinking of – sitting here drinking and moping and watching her life crumble around her? Roused, she took up her glass, threw her drink back and tossed some francs down on the table.

'You're leaving?' asked Marianne.

'Yes. There's something I have to do – to *try*, anyway. I really *am* sorry I can't help you with the magazine. I'm sure you can do this, though.' And then, an afterthought: 'You might think about the Countess de Frémont. She has plenty of cash to spare and she's . . . well . . . easy.'

## 44

SHE WAS SURE SHE'D NEVER WAITED SO LONG ON THE telephone. So much time and space in which to be nervous. To fear, to dread, to pray.

Please let him be there. Please let it be *him*, not *her*.

The delay stretched out. The operator must be doing this deliberately.

And then, at last: 'Putting you through.'

A loud click and the sound of breathing. His. She knew it was his and she loved it.

'Paolo, I'm so—'

'I know.'

'Do you think you could ever forgive me?'

'Maybe. Are you drunk?'

'Yes. I've left Robert.'

'Are you sure?'

'Of course I'm sure! Robert, the apartment, even my shoe collection . . .' A throb beneath the ribs. 'I've done it, Paolo. It's done. There's no going back.'

A breath. 'Are you all right?'

'I'm leaving Paris. Tonight.'

'Where will you go?'

'London. Come with me.'

A sound on the line. Perhaps a cough. Perhaps a laugh.

'We can start afresh there. London's a great city – maybe even greater than Paris. Your work needn't suffer at all. There'd be so much new inspiration. We'd have each other. There wouldn't be trouble from Robert or . . . or *her*. We could be happy.'

Silence.

'Alternatively you could stay here with your shoes, going to parties and sleeping with women you don't love and who don't love you. The years will go by and you'll just get more and more lonely and bitter. A life without love, that's what you'll have. You'll shrivel up like an old prune. Do you think that'll make your shoes more beautiful? I doubt it.'

Still he didn't speak. The fire in her belly was starting to waver. 'Come on, Paolo. Say yes. We can get the eight o'clock boat train.'

'It's already six-thirty.'

'So?'

'So I don't have much time to pack.'

The flames leaped again. Right into her throat. 'You're coming then?'

'Yes.'

'We'll be fine. You know that, don't you?'

'I'll see you at the Gare du Nord.'

'On the platform.'

Genevieve breathed in and out and the receiver was empty in her jewelled hand.

## 45

PIGEONS FLUTTERED ABOUT HER AS SHE HANDED OVER THE money for her ticket. They snatched at a piece of bread that somebody had dropped and went soaring back up to the vaulted steel and glass roof. People drifted. Businessmen in smart coats were scything through the crowds, clutching their hats, tutting their contempt. Steam hissed and puffed from the great dark engines, putting Genevieve in mind of her father's dogs – big black hounds pawing at the frozen ground, straining at their leashes, their breath clouding the air. She had always been afraid of them.

A sharp-looking woman with angry red cheeks and a drab hat was striding towards the trains, dragging her tiny daughter by the hand, proceeding at such a pace that the child was all but lifted off the ground. The little girl, who couldn't have been more than four or five, clutched at her rag-doll and whimpered as she struggled to keep up. The child, out of breath, was falling behind and the mother yanked her arm, causing her to drop the doll. The girl let out a squeal and a sob, lunging but failing to grab the doll as she was carried onward. Genevieve hurried to retrieve it for her but was elbowed in the stomach by an old woman with an umbrella. The old lady began to complain loudly and breathily, and when Genevieve disentangled herself and looked up, the child and her mother had vanished. For a second, she thought she heard cries in the distance, but it was impossible to distinguish them clearly from the general hubbub. The abandoned doll had wool hair, a grubby white face, and expressionless blue felt eyes. Genevieve sat it on a bench.

At a station bar, she drank a small black coffee, savouring every tiny pungent sip and reflecting that this was the last good cup she'd have for some time to come.

Back to England then. But not the England she'd left behind, she reminded herself – not the England of hushed whispers, rattling teacups, mildew and disapproval. No, they were headed for London. The theatres, the department stores, the grandeur . . . You could escape disapproval in London. You could merge with the crowd, you could lose yourself . . .

Not that they would be losing themselves, of course. It was vital that Paolo rose rapidly to prominence. After a week or two in a hotel (she fancied the Connaught), they'd find the right business premises – Bond Street, possibly – and a smart flat, perhaps one of those lovely white Georgian buildings in Kensington: large windows and balconies and a view over Hyde Park. Yes, that would be most acceptable. Her smile snagged slightly at a creeping worry about how they'd pay for all this. They hadn't exactly taken the time to consider that small issue . . . But surely Zachari must have pots of money. He certainly didn't fritter his earnings away on the art of living. Anyway, they only needed enough to get a good start. Once he was designing again, with her at his side, their shared future would be assured.

She imagined Robert reading her note. He'd be out of his mind. Perhaps he'd go to the shoe room, start pulling boxes down and hurling the shoes about. He might hack at them with knives and scissors or heap them up into a pile and set fire to them!

A shudder.

Her watch showed it was almost twenty to eight. A brass band in blue and gold uniforms was just striking up as she arrived at the platform. Cases and carpet bags were being carried on to the train. Inside, passengers were settling down with their newspapers. A boy was drawing with his finger in the filth of the window – a smiley face – until someone told him to stop and he shrank, scowling, into his seat.

Quarter to eight. Some shouting at the head of the neighbouring platform caused Genevieve to turn and peer. Someone famous had got off the train. Newspaper photographers were crowding in from nowhere with a series of flashbulb explosions, along with a gaggle of autograph hunters, fascinated children, and other desperate types drawn like moths.

Josephine Baker came clearly into view, mobbed by photographers and fans. Since her triumphant debut in *La Revue Nègre* at the Théâtre des Champs Elysées she was known to every man and woman in the city. Even those who'd never seen a show in their lives couldn't possibly have missed her wickedly sensual face and criminally short dress plastered on every kiosk on every street corner in Paul Colin's poster. Now she strode down the platform with her pet leopard Chiquita on a leash, flashing a white smile, followed by several handsome men who could equally easily have been minders, managers, lawyers or lovers.

Paul Poiret, concluded Genevieve, examining Miss Baker's gorgeous slinky, pink gown. She got on tiptoes to peer at her feet: pink and silver and sparkling – yes, those shoes could easily be Paolo's. She must ask him when he arrived. He really ought to be here by now.

Ten to eight and the Baker entourage had moved on and away. Genevieve was trying hard not to fret.

'Madame?' An elderly train guard tapped her on the shoulder. 'Perhaps you would like to board now?'

'I'm waiting for someone.'

'Perhaps you would like to wait on the train?'

'No.'

Five to eight and the doors were slamming, each bang sending a shock wave through Genevieve's body. Her head was filled with disaster. Zachari lying under the front wheels of a taxi in the Rue Denain within sight of the station, her name on his dying lips. Zachari in a dark alleyway, falling backwards with blood streaming from his head while Robert stood over him, the gun still smoking. And, perhaps worst of all, Zachari in his workroom, hammering away at Violet de Frémont's latest pair of shoes, stoically ignoring the clock on the wall.

'Madame?' That guard again. They were the only two people on the platform. Alone with the hiss of steam. The boy in the nearby carriage was drawing another face in the window filth, the mouth turned down in simplified sadness.

'Madame, you must get on the train now.'

She thought again of the sad, pink face of the child who dropped her rag-doll.

'Madame?'

She turned away to conceal her tears, and hurried to get off the platform in her beautiful but impractical shoes just as the whistle sounded.

A shunting and squealing signalled the first movements of the engine. A grinding and rolling as it inched away. A few stragglers waved and flapped white handkerchiefs.

At the head of the platform, she shut her eyes tight, dropped her case and stood hugging herself, very small and still while people surged around her. When she opened her eyes again there was a boy standing in front of her. A grubby-faced boy of twelve or thirteen with dark, greasy hair and short trousers, his shoelaces trailing on the floor around his feet.

'What do you want?'

The boy just stared.

'Are you begging?'

Hollow eyes. There was something familiar about him.

Now he thrust something at her. A folded piece of paper. She reached out and took it, and while she was still opening it, he span around and ran away.

*I can't come with you. I'm sorry.*
*I love you.*
*P*

Genevieve's heart thudded – once, twice. The boy was sprinting past the ticket office, scattering people to left and right as he went charging on – and then he was gone.

She crumpled the note in her hand. Scrunched it tight in her clenched fist while pigeons fluttered around her and fought over a piece of bread.

## 46

ROBERT WALKED TO HIS OFFICE. HE COULDN'T THINK OF anywhere else to go. This city was not his. It never had been. And he'd never felt more like a loose, dangling thread.

*Wait here*, he'd said to Genevieve. *We'll talk when I get back*. But what was there to say? Harry was right about her. The sooner he faced up to that, the better. It was time to go home. He should have gone home long ago – years ago. He should never have come to Europe in the first place.

It had been a fiasco from start to finish. He'd only travelled out of some abstract notion of romance and heroism. Everyone back home had laughed or raised their eyebrows at his fervour to join up. They seemed to see it as a sign of his immaturity, and they humoured him. *Indulge the boy. Let him get it out of his system*. They'd been right. He'd ended up as a bit-part player with no direct experience of the gore and the glory of the battlefield. He came through the war without medals or scars. He didn't even come through it with Agnes, his first love, on his arm. How different his life would have been had she chosen him over the lost-and-found Edward.

The building was empty. Everyone had gone home to their families, their nice lives. Riding up in the lift to the fourth floor, wandering down the long corridor, he thought he might stay here for the night. Lie down to sleep on the tigerskin rug she'd made him buy. Yes, why not make her sweat a little? He was in no hurry to go back to the Rue de Lota.

'Mr Shelby King.'

Robert jumped and span around at the girl's voice.

'I'm sorry to have startled you. I need to speak to you.'

Céline, the maid!

'How did you get in here?'

'I followed you.' Her pupils were dilated in the half-light. 'I didn't mean any harm, I swear.'

'You *followed* me? From the Rue de Lota?'

A nod.

'But this building is kept locked out of hours. I locked the door behind me.'

'Actually, sir, you didn't.'

He rubbed at his head. 'Come on through to my office. We may as well have a drink together and you can tell me what's on your mind. God knows I don't have anything better to do. And neither do you, from the look of it.'

Getting out the bourbon, he gestured for her to sit down. She looked anxious – not just at the situation but at the drink itself. He supposed she'd never tasted it before. For some reason he kept thinking of Marie-Claire – what she'd say if she walked in and found him drinking the hard stuff with some slip of a girl after hours; the disapproval in her soft eyes. But oddly, this only drove him on. Even as she was coughing and spluttering from the first sip, he was tipping more into her glass and sitting down on the other 'visitor's chair', close to hers.

'So,' he said. 'I gather you've left us. Now, why would that be?'

'Oh, sir. I didn't want to leave you. Not *you*. But *she* – she's been . . . I couldn't ignore it any longer.'

He almost couldn't bring himself to ask the question. And yet he had to, didn't he? 'Ignore what, Céline?'

'She doesn't deserve you. You're so good to her. And she . . .'

He sighed and drained his glass.

'It started with the phone calls. He called himself Monsieur Renard. I didn't mean to eavesdrop, but she didn't even bother to lower her voice! And then she'd be coming and going, all dolled up in her finery, sir, while you were out at work. Calling up hotels to book rooms and waltzing off when you thought she was sitting in at home. It's true. I swear it on my mother's life.'

It was almost a relief to sit here listening to this story. There was nothing the girl could say that would shock him. Not now. Look how nervous she was. Frightened of how he might react, but pressing ahead with her story regardless. Was it her sense of honour and justice that had driven her to follow him here and pour out her story? Or hatred of his wife? Or what?

'. . . She tried to buy my silence. First she gave me a pair of shoes. Then it was money slipped under my door. She was so brazen! "I'm off for a shoe-fitting, Céline." Well, nobody spends that long at the shoemaker, sir!

391

Not for a fitting, at any rate. Not even her.'

Robert looked levelly at her. There was something familiar in the words she'd just spoken . . .

'I stayed as long as I could, sir. For your sake. I . . . You're such a nice man, sir. I can see this is a shock and everything, but – well, you can't let her destroy you. We're not all false like her, sir. Not all of us.'

She looked up at him through her lashes, her face transformed. More confident and feminine. Coquettish. Was she taking her cues from him? Had his own expression changed?

'I know, Céline.' He poured out more bourbon. Pouring until the glasses were half full, and murmuring, 'You're a good girl. That's why you wrote me those letters, isn't it? On that pretty lilac paper. Out of the goodness of your heart.'

'Oh, sir.' She looked so relieved. So delighted. 'I knew you'd believe me.'

'Of course.' He pulled his chair a little closer to hers. How old was she? Sixteen? Seventeen? 'My marriage is over, honey. It's been over for a long time but I've only just realized it.' Unbidden, Marie-Claire came back into his head. Marie-Claire in her kitchen, making coffee. Turning to tell her little boy where to find his schoolbag. 'You see, I've met someone else.'

'Someone . . . else?' Her eyes shone wetly. Her expression revealing everything he needed to know.

'Yes. Now drink up. There's more in the bottle.' And he reached out and patted her knee, letting his hand remain there – on her knee – just long enough to be certain that she wouldn't push him away.

## 47

SITTING BACK IN HER TAXI, GENEVIEVE RE-READ THE PALTRY note, ripped it into tiny pieces, and scattered it along the street like confetti.

Zachari's shop was shuttered. She knocked for a while and called out his name. Then she kicked the door. Once, twice, three times. Having vented some of her anger, she stopped and tried to think.

He *did* love her. She knew he did. So why would he treat her this way? Not even coming to the station himself, but sending some boy with a stupid note?

She needed answers.

She thought she could prise open one of the upper windows. They were old and the frames looked rotten, the catches fragile. If only there was a way to get up there . . . Reminded suddenly of Guy Monteray climbing to the apartment above Shakespeare and Company, swinging up by the sign (how shocked she'd been at his behaviour, but now it seemed little different to her own), she contemplated the sign that hung above Zachari's door . . . But it was very high up – she didn't have Monteray's height and long, strong arms – and its fixings looked old and brittle. It might not take her weight.

People climbed drainpipes, didn't they? And here was such a pipe, running vertically to the left of the door. But where did you put your feet when you climbed a drainpipe? They were hardly ladders. No convenient rungs.

Genevieve walked around the corner, gazing up. The building was so closed to her that it seemed almost wilful.

Stopping before the street-level grille covering the basement window, she thought back to the night, all those months ago, when she'd paced back and forth in her Sebastian York snakeskin court shoes, hoping that Zachari would notice her tiny, delicate feet and shapely ankles, and come out to find her.

She couldn't see any way of getting in. So what now? Check into a hotel? Drink the night away in one of the Montparnasse bars with whatever distant acquaintances were around? She wished she had a friend to call, but her only close friend had turned out as faithless as her absent lover.

She'd wandered slowly all the way out on to the Rue de la Paix before something occurred to her. It was a long shot but none the less . . .

Back she went to Zachari's shop, and up to the front door. She grasped the handle and . . . it turned. The door opened.

The fitting room was sad. Those melancholy purple couches, the empty mirrors. Genevieve's heels were loud against the polished floor. Unable to believe he would have left the shop unlocked, she called out his name. Nothing. Could he be downstairs?

Another door left unlocked. Paolo's workroom was very different in the half-darkness. The streetlamp outside cast a ghostly glow over the clutter. A couple of abandoned sketches lay on the table showing shoes with strange slats in the sides and odd pointy boots with baubles on the ends like something a court jester would wear. The tools hanging from hooks on the wall were sinister, like weapons.

Wandering around this room, alone, was like reading someone's diary or going through their underwear drawers. It might all look like clutter – the beads, the jewels, the feathers, the sheets of leather, the lace, the sketches, the dyes, the almost illegible notes – but each item, each bit of fluff, had been carefully selected and kept for a purpose.

Genevieve examined notations, picked up jars, tripped over pieces of wood, but nothing seemed to tell her anything about why Zachari had done this to her, and where he might be now.

Concentrate.

Here on a stool was a pair of delicate court shoes, painted like the wings of butterflies. He'd been talking about them on the telephone just today, hadn't he? He was all excited to tell her something and she hadn't been listening. Now, who did he say they were for? The Countess de Frémont, possibly? He might be in bed with Violet right now. They might be laughing uproariously at the very thought of her at the Gare du Nord, waiting and hoping and longing . . .

No. That wasn't what was happening. Focus, Genevieve. What had he told her that first day he brought her in here? He kept all the shoes in a padlocked cupboard. He would never leave them lying around.

She picked up the butterfly shoes and sat down on the stool, convinced now that something had happened to Paolo – something that had compelled him to change his plans at the last moment, write a hasty note and send a boy to deliver it to her.

Who or what had that kind of power over him?

Back upstairs, she made straight for the reception desk. The appointments diary lay open but there was no address book. She tried the drawer – and yes, here it was.

First she looked under 'O', but there was no address listed. Then she realized she didn't know the surname, so was forced to check under every letter of the alphabet, nervously running her finger down each page, so tense and impatient that she almost tore the pages as she turned them.

Nothing.

Genevieve slumped. Her head, shoulders and back ached with tiredness. She was aware, now, of how thirsty she was, and of how much she needed to sleep. For a while, she just sat there at the reception desk. Then, with an effort, she dragged herself back to the staircase and climbed up to his apartment, immensely relieved when that door opened too. She'd get herself a glass of water and lie down on his bed for the night. He had to come back eventually, didn't he?

She was already running her second glass, the water dripping down her chin even while her thirst was still raging, when she turned and saw the half-written letter on the kitchen table.

*Dear Olga,*

*I don't know how to say this to you, after all our years together. I know it's cowardly to run away like this. I suppose I'm too ashamed to face you – to speak the words aloud and see your proud face alter just a little, that very small shift in expression that lets me glimpse the tumult beneath. I've seen it before, all those times I've treated you badly – when I've let you down and gone with other women and lied to you. I think sometimes I've been deliberately cruel just to find out how much you're prepared to take – to push you to your limits. But you're limitless when it comes to me, aren't you, dearest? You've faced whatever the world – and I – have thrown at you with stoicism, strength, and the particular kind of resignation that I just can't stand and never could.*

*I am leaving with Genevieve, as I expect you've guessed. She couldn't be more different from you and perhaps that's why I'm drawn to her. She's impatient, flighty and passionate, and there's something intoxicating about her. (See, I'm doing it even now – the unnecessary cruelty.) All I know is that I believe I've met my match in her. We're like the left and right shoes. We're meant to be together.*

*And so it's goodbye. I'm so grateful to you, Olga, for everything you've given me. You have taught me about love and about life. I would never have been Paolo Zachari without your help.*

*Don't worry about money. I'll*

And here the letter broke off. With tears in her eyes,

Genevieve took it up to read it again, and saw that there was an envelope lying beneath it on the table.

An envelope with the name 'Olga Krechnev' written on it, and a full address.

## 48

HE'S WITH *HER*.

It was her only clear thought as she dropped the letter. And then the other thoughts came rushing in.

He nearly came with me. *Nearly*. But something made him change his mind even as he wrote that letter. Something made him break off and hurry out of the shop without locking up. And he wrote the goodbye to me instead.

She asked the taxi driver to stop on the Quai des Célestins, preferring to walk from there. Dusk was turning to night. The sky above the Seine was a deep, sorrowful blue. The river was silvery and tranquil. Genevieve crossed over to the Ile St-Louis by the Pont Marie. Olga's street lay along one of her favourite walking routes, Quai d'Anjou on the Ile, one of Paris's best addresses. The tall building with the large windows, curling wrought-iron balustrades and pretty walled courtyard was one she'd gazed at hundreds of times, and coveted. A far cry from anything she might have imagined.

He's been with her for years. Ever since he arrived in Paris. All those women – they meant absolutely nothing to him. They were an act of rebellion, nothing more. It's always been her.

The street was silent but for the mewling of a cat, the rustling of the creeping vines in the walled garden, and the distant lapping of the river. A lamp glowed at one of the long windows on the third floor.

The concierge, an elderly woman with blue-veined arms, was initially grim-faced and unhelpful. But then she seemed to notice the thick rope of pearls around Genevieve's neck, and the diamond pin in her cloche hat, and became more amiable. Some dollars pressed into her palm – and then a few more – made her more amiable still. Genevieve was able to take the lift up to the third floor alone and unannounced.

The door was opened only a crack. Dark eyes peeped out at child height.

'Hello.' Genevieve bent down and tried a smile. 'I'm looking for Paolo.'

Small fingers crept around the edge of the door.

'Is your mother home?'

'She's in bed.'

'And Paolo?'

The fingers retreated. She heard a sound – the slap of bare feet on a wood floor, moving away. A creak of the door, left open.

The little girl who answered the door was wearing a nightie and clutching a moth-eaten bear under her arm. She was standing just inside, twirling strands of her long dark hair around her fingers. She must have been about eight years old. Through the open door to the salon, Genevieve could see a second girl. Younger – maybe five or so, with a curly mop-top and a sulky expression, cross-legged on a Turkish rug in the middle of the room. She was playing with something heavy and sparkly. A piece of glass, by the looks of things. They were so young, these children.

The apartment was all polished oak and thick rugs, antique *chaises longues* and long mirrors in heavy silver frames. There was a feel of old-style opulence here, and the kind of luxury she might have expected from Paolo's own apartment. The walls were crammed with books and paintings. Toys lay about, and amongst the art on the walls were pinned some brightly coloured childish daubs.

To think she'd expected mouldy walls and laundry . . .

'What do you want?'

Genevieve took a few steps into the salon to see the boy from the station sitting at a pretty walnut bureau, writing in a schoolbook.

'I need to speak to Paolo. Is he here?'

'He doesn't want to speak to you.'

'And how do you know that? Did he say so?'

'He's busy.' The boy turned back to his work.

The salon windows were open and the breeze was moving the heavy chandelier with a gentle tinkling sound.

Returning to the hallway, she crouched down to address the child with the bear, who lingered near the front door. 'Hello. I'm looking for my friend Paolo. Is he in one of those rooms?' She indicated the five closed doors.

The girl smiled and seemed about to speak.

'Leave her alone.' The boy came striding out, his chest all puffed up.

Genevieve straightened. 'Well, if you won't tell me—'

'You're not wanted here. Go away.'

They were staring at her – the girl smiling, the boy still angry. The littlest child, on the rug, carried on playing with her piece of glass, oblivious.

'Look,' Genevieve began, aware of how ridiculous it was to feel intimidated by a boy in short trousers, but intimidated none the less. But then she heard it. The coughing.

Deep, gut-wrenching, raging like a fire, and building, the way a house-fire builds, consumes. A sound barely even human.

The child in the nightie covered her ears and shut her eyes tight. The girl on the rug did the same.

Before the boy could get in her way, Genevieve made straight for the door which seemed to be the source of the dreadful sound.

A giant-size bed with a tapestried canopy sat at the centre of the room, and in the centre of the bed was Olga, thrown forward by the force of the appalling coughing. Her face was partly hidden by a white china bowl into which she hacked and spat, her hair – always so shiny in its neat chignon – a dangling mass of sweat-soaked rats' tails. The bowl was held for her by a young man. It was that barman from the Ritz! He'd waved at Genevieve from a window only yesterday. The one who'd been serving Olga on the day she and Lulu had followed her. No wonder he'd refused to take Olga's money. What nice boy would take payment from his mother, after all?

The windows were wide open but still the room reeked of sickness, sweet and rotten. A bowl of oranges sat on the bedside table.

The coughing fit began to loosen its grip and finally it let Olga go. She slumped back against the pillows, her eyes closed, her cheeks the high pink that Genevieve had seen in the faces of other sufferers, most recently Norman Betterson. The boy at her side dabbed at her mouth with a flannel, and then soaked a second cloth in a bowl of water and pressed it to her forehead.

Soothed, Olga opened her eyes, clear and glittering, and the trace of a smile appeared on her mouth. She muttered something to the boy in Russian, and he too looked up.

'What are you doing here?' he said.

'She's come to take Paolo away. Haven't you?' A voice like dead grass in the wind.

'Don't be silly, Mother.' The boy lifted the cloth from her forehead.

'I don't understand,' said Genevieve. 'You didn't seem so very ill. It was only this morning.'

'It's Mrs Shelby King, isn't it?' The boy looked confused. 'Is it you that's moved into the apartment on the fifth floor?'

'Don't, Viktor. She has come to take Paolo away.'

'Is he here?' Genevieve couldn't stop herself. 'I just want to know that he's all right.'

'Now, look—' Viktor began, but Olga put a hand on his arm.

'Go and check on your brother and sisters.' And then, more softly, 'It's all right, *zolotoi*. I'll just talk to her alone for a minute.'

Darting a suspicious glance at Genevieve, the boy left the room.

'Is he here?' Genevieve repeated.

'I told you to stay away from him.'

'I love him,' said Genevieve. 'I have to know what's happened.'

A rustling, crackling sound. Something that was almost laughter.

'We were going to leave Paris together.'

There was anger in Olga's eyes, hot and fevered, as she pulled herself forward. 'You don't know what love is until you know about suffering.'

Genevieve took a couple of steps closer. 'You know about my baby. You know I've suffered.'

'*Poor little Genevieve.*'

'Don't. Just don't.' She took a breath. 'Look, I'm sorry. I can see that you're very unwell. Perhaps I shouldn't have come here, but . . .'

'No. You shouldn't.'

She steadied herself. Tried to make herself walk out of the room, but couldn't. And then the words burst out. 'We're in love, Olga. I can't pretend otherwise, and I don't think he can either. He cares about you, I know. But you're so much older than him . . .'

'You stupid girl. You think *I'm* the one that needs *him*?' The cheeks were more and more pink. And then something seemed to distract her, and her expression changed subtly. 'Say it!'

'Say what?' Genevieve shook her head.

'You know what.'

'Mother?' The boy was back, peering around the door.

'Say it!'

Viktor turned to Genevieve. 'She needs to sleep. Let her sleep.'

'Say it,' whispered Olga, lolling back against her pillows.

'I should go,' muttered Genevieve. And, to Viktor, 'Is there anything I can do for her? Has the doctor been?'

'Just go,' said the boy. 'Please.'

'Say it, for God's sake!' hissed Olga, and her eyes opened wide again. 'That I'll have to let him go soon. That I'll have no choice. Well, I won't let him go! You hear me? I won't!'

Standing in the doorway to the salon, Genevieve saw that the younger boy was back at his schoolwork. The girl on the floor was still playing with the sparkly object – passing it from hand to hand. It was the stopper from Robert's sherry decanter. The older girl was drawing on a piece of paper, holding the pencil with her left hand. Her curly hair hung down over her face.

And now she became aware of hushed voices behind another door. Paolo's voice – unmistakable – speaking rapidly. Almost a whisper. Far too quiet for her to be able to make out the words. A pause, and then an older man replying curtly, abruptly. Genevieve moved closer, putting her ear to the door.

Paolo's voice, from inside the room, grew louder. 'Is that definite? Are you certain?'

'She's dying.' The younger boy had got up from the bureau and was standing right behind her. There was an odd look on his face – a sort of pleading, as though his mother's health was in her gift.

'But are you *sure*?' Paolo again.

'It's obvious,' said the boy. 'Isn't it?'

'I suppose so,' said Genevieve. 'Yes.'

The boy's eyes were wide and staring. And suddenly all the arrogance was gone and he seemed to crumple. A sob escaped as he barged past her and blundered into his mother's room, the door slamming shut after him.

The doctor was talking to Paolo, explaining something. Although she couldn't hear the words, Genevieve recognized the patient, professional tone. It made her think of Dr Peters – the way he used to talk to her when he explained, over and over, why she had to give baby Josephine away.

'There must be *something*,' said Paolo, from behind the door. His voice had a desperation in it that Genevieve had never heard before. She couldn't stand to hear any more – it was too awful. Alien in Paolo and yet horribly familiar.

As she moved away, back into the salon, she felt a great sadness rise up in her. It wasn't just about losing Zachari. This was about something else too. Something she'd only fully acknowledged to herself just now in that sickroom, while a dying woman sneered at her.

The girl at the table lifted up her drawing and held it this way and that. It was a woman's shoe.

Genevieve was crying, silently, as she stared down at the drawing. Her tears were for her lost baby. And for these lost children.

## 49

'COME BACK FOR YOUR SHOES, HAVE YOU?'

Genevieve froze in the act of bending to ease off the gold shoes. She had hoped, *prayed*, that he would be in bed.

'I don't feel well.' This was true. The sadness still gripped her. The stench of the sickroom lingered on in her nostrils. 'Could we talk in the morning, Robert? I'd like to go to bed and sleep.'

A squeak of leather from the salon and he was standing in the doorway staring down at her as she fumbled with the buttons on her shoes.

'But my dear, you don't live here any more. Have you forgotten?'

She dropped the first shoe on the floor and reached down to remove the second, using the wall to steady herself. 'Please, Robert. I really need to sleep.'

'So do I. But I don't suppose I'll be able to.'

She dropped the second shoe. 'I know I owe you an explanation—'

'An *explanation*? I should think you owe me a damn sight

more than that!' He was bristling with anger. His whole body was shaking with it.

Wearily, she placed the hat with its bedraggled ostrich feather on the hall table. 'I can't talk at the moment. I'm sorry.'

'You don't get to call the shots any more. That's something you don't get to do.'

Her arms ached as she straightened up and slipped off the Chanel jacket.

'So, do I take it your cobbler doesn't want you?'

She flinched. 'How did you—'

'I'm not a fool, Genevieve. Whatever you might think.'

'I know that.'

'Then why did you treat me like one?'

'Oh, Robert. For pity's sake.'

'So I'm supposed to *pity* you now? *I'm* to pity *you*?'

Genevieve tried to swallow. 'Look, if you want me to go, I'll go. I'll find a hotel.'

'You . . .' He grabbed her by the shoulders and shook her till it felt like every bone in her body was rattling. 'Damn you!' And then he let her go, and stood looking down at his own hands.

'Let's have a drink,' she said. 'Come on. Come and sit down.'

The roses on the mantelpiece had dropped all of their petals. They lay scattered at the base of the vase. Some of them had fallen on to the hearth below. She poured a bourbon for him and a cognac for herself. She took her time over fixing the drinks, fussing with the ice tongs, reluctant to face him again, though face him she had to. All she could think about was Paolo, behind a closed door, not knowing that she was there on the other side. Perhaps never finding out. All she could think about was those little girls. And *her* little girl.

'You were right – what you said. He didn't want me.' She saw Olga, her face racked with pain and fever, the wet strands of hair plastered across her forehead. She handed Robert his bourbon, seating herself on the padded stool by the hearth.

'So you thought you'd just drop by here and cosy down for the night, did you? What's your plan for tomorrow, and the day after and the day after that?'

'I don't have a plan.'

'You've never loved me, have you? No, don't answer that. There's no need to. But, you know, Genevieve, no man has ever loved you as much as I have.'

She stared down into her drink.

'You've ripped out my heart and squeezed out all the juice – like it was an orange. There's only the peel left and that's no damn good to anyone.'

'Robert—'

'What did this guy have that I don't? Was it the shoes? Didn't I buy you enough shoes?'

'Of course you did. It wasn't—'

'I hope he hurt you real bad.'

'He did.' She swirled the cognac, golden, around her glass.

'Good.'

He took out a cigar. She watched him light it. It was a fat cigar and he had to puff a lot to get it going. Oddly, he seemed in lighter spirits now, in spite of all this talk of oranges and peel and hurting real bad. The rage was no longer in evidence. He'd put it away in his jacket pocket, along with his lighter. She saw him as his business associates must see him – a confident man, rather suave. Capable. He'd shaved since this afternoon. He'd put on a crisp grey suit.

'You've behaved inexcusably,' said the new, cool and composed Robert. 'No man in his right mind would take you back after what you've done.'

Genevieve opened her mouth to start talking again about finding a hotel, but Robert held up his hand to silence her.

'Still, when all's said and done, you come from a damn strange place. They're a cold kind of people, your family. They didn't bring you up the way they should have.'

She waited, watching the smoke from his cigar clouding across the room.

'Why did you tell me you were pregnant?'

'I don't know.'

'It was a really stupid lie.'

'I know. But does it matter now? Our marriage is over anyway, we both know that.'

'There shouldn't be secrets between man and wife.' He sipped from his bourbon. 'That's where the rot starts. You were building that "path of lies" long before you took up with your cobbler.'

'It's late, Robert. In the morning I'll tell you whatever you want to know.'

'Will you?' He raised one eyebrow. His voice was cool. 'Because there *are* things I want to know.'

'Please let me go to bed.'

'It's not all your fault. Not *all* of it.' Robert gazed at the dead roses. 'I had you followed. I had a man go snooping about in your past. In your school records.'

'You did *what?*'

'I'm not proud of myself. I handled it all the wrong way. But there *is* something you haven't told me, isn't there? Something happened to you when you were a girl. That "something" turned our marriage sour.'

'Robert, don't.'

'When you're really angry at someone, you can do very bad things. I did something bad tonight. I think I wanted to get even.'

'Don't tell me any more. I'm not asking.'

He seemed, for a moment, to be deliberating over whether to say more about this – apparently deciding not to. 'Genevieve, I'm a man who likes to look to the future, always have done. I don't fixate on the past. But you have to know what's there. There are lessons to be learned – you learn them and you move on. That's how you make things good. I still love you, God help me.'

'Are you saying you want me back? Do you really think we can go back to the way things were?'

A dry chuckle. 'Oh no, honey. We're not going back. We're going forward.'

'What do you mean?'

'I have a deal to propose. And I want you to give it some proper thought. I'll say what I have to say and you can stay here tonight and sleep on it.'

Again she waited. He looked taller, as though he was actually growing, in front of her eyes.

'You'll tell me your secret. The secret that's undermined

this marriage and made you turn to another man. You'll tell it to me, and I'll listen, and then we'll move on. We won't talk about it ever again. We'll leave Paris as soon as I can wrap things up and organize the tickets. We'll go to Boston. You'll treat me the way a wife should treat her husband, with respect. We'll have children.'

'Oh, Robert—'

'No, don't say anything now. Take tonight to think it through. It's not a bad place, Boston, if you give it a chance. You'll never want for anything. You'll get to know my mother and sister. They'll be good friends to you. We'll all take care of each other. We'll leave this whole mess behind us and start again.' Another puff on the cigar. 'No more affairs, no more lies, no more secrets.'

He drained his glass. His hands were so steady now.

'What makes you think I'd come to Boston? You know I've never wanted to go there.'

'What choice do you have? Anyway, Paris isn't right for you. It's not what you need.'

'What do I need, then?'

He leaned forward. 'I know about the shoes, honey. The tiny ones with the buttons. Your little-girl shoes. Of all the hundreds of shoes in that room of yours, you packed your Mary Janes to take away with you.'

She tried to speak, but couldn't.

'You need to be someone's little girl. Be mine. It's all I've ever wanted.' He stood up again, brushed himself down. 'That's the deal. Take it or leave it. I'll see you in the morning.'

## 50

THE MOON LIT HER ROOM A SICKLY GREEN. OR WAS IT THE streetlights? She couldn't find the motivation to get up and close the shutters. She was exhausted but restless. Even closing her eyelids was an unbearable effort. They wouldn't stay shut.

She ached for the feel of Paolo's arms around her. For the lemony smell of his skin. His salty-sweet mouth.

She thought of Robert's cloying embraces. How could they go on together, in Boston or anywhere else? And how could she tell him her secret? It was impossible.

She'd have to go home, to her father.

A life of rose-pruning. Needlepoint by the fireside. Walking the dogs. Chatting with the vicar at church. Drinking alone late at night and topping up the bottles with water so the servants wouldn't notice. Pining for what-might-have-been-but-wasn't. Nursing Daddy as his health deteriorated. Sitting by his bed and talking incessantly of the minute, inconsequential goings-on in the village, because after all, what else would there be to talk about?

Avoiding the gaze of Dr Peters.

She fell asleep thinking about her Mary Janes. The buttons. The shiniest black leather that she loved so much. The way she used to lick her finger and rub the smears of dirt away. Her little feet inside them. That one precious afternoon at Fortnum's with her mother and Mr Slattery, the gentleman from New York.

Morning seemed to arrive very suddenly, yanking Genevieve from her sleep before she was ready. She pulled herself up in the bed and looked out at the grey rooftops, the chimneypots, the trees. The traffic had already started up. Shutters clanked and banged open. Someone down in the street was whistling. She sat there in the bed for a long time, listening to the sounds of the city waking up.

# 51

THE STREETS WERE PUNGENT WITH MORNING BAKING. EVERY corner was alive with flowers, sold from market stalls or simply from baskets. An old man was leading a herd of goats, bells clanking. A woman appeared from an apartment building with a jug and the goatherd stopped in the middle of the road and began to milk a bleating nanny. The scene was observed by an immaculate grey-haired woman in a pair of pink Perugia pumps with spike heels seated on a café terrace. Two gendarmes on the opposite side of the street were laughing and smoking. Only in Paris would you find a scene quite like this.

When Genevieve walked into Rumpelmayer's, the first person she saw was Lulu, at their favourite corner table, three empty coffee cups lined up in front of her. She was eating a chocolate éclair.

After a moment, she looked up and saw Genevieve.

'Want to join me, chérie?' She gestured to the empty chair on the other side of her table.

'Don't mind if I do.'

Lulu leaned forward. 'Have you seen the new waiter?'

'Where?'

'Over there.' She pointed across to where a young man was laying cutlery out on a neighbouring table. He had broad shoulders and what looked like nicely muscled arms. His waist was narrow. His hair was slicked back with rather too much oil. Genevieve imagined it to be stubbornly curly, difficult to tame.

'Do you think he's . . . ?' Lulu gestured at the baguette being served on the table next to theirs.

Genevieve pursed her lips and then slowly shook her head. 'I think he's more . . .' and she pointed at Lulu's éclair.

'Pity. Nice eyes though.'

'So who's the cake for? Camby?'

Lulu frowned. 'Him? No. He's back, as predicted. He seems to be all right but he has no memory of Violetta or of where he's been. Or so he claims. I'm too relieved to be angry.'

'And you love him. You always will. So if not for Camby, who's that cake for?'

'It's for us, Vivi. For you, my best friend. The girl who has always seen behind my make-up. I went and poisoned our friendship because I was jealous of you. And now there's nothing I can do about it, no matter how sorry I am. What I did was unforgivable.'

'Let me be the judge of that.' Genevieve reached across to squeeze her hand.

Lulu peered hard at her. 'Are you saying . . . ?'

'I was jealous too, and secretive and mistrustful. I pushed you to it. We were *meant* to be friends, Lulu. Why else have we both turned up here this morning?'

416

'For cake! And buckets of coffee. You don't believe in all that fate rubbish, do you, chérie? Don't tell me you're going all religious on me.' She was smiling all over her face.

'Well, it was *you* who said that men might come and go but best friends are for ever. You said it the last time I saw you. Before you made your confession.'

Lulu stared at the mess of éclair on her plate. 'I always confess. It's my Catholic upbringing.'

Genevieve beckoned a waitress. 'A *chocolat l'Africain*, please. And a piece of that praline cake, and one of those pastries with the cream.'

'*Two* cakes?' Lulu frowned and tutted. 'You will be enormously fat, chérie. You won't be able to get through the door.'

'One for Paolo and one for Robert,' said Genevieve brightly. 'I think that's *choux* pastry, you know. How apt.'

'So it's over with both of them? Was that completely intentional?'

'Not exactly. I was going away with Paolo. But it all went wrong.' She picked up a pencil that was lying on the table and started doodling on the back of the bill.

'Oh, chérie. This is my fault.'

But Genevieve shook her head. 'He has children. With Olga. Did you know?'

'Children?' Her eyes and mouth were open in amazement, her tongue coated in chocolate crumbs.

'Two daughters. She has two sons by the dead husband, but the girls are his.'

'How did you find out about this?'

'He stood me up last night and I went to find him. He was at her apartment. Well, it's his apartment really. That's very obvious when you see the place. And it explains a lot about him that I didn't understand. She was sick in bed. Quite possibly dying. I saw the children. I spoke to them.'

'What about Zachari? Was he there too?'

'He was talking to the doctor in another room.'

'I hope you hit him, chérie.' Lulu put her hand on Genevieve's arm. 'And not just a slap. Men like that deserve a closed fist.'

'No. I stood on the other side of the door, listening to him. And then I walked away.' She was still doodling. A sketch of Lulu – all eyes and mouth and the beauty spot.

'You mean you didn't even speak to him?'

'It changed everything, seeing those children.'

'Yes?'

'They were losing their mother. I stood there and looked into their eyes, and I knew I had to walk away. He's all they have, Lulu. I love him, but they need him so much more than I do.'

Lulu patted her shoulder. 'You're a good person.'

'No, I'm not. Really, I think I did it for *my* baby. Does that sound stupid? Anyway, he chose too. He chose them over me.' She sighed. 'I always knew that he was hiding from something, down there in that basement of his.'

'This all sounds so damn noble, chérie. *Too* noble, if you ask me.'

Genevieve shook her head. 'I can't be angry with Paolo any more than you can with Camby. I understand too well about living in hiding. I've done everything I can to hide from my past – from Josephine. But she's still there and I still wonder about her. I don't know what I'll do about that.

I'm not sure if there's anything I *can* do. But it's something I have to think about.'

'What about Robert? Does he know about all this?'

'Some of it. About Paolo, I mean. Not about Josephine. Poor Robert. I've pretty much destroyed him.'

'Ah.' Lulu flapped a hand. 'You two were all wrong from the start. You've done him a favour, ending that marriage. Now he can find a nice simple girl who'll bake cookies for him.'

But Genevieve wasn't convinced.

Lulu pointed down at the small case by her feet. 'So where are you going with that bag? London?'

'God, no. When I went to bed last night, I didn't know where I'd go or what I'd do. I've never felt so lost. I even contemplated going back to live with my father. But when I woke up this morning, I looked out of my window and saw that it's all still here for me. Paris. It's still the place I dreamed about. It's still my city. My home.' But her lip trembled. 'As to the details, I really don't know.'

'What shoes are you wearing today?' Lulu bent down to take a look. 'Ah – the red velvet Zacharis.'

'World's best shoemaker,' said Genevieve. 'I could hardly leave those behind, now could I?' There was a lump in her throat now. 'But as to the rest of my collection . . .' She had to take a sip of her drink.

Lulu wagged a finger. 'I will not hear such defeatist talk! Vivi, we will get your shoe collection out of that apartment even if we have to hold up the doorman at gunpoint! We're going straight over to the Rue de Lota after we've had this cake, and I'll distract Robert while you put all those boxes in a taxi. I'll sleep with him if I have to – desperate times call for desperate measures – and—'

'We'd need more than one taxi for my shoe collection. Anyway, where would we take it?'

Lulu shrugged. 'My place?'

Genevieve thought of Lulu's apartment, and tried very hard to smile.

'We'll do it, chérie. I won't let you down again.'

'I know.'

The *chocolat l'Africain* and cakes arrived.

'So I'm staying in Paris, but I've no clue what I'm going to do.' Genevieve stuck a finger into her cream pastry. 'I'm not a poet. I'm not a wife. I was a half-decent patron of the arts but you can't do that without money.'

Lulu shrugged. 'Who needs money? You have charm. And beauty and a good brain. You'll find a way forward. There's another kind of life waiting for you out there. You just have to reach for it.'

'Do you really think so?'

Genevieve turned to gaze out of the window. There was a touch of autumn in the air. A tree outside was dropping its leaves and they were blowing down the street. An old man in a cap was sweeping them up but they kept on escaping and throwing themselves under the wheels of passing cars, beneath the hooves of a horse dragging a cart full of junk. A woman was walking by, carrying a baguette under one arm and holding the hand of a little girl in a red beret. The girl saw Genevieve looking at her and stuck out her tongue, before being drawn on and away.

'Yes, I do.' Lulu reached for the sketch. 'Say, that's a great caricature. I didn't know you could draw, chérie.'

'I can't. Not really.'

Lulu mock-frowned. 'Take it from me, you're good. I might not know about poetry but I *do* know about art. Do you know how many times I've been drawn?'

And now two women came into view, walking arm in arm down the street. Women dressed in black. The younger one had a horsey face with big dewy eyes. The older one had softer features, but her eyes were hard, steely. Determined.

Genevieve remembers an apartment lined with books. A table covered in papers – poems that could be salvaged or lost. Two women peering together at some difficult scrawl, trying to decipher it. A feeling of peace, of deep water. A desire to help them. To join them. And now an intricate squirling pattern in three shades of green starts growing and spreading across her imagination, the way ivy sprawls and climbs over buildings.

THE END

*The Real-Life Shoemaker Behind* The Shoe Queen

In the early 1900s, shoe designer Pietro Yanturni had a shop just off the Place Vendôme, bearing the legend PIETRO YANTURNI – WORLD'S MOST EXPENSIVE SHOES. Like Paolo Zachari, Yanturni made his hand-picked customers walk up and down barefoot so he could study their feet and the way they moved, and create shoes that would be absolutely perfect for them. The women had no say in how the shoes would look, what materials would be used or when the shoes would be ready. Some customers would be kept waiting for years.

Many women, once they'd worn Yanturni's shoes, became addicted and refused to buy from anyone else. Rita de Acosta Lydig, a wealthy society woman and patron of the arts, famously bought hundreds of pairs from Yanturni, kept them in velvet-lined boxes and had special shoe horns made from the wood of antique violins.

Yanturni is something of a mystery. He was a curator of the Cluny Museum in Paris, but little else is known about his life. Sources can't agree on the spelling of his name (he's often called Yantourney or Yanturney), where he was from or pretty much anything else. The shoes, however, have survived, and Yanturni has been a major influence on shoe design, then and since, particularly in his creative, varied use of fabrics and colour.

## The Crazy Years

In reading about Paris in the 1920s, I encountered many irresistible stories and personalities. While no character in my novel is based entirely on a real figure, I should mention the following:

Norman Betterson owes much to Ernest Walsh, poet-editor of the literary journal *This Quarter*. Dubbed by Hemingway as 'The Man Marked For Death', Walsh would tell people, 'I'm fine. I've another five years to live.' He eventually succumbed to tuberculosis in Monte Carlo where he was staying with two lovers: Ethel Moorhead (the magazine's patron) and Kay Boyle (author). After Walsh's death the two women stayed on together for a time, but *This Quarter* died with its editor.

Guy Monteray bears more than a passing resemblance to Harry Crosby, a wealthy, handsome playboy and author of dubious poetry. Harry and his wife Caresse set up home in a mansion on the Rue de Lille, where they installed a vast sunken bathtub and hosted wild orgiastic parties. On a trip to Egypt the couple had themselves tattooed with a symbolic black sun, and entered into a death pact. Ultimately, though, it was with another lover, Josephine Bigelow, that Crosby shot himself. The couple were found lying across a bed in Bigelow's New York studio. The E. E. Cummings poem quoted here for Guy Monteray's suicide was written as the epitaph for Crosby and Bigelow.

Finally, Lulu is inspired by the legendary Kiki: artist's model, outrageous cabaret performer, lover of Man Ray and café companion of Kisling, Foujita and Pascin. Kiki became a model at fourteen, after blackening her eyebrows with matchsticks and fleeing a life of rural drudgery for the bright lights of Paris. The stories of her life are too numerous for this note. Hemingway said of her, 'Having a fine face to start with, she made of it a work of art.'

I won't list here all the books I read while researching *The Shoe Queen*, but would like to mention the following in particular:

*The Crazy Years – Paris in the Twenties*, William Wiser (Thames & Hudson)
*The Last Time I Saw Paris*, Elliot Paul (Sickle Moon Books)
*A Moveable Feast*, Ernest Hemingway (Vintage)
*The Bohemians – The Birth of Modern Art: Paris 1900-1930*, Dan Franck (Phoenix)
*Geniuses Together – American Writers in Paris in the 1920s*, Humphrey Carpenter (Houghton Mifflin)
*Paris Between the Wars*, Carol Mann (The Vendome Press)

*Art Deco Interiors*, Patricia Bayer (Thames & Hudson)
*Art Deco Fashion*, Suzanne Lussier (V&A)

*Heavenly Soles – Extraordinary Twentieth Century Shoes*, Mary Trasko (Abbeville Press)

*Shoes – A Lexicon of Style*, Valerie Steele (Scriptum Editions)

*A Century of Shoes*, Angela Pattison and Nigel Cawthorne (Chartwell Books Inc.)

*Shoes – Fashion and Fantasy*, Collin McDowell (Thames & Hudson)

## Acknowledgements

I am grateful to the Arts Council of England for their Clarissa Luard award, received during the writing of this book.

Big Thanks are due to the following people:
To Chris and Patricia O'Dell, the Barclay family and Susie Tiso for idyllic writing breaks in their lovely cottages; to my editors Diana Beaumont, Heather Barrett, Jeanne Ryckmans and Lauren McKenna, and my agents Carole Blake, Conrad Williams and Oli Munson, without whom this book would be in the bottom drawer; to Françoise Davis for checking my Frenchisms; to Rhidian Davis for babysitting.

And to Simon, for everything.

# THE PERSONAL SHOPPER
## Carmen Reid

**Meet Annie Valentine: stylish, savvy, multi-tasker extraordinaire.**

As a personal shopper in a swanky London fashion emporium, Annie can re-style and re-invent her clients from head to toe. In fact, this super-skilled dresser can be relied on to solve everyone's problems . . . except her own.

Although she's busy being a single mum to stroppy teen Lana and painfully shy Owen, there's a gap in Annie's wardrobe, sorry, life, for a new man. But finding the perfect partner is turning out to be so much trickier than finding the perfect pair of shoes.

Can she source a genuine classic? A lifelong investment? Will she end up with someone from the sale rail, who'll have to be returned? Or maybe, just maybe, there'll be someone new in this season who could be the one . . .

**A fabulous read. A sexy read. A Carmen Reid.**

**'If you love shopping as much as you love a good read, try this. Wonderful!'**
**Katie Fforde**

9780552154819

**CORGI BOOKS**

# THE STARTER WIFE
## Gigi Levangie

'FEARLESS AND FABULOUS'
Lauren Weisberger, author of *The Devil Wears Prada*

**There are starter jobs. Starter cars. Starter houses . . . now meet the starter wife.**

When her husband dumps her by cell phone, Gracie Pollock is left reeling. She believed that she and Kenny were different from other Hollywood couples. She never thought that she'd be a *starter wife*. But now that her marriage is over, she's a social pariah and her husband is dating a famous blonde pop starlet. What will Gracie do next?

A sexy, satirical and wickedly funny novel about life (and love) after divorce . . . Hollywood style.

'ACIDIC AND UNFORGIVING . . . I LOVED IT'
*New York Observer*

'WE WRITE ABOUT THE REAL HOLLYWOOD'
Jackie Collins

'WITTY AND INTELLIGENT'
*Newsday*

9780552771658

**BLACK SWAN**

# THE LOLLIPOP SHOES
## Joanne Harris

'Who died?' I said. 'Or is it a secret?'

'My mother, Vianne Rocher.'

Seeking refuge and anonymity in the cobbled streets of
Montmartre, Yanne and her daughters, Rosette and Annie,
live peacefully, if not happily, above their little chocolate shop.
Nothing unusual marks them out; no red sachets hang by the
door. The wind has stopped – at least for a while. Then into
their lives blows Zozie de l'Alba, the lady with the lollipop
shoes, and everything begins to change . . .

But this new friendship is not what it seems. Ruthless, devious
and seductive, Zozie de l'Alba has plans of her own – plans that
will shake their world to pieces. And with everything she loves
at stake, Yanne must face a difficult choice; to flee, as she has
done so many times before, or to confront her most dangerous
enemy . . .

Herself.

'A DELICIOUS URBAN FAIRYTALE, WHERE
KILLER SHOES AND AZTEC MYTHS BATTLE IT
OUT WITH TRUE LOVE AND THE SEDUCTIVE
POWER OF CHOCOLATE'
*Daily Mail*

9780385609487

NOW AVAILABLE FROM DOUBLEDAY

# Doubleday